DEAD
WOMAN
CROSSING

JENEVA ROSE

DEAD WOMAN CROSSING

bookouture

Published by Bookouture in 2020

An imprint of Storyfire Ltd.
Carmelite House
50 Victoria Embankment
London EC4Y 0DZ

www.bookouture.com

Written by Jeneva Rose

ISBN: 978-1-83790-126-5
eBook ISBN: 978-1-83888-728-5

To my husband, Andrew.
You believed in me when I didn't believe in myself.
This one's for you, because of you.

CHAPTER ONE

As the tires slammed onto the hot asphalt, Detective Kimberley King instinctively positioned her arm in front of her sixteen-month-old daughter, bracing her. Her sleeping child did not wake. Having been born and raised, thus far, in New York City with its constant squealing sirens and blaring car horns, it would take more than a rough plane landing to wake her resting cherub.

A few of the passengers toward the back of the plane clapped when the tires were firmly planted on the runway. Kimberley couldn't help rolling her eyes and shaking her head. *Simpletons*, she thought, but she quickly had to remind herself… simple was her life now. These were no longer the plain inhabitants of the flyover states, but rather they were now her neighbors, her new people. She would no longer be Detective Kimberley King, NYPD, but something quite different. In New York, she worked homicide, the worst of the worst cases, the things nightmares were made of, but where she was going, murders would be few and far between she presumed given the size of the town. As soon as she stepped foot off the plane, it would be official; she would now be the newest chief deputy of Custer County, residing in Dead Woman Crossing—a town named for its grizzly history of an unsolved brutal homicide. Perhaps Kimberley would feel more at home there than she thought she would. She believed she'd always be a New Yorker at heart and would cling to that as long as she could, but that wasn't her identity anymore. She was now an Oklahoman.

"Please be careful when opening the overhead bins as items may have shifted during flight. We hope you enjoyed your flight, and we thank you for flying American Airlines," the flight attendant announced via the intercom. Immediately, most passengers rose from their seats as if the stewardess had given a powerful sermon rather than simple disembarkation instructions.

Kimberley turned toward her daughter and unbuckled her. Jessica stirred awake, rubbing her sleepy eyes. Her face began to crumple as she adjusted to the unfamiliar surroundings, but Kimberley acted quickly. She knew that look, the look that signaled Jessica was about to throw a tantrum. Her daughter had seemed to learn in recent weeks that crying could be used as psychological warfare against her mother. Kimberley planted several kisses on the top of her soft head and pulled Jessica into her lap with a hug, quickly soothing her, before she erupted like a volcano full of tears. She had woken her daughter earlier than usual and opted not to put her down for a nap, all to ensure the plane ride had gone smoothly and it had.

"Jessica, baby, we're here," Kimberley said, bouncing her little girl.

Looking at her daughter was like looking in the mirror; she was the spitting image of Kimberley. Rich dark brown hair, vivid blue eyes, and pouty lips. Kimberley was thankful her daughter had taken after her and not her ex, Aaron, who looked like the poster boy for the Aryan race; blond hair, light eyes, fair skin. He was no longer in the picture. If she was being honest, he was never really in the picture, so she was happy Jessica didn't serve as a constant reminder of him. She hoped she'd get her strong personality as well, instead of her father's, who was more concerned about working out in the gym than taking care of his own child. When she told him she was moving out of state and that he could see Jessica as much as he wanted but would have to travel, he had responded with a shrug as if she had asked him something as simple as do you want bacon or sausage with your eggs?

Motherhood had changed her, but fatherhood hadn't changed Aaron. When she first had Jessica, Kimberley developed almost a sixth sense. It provided more than any police training had ever done for her. The instinct, many called maternal, translated well into her detective work. It made her notice everything, sense danger. Every situation, she could look at it and find a hundred different ways something could go wrong. Jessica changed Kimberley for the better. But with Aaron, fatherhood shone a light on his true colors: selfish, childish, and narcissistic. Kimberley quickly brushed the memory from her mind before it affected her mood, the roots of her life left behind trying one last time to pull her back into despair.

She tied her long hair into a ponytail, readying herself to trek off the plane with half of everything she owned. Kimberley stood from her seat and lifted Jessica, her little legs wrapping around Kimberley's petite, yet strong body. She was used to handling everything by herself, so grabbing her luggage from the overhead bin, Jessica's diaper bag, and her tote bag all the while holding her daughter looked like a magic act to the untrained eye, but to her it was easy. Jessica tightened her arms around her mother's neck and laid her head against her shoulder, letting out a soft coo. Kimberley smiled and kissed the top of her head while edging her way into the aisle.

A middle-aged man with a bald spot the size of a grapefruit on the back of his head stood in front of her. He turned around and gave Kimberley and her juggling act a once-over. "Do you need help with any of that?" he asked, pointing to her bags.

Kimberley's eyes widened and her brow creased. She wasn't used to others offering their help, especially coming from Manhattan. In New York City, people are just too busy to stop and help. They've got places to be, traffic to get through, subway rides to make, lines to stand in. Everything there is go, go, go. They're not mean. They just don't have the time to be nice.

"Oh, no. I've got it," she said, because she also wasn't used to accepting help either. Kimberley was the type of person that handled everything herself. It was why she didn't really have anyone to say her goodbyes to when she left New York. She lived by the cynical idea that the fewer people that were in your life, the less you had to lose.

She remembered where she was though and figured she'd have to change that mindset sooner or later as this gentleman likely meant well.

"Actually, yes. Please," she said, her own words sounding like a foreign tongue as they left her mouth.

The man smiled and grabbed the small wheeled bag from her. "You from around here?"

"No, but I will be soon, I guess." She shrugged her shoulders.

"I was born and raised here, but I didn't realize folks willingly moved to this part of the world," he said with a chuckle.

"They don't," Kimberley snorted, but quickly stopped, and looked up to read the man's face, unsure whether she had offended him.

The man let out a belly laugh. "Quick wit," he said. "Well, welcome. You'll like it here just fine after a time. Oklahoma is like the heels of a loaf of bread. It's not anyone's first choice, nor is it as enjoyable or as soft as the rest of the loaf, but it does the job it was meant to do, protects the rest of it from going stale, and hell… it's still bread."

Kimberley nodded. "I like that. By the way, I'm Kimberley, and this is Jessica." She motioned to her daughter with a tilt of her head.

"Nice to meet you both. I'm Frank." Shuffling bodies in front of him got his attention and he turned his head. "Line's moving," he called over his shoulder as he lumbered forward.

Outside the plane, Frank handed over the luggage to Kimberley on the jet bridge, while she grabbed her stroller that the flight crew had already set aside. She placed Jessica in the seat and stuffed her purse and the diaper bag underneath.

"Well, you enjoy yourself, ma'am, and perhaps I'll see you around," Frank said with a smile and a wave of his hand.

"Thanks for your help." Kimberley gave him a nod as he took a couple of steps back and turned around, walking away into the bowels of the terminal.

She bent down to make sure Jessica was secure and that she had everything she had brought with her on the plane. Grabbing her luggage and pulling it behind her with one hand, she pushed the stroller with the other down the jet bridge. This was it… a new start for her and her daughter.

Out in the baggage claim area, Kimberley spotted David, leaning one of his broad shoulders against a concrete pillar near the baggage carousel. She had never met him in person, but had seen and talked to him many times on FaceTime calls with her mom, Nicole, and he had seemed nice enough. Nicole and David had married at the courthouse a few years ago, just the two of them, so he was technically her stepfather and Jessica's grandfather. Despite being sixty, he was large and barrel-chested, the result of a lifetime of wheat farming. His skin was weathered and clean-shaven, and his hair was a mix of salt and pepper. His eyes were dark, a complete contrast to the soft facial features that gave him a kind-looking face.

David stood up straight and smiled wide when he spotted Kimberley. He made his way to her. His footsteps were heavy, and his great stature towered over hers when he gave her a half hug with a pat on the back. She didn't know him well, but hoped she'd get to know him better as he was the man her mother loved. Kimberley was grateful for him for providing her mother with a life her father had never done and for graciously opening his home to Jessica and herself.

"Where's Mom?" Kimberley asked, scanning the surrounding area of passengers hurrying to their baggage carousels. Each unfamiliar face she laid eyes on in the crowd of moving people caused her more and more disappointment.

"Nicole had one of her migraines. So, she's at home resting, and by resting I mean prepping dinner, as we both know she is incapable of slowing down." David arched an eyebrow.

"Oh… yeah, that's Mom for ya." Kimberley tried to hide her disappointment with a small smile.

She hadn't seen her mother since Jessica was born as Nicole had only come to the city once in all the time Kimberley had lived there. Kimberley didn't fault her for that, because she knew her mother didn't have the money to be traveling back and forth. And she couldn't be mad at her mother for that either, because Kimberley had never traveled to Oklahoma to visit. She had always been too busy with work.

"How was the flight?" he asked, his eyes never fully making contact with Kimberley's, always half looking, half scanning his surroundings. A carryover trait from his military days as an artillery officer in the Oklahoma Guard doing security and stability operations in Iraq.

She looked down at her daughter to check on her again. Her blue eyes were wide open, staring up at David, almost as though she was mesmerized by the giant.

David leaned down, putting out his pointer finger. Jessica wrapped her tiny hand around it, her fingers too short to reach her palm. She giggled and smiled widely.

"Hi, sweetie," David said. "I'm your Grandpa Turner. But you can call me Papa," David said, smiling back at Jessica.

Jessica opened her mouth wide almost as though she was going to say "Papa" but instead gave the biggest, goofiest grin her sweet little face could conjure up.

"She's adorable," David said, his face mimicking hers to get her to laugh and smile more.

The two of them had never met before, and Kimberley was unsure as to how warm his welcoming would be to Jessica as he had grandchildren of his own. But this interaction was a pleasant surprise and made her more confident in her decision to move to Oklahoma.

David gently pulled his finger out of Jessica's grasp. He straightened up slowly into a standing position. "She's my first granddaughter," he said proudly.

Kimberley gave a small smile. "She is, isn't she?"

David nodded. "Your mother mentioned she was a good baby."

It wasn't like she'd know firsthand, Kimberley thought to herself. "She is."

"Expecting any bags?" David looked around again.

A couple of the baggage carousels had started up.

"Just a few. We packed light." Kimberley had only brought along what she and Jessica needed. Her apartment in the city was small, so they didn't have much to begin with—and with how demanding her job at the NYPD was, she barely had any street clothes because she was almost always in uniform. Detectives were allowed to wear business casual attire, as opposed to the full blues, but Kimberley liked the immediate authority the uniform signaled. A bitter taste rose in the back of her throat as she thought about her former job and the well-deserved promotion she was passed over for. There was no good reason for her to have not gotten the job, but she was sure it had to do with Jessica. Her career had been soaring up like a helium balloon released from a child's grasp... until she got pregnant. Then the balloon popped. Her male counterparts treated her differently, like she was fragile, like she'd break at any moment. It was understandable in a way, but Kimberley thought that after she gave birth and returned from maternity leave, things would go back to the way they were before her uterus was occupied. It hadn't. They viewed motherhood as a weak spot, but for her, it had become her source of strength. She swallowed the resentment hard, following behind David toward her designated baggage carousel.

Kimberley finished buckling the car seat and ensured Jessica was safe and secure. She double-checked everything once more before closing the back door of the Chevy Impala sedan. She knew it was her mother's car because her mom had told her about it when she purchased the used vehicle a year before. Kimberley sat down in the passenger seat.

"We got that car seat from my daughter, Emily," David noted. "It's yours to keep. Her boys are too big for car seats."

"Thanks. That was nice of her." Kimberley looked over at David.

She turned back to check on Jessica once more. Jessica's blue eyes were still wide, bouncing around the vehicle that sat idle in the parking structure. Kimberley thought for sure her daughter would cry now that she was wide awake and taking in unfamiliar surroundings, but she didn't. The concrete structure surrounding them must have comforted her. It was after all what she was used to in the city.

"Ready?" David asked, turning on the engine.

Kimberley took a small breath and nodded.

"Let's hit the road. It's about a seventy-mile drive—should take a little over an hour," he said confidently, backing the vehicle out of the parking spot.

"Takes me an hour to travel two miles in the city sometimes," Kimberley noted.

David arched an eyebrow. "Well, you'll feel like a time traveler in Oklahoma." He let out a chuckle and Kimberley gave him a courteous smile.

One hour separated Kimberley from Dead Woman Crossing, her new home. She was looking forward to a fresh start and bringing Jessica up close to her mother, surrounded by wheat fields and flowing creeks, what she gathered Oklahoma looked like from the photos she had received from her mom over the years. No more soaring skyscrapers and endless concrete.

"Your mother tells me you and your boyfriend broke up," David said coolly, as if he were talking about the weather and not the ruination of her love life.

"Yep. We did a while ago."

"Why's that?"

"He didn't want to be a father."

David shook his head and quickly glanced over at Kimberley with a somber look. "That's a damn shame." He returned his focus to the traffic in front of him as they weren't out of Oklahoma City yet.

Kimberley could tell he wasn't used to driving on roads with more than a few vehicles as his shoulders were high and tense, his large hands wrapped around the steering wheel at ten and two and he leaned forward a little. He looked rather uncomfortable. A white sedan in front of them slammed on its brakes.

David pounded his fist against the horn. "Damnit!" he yelled.

A blood-curdling wail came from the backseat as Jessica erupted into tears. Kimberley turned around, reaching back, she tried to comfort her.

"I'm sorry," David said. "I can't stand these city drivers."

"It's okay. She was due for a tantrum anyway." Kimberley grabbed her stuffed elephant and a pacifier from the diaper bag at Jessica's feet. She had been weaning her daughter off the pacifier, and it was now only used for emergencies like tantrums in hour-long car drives.

"It's okay, Jessica," Kimberley said in her soothing motherly voice as she handed over the little gray elephant and the pacifier. Jessica cried a little more before taking the pacifier with her tiny hand and popping it between her pouty lips. She held Ellie underneath her arm and against her chest. Her eyes were still wet.

Her face was still red. Her nose pushed air in and out quickly as she began calming down.

"Good girl," Kimberley said with a smile as she faced forward in her seat.

Traffic was moving again. She glanced over at David who appeared more comfortable. His raised shoulders had fallen. One hand had released itself from its steering-wheel death grip and was now fiddling with the radio station.

"Sorry about that."

"It's quite alright. It's not the first time she's heard someone raise their voice in front of her," Kimberley admitted.

David glanced over at Kimberley and then back at the road again.

"Don't worry. Jessica's too young to remember anything that happened between you and that ex of yours."

Before she could say anything, like thank him for saying exactly what she needed to hear, he changed the subject.

"You like country music?"

She didn't but she said yes anyway.

David turned the radio to an oldie's country station. A song by Alan Jackson played softly, while David tapped his fingers on the steering wheel to the rhythm of the music. He wasn't a man that could sit still, always fiddling with something.

When the song ended and a loud commercial started up, David turned down the volume slightly.

"I think you and Jessica are going to like living on a farm," he said.

"Yeah, I think so too. I know Mom loves it."

With Oklahoma City behind them now, all that lay ahead was a long stretch of highway that seemed like it had no end. Kimberley looked out her window. The wheat fields were a blur of gold. When she thought of the country, she thought of the color green. But not here in Oklahoma. It was gold. Heck, New York City had more greenery than this.

"The farm's been in our family for generations and generations," David said with a pleased smile.

"That's impressive." She knew that tidbit already, but she let David think it was the first time she had heard it. He was clearly proud of his family farm.

"I'm glad my daughter Emily found a man like Wyatt who was willing and wanting to take over the farm. Most men these days are soft. Buncha whining pussies, if ya ask me."

"Based on my ex, I'd say you were right," Kimberley joked.

David gave a wry smile. "I think you and my daughter will get along real well. You're both about the same age."

"I hope so," she said with little conviction in her voice. Kimberley had never been good at making friends. She was a bit of a loner, but she knew she had to change. Keeping everyone at arm's length wasn't doing her any good and it wouldn't do her daughter any good either.

"The Thunder Rolls" by Garth Brooks came on the radio, and David turned the volume back up. He clearly liked the song as he began to sing along with it, tapping his fingers on the wheel. Kimberley looked back out her passenger window at the big blue skies that were slowly cascading into hues of pink, yellow, and orange, thanks to the sun that was falling behind the horizon. Everywhere around them was wide-open spaces and far-reaching fields that appeared to go on and on forever. For many, they would see this as nothing. But Kimberley saw something. She saw opportunity, a new life, a fresh start. She now knew what the frontiersmen must have felt when they "headed out west." Hope. This would be her better life.

On top of a slower-paced life, she expected her new job as chief deputy would also be less time-consuming and demanding, allowing her more time to spend with Jessica. Her life in New York had become near impossible, but in Oklahoma, there was possibility. She'd miss the energy that the city radiated, the hustle, the fact that anything she could ever want was available like Chinese food at 3 a.m. However, she had learned that New York City couldn't give her everything she wanted. It couldn't give her time with her daughter or a close relationship with her mother. She needed it now more than ever. She tried to make the city work while being a single mother, and she had for sixteen months... barely.

The song ended and once again, David turned down the radio.

"How ya feeling about the new job, Chief Deputy King?" He raised an eyebrow.

"Good. It'll be different than the city, but I'm looking forward to a change. Sheriff Walker seemed great during my phone interviews."

"He's a good man... His views are a bit modern for my taste. Regardless, he does a good job at keeping our town safe."

"Modern?" Kimberley tilted her head.

"Well, he hired you. We've never had a female on the force before."

Kimberley bit her lower lip, mulling over what to say in response to his outdated beliefs. This wasn't a point of view she had ever really encountered in the city, but she was sure it was one she'd be seeing a lot more of in the South.

"We have different definitions of modern then," Kimberley settled on.

David glanced over at Kimberley.

"Oh, I don't mean anything by it. I just believe in taking care and providing for my family. I think that's the man's job. But you... you've gotta step up because your boy stepped back."

He returned his focus back to the road.

"Well, regardless, I think you're going to like it here. Us Oklahomans are the salt of the earth, not too good for nothin' like them coastal elites out by y'all," David said with a smile.

Kimberley forced a smile back as a new song came on the radio.

"I'm just teasing ya." He turned the volume back up, his fingers drumming against the steering wheel once again.

The sun had fallen completely below the horizon when they pulled into the town, which was marked by a sign that read "Dead Woman Crossing—Unincorporated." The town was so small it didn't even have a population. *How strange*, Kimberley thought.

"Almost home," David said over the song.

Kimberley's eyes followed the smattering of various house styles, all very old and collapsing in on themselves, like a row of dying stars, dim and lifeless. The wheatgrass was everywhere: on the edge of the road, in between houses, running off into the distance across the horizon. It looked like a virus, centered here but spreading its tendrils throughout the land, choking everything out that wasn't exactly like it.

David pointed toward Kimberley's passenger window. "Over there is our little downtown, I guess you'd call it. Coffee shop, laundromat, pharmacy, and a convenience store. All the basics."

Without David naming them off, she wouldn't have known what any of them were as their lights and signs were turned off, just little brick buildings full of glass windows.

Dead Woman Crossing appeared rather deserted save for the lit-up windows of the local bar, The Trophy Room, which was in the center of the town at its only four-way stop. The siding of the building was an unintentional off-white, presumably because it was dirty. Various tacky neon beer signs were hung in the windows. The gravel parking lot was around half full of trucks and motorcycles. She could see people shuffling around inside. Several picnic tables were set up off to the sides of the front door. A few men sat at a table, smoking what she thought were cigarettes but couldn't be sure, and they clearly noticed her, as their eyes were fixed on her. David rolled down his window and waved at them, but their line of focus was like a laser beam with their target being Kimberley. She might not be from a small town, but Kimberley knew that look. It was suspicion. It said you don't belong.

"That's The Trophy Room," David said proudly. "A nice place for us men to blow off steam."

"I guess I'll have to check it out sometime," Kimberley said with a smirk.

David drove through the four-way crossing, continuing through the town.

Dead Woman Crossing would be quite a change for her. In Manhattan, Kimberley could walk past a thousand people in a day and not one of them would look at her, let alone notice her presence. But here, she already had a sense that everyone was always watching.

Kimberley turned around, checking on Jessica again. She had fallen asleep, the pacifier in her lap, her head craned to the side and her hands crumpled up in tiny little fists. She glanced through the back window at The Trophy Room; the men's necks were twisted in her direction, their eyes lit up like tiny yellow orbs, still watching her. She turned in her seat, facing forward again.

"Over there is our grocery store. Pearl and Bill own that. It's small, but they have most of what we need." David pointed to the small shop on the corner that was also closed.

It seemed Dead Woman Crossing shutdown early, save for The Trophy Room.

"There's a Walmart in Weatherford, about fifteen minutes from the farm, but we try to support local first and foremost," he added.

"I was the same way in New York City, local first," Kimberley said with a nod.

"Good. You'll fit in just fine around here then."

David pulled the car into the long gravel driveway of the family farm. She could only see as far as the headlights shined at first until the spacious white weather-boarded house with a wraparound porch came into sight. David put the car into park right in front of the home, and Kimberley couldn't pull her eyes from the beauty of it all. She definitely wasn't in New York City anymore, as her entire apartment there could have fit within the porch alone. Excitement for her new life and her temporary home swelled inside of her as she thought about Jessica running back and forth across the large porch, rolling around in the wheatgrass fields, and jumping in the dark with hands splayed trying to catch fireflies. A large gust of wind swayed several of the wooden rockers on the porch, almost like a ghostly greeting for Kimberley and her daughter.

CHAPTER TWO

Kimberley climbed out of the passenger door and made her way to the back to grab Jessica, who was still sound asleep. She couldn't believe how exhausted her little girl was, but she welcomed it; it made for a smooth transition and easy travels. She thought of her little girl waking up in a new house. No more sirens. No more loud neighbors banging and clamoring around at all times of the day. No more crammed subway rides. No more absentee mother and deadbeat father. Here, in Oklahoma, she would have peace and quiet, space to run around and be free in, a family, and a more attentive mother. With a less demanding job, she'd have more time to spend with her daughter.

David killed the engine and meandered to the trunk, loaded up with Kimberley's belongings, before returning to the front of the car. He waited and watched the process unfold as Kimberley removed Jessica and all the accessories and equipment required to keep a small child running smoothly and cleanly.

"That's a lot of stuff for such a little girl," David said with a small grin.

Kimberley looked down, noting everything she had in tow—a diaper bag, a stroller, a tote bag, a backpack and Jessica.

"They say it takes a village to raise a child, but I think it takes a caravan of random products." Kimberley returned his smile.

David let out a small laugh.

Jessica barely stirred, still tired from all her travels, while Kimberley lumbered forward. With her daughter in tow, she eyed the large white farmhouse with excitement. While Oklahoma wasn't her first choice for relocating post–New York City, a house would be a big upgrade from her dingy five-hundred-square-foot apartment that was, in all honesty, not enough room for both her and her daughter. But like everything else in her life, Kimberley made it work, and she'd make Oklahoma work too. She had considered moving to the Midwest, but she was over cold, snowy winters. She had considered another southern state, like North Carolina, but her motivation for moving was to give Jessica a better life and childhood, and she knew Jessica needed more than just Kimberley. She needed a family, people that loved and cared for her. That was why she had landed on Oklahoma.

"Alright, I'll show you to your room then," David called out from the front of the vehicle, a tacit cue to follow his lead.

Kimberley nodded, but her eyes searched the large windows of the white farmhouse. Where was her mother? Why hadn't she come out to greet her?

Kimberley began making her way toward the front door with Jessica held against her chest, her little legs wrapped around her mother's waist, assuming she and David would meet at the pathway heading up the front lawn before ceding his lead forward, but David called out, "The entrance is around back, this way."

Perhaps the room had its own private doorway to the backyard, Kimberley thought. That would be perfect for her actually. Jessica could play outside just within view and Kimberley could come and go from work without disturbing anyone. They made their way around the side of the house and then veered left down a rock-lined dirt path, deeper into the land. That's when Kimberley saw it, the little cottage tucked in the crook of the property line. A skin tag that was conveniently hidden within the armpit of this body of land. Compared to the massive farmhouse, the cottage was so small, it looked like a scale model of it. It didn't have the big wraparound porch, but it was a weathered white-boarded house.

Kimberley stifled a laugh when she thought of a line from the movie *Zoolander*, "What is this? A center for ants?" Such a silly movie, but it was one she had seen nearly a dozen times thanks to her ex-boyfriend. That should have been a red flag on date one.

"So, what's your favorite movie?" she had asked.

Aaron had replied confidently without skipping a beat. "Easy, *Zoolander*. For sure."

She had first laughed until she saw the confused look on his face and realized he wasn't kidding. She should have tossed her napkin down and walked out of the restaurant, right then and there. Kimberley immediately erased the thought when she looked down at Jessica, her face smushed against her chest. Red cheeks. Messy hair. Those pouty lips still pouting even when her baby girl was asleep. She kissed the top of her head and returned her gaze to the cottage and then her own feet, careful not to trip.

Kimberley had already figured out exactly what was going on, but she wanted to hear it from David. She wanted to hear the reasoning why she and her daughter had to live in quarantine, separated from everyone else. Why she was being viewed as a pariah before even stepping foot on this little slice of David's paradise?

"Not headed into the house?" Kimberley cocked her head even though David wasn't looking at her.

"Nope."

"So, Jessica and I are being kept in timeout?" A tinge of sarcasm and venom dripped from the words. She couldn't help herself. Her New York directness was coming out in full force.

David stopped in his tracks and turned to face Kimberley. "I think you have the wrong idea here, Kimberley. Your mother and I live in the cottage as well. So, if you wanna call it a timeout, be my guest, but it suits us just fine."

Fuck, Kimberley thought to herself. She looked ungrateful, rude, and like an idiot. She bit at the corner of her lower lip, like she usually did when she had said something uncouth. In New

York, that type of directness was the norm, but here she feared she'd end up biting a hole through her lip. She'd have to learn to be like them. *Time to one-eighty the tone*, Kimberley thought, and maybe ask before assuming, without all the New York attitude and directness.

"I was just joking. I think it looks lovely, and the property back here is beautiful," she said, forcing the corners of her lips to move upward and outward. The muscles in her face were already tiring as she wasn't used to masquerading this many pleasantries.

"Good, glad to hear it," David turned back round and called over his shoulder. The whole misunderstanding smoothed over quicker than it occurred.

Kimberley hesitated but followed behind and tried to keep some sort of conversation going, so her stepfather would forget she had offended him and his generosity.

"So, uh… who's in the big house then if you and Mom are out here?" Kimberley asked.

"Emily, Wyatt and the boys."

"Makes sense."

"That's right. They needed the space, especially them boys." David chuckled. "They'd run up the walls if they could."

"I can't wait to meet them."

"They don't sit still long enough to meet them." David chuckled again. "Heck, I've got three hundred acres of farmland, and I don't think that's enough space for them."

"Well, I really appreciate you opening up some space for Jessica and me," Kimberley said, remembering to thank him.

"Not a problem. You're family, and your mom said it was just until you got on your feet. A couple of paychecks and you'll be standing upright." David looked back and gave a quick nod.

She gave a small smile and swallowed hard, caught off guard by David's comment. She hadn't realized she was already on the clock to find a new place. Before even stepping into the cottage,

Kimberley already felt like she had overstayed her welcome...
but those feelings quickly subsided when the front door of the
cottage swung open.

There stood her mother, Nicole. She was thin and tall with a
bob of gray hair. Dressed in a clean cream-white nightgown and
a pair of slippers, she ran to Kimberley and wrapped her arms
around her and her granddaughter.

"I missed you so much," Nicole whispered into Kimberley's
ear. She sniffled.

"Missed you too, Mom."

The fact that Kimberley could wrap her arms around her
mother while holding her daughter made her realize how thin
Nicole had gotten. She rubbed her mother's back, feeling each
vertebra, like small rocks placed evenly down her spine. She
wondered if she was sick. Her mother would have told her, right?
As she pulled away, Kimberley took a closer look at her mom. The
only solid source of light coming from the moon made it difficult
to see her clearly, a shadow cast across her frail face, making her
look like a figment of herself, a drawing of her mother not yet
fully colored in. The eyes she remembered as being vibrant were
dull and bloodshot. Beneath them, sunken and dark bags, like
two freshly dug holes waiting for the eyes to close permanently
and bury themselves within. Her mother had to have been sick or
at the very least not taking care of herself. Kimberley felt a small
sense of relief that she had had the foresight to enroll Jessica in
a local daycare ahead of time, especially now that she had seen
how unwell her mother looked.

Nicole rubbed her granddaughter's sleeping back, swooning
over her. She hadn't seen her since she was a baby.

"She's gotten big," Nicole said, her voice just above a whisper
with a waning sadness held within. Her eyes widened, revealing
more of the red veins that appeared to have no end, like the roots
of an ancient tree.

Kimberley nodded, her eyes still searching her mother's face, absorbing it in its entirety as well as each section of it.

"Let's get her inside and in bed," her mother said, beckoning Kimberley with her hand.

Kimberley ran her fingers through Jessica's hair as she slept peacefully in an old wooden crib she was sure was either passed down from David's family or had been picked up from a local garage sale. The bedroom she and her daughter would be sharing for the foreseeable future was small, but it would do. It was big enough for a full-size bed, a bedside table, a crib, and a tall dresser. That was all she needed. Well, all she really needed was Jessica, so anything beyond that was a luxury. She tucked the small stuffed elephant beneath her daughter's arm. It was dingy, old, and gray with a missing eye, but Jessica loved it more than anything. Kimberley pulled the pink blanket up a little higher and leaned down, planting at least the twelfth kiss on her daughter's forehead for the night.

She took a look around the room, at the two suitcases beside the closet, the bag on the floral bedspread, and then decided she'd unpack it all in the morning. This was hers and Jessica's home now, a nine-by-ten bedroom with popcorn walls and vomit-green shag carpeting. It definitely must have been last updated in the 1970s, when dangerous, textured walls met comfy, ugly floors—a time when people clearly didn't know what they wanted, and it was evident in their choice of interior design. Kimberley walked to the door and reached for the light switch, her hand hovering near it for a moment, one final glance at Jessica. As she turned off the light, the back of her forearm slid down the wall.

"Ouch," she said as her brain registered the searing pain. She brought her arm up to her line of sight, a thick, red scratch stretched three inches long. The popcorn walls had already gotten her; the house drawing the first drop of blood. Kimberley rubbed the blood away and reminded herself to keep Jessica away from the walls, if that were even possible. She rubbed her arm again, trying to polish away the stinging pain.

"She fell right asleep," Kimberley said to her mother as she gently closed the door to the bedroom.

"Oh, that's good." Nicole smiled. "She had a long day."

"Yeah, and she slept for a lot of it. Made it through the trip with only one tantrum."

"You're a lucky mom. When you were little, the only way I could get you to sleep was with a nip of rum."

"Mother of the century." Kimberley rolled her eyes, but her tone was light, and she smiled. It was so good to see her mom.

"Oh, I'm mostly kidding, honey." Nicole gave her daughter's hand a squeeze. "Come, dinner's ready."

Kimberley followed Nicole down the hallway and into the small dining room that fit a square table, four chairs and a buffet filled with white china. The plates on the table were plastic, so she assumed the china was for special guests, of which she clearly was not. David padded into the dining room and took a seat at the table.

"Everything looks great," he said, planting a kiss on Nicole's cheek.

Her mother smiled at David and turned her attention to Kimberley. "Sit. Eat," Nicole said while she took her own seat.

The plates were already pre-served with a scoop of buttery Brussels sprouts, a large cut of flank steak, and an even larger helping of mashed potatoes. A glass of red wine was placed at her and her mom's plates, with an open bottle in the center of the table. Kimberley took a seat across from her mom and next to David.

"No wine for you, David?" Kimberley asked, mostly out of curiosity.

"Wine's for women," David said, pulling a beer from his overalls and opening it before setting it on the table.

Kimberley nodded. No use arguing that line of thinking. She picked up her fork and dove it into the Brussels sprouts.

David cleared his throat. "We say grace in this house, Kimberley." He held her mother's frail hand in his and bowed his head. Kimberley went to reach for his hand out of politeness, but it wasn't in sight and his eyes were already closed. She sensed he had done it on purpose, perhaps displeased that she had eaten a bite of food before giving thanks. Her mother's hand found hers and she held it.

David cleared his throat. "Dear Lord, we thank you for this food and all our blessings. We ask nothing of you as you have already given us so much. Amen."

"Amen," Kimberley and Nicole repeated.

Nicole let go of Kimberley's hand and shot her a sympathetic glance.

David let go of Nicole's hand and brought his other hand up from beneath the table. Without missing a beat, he cut into his rare steak; blood oozed out of it, pooling in the center of his plate. He immediately popped the hunk of meat directly into his mouth. Kimberley watched him for a moment from the corner of her eye. She wasn't the godly type, but his prayer said more about him than anything else he had said this evening. He was a proud man, straight to the point, direct, and he didn't ask for things; he took them himself.

"Don't say grace in your house, Kimberley?" David asked with food still in his mouth.

"I'm usually too hungry for that," she said with a laugh.

David stared back, methodically chewing his food. Kimberley couldn't tell if he was thinking of a response or trying to burn a hole through her head by staring at her and culling some divine power from up high. Thankfully, Kimberley's mother intervened first.

"I'm so happy you and Jessica are here." Nicole beamed as she picked up her fork.

"Me too, Mom." Kimberley dove her fork into the Brussels sprouts she had her eyes on. All day long, she had only eaten peanuts from the plane and an old Larabar she found lying in the bottom of Jessica's diaper bag. Her stomach rumbled as the forkful of food entered her mouth. A homecooked meal. She almost moaned over it. In New York, takeout food and protein bars were the norm, but this, this she could get used to.

"So, David told me Wyatt and Emily live in the house."

David let out a small grunt as if he thought Kimberley was poking the bear.

"They do. You're just going to love them and their two boys. They're a handful," Nicole said, taking a sip of red wine.

"Boys are meant to be handfuls. That's why they're boys," David said as he brought the beer up to his mouth. He took a long swig and set it back on the table with a thud. His eyes never leaving his plate.

Nicole gave a tight smile as she cut her steak up into tiny pieces.

Kimberley made a "hmph" sound. She figured David was the type of man that would explain away all actions of the male sex with "boys will be boys," so his comment didn't come as a surprise to her. David seemed like a simple man with outdated views. She decided she'd lighten up on him, try to be a little nicer, but she'd still keep a close eye. You could never be too careful, especially with men. Kimberley had learned that the hard way.

"You'll meet them tomorrow," Nicole added. "They were supposed to come over tonight, but their youngest, Jack, was running a fever, so she put him to bed early."

"Is he okay?" David asked, his voice full of concern.

"I'm sure he is. Kids get fevers all the time. But Emily didn't want to risk passing anything onto Jessica, just in case it's more serious. Hopefully, he'll sleep it off," Nicole explained.

"He's a tough kid. He's got them Turner genes." David popped another piece of steak in his mouth, chewing proudly.

Nicole smiled and took a sip of her wine. "So, when do you start work?"

"The day after tomorrow." Kimberley took a bite of mashed potatoes.

"Sheriff Sam Walker is highly respected in this community. I'm sure you'll learn a lot from him," David said with a crooked smile.

Kimberley tilted her head. "I'm sure I can teach him a thing or two as well."

Nicole interjected. "Well, Dead Woman Crossing is nothing like New York City, I'm sure. It's rather quiet here."

"You working the first shift?"

"Yes, unless I'm needed otherwise."

David nodded. "Day shift is good. They've got a pretty solid team. Nothing all that exciting though. You might get bored." David picked up his steak with his hands and bit into it like a caveman. He chewed and swallowed, grease and blood from the piece of meat covered his lips and around his mouth. "Might want to move back to the Big Apple after a few months of gangbangerless streets."

"I'm sure I'll be just fine here. I'm looking forward to some peace and quiet. More time with Jessica and my mother, less time with gangbangers," Kimberley said with a small smile directed at her mother.

Nicole smiled back.

"That's good, then. Sounds like the Custer County Sheriff's Office is going to be a good fit for you." David took a long swig of his beer.

Kimberley looked away from her mother's plate and back at David. "I hope so. I'll miss the excitement of the NYPD, but this is what's best for Jessica."

"If you ever get too bored and want a thrill, I'll take ya hunting. Ever been?" David raised an eyebrow.

"For animals? No. Humans? Yes." Kimberley chuckled, but stopped when she saw the confused look on David and Nicole's faces. "Sorry, homicide humor."

Nicole took another sip of her wine. David's mouth curved into a grin when he finally got the joke. "Ha," he said. "That's a good one."

"What do you hunt around here?" Kimberley asked.

"Depends on the season. But deer, bobcats, hogs, turkey, and rabbits are the main ones."

"I might have to take you up on that hunting offer. I'll have to see how thrilling the job is first."

David took another swig of his beer and nodded.

"What's on your agenda for tomorrow?" Nicole asked, changing the subject as she was clearly bored with the hunting conversation. She placed her fork beside her plate.

"Aside from unpacking and meeting Wyatt and Emily, I've got to run to the daycare to meet the staff there." Kimberley cut into her fleshy steak.

"Of course. I'll go with you since I'll be doing some of the pick-ups and drop-offs. You know you don't have to pay for daycare? I'm home all day; I could watch Jessica. Actually, I would love to," Nicole said, the vivacity in her eyes growing.

"Well, Mom, you could have always hopped on a plane?" Just as the words left her mouth, she immediately regretted it.

Nicole pursed her lips together. The light in her eyes dimming slightly.

Kimberley tried to smooth things over. "Actually, no, I don't want to impose. It's good for Jessica to interact with other kids and socialize. Plus, she's a handful," she quickly added.

"She didn't seem like one tonight…" Nicole took a sip of wine.

"That was only because I woke her up early this morning and played with her all day until we had to leave for the airport." Kimberley chewed on a piece of steak.

There was no way she was going to burden her mother with Jessica, especially after witnessing her not eat anything at dinner or seeing how frail and tired she was.

"Oh, alright." Nicole flicked her hand. "But if you change your mind."

"She said no, Nicole. Plus, you have a house to take care of," David argued.

Nicole gave a slight nod.

"I can help around the house," Kimberley said, jutting her chin up at David.

Who was he to tell her mother what she could and could not do?

"That is expected, but I appreciate you offering," David said, setting down his now empty bottle of beer. "Well, I've gotta get up early, so I'm going to head to bed. Good night, you two."

He rose from his chair, leaving his empty plate and beer bottle on the table, and walked down the hallway toward their bedroom.

"Good night," Nicole and Kimberley called out.

His footsteps were heavy and loud throughout the small house.

"Is he alright?" Kimberley asked.

Nicole nodded. "He just doesn't like change. Don't worry. He'll get used to it."

Kimberley searched her mother's face again, but it remained neutral.

"Do you need help cleaning up?" she offered.

"No, of course not. You've had a long day. Please go to bed," her mother said, standing from her chair and picking up her full plate of food and David's empty plate. She stacked them on top of each other.

Kimberley slowly rose from her seat.

"Are you sure?"

Nicole hesitated for a moment. "How about you help me finish off another bottle of wine instead?" she said with a smile.

Her mother prided herself on taking care of her family in every way she could, which to her was cleaning and cooking. Growing up, it seemed to be the one thing Nicole *could* do that wouldn't infuriate Kimberley's father, so she put all of her energy into having a spotless home and preparing the best meals she could, despite only being able to afford the cheapest of ingredients. Her father worked in a factory and her mother was a secretary and, with only one child, they should have been financially stable at worst. However, her father's drinking consumed a large portion of their income, dropping them from middle class to just scraping by.

"Deal," Kimberley said, smiling back.

"I figured that was an offer you couldn't resist," Nicole said over her shoulder as she left the dining room carrying the plates, silverware, and empty bottles. She returned only a moment later with a bottle of red wine and a corkscrew.

"You know I can help with more than just drinking the wine?" Kimberley teased.

"I know. That's why I brought the corkscrew. Open and pour. I'll just be a moment," Nicole said with a laugh, disappearing back into the kitchen again.

Kimberley shook her head and smiled. She missed moments like this. Her and her mom hadn't had nearly enough of them. From the kitchen, she heard water splashing and pans banging, while she uncorked the bottle. Nicole was clearly rushing to get back to her daughter. Just as she finished pouring the two glasses of wine, her mother emerged into the dining room, slightly out of breath. A couple of beads of sweat clung to her hairline.

"See, I told you it would only be a moment," Nicole said, taking a seat.

Her mother raised her glass. "To having my babies home." She smiled, but a glossiness formed in her eyes.

"To being home," Kimberley added. They clinked their glasses together and drank.

"I was really sad to hear about Aaron." Nicole set her glass down. "When I met him, it seemed like you two made a good team."

It had been a couple of days before Kimberley's due date when Nicole had met Aaron in person.

"Wow, I can see where Kimberley gets her good looks from," Aaron had said, smothering her mother with charm. He had won Kimberley over the same way. Her mother blushed and hugged Aaron, officially welcoming him into the family despite the fact that he and Kimberley weren't engaged and he had only recently decided to step up as a father.

Her mother had stayed with her for ten days, helping with last-minute preparations for Jessica, being there for the birth, and then helping care for a newborn baby. During that time, Aaron had been on his best behavior, attentive in every sense of the word. Feeding and changing Jessica, waking up with her, rocking her until she stopped crying. He even gave nightly foot rubs to Kimberley and prepared her and Nicole nutritious and hearty dinners. So, did Kimberley and Aaron make a good team? It sure seemed that way.

"Looks can be deceiving." Kimberley shrugged away the memory, taking another sip of her wine, careful to swallow it completely. Aaron was like a gag reflex. Just thinking about him made her want to throw up.

"What do you mean, sweetie?" Nicole's eyebrows drew together with concern.

Kimberley looked around the dining room, then back at her mother. She'd never uttered the words aloud, never told anyone how awful or selfish Aaron really was.

"Aaron walked out on Jessica and me well before she was born." Kimberley still couldn't say it. Her words faltered. She was embarrassed she had picked a partner that had been so selfish, so like her own father—minus the addiction. It was true, the apple didn't fall far from the tree, and it was why she had never told her mother.

Nicole tilted her head in confusion.

"He pushed me for an abortion when I told him I was pregnant. He pushed for it all the way up until I was twenty-four weeks."

Nicole gasped. Reaching her hand out for her daughter's, she held it. "I wish you would have told me this before."

"I know. I didn't want to tell anyone, because I don't want Jessica ever finding out that her father wanted to abort her."

"What changed? Why was he there for the birth?" Nicole creased her brow.

"I'm not sure. Trying to clear his conscience or something. He was gone two weeks later, claiming it was too much for him to handle, and he never wanted her anyway. But he still manages to send a text here and there to ask how she is, as if he cares." Kimberley shrugged her shoulders and took a long sip of her wine.

Nicole refilled both their glasses.

"Jessica is better off without him and so are you. He's an asshole," she said with a stern nod.

Kimberley let out a small laugh. She always loved when her mother would get a little tipsy and crass. It was completely out of character for her, but it was refreshing to Kimberley.

"He is."

"You'll find a nice man here in Oklahoma, a real southern gentleman," Nicole said encouragingly.

Dating was the last thing on Kimberley's mind. Unlike her mother, she was okay with being alone; maybe not for always, but for now, alone was just fine. Kimberley shuddered at the thought of dating a southern gentleman. She could open her own damn doors, pull out her own chair, pay for her own meals, and hold her own umbrella.

"Anything I should know about Dead Woman Crossing?" Kimberley asked, quickly changing the subject before her mother tried setting her up or started detailing all the local bachelors.

"People are nice around here. Striking up conversations with strangers is just what they do in the South. Might seem odd at first, especially coming from the New York. I felt the same way when I moved here from Jersey. But, after a while, you'll start to embrace and enjoy it."

"Enjoy? I don't know about that," Kimberley teased.

"Oh, just wait and see. You'll be out and about saying 'Hey y'all,' to strangers in no time." Nicole laughed.

Kimberley took another drink of her wine, finishing it. A yawn forced its way out of her.

"Sweetie, you're tired. Go on and head to bed."

"I've got a set bedtime again," Kimberley teased.

"Yes. Now off to bed." Nicole smiled.

Kimberley rose from her chair and smiled back. "Night, Mom."

"Good night, Kimberley."

Kimberley pushed her chair in, trying to leave as little mess as possible. She was about to pick up her empty glass to go clean it, but she knew her mother would tell her to put it down and leave it for her.

"I'm so happy you and Jessica are here," Nicole added.

She had said that to her already. Her mom had always been that way. When she meant something, she said it more than once.

"Me too, Mom." Kimberley glanced again at her mother and then left the dining room.

She walked down the dark hallway, the floorboards creaking beneath her with each step, careful not to run her hands along the hazardous walls. Standing in front of her bedroom, she slowly opened the door and, without turning on the light, she entered and closed it gently. She felt her way to the bed, removing the bag from it, pulling up the covers and sliding underneath them. Kimberley had already memorized the layout of most of the house, where every item and piece of furniture was, just by walking through it. She was good at that sort of thing.

CHAPTER THREE

Kimberley sat up from her bed, still dressed in her travel clothes from the day before. She had been too tired to change, too tired to brush her teeth, too tired to wash her face. As soon as her head hit the pillow, she was out like a light. She reached for her phone, noting the time, 7 a.m. Kimberley hopped out of bed and walked to the crib, expecting to find Jessica, but the crib was empty. Panicking, she ran out of the room, down the hall, and into the kitchen. Relief hit her just as quickly as the panic did when she spotted Nicole holding Jessica while she poured herself a cup of coffee. Kimberley smiled at the sight of grandmother and granddaughter. Jessica was awake, holding and petting her toy elephant, saying "Ellie," over and over again. It was as close as she had gotten to saying elephant.

"Good morning," her mother said as she turned around and spotted a frazzled Kimberley. Her entire appearance was disheveled thanks to a deep, deep sleep—the first in a very, very long time.

She was surprised she hadn't heard her mother come in and get Jessica. Kimberley was used to waking to any and every sound. She had always been that way. Growing up with a father that was like an atomic bomb, ready to explode at any time, day or night, had heightened her sense of awareness, whether she was asleep or awake. But it had gotten more intense since becoming a mother herself.

Kimberley and Aaron had lived together the first two weeks of Jessica's life. He had helped out, waking up in the middle of the night to tend to her when she was crying as Kimberley was still healing from giving birth and was dealing with a bout of postpartum blues. She remembered the night that changed her. Jessica had begun to cry sometime in the wee hours of the morning. Kimberley stirred awake almost immediately.

"Go back to sleep. I've got her," Aaron said, rubbing his hand across her swollen belly.

Kimberley smiled, relief rippling through her, grateful Aaron had finally decided to step up as a man and a father. People could change, she remembered thinking.

Aaron slid out of bed and softly padded out of the bedroom, closing the door behind him. Kimberley rolled over and let her heavy eyelids close, drifting back to sleep.

She stirred awake sometime later from the piercing cries coming from the living room where Jessica's crib was. She had wanted to put the crib in the bedroom, but there was barely room to walk around the bed, let alone space for a baby. Kimberley wasn't sure if Jessica was crying again or the crying had never stopped. She glanced over at the clock, 3 a.m. The space beside her was empty, so she assumed Aaron was tending to Jessica and she opted to wait a few minutes. She didn't want to make him feel as though he couldn't handle it as Kimberley believed it would push him away. She watched the clock, waiting for the numbers to turn over, while her baby cried and cried on the other side of the door.

3:01 a.m.
She held her breath, trying to hear Aaron's footsteps or whispers. She listened for running water, the fridge door opening, cabinets closing, any sign that he was prepping a bottle.

3:02 a.m.
Kimberley exhaled. Jessica's crying hadn't become any louder, but it felt louder to Kimberley.

3:03 a.m.
She sat up in bed slowly. The metal frame creaked.

3:04 a.m.
Her bare feet touched the worn hardwood floor.

3:05 a.m.
She stood up. Creak. Creak. Creak. As she walked to the door, Kimberley took a deep breath. She still hadn't heard Aaron, but how could she when the only thing she could hear was her baby crying?

3:06 a.m.
Kimberley threw open the door, running to the crib right outside of it. When she looked inside, she gasped. The world around her went silent. Inside, there was nothing but a small stuffed elephant. Where was her baby? The dark room spun. Was she dreaming? Was this a dream? Would she wake up soon?

A crying scream from the other side of the room brought her world back. She flipped on the light switch beside her, squeezing her eyes closed for a moment. She blinked them open slowly, adjusting to the brightness. The apartment was small, one room contained both the kitchen and the living room and all that fit inside of both of them was a loveseat, a table for two, an end table and a TV stand. The recliner was given away to make room for the crib. She stumbled past the loveseat and there on the other side, lying on the hardwood floor was Jessica wrapped in a blanket, alone. Kimberley's eyes filled with tears as she scooped her daughter up into her arms, holding her close. She walked to the crib, grabbing the stuffed elephant her mother had given Jessica the week before and tucked it between her and her baby. It seemed to almost immediately comfort her crying child. Kimberley collapsed onto the couch, apologizing profusely to the little girl that would

never remember. But Kimberley would. That night had triggered
something in Kimberley, and as she rocked her daughter back to
sleep, she remembered thinking, people could change.

Kimberley shook her head slightly, brushing the memory away.
"Morning, Mom," she said.

Kimberley walked over to her mother and Jessica. "Good
morning, baby girl." She pinched at her chubby cheeks. Jessica
smiled and laughed. "Mama," she said, reaching out her arms.

"Want me to take her?" Kimberley offered. Jessica was around
twenty-two pounds, according to her last doctor visit, which was
just before leaving the city, but she looked much larger in her
mother's arms.

"Oh no. I've got her. Have some coffee. I just brewed a fresh pot
and there's cinnamon rolls on the counter," Nicole said, bouncing
Jessica up and down, while she paced around the kitchen.

The kitchen was small, with a bar top counter and some stools
that were never used, based on their accumulation of dust. A
tacky rooster backsplash lined the back of the counters jutting
up toward white cupboards that mirrored the façade of the rest
of the house. The appliances looked old and outdated, as if they
had been installed back when the shag carpeting in Kimberley's
bedroom had been in style. From the appearance of the cottage, it
really hadn't been made a home yet as it lacked any sort of personal
touch that she knew her mother to have, like florals. Their home
growing up had floral drapes, floral pillows, a floral backsplash.
If it had petals, her mother would purchase it. Kimberley always
believed her choice of décor was her mother's way of brightening
up a dark home with a dark secret.

Kimberley grabbed herself a mug and poured a cup of coffee,
which smelled like Folgers, America's cheapest well-known coffee.
Her mom had never been a picky coffee drinker. If it was brown
and hot, to her it was coffee and she'd drink it. She walked over

to the counter and took a seat at one of the stools, quickly wiping away the dust with her hand while her mother's back was turned. She grabbed a gooey cinnamon roll, her mother's specialty once she was rested in place. Kimberley noticed only one other roll was missing from the pan, so she assumed David had eaten it and her mother had only consumed the brown water she called coffee. Taking a bite out of it was like having a vivid flashback of her own childhood. Her mother up at the crack of dawn, while the home was still peaceful. Her dad still sober or at the very least getting there while he was passed out on the couch with his tongue hanging out. As a child, her mother could pretend her marriage was good and she was happy in the mornings, smothering cinnamon rolls with creamy frosting. Making coffee. Cleaning. Tidying up. Doing everything she could to create a façade for her daughter that their life was perfectly normal and that the father that chose his vices over his own family wasn't a threat, even though Kimberley knew he was, like a sleeping dragon living within their own home.

"How'd you sleep?" Nicole asked, pulling Kimberley from her vivid flashback.

Jessica wiggled and giggled while her grandma bounced her around the kitchen. She reached out her hands when Nicole walked past the pan of cinnamon rolls like she was drawn to them. Her little hands grasping in the air.

"Oh, you want Grandma's famous cinnamon rolls?" Nicole said cheerily to her granddaughter. She grabbed a chunk and as soon as it was in Jessica's reach, it was basically already in her mouth. Her eyes lit up as she devoured it.

"A little too well. I didn't even hear you come into my room this morning. I haven't slept that well since Jessica was just a couple weeks old." Kimberley set the half-eaten cinnamon roll down on a napkin her mother had placed in front of her while she was caught up in her own thoughts.

"I was as quiet as a mouse," Nicole said. "Not like this elephant. Right, Jessica? Can you say 'elephant'?"

"Ellie," Jessica said with a giggle.

"That's close. Can you say 'Nana'?" Nicole grinned while smothering Jessica with kisses on her cheeks.

"Na… na," Jessica said, sounding it out.

Nicole nearly leaped up and down. Her smile stretched so far; Kimberley feared her lips would split down the center. "Did you hear that? She said 'Nana'!"

Kimberley couldn't help but smile too. "Thanks, Mom, for helping out."

"It's my pleasure," she said, never taking her eyes off Jessica.

Kimberley had never seen her mother happier than she was in that moment. It brought a warmness to her heart, and she knew she had made the right decision to move her and Jessica to Oklahoma. The annoyance toward her ex was still there and the anger about being passed over for a position she had rightfully earned was still present. But those feelings were miniscule compared to what she was feeling right now: contentment.

"She's going to be stringing together sentences in no time," Kimberley said.

"Is she behind?" Nicole asked, raising an eyebrow not in a judgmental way, more so curious than anything else.

A wave of guilt hit Kimberley just as she took a sip of the piping hot coffee. The burn on the tongue was well deserved, she thought to herself.

"No, but she's not ahead either," Kimberley said.

She knew the long hours, coming home too tired to interact with her baby, and only being able to afford substandard daycare, and by that she meant the old woman that lived in her building, wasn't giving Jessica the life she deserved. And she had vowed to get her into the best daycare in Oklahoma—whatever that looked like—and spend as much time with her as her job allowed. Plus, having her own mother around would help.

"That's alright. You were a late talker too," Nicole said. "And then when you finally started, I couldn't get you to shut up." She smirked at Kimberley.

"Ha-ha," Kimberley mocked while she pulled the cinnamon roll apart and popped another piece in her mouth.

"I'll get you talking in no time," Nicole said to Jessica while she nuzzled her neck.

"Where's David?" Kimberley asked.

"He's somewhere out on the farm, pitter-pattering with something."

She placed Jessica in a wooden highchair, strapping her in with two straps she tied into a bow, and locking in a tray. Kimberley hadn't even noticed it. It was clearly old, like everything else in the house, and definitely wasn't up to the child safety standards of present day, but it was better than what she had in the city. Living in New York with sky-high rent and raising a daughter on her own, never afforded Kimberley the privilege of saving money. Oklahoma would change that and, with that, she'd provide Jessica with the best.

"I thought he was retired, and Wyatt was running the farm?" Kimberley raised an eyebrow over the top of her coffee mug.

"Ha. David won't retire until he's dead. He's a hardworking man that can't seem to sit still. If he's not working on the farm, he's helping out a neighbor or running errands."

Nicole opened the fridge, pulling out an apple and a yogurt. On top of the fridge, she grabbed a box of Cheerios and a loaf of bread. "Anything she's allergic to?" she asked before proceeding.

Kimberley shook her head. "Not that I know of. She's been good with what I've given her, which is everything from takeout Chinese to takeout pizza."

Nicole slightly frowned, but quickly rotated it into a small smile for her granddaughter.

"Such a good girl," Nicole said, leaning over Jessica. "You get only the best in this house." She scooped a handful of Cheerios from the box and set them on the tray table of the highchair. "Yummy, yummy. These were your mom's favorite snack when she was a kid."

Jessica immediately smacked her hand against the tray, making all the Cheerios bounce. She giggled uncontrollably until she popped a few in her mouth. "Ummy," she said with glee.

"That's right. Y-ummy," Nicole said over pronouncing the "Y" for Jessica.

Jessica grabbed a few more and splatted them into her mouth. "Yummy," she said.

"Good girl." Nicole turned to Kimberley with a smile. "See, talking in no time." She winked.

Kimberley couldn't help but smile back. Her mother had come alive overnight. She was still frail, but she had a strength to her. The bags were still under her eyes, but the red veins had faded slightly. And her smile was so infectious that it made Jessica and even herself light up. In this moment, her mother appeared genuinely happy, and she hoped it would continue.

Nicole sliced up the apple into small pieces for her granddaughter and put them onto a small plate. She scooped a couple of spoonfuls of yogurt from the container and put them on the plate too. Jessica had finished clearing the Cheerios from the tray and was now slamming her hands on the tray saying, "More."

"Just like your mom," Nicole joked, setting the plate on the tray. "I like to dip the apple in the yogurt," she said while she picked up a piece, smothered it in yogurt and popped it in her own mouth.

Jessica laughed, picked up a piece of apple, dunked it into the yogurt and put it into her mouth, copying everything her grandma had just done. "Yu… mmy," she said.

"That's right. Yummy." Nicole beamed.

She turned toward Kimberley. "I've got everything under control for now. Why don't you go get ready for the day and pop over to Emily's? She's expecting you."

"She is?"

"Oh yes. She stopped over while you were asleep, and I told her I'd send you over when you woke up."

Kimberley stood up apprehensively, looking over at Jessica who was devouring everything on her plate and then back at Nicole.

"Don't worry. I got it," her mother reaffirmed.

She nodded. "Thanks, Mom."

Her cautiousness had nothing to do with her mother. It ran deeper than that, threaded through a dysfunctional childhood, ensnared around an alcoholic, abusive father, and tied in a sloppy bow by an ex that abandoned their daughter, leaving her lying on a floor, too inconsiderate to put her back in her crib or wake Kimberley and tell her to her face that he was a fuckwad.

CHAPTER FOUR

Kimberley pushed back the yellow shower curtain, immediately wrapping a towel around her. She carefully stepped out of the puke-green-colored tub onto the peeling linoleum tile. Tousling her hair with her fingers, she walked to the pedestal sink, which matched the puke-green tub and the puke-green toilet. *What the hell were people thinking in the 70s?* Smearing a section of the steam-fogged mirror with her hand, she revealed her face and studied it for a moment. She didn't look different, but she felt different. Her wet dark brown hair hung heavily around her heart-shaped face. Tiny droplets of water slid from her long tresses down her bare skin. Her eyes were still as blue as they were back in the city, but outside against the Oklahoma blue skies, they'd probably pale in comparison. Her full lips had started to crack. She'd credit dusty, dry Oklahoma for that. Less than twelve hours in the state, and it had already left its mark on her. Leaning closer to the mirror, she pulled at her porcelain skin that had a pink hue to it thanks to the scalding hot shower. She inspected it closely. It too was dry. *Thanks, Oklahoma.*

Dressed in a white T-shirt and black pants, Kimberley walked down the rocky path toward the large farmhouse. Her hair was still damp and pulled back in a low ponytail and a pair of black Wayfarers sat on top of her head. She had showered and unpacked and checked on Jessica at least six times before her mother finally shooed her out of the house. The sun was set high in the sky, its rays scorching Kimberley and the land. She pulled her glasses down in front of her eyes, blocking out the light but not the heat. Her mother had told her she was going to burn up in those pants, but it was all she had. She'd never be caught dead in a pair of shorts in NYC. Too many nasty things to get on you, like bodily fluids. It was always best to cover up no matter how blisteringly hot it was.

Walking around the side of the house, she came upon the large white wraparound porch. It looked even better in the daytime, like it was straight out of a movie set. Before she was done admiring the house, the screen door flung open, slamming against the siding.

At first glance, she thought it was David, but the man was much too young to be David. The man was holding a glass of water, dressed in a white T-shirt that appeared damp with what she assumed was sweat. His blue jeans looked brown thanks to the dirt that was plastered to them. He tipped back the glass of water, drinking the whole thing in two large gulps. With his chin raised, she could see a part of his beard that hadn't grown in thanks to a thick scar about an inch in length. His hair was dark and cut short, almost like a buzz cut. She was sure it hadn't been professionally done because there were areas that were cut a bit too close. The bags under his eyes were the only thing soft and round. Everything else about him was chiseled with sharp edges, from his jawline to his cracked knuckles.

"You must be Wyatt," Kimberley said smiling.

He set the glass on the railing of the porch and wiped his mouth with the back of his hand.

"Emily, come get this glass," he called over his shoulder.

His face was a mix of tan, red, and stubble. Although, Kimberley saw a bit of paleness there as well. He was clearly exhausted, evident due to his red-rimmed eyes and the breath he just couldn't seem to catch no matter how cool and calm he tried to appear. Kimberley assumed he had been up and working for hours… and, perhaps, he hadn't slept at all.

"Yeah, I'm Wyatt. You must be Kimberley," he said, walking down the steps.

Kimberley nodded. "Great house you have here."

She looked up at the large white weather-boarded farmhouse, taking it all in again. It was clearly a source of pride as the outside of the home was well taken care of. No peeling or cracked paint in sight. Yellow and white flowers lined the wraparound porch, planted evenly apart. The outside of the home had both a man and a woman's touch, and Kimberley wondered if that continued inside of the house.

"Sorry, I don't really have time for the small talk. I've got work to do, but I'll catch up with you later." He took a sharp turn at the bottom of the stairs toward the field.

Kimberley watched him walk away. He glanced back once, and she tipped her head at him. It wasn't exactly the southern hospitality she was expecting.

"I'm sorry about him," Emily said, picking up the glass Wyatt had left. "He's overworked and overtired." Her voice was mousey, and she gave a pleasant smile.

Emily was dressed in a floral-print dress that went down to her knees. Her dirty blond hair fell above her shoulders and was perfectly in place. Her makeup was minimal, if she was wearing any at all. Kimberley couldn't really tell if the rosiness of her cheeks and lips was natural or not. She was very pretty, but with the way she dressed, she appeared to be muting her own appearance, like a woman in the 1950s.

"I'm Emily," she said, extending her hand and walking across the porch.

Kimberley quickly jogged up the stairs and reached for hers, shaking it. "I'm Kimberley."

"Well, it's nice to finally meet you," she said with a wide smile, taking a step back. "Your mother has been telling me all about you and your daughter... Jessica, right?"

"Yeah, that's right."

"She's just a little one. How old again?"

"Sixteen months."

"Oh, yeah. Such a good age. She'll be having you pull your hair out in no time though. When they hit two, all hell breaks loose, and I don't think it gets better until they're thirty," Emily said with a laugh.

"I heard your boys are a handful."

"A handful? That's putting it lightly. Let me guess, my dad said that? To him, those boys can do no wrong. Grandparents, am I right? Oh... where are my manners?" She flicked her hand. "Would you like some lemonade? I'll get us some," Emily added before Kimberley could refuse.

Kimberley typically only drank coffee, water, beer, and cheap whiskey. The occasional glass of wine at dinner was the only other liquid that ventured into her life. Emily disappeared inside, telling her she'd be right back. Kimberley walked to a pair of rockers with a small table between them and took a seat. She slowly rocked back and forth, taking in everything she could see from the wraparound porch. It really looked like a scene out of *The Grapes of Wrath*. Beyond the sparse wild grass of the front yard, the dirt road marked the edge of the property, and tall fields of wheat stretched as far as the eye could see. A few trees were randomly scattered throughout, as if they were there only by accident. It appeared as if the birds had an unspoken rule not to defecate on this stretch of land and scatter seeds throughout, and only a few rulebreakers who couldn't hold their bowels had left permanent remembrances of their poor planning.

Not more than a couple of minutes later, Emily emerged from the house with two glasses and a pitcher of lemonade that looked as though it was freshly squeezed. She poured Kimberley a glass first and handed it to her before pouring herself one.

"Cheers to new neighbors." Emily smiled holding up her glass.

Kimberley pulled the glass from her mouth and tapped it against Emily's. "Cheers."

Emily beamed, took a small sip and sat down.

As soon as the liquid hit her tongue, the sweetness perfectly balancing the bright sour acidity, Kimberley knew the lemonade was freshly squeezed. *This* was the southern hospitality she was expecting. She immediately liked Emily. She was kind and welcoming, albeit a little old-fashioned, but so far from what she had seen in Oklahoma, everything here was a bit antiquated.

"Must be different here… ya know, from the city," Emily said as if she were just making small talk, but Kimberley noticed she had said it in a way like she was missing out from a whole big world outside of Oklahoma, dying to know what lay beyond the amber waves of grain.

"It is. It doesn't have the energy that the city has. It has a calmness to it instead, which is nice. It's good to slow down, take a look around, smell the roses as they say." Kimberley took another sip of the refreshing lemonade.

The energy from the city wasn't always exhilarating for Kimberley. At times, it was downright chilling. The fact that a single person could move undetected in a sea of millions taking life, as if they were the Grim Reaper, was haunting. Kimberley had finished pinning up a handful of the crime scene photos across from her desk in her small cubicle. She stared at them intently, hoping something would jump out at her. A woman in her mid-twenties with a blond pixie haircut was shackled to a mattress. A slit six inches in length ran horizontally across her lower abdomen.

Detective Lynn Hunter stepped into the cubicle, taking a seat across from Detective King, blocking the view of the crime scene photos that Kimberley couldn't take her eyes off of. She had golden blond hair that was pulled back in a low bun at the nape of her neck and dark blue eyes that looked like blueberries. She was five years older than Detective King and had been her mentor since she joined the NYPD. Unlike Kimberley, she dressed in a black pants suit, muting her striking appearance. Detective Hunter set a couple of files on the desk in front of Kimberley.

"What have we got?" Kimberley asked, opening them.

"Victim's name is Jenny Roberts. She's a twenty-six-year-old waitress from Harlem. She worked at the Blue Devil Diner. Her boyfriend reported her missing two nights ago, but apparently she had been missing for three days prior to that."

Kimberley arched an eyebrow. "Odd. Why didn't he report it sooner?"

Lynn shook her head. "I've got a couple officers verifying his alibi. Cause of death is the cut on the abdomen. She bled out after that."

Kimberley took a deep breath. "So, the boyfriend is looking like our main suspect?"

"As of now, yes. But what have I taught you?" Lynn tilted her head.

"Never jump to conclusions."

"Exactly. This wasn't a crime of passion—whoever did this took their time. This was planned well. Snatched her after a work shift. Last person to see her was a cook at the restaurant by the name of Mario."

Kimberley flipped a few more pages. "What about him?"

"Pulling background check and verifying his whereabouts the night she went missing."

Kimberley nodded.

"There's one more thing. She was pregnant. Around fifteen weeks. She wasn't showing yet."

"Fuck. Did the boyfriend know?"

"He says he didn't know."

"Do you believe him?" Kimberley leaned forward in her chair.

"It doesn't matter what I believe. It matters what we can prove. Remember that, Detective King."

Kimberley loosened the grip on her glass of lemonade when she realized how tightly she had been holding it… it was how she held onto the past. She shook the memory away.

"Calmness. Yeah, that's a nice way of putting it." Emily rocked in her chair while glancing between Kimberley and the endless fields that made it look like there was nothing else in the world but rolling golden wheat.

Loud footsteps pounded inside the house faster and faster, and suddenly the porch screen door burst open. Two young boys ran across the porch, down the steps and toward the field, laughing and yelling at one another, one saying "Slow down!", the other saying "Hurry up!" They were both lanky with tanned skin, which Kimberley presumed was from playing outside on their big farm all the time. The older one had brown hair and the young one had blond hair with a splattering of freckles on his face. It looked as though they each took after one of their parents.

"I said no running in the house," Emily called out, but they were already too far away for them to hear her.

"Those are my boys. Jack's five and Tom's seven. I love them, but they're making me go gray already," Emily said with a smile.

"Jack seems to be feeling better. My mom mentioned he had a fever." Kimberley nodded.

"He is. I swear he just works himself up at bedtime. That boy's scared of his own shadow. Thinks there's some sort of boogeyman living on the farm. Says he hears things outside at night."

"Kids have quite the imagination," Kimberley said as she watched the boys run around in the tall wheat grass.

"I think he's been watching too much TV. We should have never let him watch *Stranger Things*." Emily shook her head.

"I'll be sure to keep that off the watch list for Jessica," Kimberley said with a smile.

"Oh yes. Where is your little girl?" Emily's face lit up. "I've been dying to meet her."

"Over in the cottage with my mom. She's getting her ready to go visit the daycare center."

"The boys and I'd be happy to tag along if you need company. They have the day off school today because of teacher conferences. They love Happy Trails Daycare and were devastated when we pulled them from the after-school program. Didn't make sense to spend the money anymore now that they're a little older and there's four adults here on the farm."

"Makes sense and, yeah, that'd be great."

Kimberley had wanted it just to be her, her mom, and Jessica, but she wanted a close relationship with Emily and her boys more. That was, after all, why she had moved here... for family. She'd have to put her loner tendencies aside.

They sat and rocked in silence for a few more moments looking out at the field where Jack and Tom ran to and fro, kicking up dirt and wheat and crying, "You're it!" as they tagged one another.

"What's it like?" Emily interrupted the silence, turning her head to look directly at Kimberley.

Emily's eyes were as large and blue as an Oklahoma sky. And she looked at Kimberley like she was a young naïve girl that hadn't set foot out of her town but daydreamed regularly about what the world was like outside of her own bubble.

"What's what like?" Kimberley asked, taking another sip of lemonade.

"New York City. Is it like the movies?"

"Depends what movies you're watching." Kimberley smirked.

Emily looked up and twisted her lips, trying to recall the films.

"Is it dangerous?" she asked.

"No. I mean, parts of it are. But, overall, it's a safe city, especially for its size," Kimberley said proudly as she had been a part of keeping that city safe.

She had seen the ugly side of NYC, the underbelly of the beast, but she had also seen its beauty. New Yorkers were tough and direct, but these same people were the ones that ran toward two falling towers. They were the same ones that rebuilt, that mourned, that helped their fellow neighbors. They were tough, but they were also real. Kimberley hadn't lived in New York City when September 11 happened. She and her family lived across the Hudson River over in New Jersey—something more affordable than Manhattan or Brooklyn. But they could see the skyline from where they lived, and especially those two buildings. How could you not? She was sixteen when the towers fell and remembered it vividly. What happened that day changed New Yorkers and they were certainly close enough to feel that. Heck, people in Alaska were close enough to feel what it had done to the city, how it had changed the people… how it had changed every American. It was the first time in their lifetimes that they were truly "One Nation Under God" or whatever god you believed in. You were one nation under something. But what mattered was the one nation. Nineteen years after the attack, she could still see the effects it had on the people, whether they were there or not. It made you walk a little faster. Be a little nicer. Take a second look at something out of place. The city radiated energy and strength. She had fed on it for a decade and in Oklahoma, Kimberley would have to find a new energy to feed on.

"Are the people mean?" Emily asked meekly.

"No, not at all. They're busy and direct but not mean. They just say what they feel. It may seem mean if you aren't used to it, but the good thing is you always know where you stand with someone. No sugar-coating anything." Kimberley nodded. "What's Oklahoma like?" she asked, changing the subject.

"Well, plain, I guess. You've probably already seen everything we have to offer on the way in. But we do get tornados. Lots of 'em. Ever seen one of those?" She widened her eyes.

"Only in the movies." Kimberley smiled.

"Fairly accurate if you've seen *Twister*. They're scary but they pass quickly."

Kimberley nodded. She had described her own father like that at one point. So, she too had experienced a tornado.

"Your mom tells me you'll be working with Sheriff Sam Walker?" Emily raised an eyebrow.

"That's right. Got any intel on him?"

She had spoken to Sam on the phone a couple of times for interviews and then, after she was hired, just to chat about expectations of the job. He seemed genuine on the phone, like he was happy and proud to have an NYPD detective join his force—at least that's how it sounded. Kimberley had never met him in person, but she would later in the afternoon. She would find out more about him then, when she could look him in the eye while they spoke, study his body language, size him up.

"Sheriff Walker is a wonderful man. He works hard for this community and hasn't let any of his"—Emily looked around searching for the right word—"circumstances hold him back."

"Circum—"

"We're ready!" Nicole announced, walking up the side of the porch with Jessica in tow. Jessica was wearing a floral summer dress that Kimberley had never seen, and it kind of matched Nicole's dress, which hung on her like a potato sack thanks to her small frame.

"Ma… ma," Jessica said as soon as she laid eyes on her mother. Kimberley's heart flipped at the sound of her daughter's voice and the sight of grandmother and granddaughter bonding so well, just as they should.

Kimberley set the empty glass down on the table beside her and rose from her seat, happy to see her daughter but disappointed to not learn more about the circumstances surrounding Sheriff Walker. She made a mental note to ask Emily about it later. It seemed to her that they were getting along well enough. Kimberley wasn't a "let's sit on the porch, gossip, and drink fresh-squeezed lemonade" type, but she could learn to be.

"Emily and her boys are going to come with us," Kimberley said as she jogged down the porch steps toward her mother and daughter.

"Oh, wonderful." Nicole beamed. "I knew you two would get along swimmingly. Emily's too sweet not to love."

Kimberley raised an eyebrow. *Swimmingly?* She must have picked that lingo up around here.

"Hi, sweetie. You look so beautiful in your new dress." Kimberley ran her hand through her daughter's hair. Jessica's eyes were laser focused on the silver watch on Kimberley' wrist. She opened her mouth and sunk her gummy smile into it.

"Ah-ah." A string of sticky saliva dribbled as she pulled her hand out of reach from Jessica.

Kimberley wiped her daughter's mouth with her fingers and wiped away some of the drool that landed on her dress. "You're ruining your new dress, sweetie."

Turning her attention to her mom, she mouthed, "Thank you."

Nicole nodded. "I've got lots more for you. Can't have my sweet granddaughter dressed in black, gray, and white all the time."

She nuzzled Jessica before setting her down. "You're not a New Yorker anymore. You're an Oklahoman."

Kimberley rolled her eyes. "She was stylish in New York," she whispered.

"They'd think she was a goth or a punk round here," Nicole whispered back.

As soon as her feet were firmly planted, Jessica started walking, albeit a little wobbly, but well enough. She reached down and picked up blades of grass, pulling them from the ground and throwing them in the air. Jessica had seen grass before, but rarely as trips to the park were few and far between thanks to Kimberley's demanding work schedule and the fact they didn't live all that close to a park.

"Look at her go. She's adorable!" Emily said.

Kimberley noticed Emily rub her belly, and she wondered if Emily was pregnant or just daydreaming about a little girl of her own.

"BOYS! TIME TO GO!" Emily dropped her hand from her stomach and yelled out toward the field. "Children sure are a blessing," she said back to Kimberley with a smirk.

Kimberley leaned down, picking up Jessica, and just as she hoisted her up, Jessica rocked forward quickly smacking her forehead into her mom's mouth. Kimberley closed her eyes for a moment until the sharp pain faded. "They sure are."

CHAPTER FIVE

Emily sat in the back with Jack on her lap, Tom strapped in beside her on one side of her and Jessica in her car seat on the other. Kimberley had suggested taking two cars, but Nicole and Emily said it was fine as it was a short ride to the daycare center. Nicole drove, while Kimberley sat in the front seat, keeping a close eye on Jessica in the rearview mirror.

"Mom, I want to go back to Happy Trails," Tom whined.

"We are."

"No, for good, like we used to. I miss my friends."

"Me too," Jack added, pushing out his bottom lip.

"You two are grown now. You don't need daycare. I thought you were my big, strong boys?" Emily said.

"I am a big, strong boy," Jack said, holding up his tiny arm to flex it.

"Wow! I had no idea how strong you had gotten. You definitely don't need to go to daycare," Emily said, pretending to admire her boy's muscles.

"Mom, look at mine. I'm even stronger, so I don't need to go to daycare even more than Jack," Tom said, flexing his arm.

"You're both right. So proud of my strong boys." Emily wrapped her arms around both of them, pulling them in for a quick embrace.

Jack looked over at Jessica who was sucking on the trunk of her stuffed elephant, completely content in her car seat. "Jessica, you gotta get stronger," he said.

"And she will." Emily nodded as they pulled into a parking place.

The door slammed behind her as Kimberley hoisted Jessica onto her hip. Nicole grabbed the diaper bag, while Emily took off after her two boys, who were already sprinting toward the front door of the daycare center.

Tom stopped before pushing open the door and flexed both of his arms. "I think I might be too strong to enter, Mom."

"Oh get in there, you goober." Emily laughed, tousling his hair and pushing open the door for her sons to enter.

Kimberley stopped on the sidewalk, taking in the daycare center, which was clearly someone's house that had been transformed for business purposes. The windows were decorated with kids' artwork and colorful window clings. The bushes lining the house were well maintained, appearing to have been recently hedged. Inside, she could hear the laughter of children.

"You really don't have to bring Jessica here. I'd love to watch her," Nicole said, making one final plea to Kimberley.

"I know, Mom. But it's too much to ask of you. You'll still have her for a couple hours after daycare before I get home from work, and I'm sure you'll find that exhausting enough," Kimberley said, walking toward the front door. She was tempted to say yes after having seen the way her mom had bonded so quickly with Jessica. She even thought it'd be funny to tell Emily's boys that Jessica was also too strong for daycare and wouldn't be attending, but she wanted her daughter to interact with kids her own age. Besides, taking care of a sixteen-month-old all day was a lot of work, and she didn't want to burden her mom any more than she already had.

Nicole walked alongside her, a slight frown on her face. "Okay," she said defeated, while she opened the door for Kimberley to step in.

Inside, Kimberley was met with a front foyer that was set up to look like a waiting area. Chairs had been lined along the wall for visitors to sit, and a table sat in the middle acting as a make-shift check-in desk. A plump woman with curly red hair and a permanent smile sat in one of the chairs holding a clipboard. She immediately rose when she saw Kimberley, Jessica, and Nicole.

"Hi, you must be Kimberley," the woman said, holding out her hand. "I'm Margaret, the daycare teacher for our toddler program."

Kimberley nodded, while she shook her hand. "This is Jessica."

Jessica turned her head away from Margaret and rubbed her eyes.

"Oh, she's just being shy. Say hi, Jessica," Nicole said, rubbing her granddaughter's shoulder.

"Hi," Jessica repeated with her head still turned away.

Margaret laughed. "Oh, that's alright, sweetie. You'll warm up in no time."

She redirected her attention to Kimberley, while glancing down at her clipboard and flipping through the pages.

"I think over the phone and via email, we got all the logistical stuff squared away—medical form is filled out, emergency contact form is good, scheduling good, payment is set. So, I guess I'll just show you around."

"That sounds great. And you have my mother down for drop-off and pick-up?" Kimberley asked.

Margaret scanned the pages. "Yes, Nicole, you're good to go. If you'd like to add anyone else, you can do that now or at any time." She nodded and then turned on her foot. "Right, this way."

Kimberley and Nicole followed behind down a hallway, passing by a couple of colorful rooms. Margaret pointed out each room, noting the age groups. She pointed out where the bathroom was, cubbies for the kids, and a kitchen that only staff used to prepare lunches and snacks.

They entered a large three-season room at the end of the hallway that had been insulated for year-round use and converted into a classroom. It looked as though a rainbow had exploded inside of it, with pastels and artwork adorning every square inch of space. Nearly a dozen children were scattered throughout the room. A couple were coloring at a large table. Some were lying on the massive rug flipping through picture books. There were several beanbags and bookshelves surrounding the rug. A couple of kids were playing with toys near an area that had Little Tikes kitchens, stores, and workshops set up.

Jessica wriggled in Kimberley's arms wanting to get down, so she set her down and immediately Jessica walked toward two little girls sitting at a table coloring.

"It's free play right now. We have it for an hour each day to encourage the children to explore their own interests. It's a nice way to observe the kids as well, to see what they like and how they freely interact with others, which will be noted in the weekly reports," Margaret said with a smile.

She pulled a piece of paper from the clipboard and handed it to Kimberley. "This details their daily schedules for this week. We'll also send your little one home with a lunch menu and schedule every Friday for the next week. Jessica will be in great hands here at Happy Trails Daycare."

Kimberley nodded and gave a tight smile. She couldn't argue with what she saw. It all seemed wonderful, and Emily had had nothing but amazing things to say about the place on the car ride over. She watched Jessica laugh and giggle as she colored a sheet of paper with a crayon. She and one of the other little girls exchanged a couple of words back and forth as if they were having a full-blown conversation. Nicole walked over to Jessica and kneeled beside her, helping her hold the crayon properly and pronounce some of the words she was trying to repeat from the other little girl.

"Do you have any questions?" Margaret asked with a beaming smile.

"Can I just look around the building?"

"Umm… sure," Margaret said a little taken back.

"I'm a cop, so it's a bit of a habit to case a place."

Margaret opened her mouth slightly and nodded. "By all means, have a look around."

Kimberley nodded and signaled to her mom that she'd be right back. She left the room, walking down the hallway, passing each of the other daycare rooms again. She wanted to have a clear layout of the house, already considering more than a hundred different things that could go wrong. Kimberley took inventory of everything and double-checked doors, windows, ensuring they all had proper locking mechanisms on them. In one room, she spotted Emily trying to round up her two boys, who were adamant about staying and playing with their friends. Emily waved as Kimberley passed by, saying she'd be out in a minute.

Out in the foyer, Kimberley looked around, specifically at the front door, ensuring it was strong and had several locks on it in case, God forbid, they'd have to keep somebody out. Years and years ago, this sort of worry would have never crossed her mind, but she had learned that even in small-town America, the worst could happen. She gave the solid oak door one final look, bending down to check the bottom of it, but before stepping away, the door swung open, thumping her in the head. A couple of stars burst in the corner of her eyes as she backed up and grabbed the top of her head, pressing her palm against it.

"Oh my God, I'm so sorry," a woman carrying a large diaper bag and holding her child on her hip said.

The woman's eyes were wide and green like emeralds. Her hair was long and dark, and the baby girl had entangled one of her hands in it, wrapping it round and round. She had creamy skin, like a fresh scoop of vanilla ice cream, waiting to be dived into. In this part of the country, that told Kimberley that she spent very little time outside.

"I'm such a klutz," the woman added.

"No, no, no, that was my fault. I shouldn't bend down in front of a door," Kimberley said, lowering her hand from her throbbing head.

"No, it's my fault. I'm running so late… again. Ugh, I'm such a mess," she said, shaking her head.

It was then that the woman realized her daughter's hand had her hair wrapped around it like a spool of thread. "Isobel, what did you do?" she said, trying to get her hair free.

"Let me help." Kimberley stepped forward, taking the bag from the woman and distracting the little girl long enough so the woman could free herself.

"Thanks," she said, switching the child to her other hip. "I'm Hannah, and this little monster is Isobel." She smiled.

Isobel looked like a mini version of her mom: the same green eyes, the same dark hair, although much shorter than the mane Hannah had.

Kimberley shook her hand. "I'm Kimberley. My little one is with my mother in the toddler room. I was just taking a look around."

"You have one too? How old?"

"Sixteen months."

"How is she?"

"She's a handful," Kimberley said with a smirk.

"So, that's what I have to look forward to. Isobel here is fourteen months, and she's been a handful since she learned to crawl." Hannah let out a strained laugh.

"Wait 'til she can walk," Kimberley added with a laugh.

"Oh God." Hannah looked at her daughter and then back at Kimberley, slightly rolling her eyes jokingly.

Kimberley scanned the woman's face, seeing more than what met the eye. She was naturally beautiful and young, no more than twenty-five. She was exhausted, scatterbrained, the telltale signs of a mother with a young child. But there was something else there: a tinge of frustration, perhaps? Something that said, "Can't you see everything I'm trying to deal with here?" Kimberley recognized it, because she had it too. Single mother.

"You must be new in town. Haven't seen you around," Hannah said, gently bouncing her baby who had begun playing with her mother's long, thick hair again.

"I am. Just moved here with my daughter yesterday."

"Your husband didn't move with you?" Hannah asked, obviously fishing to see if she could finally meet someone who shared the commonality with her.

Kimberley picked up on it right away.

"It's just me and Jessica," she said with a wide and inviting smile.

Hannah gave a tight smile and a nod. "It's just me and Isobel too."

She shuffled her feet slightly, unsure of what to say, so Kimberley broke the silence. "You said you were running late?"

Hannah put her hand over her face and shook her head. "Oh yeah, duh. I work part time over at the pharmacy. What about you? What brought you here to Dead Woman Crossing?"

"Well, my mom. Plus, I took a job as the new chief deputy," Kimberley said with a nod.

Hannah opened her mouth and then closed it as if she didn't know what to say. "That's impressive. Congrats." Her enthusiastic tone matched her lit up face.

"Thank you."

"Well, I better get going before I get fired," she said with a slight laugh as she stepped around Kimberley.

Kimberley backed up so she could get through to the back of the house where the childcare rooms were.

"It was really great meeting you, Chief Deputy Kimberley…"

"King," Kimberley added.

"Kimberley King. That's got a nice ring to it. Keep your last name if you ever decide to throw in the towel," Hannah said with a grin.

"Noted." Kimberley smiled back.

Hannah nodded and ducked out of the foyer with Isobel and her bag in tow. She already felt a kind of connection to Hannah, as silly as that sounded. Both of them were very different, coming from two opposite worlds, but they were one and the same. Two women raising children alone.

Hannah briskly walked back out of the childcare room, arms now free of any burden. She sidestepped Kimberley and opened the door but stopped to turn back.

"Ya know, it can be real tough moving to a new town and fitting in or finding friends. I'm sure you're real busy what with Jessica and being a sheriff and all, but... if you ever wanna grab a coffee or, hell, a drink sometime, don't be a stranger, okay?"

Kimberley could tell this was less of a kind and welcome invitation for the sake of being inviting and altruistic and more a woman who desperately wanted a friend of her own. Someone who had lived in this town for quite some time but still felt out of place and like she didn't belong. But a friend wouldn't hurt one bit. It would give her mother and David some space, and it would give more time for Nicole to spend with Jessica.

"Sure," Kimberley said. "I'd like that."

"Okay." Hannah bashfully nodded as she walked away, leaving the daycare and heading to her car.

They hadn't exchanged information, but she knew where to find Hannah—here or at the pharmacy. Plus, Kimberley got the distinct feeling that in this town, everybody knew everybody else.

Nicole and Emily walked together into the foyer where Kimberley was still standing thinking about her conversation with Hannah.

"Hey, where are the kids?" Kimberley asked, looking at them.

"You've got to go down the sheriff's station, and I have some errands to run. I know you weren't going to start until tomorrow, but Margaret said you had a free trial day included," Nicole explained.

"And my boys begged to stay today. Said they were feeling too weak to leave. I guess my whole 'strong boy' approach backfired on me. Kids are too smart for their own good, so I just paid for the day for them. I have a hard time telling them no. Nicole or myself can pick them all up later today," Emily said with a defeated smile. Although, she looked slightly relieved to have her boys out of her hair.

Kimberley assumed Emily didn't get much free time for herself.

"Mom, why didn't you ask me first?" Kimberley tried not to sound annoyed, but she was; she found it all a little odd since Nicole had been begging to watch her granddaughter.

"Oh, I'm sorry. You're right, I should have asked. You're her mom, and it's not my place to make decisions like that for her."

Kimberley paused for a moment, deciding what to say, whether or not to press it. "It's fine. I've gotta head to the sheriff's station and you've got errands to run. So, it all works out," she said, making amends.

Not wanting to get involved, Emily walked ahead, pulling open the door for Kimberley and Nicole.

"Are you sure, sweetie?"

"Yes, Mom. It's completely fine," Kimberley said, walking outside. Nicole and Emily followed behind.

"Here," Nicole called out.

Kimberley turned around just in time to catch a set of car keys. "What's this?"

"Grocery store is just a few blocks away, so Emily and I will walk and have David come get us. You go ahead and take the car," her mother said with a smile.

"You sure?" Kimberley raised an eyebrow.

"Positive. Go on. Make sure you're home for dinner so I can hear all about it."

"And don't let any of them boys give you any grief either," Emily added with a wink.

"Thanks, and you know I won't."

CHAPTER SIX

Kimberley parked in front of the Custer County Sheriff's Office. It was a twenty-five-minute drive from Dead Woman Crossing over to Arapaho where the office was located, but it was a straight shot on a few country back roads and was easier than a three-train subway transfer into Manhattan by a long shot. The building was plain and unassuming. Mostly poured concrete and some beige accent bricks for a bit of aesthetic relief, but it looked roomier than her previous precinct, likely with far fewer bells and whistles on the inside.

Through the double front doors Kimberley was greeted by a sweet and homely woman behind the front desk. Her hair was gray and curly, sitting on top of her head, most likely from a fresh perm. She was average-sized, around seventy years of age and dressed in a floral-print top and navy-blue chinos; a mix of professionalism and her own personality, Kimberley presumed. She looked as though she was a permanent fixture in the building and had likely seen more elected sheriffs come and go than she could even count anymore. Kimberley was going to be floored if her name wasn't Esther or Barb or some other extinct name.

"Well, hello! You must be Kimberley!" The woman leaped up from her desk and glided over to Kimberley with a speed and lightness of foot that she frankly found alarming.

"How did you know?" Kimberley asked, as she hadn't announced when she would be coming in for the day to do meet-and-greets.

"Oh, you can just tell these things. You don't look like someone from around here, and we don't get many visitors who aren't in handcuffs. So, I just put two and two together." She beamed up at her.

"Good hunch. Maybe you should be the new chief deputy," Kimberley said with a smile.

The woman let out a roaring belly laugh. "Who me? No way!" She flicked her hands.

"What's all the racket out there?" a man's voice called out from the back, followed by footsteps. Behind a cubicle partition, a tall man came around the corner.

"Oh, Sheriff Walker. I was just introducing myself to Kimberley here. Silly me, I forgot to tell you my name. I'm Barbara Anne." She shot out a hand to Kimberley.

Kimberley grabbed it in kind and returned the gesture. "Pleased to meet you." *Fucking called it*, she thought to herself.

"Kimberley, eh? Nice of you stop in a day early to get a lay of the land."

Sheriff Sam Walker strolled over and sized her up from her tennis shoes up to her face, where a pair of discerning and sharp eyes stared back at him, giving him the exact same treatment. He shook Kimberley's hand and gave a pleased smile.

"Barb, would you mind getting Kimberley a cup of coffee?" Sam asked.

"Oh, of course. Where are my manners? Do you take cream or sugar?" Barb smiled.

"Just black." Kimberley nodded.

She wasn't used to people taking her coffee orders. Even as a detective in the city, she got her own coffee, but this she could get used to.

"That'll be an easy one for me to remember," Barb said as she walked away.

Kimberley returned her attention to Sheriff Sam Walker. The man in front of her wasn't the one she had pictured when they had spoken on the phone. In her mind, Sam was fifty and potbellied with graying hair and a "who gives a shit" attitude about his job. But that wasn't the case at all. The man standing in front of her clearly took care of himself and couldn't have been older than late thirties. He was a rugged, six-foot-three man with some facial stubble. His ash-brown hair was military cut, and he sported a strong square jaw with a clean smile. Despite being younger than she expected, Kimberley noticed he was a little worn-looking. Perhaps it was due to the demands of the job. But something in his eyes told her it wasn't just that. His dark eyes had a sadness to them, as if he had endured more in his life than most others. Sure, the job can do that to you—dead bodies, missing children, rape, all the worst parts of humanity rolled into one lovely package, delivered to your doorstep daily that you get to keep opening again and again—but this wasn't that, this was… personal.

"Officially, and in person, I'm Sheriff Sam Walker," he said, holding out his large hand.

Kimberley shook it. "I'm Kimberley King, or I guess Chief Deputy King now."

"In here, I'll call you Detective King. I know what that means out where you came from, and it was no simple feat, especially in the NYPD, the most respected police force in the country, maybe the world. In my book, once a detective, always a detective," he said with a wink.

He was clearly impressed with her credentials. He had mentioned on the phone that they never had anyone on the force come from the NYPD before. She assumed it was a major reason why she got the job. The NYPD immediately garners respect, as does the title of detective. Put them together and people look at you like you're some sort of action hero.

"Let me show you around," Sam said, motioning with his hand.

They walked through a couple sets of doors before coming into a large room with two rows of three desks. A deputy sat at one of them, typing vigorously on his keyboard. He glanced up and nodded at the sheriff. He looked young, maybe early twenties, with blond hair and a goatee that was barely visible, just like his presence.

"Deputy Burns. This is our new chief deputy. Kimberley King," Sam introduced.

Deputy Burns stood from his seat. Kimberley could see now he was average-sized. His features were soft, almost feminine. He gave a crooked smile and saluted Kimberley, like a toy soldier.

"Burns, what the hell are you doing?" Sam let out a sigh, shook his head, and scratched at his eyebrow.

The deputy lowered his hand and dropped his smile. "Uhh… sorry."

Kimberley let on a smile and shook the deputy's hand. "Nice to meet you. If you feel more comfortable saluting me, I won't stop you," she teased.

He cracked a smile back.

"Almost done with those reports?" Sam asked.

"Just about. They'll be on your desk before end of day."

Sam gave an approving nod.

The deputy returned to his desk, immediately diving back into his work.

Kimberley looked around the large room. A couple of the desks were tidy. A couple were messy with papers strewn about on them. The walls were covered in several large bulletin boards. One was plastered with posters of lost animals. One was a splattering of information related to unsolved crimes, like hit-and-runs and robberies. And another was probably the handiwork of Barb: deputies' birthday, kudos, events in the community. Unlike the other bulletin boards, it was colorful, well organized, and up to date. She didn't know Barb, but she suspected that this was definitely Barb's touch.

"Here you are, Kimberley," Barb's voice called behind her.

Kimberley turned around to find Barb with a wide smile holding two cups of coffee. "I got one for you too, Sheriff. You both take your coffee the same way," she said with a wink while handing each of them a steaming hot mug of black coffee.

"Thanks, Barb," Sam said with a slight tilt of his head.

"Thank you," Kimberley said, taking the cup.

"Anything else I can get for you two?"

"Nope. All good here." Sam nodded.

She upheld her smile as she backed away and exited through the set of doors she came through.

"She seems great." Kimberley took a small sip to test if the coffee was temperate enough to drink it.

"Barb? She's worked here longer than I've been alive. If you don't like celebrating your birthday, don't tell her when it is. She brings in balloons and cake and gets everyone to sing 'Happy Birthday,'" Sam said with a grin.

"Noted."

They stared at one another for a moment too long; the moment beyond that one single moment that makes the moment a little awkward. Sam cleared his throat and gestured with his free hand around the room.

"So, bathrooms are on the right and the door on the left side leads to a small kitchen break room with a fridge, microwave, table, and chairs. Most people eat at their desk or on the road, but it's there if ya want to use it."

Kimberley followed Sam, walking down the aisle that separated the two rows of desks.

"Most of the daytime and nighttime deputies share desks— we've got four on days and five on nights. Deputy Bearfield is our most senior deputy, so he's got his own space."

"Where's the rest of the deputies?" Kimberley asked, glancing around.

"Patrolling. Burns is our newest deputy, so he's on paperwork."

Kimberley nodded, following behind.

At the far end of the room were two side-by-side offices with big glass windows so they could look out into the rest of the sheriff's station. On the left, a nameplate on the door read "Sheriff Sam Walker." The office on the right had a nameplate that read "Chief Deputy Kimberley King." He walked into the office and flicked on the light. Inside was a desk with a computer, a swivel chair and two chairs on the other side of it. A filing cabinet and a storage wardrobe were against one wall, and the other wall had several shelves filled with random books and binders. On the desk sat a large succulent with fleshy, thick green leaves in a black pot.

"The succulent is from Barb," Sam commented.

Kimberley smiled. "Of course it is."

"Nothing special about the office. It doesn't have a window or anything, but it's your own space. You can store clothes in the wardrobe rather than having to use the locker room. The desk chair is comfy. We can get rid of all these books for you." He pointed to the shelves on the wall filled with books and binders. "Some of the deputies here think those shelves are for storage," he said, shaking his head.

"It's perfectly fine. I mean I never had an office in the NYPD, so this is a massive upgrade." Kimberley nodded, taking a sip of her coffee.

"Really? Even as a detective?"

"Yup. No room for it. Detectives sit in cubes. Patrol officers don't even get that usually. They have to share space. Only captains and above got offices and those were still smaller than this."

"Well, welcome to your mansion then. At least we were able to one-up the NYPD in one area," Sam quipped. "I'll issue your badge and gun tomorrow. Your car is in the shop for inspection and won't be ready 'til the end of the week. Sorry about that. Do you have a way to get around in the meantime?" Sam raised his mug to his lips and took a large gulp, peering at her over the cup.

"I'll make it work."

Kimberley walked to the other side of the desk and set her cup down. She looked over everything, pulling out drawers, and inspecting the chair. She sat down and adjusted it to the height that was most comfortable, while the sheriff observed her.

"Good." Sam rocked back on his heels and then opted to take a seat in the chair in front of her desk, facing Kimberley. "So, let me tell you a little bit about the team first."

Kimberley looked up at him, eager to know more about the people she'd be working with.

"You met Burns out there. He's a good kid, just a bit green."

"I gathered that from his toy-soldier salute."

Sam cracked a smile but continued on. "I also mentioned Deputy Bearfield. He's been on the force for about eight years. He's thorough and reliable, but I must warn you, he's got a bit of a chip on his shoulder right now."

Kimberley raised an eyebrow. "About what?"

"You. He applied for the position of chief deputy, and obviously I went with an outside hire." Sam gestured to Kimberley. "He's a good deputy, but let me know if he gives you any grief."

Kimberley slightly narrowed her eyes. She didn't like coming into a situation where people she didn't even know had an issue with her.

"Will do. Anyone else already have a problem with me?" Her tone was a mix of sarcasm and her New York attitude, which sometimes she just couldn't help.

Sam sighed. "No, and his issue should be more with me than you. I'm the one that didn't hire him. We also have Deputy Hill. He's new to day shift. I had to remove him from the night shift after he accidentally discharged his weapon during a suspected DUI violation." Sam rubbed his forehead.

"Jesus. Did he shoot anyone?" Kimberley sat forward in her seat.

"Yeah, his own foot. He's recovered now, got a bit of a limp and a severely bruised ego, but he's determined to work his way back up, so he'll fall right in line."

"You got quite the team here," she said sarcastically.

"Now you can see why I hired you." Sam smirked. "And let's not forget our crown jewel, Deputy Lodge. You won't meet him for a while as he's on suspension."

"They just keep getting better." Kimberley shook her head. "What's he on suspension for?"

"Domestic violence."

"And he's still working here?" Kimberley already hated the man, and she hadn't even met him.

"Trust me. If I could have fired him, I would have. His dad is on the county board and I know that doesn't sound like anything where you're from, but here it means something. Like I said, you won't meet him for a while though, so no need to worry."

"How long is his suspension?"

Sam looked down at his watch. "He's got another five weeks, pending AA and therapy completion."

"Good." Kimberley nodded. "I respect that you're holding him accountable."

Sam folded his arms in front of his chest, not commenting any further on the matter. "So, that's the daytime team. Any questions?"

"Not about the team. I'm sure I'll get to know them all well in due time."

Sam nodded and scratched his head as if he were thinking of what more to tell Kimberley.

"Oh, yes. Barb's got a map in that binder you'll get tomorrow of the area of Custer County we patrol, so you'll have that for a visual. There are twenty-seven thousand residents in the county, but we tend to stay away from Clinton and Weatherford as they have their own dedicated police departments. Those two communities account for twenty thousand residents. We help them when needed, but otherwise we leave it to them."

"This department is responsible for only seven thousand people?"

Sam nodded. "Yeah, I know. A big dip from NYC's eight million plus residents. We cover the smaller towns and everything between them, so Anthon, Thomas, Custer City, right here in Arapaho, Butler, and good old Dead Woman Crossing."

"Well, alright then." Kimberley clapped her hands together.

"And you mentioned on the phone, you're living over in Dead Woman Crossing on the Turner Farm?"

"That's right." Kimberley nodded.

"Well, since you're living there, let me tell you a little bit about Dead Woman Crossing."

"What's there to know?" She raised an eyebrow.

"Not a lot." Sam chuckled. "But I'll give you the basics. This ain't New York. I'll shoot straight with you. You and I both know that in New York you saw more shit in a one-week period than most of my boys have and will see in their entire careers. Your expertise and experience will be highly valued and don't ever forget that. Around here most of the crimes we come across are traffic incidents, DUI's, some burglaries, domestic abuse incidents, a little bit of drug possession, mostly meth, and every now and than a missing/stolen livestock incident."

"Livestock and meth? Sounds like a riot." Kimberley smiled.

Sam squinted his eyes slightly, caught off guard by her directness. He brought his foot up and laid it across his knee, getting a little more comfortable in his chair.

"We have some town troublemakers. You'll encounter them plenty, I'm sure. I had Barb put together some of the main ones with past offenses, photos, where they live, etc. You'll get those with the rest of the paperwork tomorrow. Then, we got The Trophy

Room. It's our local bar and the town trouble spot. I'm sure you'll be there at least once a week breaking up a brawl or escorting a drunkard out."

Sam drained the rest of his coffee. "Any questions?"

Kimberley hesitated for a moment, thinking of the high-octane pace of her NYPD job. How every day was different, and she never knew if a call would lead to an intense situation like a chase or a murder scene, or if it'd be something mundane like a suspicious person report or a disturbance. A slight pang ensued as she remembered the excitement, but she quickly forced it to subside, reminding herself of all the reasons she came here. Repeating them over in her head. *More time with Jessica. Predictable hours. Mom. More time with Jessica. Predictable hours. Mom. More time with Jessica. Predictable hours. Mom. To forget. To move on.* The words slipped into her mind just as quickly as the memory tied to it.

"Are you sure you two want to see this?" an officer with a potbelly and a bald head asked.

Detective Hunter looked at Kimberley and shook her head, giving her a smirk. "Yes, Officer Richardson," she said, holding up her NYPD homicide detective badge. Kimberley followed suit, flashing hers.

"Oh, sorry," he stammered. He pointed to the ladder that led up to the attic. "Right up there."

Detective Hunter started up the ladder first with Kimberley following behind. The attic was almost entirely empty, save for the victim, a forensics team, and a couple of officers. A Hispanic woman with long dark hair and high cheekbones was strung up by her neck and wrists with the ropes tied to the rafters. Dozens of rope burns and bruises revealed he had pulled her up, strangling her, and then let her down again, up and down, and up and down, for as long as her body could take it, as if she were some sort of string puppet.

"Fucking Jesus," Kimberley said.

"Jesus didn't have anything to do with this."

"Has this been photographed?"

"Yes," a young officer replied.

The camera flashed over and over and over again.

"What do we know about the victim?" Kimberley asked. She always wanted to get to know the victim as best she could. It was her way of remembering and honoring the person. Detective Hunter had taught her that.

"Maria Velasquez, age thirty-two, legal secretary, lived on the lower eastside," an officer holding a notepad said. "We've been looking for her as her husband reported her missing a week ago."

"You think this is tied to the Roberts case? Were they both pregnant?" Kimberley wiped the sweat beads that had formed at her hairline.

"I fucking hope not." Detective Hunter shook her head.

"Sounds breezy," Kimberley finally landed on, pulling herself from her thoughts, sweat trickling down her spine.

He nodded. "On the whole, Dead Woman Crossing and the surrounding areas are pretty safe and quiet, so I hope you'll feel at home."

He stood up from his seat. "I can show you the holding cells, if you'd like. We don't have anyone in them."

"If you've seen one, you've seen them all," Kimberley said, rising from her chair.

Sam gave a rueful smile and left her office.

Kimberley smirked. There was something about Sheriff Walker that she liked. He seemed bigger than this town; not too good for it, but not made from it either. He carried himself like someone with more experience and confidence than this job would lead on. Maybe that's just the type of guy he was, or maybe he had something more to him. Kimberley added that to her list of "things to dig into more". A list that was growing larger in Dead Woman Crossing than she would have thought it would.

CHAPTER SEVEN

Kimberley pulled up to the front of The Trophy Room in her mom's Chevy Impala. She couldn't wait to have her very own police car. The tires crunched the loose gravel as she lined it into an unmarked spot and put the car in park. As Sam had said, it was the town trouble spot, which stood to reason since it was also the *only* spot in town. She figured she'd get acquainted with the place, seeing as the sooner the townsfolk saw her as a neighbor, or at least someone familiar, the sooner they'd respect her—or so she hoped.

Before getting out of the vehicle, she sent a quick text to her mom. *You're picking up Jessica from daycare. Right?*

Nicole had already agreed to do so, but it didn't hurt to double-check.

Her phone buzzed with a reply from Nicole. *Yes, of course.*

Satisfied, Kimberley slid her phone into her pocket and killed the engine. Several tacky neon beer signs lit up the windows of the bar and patrons shuffled around inside. Like the night before, some of the same men stood outside puffing on cigarettes. They hadn't noticed her yet, but she was sure they would as soon as she stepped foot out of the vehicle.

Kimberley took a deep breath, opened the door, and crossed the threshold into the mild evening air. Without even looking, she knew their eyes were on her. She could feel it. She stood up tall, pushed her shoulders back, and walked toward the entrance. Before entering, she eyeballed each of the men with purpose and nodded. Kimberley had learned back during her time in New York to not show weakness, to not cave to others' intimidation. The moment you do, they own you, and you never have a shot at being the true authority figure. Their eyes quickly averted. Kimberley smiled and strolled inside.

Immediately, she could see where the name The Trophy Room had derived from. It was the hundreds of glassy black eyes that seemed to be looking at her and only her. The heads of antelopes, boars, hogs, deer, and bobcats hung on all the walls, haphazardly placed wherever there was room. Taxidermy hawks, pheasants, ducks, and quail forever perched on branches that had been turned into shelves. In the far corner, a black bear stood still, her eyes the blackest of them all. Despite the onslaught of dead animals, The Trophy Room was the epitome of a dive bar. Even the New York City dive bars that were dive-y for the sake of placating to a bunch of hipsters who wanted to drink PBR because it was "ironic" couldn't even come close. A couple of pool tables were off to the side with men tossing money on their next game. Gambling machines ran partially along the side of one wall. Each of them had an older man perched up to them with backs that appeared to be permanently curved. Ashtrays with small plumes of smoke emanating from them rested near the men. Kimberley coughed when she breathed in the thick cigarette smoke that created a haze over the entire bar.

The bar was full of local regulars that were proud to have a place they belonged. It didn't take long, only mere seconds, for all eyes to be on Kimberley as if she were the main act of a performance who had just walked out on stage.

As Kimberley surveyed the bar, she knew Sam was right about one thing. This was the hot spot of Dead Woman Crossing, and like any hot spot, it attracted trouble. She could see it in some of the patrons, but most of all, she could see it in the bartender that stood behind the wraparound bar top. He was tall and lean save for the start of a beer belly that protruded from his ratty T-shirt. His hair was greasy and unkempt, just like the rest of his appearance.

But what Kimberley noticed most about him were his eyes. They were like two large pieces of coal burning a hole into her.

Kimberley walked toward the bar unafraid of the barkeeper nor anyone else in the establishment. She had stared murderers and rapists in the eye back in the city. Some townie sleazeballs were nothing by comparison.

"You're new here," the bartender said, tossing a dirty stained rag over his shoulder as Kimberley bellied up to the bar.

It wasn't a question, so Kimberley didn't answer it. "What do you have on tap?"

"Miller Lite or Bud Light. But I'd recommend Bud if you want to fit in round here," he said.

Kimberley couldn't tell if he was trying to be friendly or combative, but she heeded his advice anyway. There was no sense in ruffling feathers right off the bat. There would be time for that should it come to it. "Bud it is."

"ID?" The bartender raised his brows and held out his hand.

Kimberley rolled her eyes as she knew now he was giving her a hard time. "Really?"

She grabbed her ID from her back pocket, which was sand-wiched between two credit cards, wrapped in a small wad of cash, and handed it over.

"Just making sure to uphold the law," he jibed back. "Kimberley King," he said, looking at the ID and then at her. His mouth curved deeper into a full sleazy grin.

"Chief Deputy King," she corrected. "And your name?"

"Oh, we got ourselves a new badge in here, folks!" he yelled to the room. "Interesting." He looked her up and down and licked his lips. "The name's Ryan, and the pleasure is definitely all mine." Ryan handed back her ID with a leer.

"Ryan, knock that off," an older man sitting on a stool behind the bar said. He was potbellied with a bald head and broken capillaries on his face and nose.

"Sorry, Dad," Ryan said in a hushed voice as he pulled a pint glass from beneath the bar, filling it to the brim with Bud Light. He set it down in front of her.

The old man got off his stool and walked the few steps over to Kimberley, standing beside Ryan. "Sorry about my son. I'm Jerry and I own this 'ere establishment. First rounds on me."

"Thanks, Jerry. Appreciate it," Kimberley said with a nod.

He gave a nod back, grabbing a few empty bottles of beer from the bar top and shuffled through a door into the back.

Kimberley took a seat at the far corner of the bar, as far from Ryan as possible. She wanted to leave right then and there but didn't want to give any of them the satisfaction of making her feel uncomfortable, so she forced herself to stay, at least to finish her beer.

She wanted to drain the whole thing but instead sipped it carefully, watching her surroundings, observing how the patrons interacted with one another. Kimberley noticed that everyone in the bar essentially knew one another.

She caught nuggets of conversations as she surveyed the room.

"Where's your old woman?"

"I left her home with the kids. This is me time. I've been working out on that damn farm all day."

All of it sounded the same to Kimberley, complaining about their wives, their farm, or their sports team.

How could they live this way with everyone knowing nearly everything about you? Where you went to school. Who you've dated. Where you worked. All of their transgressions and flaws might as well be tattooed across their faces.

She took another sip of beer, her eyes peering over the pint glass at the pieces of coal staring back at her from across the bar. Ryan winked at her, causing Kimberley to visibly shiver. She looked away, but she still sensed him and all his smarminess. She turned the swivel part of her stool, focusing on the other side of the bar where the pool tables, dartboards, and gambling machines were set up. Nearly everything was in use aside from one lone slot machine that had a sign on it that read "Out of Order" in black marker.

At one pool table, two men and a woman played, although it appeared the woman was merely there for show, not to actually participate. She held the pool stick, but Kimberley never saw her shoot once, just a fixture for the men. At another table, two burly men that looked like bikers thanks to their leather vests, long hair, and tattoo-covered arms taunted one another as each of them took their shots. A small stack of money sat on the edge of the pool table, and as the game progressed, they became more and more tense and volatile, hurling insults at one another. Two men in their late twenties with dirty jeans and shirts took turns throwing broken darts at a dartboard. For this place being the best Dead Woman Crossing had to offer, they sure didn't take care of it, Kimberley noticed. Nearly everything was damaged in one way or another, which most likely was caused by the brawls the place was known for.

One of the men at the dartboard smirked when he made eye contact with Kimberley. He sported a full beard and his hair was ash-brown and messy, like he used only his fingers to style it. He was muscular and his jeans were torn not for style, but from hard work on a farm Kimberley assumed. She made sure not to acknowledge him and immediately looked away. She wasn't in the mood for company. She was just here to observe and get familiar with her new surroundings.

"Haven't seen you around," the man said. He had approached her despite Kimberley's efforts to ignore him.

"Haven't been around." She took a sip of her beer. She tried to appear as uninterested as possible, only glancing at him for a second before scanning the room as if everything else was more remarkable than him.

"You're a feisty one, ain't ya?" he said with the same smirk he had delivered from across the room.

Kimberley knew what "feisty" meant. It was what a man called a woman when she was unwilling to do what she was told and used her voice for something other than, "Yes, of course." Kimberley nodded and took another drink of her beer.

"What's your name?" he asked.

"Chief Deputy King," she said.

"Very formal. Well then. I'm Mr. Colton. But my friends call me Henry."

"Mr. Colton it is," Kimberley retorted.

"Ouch." Henry placed his hand against his chest dramatically as if she had actually hurt him. "Can I get you a drink?" he asked.

"I already have one thanks to Scooter over there," she said, lifting her pint glass and nodding toward the bartender.

He looked over at Ryan and then exchanged nods. "I'll leave you to it then, Chief Deputy King. But I'm sure I'll be seeing you around," he said with a wink as he walked away, rejoining his friend at the dartboard.

Kimberley watched the two men chat, look over at her, waggle their eyebrows, high five, and return to playing their game. She was glad she was out of earshot because she was sure whatever they were saying wasn't something she wanted to hear.

That's enough of The Trophy Room for me, Kimberley thought to herself as she turned her seat back around toward the bar and drained the rest of her beer. She came, she saw, she cringed. But she was ready to get back home to Jessica in time for her bedtime. Kimberley stood from her bar stool and pulled the cash from her back pocket. She tossed a dollar on the bar top and when she looked up to see if Ryan was watching, she noticed David's son, Wyatt, having a furtive conversation with him at the other end of the bar. How had she not noticed him come in? Why hadn't he come over and said hi?

"Hey, Wyatt," Kimberley called out as she walked around the bar toward him.

Wyatt glanced over at her without any acknowledgment of her presence. For a second, Kimberley felt like she was back in New York City. Wyatt turned toward Ryan, lowering his voice to finish his conversation.

"Hey, I was heading back home. Do you want a ride?" Kimberley asked as she stood beside him, glancing at him then at Ryan and back at him.

"No," Wyatt said abruptly, tightening his jaw.

"Okay then."

Wyatt hadn't been welcoming in the slightest, but she didn't know him well enough to know why he was so cold. His whispered conversation with sleazy Ryan didn't sit well with her, but she pushed the thought aside before she went down a rabbit hole of what it was they could be talking about.

"See ya at home then," Kimberley added as she took a step back and turned toward the door.

Just before she exited, she looked back at Wyatt and Ryan. They had resumed their conversation, ignoring the rest of the world around them, drowning out the chimes of the slot machines, crashing of pool balls, and the honky-tonk from the jukebox. They were speaking with purpose.

CHAPTER EIGHT

Kimberley pulled Jessica's highchair a little closer to her after sitting down at the dining-room table. David took the seat beside her like the night before, cracking open a bottle of Bud Light against the table and taking a swig of it. He was dressed in dirty overalls, but his face and hair were clean, like he had made an effort to freshen up before dinner. Jessica wiggled and giggled in her chair, slapping her hands against the tray—her way of demanding food.

"Just a second, sweetheart. The food's coming," Kimberley said as she pushed some of her daughter's locks out of her face.

"Hungee," Jessica squealed.

"How was your day?" David asked.

"It was good, actually. Emily and the boys came with us over to Happy Trails Daycare and then I went to meet Sam at the station."

"Glad you and Emily are getting along. How were the boys?"

"Great. Exactly as you described… a handful."

David smiled. "They're good kids though. And my granddaughter? How'd she like Happy Trails?"

Kimberley hesitated for a moment, surprised that he had called Jessica his granddaughter again. She thought when he said it at the airport, he was just being nice. But maybe he really did care about her and Jessica. Maybe he did see himself as her grandfather. A small smile crept on her face, considering Jessica having a grandma and a grandpa. Even if her father hadn't died, she would have never allowed him to be a part of Jessica's life.

"She was happy as a clam. I'm sure she'll love it there, being around kids her age. In the city, I had an elderly neighbor lady in my apartment building watch her. It was what I could afford and she was good with Jessica, but I think she'll get more out of a daycare center."

"That's a shame." He slightly shook his head. "Well, she'll have cousins living next door and there's the kids at daycare. Dead Woman Crossing is a close-knit community. She's going to grow up nicely here."

In front of her was a glass of red wine and an open bottle on the table. Her mother had taken her glass into the kitchen to sip at while she finished up with dinner. Kimberley had offered to help, but Nicole had insisted on taking care of it herself.

Kimberley took a long sip from her glass of red wine. It was medium bodied, lighter than she liked, and had notes of berries and pepper. She wasn't a big wine drinker, but she had a strong palate that could pick apart the flavors in any drink or food. Just as she placed the glass back down, Nicole entered the dining room carrying two plates of food. She was wearing a floral apron and her hair was pushed back behind her ears.

She placed a plate of meatloaf and peas in front of David and Kimberley.

"I have rolls too," she said, dashing out of the room.

A moment later, she reemerged with a basket of freshly baked rolls and a small bowl of peas. She placed the basket in the center of the table and the bowl of peas on Jessica's tray.

"Here you are my little hungry, hungry hippo, even though you ate all your snacks earlier," Nicole said, smiling at her granddaughter.

Jessica immediately dove a hand into the peas and before Kimberley could help her, she had smashed a handful into her mouth.

"Yu… mmy," she said. Her eyes lit up.

"That's right. Yummy," Kimberley repeated.

"Looks good," David said. "Hurry, so we can say grace. I'm famished," he said to Nicole.

She nodded, disappeared and reappeared faster than Kimberley could bow her head. Nicole placed her empty glass of wine on the table and her plate that had less than half the food that Kimberley had. She quickly sat down and placed her palm in David's and then reached for her daughter's.

After David finished his prayer, Nicole poured herself another glass of wine, while Kimberley and David began eating. Kimberley made sure to keep a close eye on her mother to see if she would eat anything this time.

"She likes the peas." Kimberley smiled at Jessica and then at her mom.

Nicole nodded with a smile, looking over at her granddaughter. "I couldn't get your mom to eat a single vegetable when she was a child."

"Yum... my," Jessica said again, smashing more peas into her gummy mouth.

"That's not true. I loved mashed potatoes."

"That's hardly a vegetable," Nicole said with a laugh. "Especially when they were smothered with gravy and butter."

"Touché." Kimberley smirked. She brought her wine glass to her lips and took a long drink, slightly closing her eyes for a moment.

Her father sat at the end of the table, his greasy blond hair pulled back in a ponytail, his sharp blue eyes staring back at her, and a beer perched between his lips. Her mother set a plate of food in front of him like a zookeeper would with a wild animal, cautiously. She then set a plate in front of eight-year-old Kimberley.

"Eat up, sweetie," she said, just above a whisper.

Her father didn't wait for Nicole to sit down. He didn't say a prayer. He dove into the goulash, shoving a forkful into his mouth, the grease from the chunks of ground beef dripping down his chin.

"I said I wanted steak tonight. What is this shit?" He spat as he spoke.

"We don't have money for steak," Nicole said meekly.

Kimberley took a couple of small bites, chewing slowly and quietly, wishing she was invisible. She didn't want to sit down for dinner, but her mother insisted as a way to seem like a normal family. But all it did was give Kimberley a front-row seat to her father's dark side.

"Well, then, stop spending money on stupid shit like books for her," he said, pointing at his daughter. "Or those goddamn CDs."

"Those were Kimberley's birthday gifts."

"What the fuck does she need a birthday gift for? I'm the one that brought her into this world. I should get a gift on her goddamn birthday."

Her father took a long swig of his beer, swishing it around in his mouth, and slammed the empty bottle on the table.

Nicole rose immediately to get him another, disappearing into the kitchen.

"You think you're special?" he said, leaning forward and narrowing his eyes at Kimberley.

She shook her head.

"Good. Because you're fucking not. That's what's wrong with your generation. Every last one of you thinks you're so goddamn special. You're an ant. A fucking nothing." He clenched his jaw.

Nicole set the open beer in front of him and gave a small smile to Kimberley.

"Ain't that right, Nicole?"

"What?" Her mother looked over at him.

"She's not fucking special." He pointed at Kimberley. "Tell your daughter, she's nothing."

Nicole pressed her lips firmly together.

"Tell her." He slammed his fist against the table, making the silverware bounce.

Nicole and Kimberley flinched.

"Tell her." He raised his hand, smacking her mother in the back of the head.

Nicole squealed. She looked at Kimberley, her eyes filled with tears. "You're nothing," she said, her lip trembling.

Kimberley opened her eyes and set her glass of wine down. Her father was gone, just a dark memory that haunted her from time to time.

"She is a good little eater. I fed her half my banana when she got home from daycare. I tried giving her just a small piece and she just kept reaching out her hands, saying, 'More,'" David said with a chuckle.

Kimberley ran her hand over her daughter's soft head. "You're going to be such a big, strong girl."

"How was it today at the station?" Nicole picked up her fork, spiking three peas. She slowly brought them to her mouth and chewed.

"Good. Sheriff Walker, Sam that is, gave me the rundown of the department, surrounding areas and Dead Woman Crossing."

"Did you meet Barb?" Nicole's eyes lit up. It was clear Barb had the same effect on everyone she met.

"Yes. She seemed great. Got me a succulent for my office."

"They don't make women like Barb anymore," David commented. He took a swig of his beer.

He was right. She had never met a woman like Barb before.

"Meet anyone else on the force?" David added.

"Just Deputy Burns. The rest of the day-shift workers were out patrolling or out on suspension." Kimberley raised an eyebrow, looking up at David and then glancing at Nicole, gauging if they had heard anything about the woman abuser on the force.

"So, you've heard about Deputy Lodge?" David tilted his head.

"Yeah, Sam filled me in."

"It's wild. You think you know your neighbors. But what goes on behind their doors… you just never know," David said, shaking his head.

"Yeah, it's awful," Nicole said just above a whisper.

"Did he tell you what happened?" David shoveled a hunk of meatloaf into his mouth.

Kimberley shook her head.

He took a swig of beer, rinsing out his mouth and cleared his throat.

"Apparently, Lodge got wasted at The Trophy Room and came home to his wife, Sarah. She had discovered he was having an affair, and when she confronted him, he beat her up pretty bad. He claimed he was drunk, and it had never happened before, but who knows?" David shrugged his shoulders.

"I actually stopped over at The Trophy Room on my way home. Quite the interesting place."

Nicole nodded while taking a sip of her wine. David grabbed a roll from the basket and tore it in half.

"The Trophy Room is really a man's place. No sense in you going there," David said, stuffing a piece of bread in his mouth. "Besides, Lodge hangs out there and you just heard what kind of man he is."

"I'm not afraid of Lodge. Plus, when his suspension is up, he'll be working under me."

David raised his brow. "I'm just saying, it's more of a man's place. There's a nice coffee shop over on the strip and a beauty parlor next door. That's where the women around here hang out."

Kimberley cocked her head. "I go where I like, David."

"Figured you'd say that. No stopping the East Coast from doing what they want here in Podunk, Oklahoma," David replied, not raising his eyes from his plate.

"What's that supposed to mean?"

"I am woman, hear me roar. You got a point to prove?"

"Not trying to prove any points. I'm the chief deputy of this county. No place is off limits."

"Just cause you're a cop, don't mean ya need to go stickin' your nose everywhere. It's like that saying—just cause ya can, doesn't mean ya should."

Kimberley was fuming. Who the fuck was this sexist, backward-ass man to tell her how to live and how to do her job? She was about to unload on him with both barrels and chew his ear off until he inevitably lumbered his ass back to bed. But no. That's exactly what he wanted. He wanted to see the temperamental woman. The one who couldn't keep her emotions in check. To make her look hysterical in front of her mother and upset her daughter. Kimberley wasn't about to give him what he wanted.

"Ya know, maybe you're right, David. I hadn't thought about it like that. The more time I spend poking my nose into everything, the less time I have to do productive things. Maybe I can start patching up all the uniforms at the station and making the other deputies apple pies from time to time. And hell if I get off real early, I could head straight home, with a cold six-pack of Bud Light ready for you and I can get right down to the most important task of the day, making you dinner and then cleaning up after you. I guess this town won't be so bad after all."

"No sense in getting your panties in a bunch. I'm just warning ya. The Trophy Room ain't the place for women." David stabbed his fork into the meatloaf.

"The Trophy Room is child's play to what I've seen in the city." Kimberley narrowed her eyes and stuck a forkful of meatloaf in her mouth. She chewed on the meat while she chewed on the memories of her past... One stuck out most.

Kimberley remembered walking into the dark NYC studio apartment alone as her partner, Detective Hunter, was at a doctor's appointment. Several officers had warned her that she'd never be able to unsee what she was about to behold, but that never swayed her. She owed it to the victim. The first thing that hit her was the smell: a mix of rotting eggs and iron. She had smelled dead bodies before, many times in fact, but this was different. It had its own brand to it, something else that had crept into the regular smell of rot and death. It hung thick and heavy in the air. She covered her mouth with her hand, but it was already inside of her lungs, wrapping in a coil around her bronchioles. The apartment was abandoned, with one room and then a bathroom off to the side. A forensics team was collecting samples from the spoiled food scattered on the counter and the dirty dishes stacked a couple feet high in the sink, hoping to pick up any traces of DNA. Thick, large cockroaches ambled over the counters. They didn't scatter like most roaches do when people are around. They had staked their claim, as this was now their home. She closed her eyes before heading toward the bathroom, prepping herself for what she was about to find. She turned the corner slowly, pushing open the cracked wooden door. Her eyes stared at the linoleum floor that had a pinkish color to it. Areas where it was peeled up were a deep red. It was obvious the blood was both old and new. She looked at the sink, an old pedestal full of red water. More blood. It was clogged as the lift rod for the drain wasn't pulled up. Her eyes went to the mirror. Written in blood across it read, "Who's the King now?" It was a message for Detective Kimberley King. Her fist clenched so tightly that her fingernails drew blood on her left palm. She wiped the palm of her hand against her pants. Her eyes went to the bathtub. A naked woman lay inside of it. Her body covered in hundreds of cigarette burns, thousands of small cuts, massive deep, almost black bruises. Clumps of curly red hair pulled out revealed small barren patches of tiny red dots where the scalp had bled. Her nose was crooked with the bone sticking out, several teeth were missing, and her other eye had been burned in, probably with a cigarette as well. There was so much damage her body looked like one massive wound. The killer had taken his time with her. It was a part of his MO. He liked control, liked feeling as though he were a god. They didn't know much about him, but they knew that. A long incision, nearly a foot long, ran across her lower abdomen.

She heard footsteps behind her. Two uniformed officers stood in the doorway.

"What is it?"

Kimberley stepped out of the way, so they could see the horror she had seen.

Kimberley blinked several times, washing the memory away. She had lost her appetite. She set her fork down and poured herself a full glass of wine, taking a large gulp of it, before setting it back down.

David chewed on his food and on his next words for a moment. "That's cuz y'all ain't got God up there."

Kimberley couldn't argue with that.

Nicole quietly pushed her food around her plate, taking intermittent sips of wine and giving strained glances to both David and Kimberley.

"Maybe we should change the subject," Nicole said meekly, refilling her glass again.

Kimberley noticed her mother hadn't eaten much, but she had drunk half the bottle of wine. Her red eyes now had a sheen to them, as if there were little tiny windows in front of each one. Kimberley drained the rest of her glass, ready to test her mother's method.

"God isn't a subject, Nicole." David pressed his lips firmly together.

"Correct, he is not. He is just one character in one great work of fiction. Hardly important enough to deserve a whole subject," Kimberley said pointedly.

David thinking she was dead serious would rile him up even more than if it were a joke. He dropped his fork, the silverware clanging loudly against the porcelain plate.

"I can't stop you from thinking whatever devilish nonsense you want to think, but while you're living here, in my house, I don't want to hear that kind of talk again." His skin was flushed red, and not from his work outside or the beer.

"Duly noted, massa. After all, the Bible does say a woman is only worth half as much as a man, so you must be twice as right as me. It won't happen again." Kimberley loved this sort of banter.

In the NYPD, it was how you made light of all the darkness that tried to seep into your life every day. Was it a defense mechanism, designed to mask the real issues? Of course, but it was the best weapon at her disposal for now, so why not go with it?

David let out a grunt, an acknowledgment of her agreement.

"Perhaps you and Jessica could come to church with us one of these Sundays?" David said airily.

Mercifully, Kimberley didn't have to answer this because at that moment, Jessica let out a piercing scream. Kimberley immediately tried to soothe her.

"What's wrong, baby girl?" she asked, rubbing her back.

Jessica banged her hands on the tray, pushing the bowl off of it. It hit the floor with a thud. Kimberley bent down and picked it up, noticing it was empty.

"Are you still hungry?" she said as she sat back up.

"Here give it to me." Nicole reached out her hand, taking the bowl from Kimberley and tossing a spoonful of peas into it. Jessica screamed louder, tears streaming down her face.

Nicole placed the bowl of peas in front of her. "Jessica, baby. Look, more peas," she said.

Jessica looked down, her cries began to taper, until she was just sniffling and breathing heavily. As soon as her handful of peas landed in her mouth, she was smiling again.

Kimberley took a deep breath.

"Crisis averted," Nicole said with a laugh.

"For being so little, she's quite loud." David chuckled.

"That scream of hers has nearly given me a heart attack at least a dozen times," Kimberley said, taking a drink of wine.

David picked up his fork and returned to eating his food, while washing every few bites down with a swig of beer. When it was empty, without asking, Nicole immediately got up and retrieved him another. Her mother had always taken care of everyone in her life, even the men who treated her poorly. Kimberley thought of her mother as strong, but this part of her, she found to be weak and subservient.

"After meeting Sheriff Walker, you think you'll like working with him?" David asked.

"Yeah. He seems nice. Very professional."

David nodded his approval. "He is a good man. It'd do ya well to pay attention to him. I know you're from the big city and all, but like I said before, you could probably learn a thing or two from him."

He might be trying to be condescending or dismissive of her skills, but Kimberley wasn't sure. Plus, he was right, you could always learn something from others. That was one of Kimberley's core drivers to keeping her sharp and progressing in life. Always keep learning.

"No, you're right. I'm sure I can, and I'm sure I will."

Jessica let out a massive yawn, her mouth widening almost large enough to swallow the whole bowl before her. She had eaten her weight in peas. Kimberley leaped from her seat, seeing an escape route.

"I'm gonna go put her to bed. I'll be back out to help you clean up in a bit, Mom."

"Nonsense. I can handle it myself. Go take care of your daughter." Nicole's tone was dismissive but loving.

"Thanks, Mom. Come on, you little stinker. Time for bath and bed." Kimberley hoisted Jessica out of the highchair and walked into the kitchen to the sink to wash her pea-covered hands. She then made her way to the bedroom.

"Good night, you two," she called out as she passed by the table again.

"Good night, sweetie," was her mother's reply.

A slight raising of his bottle of Bud Light and a "Night" was David's.

Back in the bedroom after Jessica's bath, Kimberley shuffled her feet across the deep stalks of the shag carpeting over to the crib. She put Jessica into her pajamas. A bit of tussling and horseplay ensued, trying to calm her down fully before bed, but eventually she won out and was able to rest her tired girl into the crib, blanket and elephant following shortly after.

Kimberley looked down at her daughter, admiring how perfect she was in her innocence and love of life, if only that was something she could capture again. She leaned down to kiss her forehead, hoping maybe a piece of that perfection would transfer to her lips and into her, if only for a moment. She leaned her belly into the bar of the crib…

CRACK! The smashing of glass against glass shot through the window and into the bedroom, shaking Kimberley through her core and shot her straight back up. She made her way to the window, her ears on full alert. She heard grass rustling and twigs snapping beneath the weight of something moving across them and then fading off into the distance, silence filling back into its rightful place, followed by crickets and the slight whistle of a light wind across the plains. The noise sounded like it started not far from the cottage. Kimberley hurried back out to the dinner table. David was still sitting there sipping on another beer while Nicole was cleaning everything up, including her nearly full plate of food.

"Did you two hear that?" she asked, trying to keep her anxiety in check to maintain the cool NYPD detective façade. Normally she was never rattled, but this was unfamiliar territory and she didn't care for unpleasant surprises so close in proximity to Jessica.

"Hear what?" David asked.

"Like glass breaking and some rustling of grass and wood snapping, like there's someone outside." Kimberley stood still, trying to hear it again, but her mother was clanking dishes and running water in the kitchen.

David tipped back his beer and shrugged his shoulders. "Didn't hear anything."

"Oh, honey. It's probably just some raccoons or coyotes. We get a lot of them on the farm," Nicole said, scraping her plate of food into the garbage.

"Nicole's right. We got lots of animals out here in the country. They make a ton of noise at night."

Kimberley's shoulders stayed tense, but she accepted her mother and David's answer.

Nicole walked into the dining room with a tied-up bag full of garbage.

"Oh, Mom. Let me get that," Kimberley said, immediately sticking her hand out to take it. She had accepted their explanation for the noise outside, but that didn't mean she wasn't about to check it out. Things go bump in the night, but so do detectives.

Her mother looked as though she was about to say no, but when she saw the strained look in Kimberley's eyes, she obliged, saying thank you.

Kimberley took the bag of garbage and headed out of the dining room, into the living room toward the front door.

"The garbage cans are behind the farmhouse," Nicole said.

She slipped on a pair of tennis shoes and opened the front door, closing it behind her. The outside was quiet, save for crickets that sounded like they were all around her. The air was dry and dusty, pulling the moisture out of her lungs with each breath she took. Kimberley followed the stone path nearly up to the farmhouse, but cut away from it, heading toward the back of the home. A couple of spotlights provided areas of light, but not enough to look out behind the cottage nor any of the buildings on the property. Howls echoed in the distance. Kimberley carefully trudged to the back of the farmhouse and found four large black garbage cans. She opened the first one and tossed the bag inside. Taking a couple of steps away from the house, she stood quietly, listening. Crickets. A rustling sound all around her, the wheatgrass swaying in the soft night wind. Whatever the sound she heard earlier was gone, along with the thing that caused it.

Back inside, Kimberley slid off her shoes.

"I'm going to bed," she called out, turning toward the hallway that led to her bedroom.

David entered the living room with a smirk on his face and a beer bottle in his hand.

"I guess round here ain't child's play after all, since we got our wildlife spookin' an NYPD detective," he said with a chuckle.

Kimberley rolled her eyes and decided against quipping back at him.

"Good night, David," she said curtly.

"I'm just teasing ya, Kimberley. Good night." He took a swig of his beer.

Inside the bedroom, she closed the door and turned off the light, feeling her way to the bed. Kimberley pulled the covers over her and laid still, listening to her daughter's breathing. She closed her eyes, but the sleep didn't come. Instead, her thoughts raced. One after another. What the hell was that noise outside? Did she do the right thing for her and her daughter by coming here? Should she have left the city? Should she have moved to Dead Woman Crossing? There was a whole world out there, and she chose Okla-fucking-homa. What was she thinking? Oh, yes. She was thinking of her mom, her daughter, their future. But would her new job be enough for her? Would this town respect her? Would David and his family accept her? Is this simple place even where she wanted Jessica to grow up? No exposure to anything besides this little bubble? Worry after worry. Thought after thought, each its own vehicle, speeding along a twelve-lane highway at one hundred miles an hour, flying in both directions and just narrowly missing one another, cutting each other off, vying to be in the front of her mind, an impending collision bound to happen. The one thing she was sure of at that point was that she wouldn't be sleeping at all. And before her first day of work, no less. It was just gonna be one of those nights. Kimberley let out a sigh and pulled out her cell phone, opening the Hallmark movie app. With a couple of scrolls, she quickly settled on the film, *The Lost Valentine* starring Betty White and Jennifer Love Hewitt. She had seen it many times, but that didn't bother her. She liked it for what it was: predictable and heartfelt. Kimberley dimmed her phone's brightness, slid her AirPods into her ears, and pressed play.

CHAPTER NINE

Kimberley waved goodbye to Jessica a third time. Her daughter was already so preoccupied with colorful blocks and new friends that she didn't deliver another bye-bye beyond the first one. A small ache settled in Kimberley's heart at leaving Jessica at daycare. In the city, Jessica would cry when she left, but here she didn't even notice. Then again, in the city, she left her with a seventy-year-old woman named Agnes that Kimberley was sure watched soap operas all day. Regardless, Jessica was growing up before her eyes. Kimberley nodded at Margaret, who gave her a reassuring smile back. She left the room and made her way down the hall, through the foyer and when she went to open the front door, it was pushed into her with greater force than she had provided. On the other side, holding the door handle, stood a disheveled Hannah with her daughter, Isobel, propped up on her hip.

"Oh, I am so sorry," she said, taking a step back and looking Kimberley up and down. Recognition hit from the day before and she gave her a clumsy smile. "We have to stop meeting like this." She laughed awkwardly.

"They didn't fire you yesterday?" Kimberley said with a smirk, holding the door open so Hannah could get by.

Hannah crossed the threshold out of breath like she had been running. Her hair was haphazardly pulled back in a messy ponytail and her eyes were dark and heavy. Kimberley assumed she looked similar as she hadn't slept well either. She released the handle, allowing the spring-loaded door to close, keeping the air conditioning and the children contained.

"Unfortunately, not. I keep trying but they just can't seem to cut the cord," she said sarcastically, walking into the foyer.

Hannah bounced Isobel on her hip a couple of times. "You just drop your daughter off?"

Kimberley nodded.

"I need to get here on time one of these days, so our little ones can meet," Hannah said with a strained smile, the smile someone gave when they needed a friend, someone to talk to.

Kimberley recognized that look. She had seen it many times before.

"Well, I'll keep being here at the same time, so maybe five minutes earlier on the old alarm clock and our girls can finally say hello."

"Ha, I've tried that. Hell, I've tried an hour earlier. I just keep hitting snooze. It's like my mind won't let it trick itself. It knows the exact time I need to wake up and be in a constant state of anxiety and rush so we can haphazardly sprint through the morning, not showing up on time to anything and alienating everyone around us. It's really a lovely way to start the day—you should try it sometime."

Kimberley could hear the sarcasm mixed with actual regret and stress. A sad love song, begging for help.

"I just might have to do that. Maybe take a walk on the wild side," Kimberley joked back. She liked Hannah. "Well, I'm off to work, really shouldn't be late on the first day. It was nice seeing you again."

Kimberley made her way toward the front door. As she grabbed the knob, twisted, and pulled the weight in toward her, she felt a hand land on her shoulder and give the slightest suggestion of pressure, urging her body to please turn back around. Hannah was still in the foyer, staring at Kimberley's face.

"Ya know, my offer still stands by the way. If you wanna grab coffee or a drink some time I would be more than happy to." This time the pretense of a warm invitation was gone. The sentence could just as easily be translated as "Please spend time with me. I need a friend. Please."

And Kimberley suddenly knew more about this woman than words could ever say, yet she still wanted to learn more.

"I didn't forget," Kimberley said with a soft smile, trying to keep the situation light. "Look, I'm over at the Custer County Sheriff's Office. How about you call me today on one of your breaks? I'll have a better idea of my schedule, and we can set up some time. Sound good?"

"Sure! Yeah. I can do that. I mean, I will. I'll call." Hannah lit up, giddy as a schoolgirl going to her first dance.

Kimberley gave her a nod and left the daycare center, jogging back to her car. She looked down at her watch... She was going to be late for work, her first day of work.

CHAPTER TEN

Just like the day before and like her days would be from that point on, Kimberley opened the first set of doors to the Custer County Sheriff's Office. She carried in a cardboard box of personal items for her office. Behind the front desk, Barbara sat knitting something out of thick forest-green yarn. She looked up; a smile bloomed on her face as soon as she saw Kimberley. She dropped her needles and stood from her desk.

"Chief Deputy King," Barb greeted. "I've been expecting you."

Shit. She was hoping they wouldn't notice she was late. It was only a few minutes. But in this line of work, a few minutes could be the difference between life and death.

"Sorry about that. I got held up at my daughter's daycare," Kimberley admitted. "But it won't happen again," she quickly added.

"Your secret is safe with me." Barb pretended to zip her lips, lock them, and throw away an imaginary key. She let out a little giggle as she walked around the desk carrying a couple of binders.

"Come with me," she said, walking toward the office area.

Unlocking a set of doors and scanning her badge at another set, Barbara led Kimberley back to the desk area. A deputy with a strong jawline and dark brown skin that had almost a peach undertone sat at the far back left desk. He looked up quickly, his features were sharp and his piercing dark eyes met Kimberley's.

"Deputy Bearfield, have you met Chief Deputy Kimberley King?" Barb asked. Her tone was light and airy.

Bearfield rose from his desk and stepped out from behind it. His long, black and silky hair was pulled back in a low ponytail. He took a couple of large steps, stopping just in front of Kimberley and Barb. His soaring height and broad shoulders contributed to his strong, stern presence. Bearfield slightly lifted his chin and sharpened his eyes in a way that said, "I was here first." Sam was right, he clearly had a chip on his shoulder, but despite that, there was still something calming to him. Kimberley recalled what Sam had told her about Bearfield—reliable and thorough.

He held out his large hand, looking Kimberley up and down for a moment, sizing her up. Then his dark eyes landed on hers. "I'm Deputy Drew Bearfield. Been on the force for eight years."

Kimberley shook his hand. There was no point in getting into a pissing contest with him. The best route was just to get him to like working for her, win him over. "I'm Chief Deputy Kimberley King. Been on the force for eight minutes."

Bearfield tilted his head, the corner of his lip perking up into a half-smile.

"She's funny," Barb said with a laugh.

"She is," Bearfield said. "I hear you came here from the NYPD."

It was obvious to Kimberley he was trying to determine whether or not she had earned or would earn his respect. But she'd play along.

"That's right. Ten years in the NYPD, the last seven of them as a homicide detective."

He brought his hand to his chin, rubbing it for a moment. "Impressive. Why d'you leave then? Chief Deputy of Custer County, Oklahoma, is quite the step-down from an NYPD homicide detective." Bearfield tilted his head, slightly squinting the black marbles between his lids.

"You're right, it is a step-down," Kimberley raised her chin, "but it was a step-up for my daughter."

The intensity in his eyes melted away. He bit at the inside of his lower lip, seemingly unsure as to what to say to that.

"Well, welcome. As far as cases go, I'm working on paperwork for a DUI and a disorderly conduct. Then I'll be back out patrolling." He gave a slight nod.

"Good. I look forward to working with you, Bearfield. It was nice meeting you." Kimberley sidestepped around him with Barb following behind.

"Hey," Bearfield called out.

Kimberley turned back.

"I look forward to working with you too," he said with a small smile.

She had won him over for now. Kimberley gave a small smile back and turned around.

She noticed the lights in Sam's office were off before entering her own office to the right. On her desk sat a large blueberry muffin and a mug of steaming hot coffee. Barb set the binders beside it and closed the office door behind her.

"Bearfield is a very nice man, not like that jackass Lodge," Barb said, shaking her head and twisting up her lips.

"So, I've heard."

"Black coffee just the way you like it, and I baked muffins fresh this morning." Barb motioned to her desk, "There's more in the break room," she whispered, as if it were a secret just for Kimberley.

"Thank you, Barb. You didn't have to do that." Kimberley was taken aback by how kind this woman was, like a grandma for the sheriff's station.

She walked around her desk and set her box of stuff down.

"No one has to do anything for anyone else… but where's the fun in that?" Barb smiled.

Kimberley assumed Barb was the type of woman who had a piece of wisdom for every situation and if it came with coffee and baked goods, she could get used to it. Though the waistline of her clothing might not.

"I've stocked your wardrobe with several uniforms, undershirts and shoes." Barb gestured with her hand toward the closet. "I estimated your size, so let me know if I'm wrong. I'm usually not." She winked.

Kimberley walked to the wardrobe and opened it, revealing five hanging perfectly pressed sheriff's uniforms. A utility belt hung on the hook of the door. Handcuffs, a baton, radio, taser, pepper spray and a few other items were sitting inside a box. The bottom shelf had two pairs of black Galls athletic shoes and one pair of tactical boots. Kimberley thumbed through the uniforms, checking the sizes of the tops and pants. She bent down and checked the shoe sizes. Barb was spot on with everything.

She turned and smiled at Barb. "These are perfect."

"Told ya, I'm rarely wrong," Barb said.

"I hung that mirror up for you too." Barb pointed at the long mirror hung on the inside of the left door.

Kimberley caught her reflection in it. She was right about how she thought she looked: tired. Like she hadn't slept at all. Her long dark hair was pulled into a mess of a ponytail. Her full lips were still chapped, despite having applied Carmex to them half a dozen times this morning. The little bit of mascara she flicked over her eyelashes and the tinted moisturizer she rubbed all over her face made her look a little put together. Dressed in blue jeans and a white tee, she didn't look the part of a chief deputy yet.

"One of the binders contains all the typical HR-type stuff. Employee handbook. Rules and regulations. Yadda yadda, it's a bore of a read. The smaller one is what Sam mentioned yesterday. It's a bit more exciting, so I'd recommend switching it up between the two." She smiled. "It's pertinent information for you concerning the town and the town hoodlums, as I like to call them." Barb twisted up her lips. "Always a bad apple or two in the bunch," she said, instantly untwisting her lips and returning a small, welcoming smile to her face.

"Thanks for the advice and the hospitality." Kimberley nodded, walking away from the wardrobe and pulling her box from the floor to set it on the desk.

Barb took a seat and looked up at Kimberley, her face completely lit up. "So, you mentioned you had a daughter? Tell me all about her."

Kimberley hesitated for a moment. She wasn't one to open up about her personal life. "Well, her name is Jessica."

"Ohh, I just love that name."

"She's sixteen months old."

"Such a good age." Barb clapped her hands together.

"Umm... she loves coloring and always wants to play with anything I have in my hands," Kimberley said with a laugh.

"That doesn't change with age." Barb shook her head. "I've got a five-year-old grandson. He damn near poked his eye out with my knitting needle one time and he's unraveled my yarn balls on numerous occasions. It's why I'm so gray." Barb pointed to her curly gray hair. "I swear it'd be a beautiful blond if it weren't for that little rascal." She laughed.

"Looks like I have a lot to look forward to." Kimberley cracked a smile.

"Jessica sounds sweet. I'd love to meet her sometime."

"Of course."

Barb stood from her chair. "I'll leave you to get settled. I'm sure I've missed a half dozen calls already. Sam will be in soon to issue your badge and firearm. He got caught up with a traffic violation on his way in, so he's running later than you." Barb raised an eyebrow. "Anything else you need right away?"

Kimberley looked around the room and then back at Barb. "Nope. All good here."

"Great. I'll be in the front or just press zero on your desk phone. Go ahead and get settled in," she said, backing out of the office.

"Detective King, settling in I see."

Kimberley glanced up to find Sam standing in the doorway of her office. He had a box in one hand and a cup of coffee in the other. A small smile spread on his face as their eyes met.

"I am." She nodded. "Just giving the office a little bit of a personal touch." She motioned to the frame and box of stuff on her desk.

Sam took a couple of large steps into the office. He set down his mug of coffee and hovered his hand over a framed picture of Jessica. "May I?"

Kimberley nodded. He picked it up and turned it over, looking at the photo. His eyes tightened for a brief second, so brief Kimberley almost missed it.

"She's beautiful," he said, scanning the photo once more before returning it to its original position. "I bet she keeps you busy."

"You have no idea," Kimberley said wearily.

Sam's eyes tightened slightly once again, but he relaxed them and cleared his throat with a small cough.

"You met Bear?"

"Yes." *Bear.* She liked the shortened nickname.

"And he didn't give you any grief?"

"A small amount of grief was given, but it's all good," Kimberley said.

"Good."

Sam tapped the black box with his fingers and then held it out to her.

"Sorry, I didn't have time to wrap it," he said with a smile.

Kimberley took it from him and lifted the cover, revealing a silver .38 caliber Smith & Wesson revolver tucked inside.

"What's this?" She looked up at him.

"Your service firearm." He gave her a quizzical look.

"You guys don't carry pistols?" Kimberley raised an eyebrow.

"No, revolvers are traditional for a sheriff's office and they're reliable, since they never jam." He folded his arms in front of his chest.

"What if you need to reload quickly?"

"Ha. Most of the deputies on my force have never even fired their gun, let alone needed to reload it. Aside from Deputy Hill, our sharp foot shooter."

"Then you won't mind if I carry this instead?"

Kimberley pulled a black case from the box on top of her desk. She unclipped the clasps and opened it, revealing an all-black Glock 9mm.

Sam eyed the gun with an air of suspicion. "I suppose not, but what's wrong with this one?" He motioned to the revolver.

"Oh, she's been with me ever since I joined the force and, unlike your men's firearms, she's gotten me out of quite a few jams and I don't mean toe jams," Kimberley said with a laugh, running her fingers over it.

"Well, I hope I'll never have to hear her, while you're with us." He smiled. "And if it makes you more comfortable, be my guest. Just make sure you have Ms. Glock registered with the department."

"It's actually Ms. Betty," Kimberley said sarcastically.

Sam uncrossed his arms and raised an eyebrow. "Ms. Betty?"

"No one ever suspects a Betty."

"Well, alright then. Go ahead and keep Mr. Reliable." Sam pointed to the revolver. "He's already registered to you, so he's yours anyway."

Kimberley picked up the revolver and the Glock and held them out. Pointing them at the side wall, she stared down the barrels of both guns, feeling the weight of them in her hands.

"I think Ms. Glock and Mr. Reliable will make a great team." Kimberley raised an eyebrow, looking back at Sam. She perked up the corner of her lip while she put the guns back in their cases.

Sam picked up his mug of coffee and took a drink of it. "I reckon they will. Before I forget." He pulled a badge from the front pocket of his shirt and extended it out to Kimberley.

The badge was a shiny gold six-pointed star. At the top of it read, "Chief Deputy." At the bottom, "OK." Text wrapping around the middle in a circle read, "Custer County Sheriff's Office."

"Welcome to the force… officially, Detective King," Sam said with a nod and a smile.

Kimberley slowly took it from him, reading the few words on it over and over, running her fingers along the points of the star. It was heavier than it looked. This was it. She was formally Chief Deputy King of the Custer County Sheriff's Office.

Kimberley looked back at Sam. "Thank you… It's an honor," she said with a tight smile.

He nodded and exited her office, walking toward his own.

There was only one thing left to do, she thought to herself, looking down at her blue jeans and white tee. She walked to the door and closed it and then drew the blinds blocking her window that saw out into the rest of the sheriff's office.

The long-sleeve tan button-down shirt fit her perfectly and Barb had thoughtfully already pinned the stars to her collar and her nametag to the right side of her chest, just above the front pocket. Engraved in the gold bar was 'K. King.' Her olive-green pants fit flawlessly. Barb must have had them tailored, however, Kimberley assumed she had done it herself, because it seemed like that was the kind of woman she was. Everything she had encountered in the sheriff's office had a personal touch from Barbara. Kimberley rocked back and forth in her boots. They'd need a little working in. She smoothed out her hair that was tied back in a low ponytail, a memory flashing into her mind.

Kimberley turned side to side, ensuring everything was perfectly in place. Looking at herself in the mirror, she found herself looking through it. She always did. Like it was a portal to a past she'd never forget.

"Kimberley, this is not okay," Detective Hunter said, holding up a photo. It was the photo of the mirror with the message written to Kimberley from the crime scene. "I think you need to get off this case." She slid the photo in front of her and took a seat.

Kimberley folded her arms in front of her chest. "Why?"

"He is taunting you. He knows who you are. This is unfamiliar territory to me, so as your mentor and your partner, I can't be like this is fine. Because I don't know if it's fine." Lynn furrowed her brow.

"I'm not going to drop this case because of some asshole. I owe it to these victims." Kimberley grabbed three photos from her desk and slid them in front of Lynn. They weren't crime scene photos. They were pictures of the women before they were murdered. Jenny Roberts seated in Central Park eating a piece of bread on a bright sunny day. Maria Velasquez stood beside her husband in front of a lit Broadway marquis for Cats. Stephanie Weisman lying out by a pool wearing a two-piece bikini, a beach hat and oversized sunglasses reading a book.

Lynn glanced at each photo and back at Kimberley. "I know. But it's not safe. We have no idea who this man is. He seems to know more about us than we know about him, and we're the detectives!" She shook her head.

"I'm staying on the case," Kimberley said defiantly.

Lynn took a deep breath and winced. "Ugh." She pushed at her lower abdomen, leaning slightly forward.

"Are you okay?" Kimberley half stood.

She waved a hand at her. "Yeah, I'm fine. It's these IVF injections. They bloat me up like a balloon and it's just tender and uncomfortable."

"*Here.*" *Kimberley handed over a bottle of water and a couple of Tylenol.*

"*Thanks.*" *Lynn tossed the pills in her mouth and washed them down with the water. She took another deep breath and looked directly at Kimberley.*

"*Tell me about the latest victim, Stephanie Weisman.*"

Kimberley nodded, giving a tight smile. She knew this was Lynn's way of saying, "I won't recommend your removal from the case."

"*Stephanie Weisman is a thirty-two-year-old investment banker. Worked at Wells Fargo and lived in Greenwich Village. Married. Pregnant with her first child, and she was seven months along. She was missing twelve days before we found her.*"

"*A waitress, a legal secretary and an investment banker. All from different classes. Stephanie and Jenny were white. Maria was Hispanic. They lived vastly different lives. What's the connection?*" *Lynn was thinking out loud.*

"*Pregnancy?*"

"*Maybe.*" *Lynn scratched her chin. "What do we know about the killer?*"

"*He's a ghost. The places he's picked are always abandoned. No CCTV. We have no witnesses from when the women are taken. He must watch them for a while, get to know their routine, and he finds an opportunity. A window in their life when no one else is looking,*" *Kimberley said as she looked at the photos of each of the women.*

"*What are you thinking for a profile?*" *Lynn asked like a teacher would with their student, and that's what she was to Kimberley. Lynn was the reason Kimberley had risen through the ranks so quickly. She had taken her in under her wing when she first joined the force because Lynn had seen so much potential in her.*

"He likes control, feeling like a god. Could be a sexual thing. I'd say he's in his early thirties, white, well-educated. He takes care of himself, works out. The way he targets pregnant women… something must have happened to him as a child, perhaps childhood abuse," Kimberley rattled off.

"That's a solid profile, Detective King. But I want to know who Jenny Roberts, Maria Velasquez, and Stephanie Weisman were. They're the key to discovering who murdered them. Find their connection." Lynn stood from her chair, giving a tight smile, before leaving the cubicle.

Kimberley refocused her eyes, bringing them back to the present and to her reflection in the mirror. For the final touch, she secured her new badge to her shirt just above her heart. She pressed her lips firmly together, taking her whole image in one final time before closing the wardrobe closet door.

CHAPTER ELEVEN

Kimberley walked through the doors into the desk pit of the sheriff's office. Her chief deputy uniform was perfectly pressed and clean, like her old blues used to be, and her hair was pulled back in a low ponytail. Deputy Bearfield and Deputy Burns were seated at their desks, typing away at their computers.

"Good morning," Kimberley said.

Burns looked up first, stopping his work immediately. "Morning, Chief Deputy King."

Bearfield finished up his typing and then looked up, greeting Kimberley.

"Whatcha guys got?" Kimberley stopped in the middle of the room, just before Burns's desk.

"Some paperwork from the night shift. DUI, traffic violation and a couple of assault charges from a fight that happened over at The Trophy Room late last night," Burns said, reading them off several sheets of paper.

Kimberley nodded and looked over at Bearfield.

"I'm taking care of some quarterly reporting for Walker," he said, slightly raising his chin.

Before Kimberley could ask about the reporting, the doors behind her opened and closed. Immediately, Burns pulled out his phone and clicked a few buttons. The song "Footloose" played loudly.

"Goddamnit! It's been four months. When are you two going to let that go?" Deputy Todd Hill whined.

Kimberley hadn't met him yet as he had been out on vacation the past few days. She turned around to find a tall, lanky man with a long face and a pointy nose. He was clean-shaven with a well-quaffed haircut, mid-to-late thirties, she presumed. He walked with a slight limp that was almost unnoticeable.

Bearfield and Burns let out belly laughs. "You're never living that down," Bear said.

Kimberley couldn't help the slight smile that creeped onto her face. She loved the banter. It was necessary for a job like this.

Deputy Hill walked slowly to his desk, trying to show no signs of his self-inflicted foot injury. "It was an accident. It could have happened to anyone," he groaned, but he didn't actually seem all that annoyed.

"Deputy Todd Hill," Kimberley greeted. "I've heard a lot about you. I'm Chief Deputy Kimberley King."

Hill walked the extra few steps to Kimberley and shook her hand. "Nice to meet you. The boys filled me in. I'm looking forward to working with you."

"Yeah, we didn't want him to get off on the wrong foot," Burns howled.

Bearfield slapped his knee as he erupted into a fit of laughter that was deep and controlled.

Hill rolled his eyes. "You'll have to get used to them." He looked at Burns and then Bearfield with a smirk. "Well, glad to have you on the force," he added with a nod.

"Likewise." Kimberley nodded. "Carry on," she added as she walked toward her office.

Kimberley took a sip of her coffee. The mixture of heat and acidity biting at her tongue and throat helped to keep her alert and focused while sorting through papers at her desk. The rest of the deputies had taken off to patrol, while Kimberley sat finishing up some paperwork before heading out to join them.

"How's it going?" Sam entered her office with a cup of coffee in his hand. His walk was slow, but his presence made it clear that this was his domain. His permanent five-o'clock shadow and buzz cut made him look rugged and authoritative. The past few days she had worked with Sam, Kimberley had found him hard to read. He was kind, but any hint of a smile was few and far between, only appearing when he was truly amused.

Kimberley looked up and tilted her head to the side. "Same old, same old."

"You've been here four days and you're already at 'same old, same old.'" Sam chuckled, half amused by her blasé response.

Kimberley leaned back in her chair and smiled while shrugging her shoulders.

"You met the crew?"

"All of them, except night shift and Lodge."

Sam nodded.

"How have the first few days been?" Sam half sat on her desk, one leg on the ground, one cheek on the table.

"Exactly as you said it'd be. Quiet with a sprinkling of paper-work and a dollop of DUI." Kimberley tilted her head.

Sam nodded, set his coffee down on her desk, and folded his arms across his chest. "Look I know this job isn't going to be the—" He stopped abruptly as his phone began to ring, and he quickly pulled it from his utility belt. "Sam."

Kimberley watched him carefully as he pressed the phone to his ear and stood up straight. He nodded several times.

"I'm on my way," he said into the phone, ending the call. Sam looked at Kimberley. "Let's go. A fisherman found a body near Big Deer Creek."

"A body?" Kimberley rose from her seat immediately, excitement swelling up inside her. Now, this was more like home, she thought.

In the car, Sam immediately flicked on his sirens and sped off toward the outskirts of the town. The tires of the squad car spit up gravel, leaving a trail of dust behind it. Kimberley buckled up and held the handlebar on the passenger's door to brace herself.

"Wait, you said Big Deer Creek?" Kimberley confirmed.

Sheriff Sam nodded. She looked at him and then back at the road.

"Like where Katie DeWitt James was found?"

"You know the story." Sam cocked his head.

Kimberley nodded. She had learned about Dead Woman Crossing's gruesome history well before she applied for the position at the sheriff's station.

"A Google search told me all I needed to know. Young local woman by the name of Katie DeWitt James was murdered back in 1905 down by Big Deer Creek. Shot in the head. Decapitated. Young daughter found alive in a stroller nearby." Kimberley recited it as if she were reading it verbatim. She'd read the short Wikipedia page over a dozen times.

"Yep. That's the story," Sam said, keeping his eyes on the road.

"It's strange the town took its name from the unsolved murder." Kimberley creased her brow, looking over at Sam for a moment. "It's just awful."

He gave a slight nod, not saying anything more, too focused on the open road ahead of him as he sped toward Big Deer Creek, the horizon and surrounding wheat fields a blur of color. His shoulders were high, his hands gripped tightly around the steering wheel and his jaw was clenched. She understood why Sam was tense. This was his town, his responsibility.

"Think this could be a copycat?" she asked, trying to pull Sam out from the hard exterior he was hiding in, like a turtle crawling back into its shell.

"I don't wanna jump to any conclusions," Sam said. "Not until we see the crime scene."

"Homicide is rather unusual for Dead Woman Crossing, right? Aside from the 1905 case?" Kimberley arched an eyebrow.

"It's very unusual." He briefly looked at her with tight eyes and then redirected his attention back at the road ahead of him.

Sam pulled the car a little off the road, right behind another squad car. Several police cars were parked up and down the street just before the bridge.

Kimberley stepped out of the vehicle and took in the surroundings. Dead, leafless trees. The twisting creek running off into the distance. The slanting hills jutting up from the bed of the creek, covered in tall, rolling wheatgrass. And the bridge. The ominous concrete aperture like a massive mouth swallowing the creek, a slight fog rising to its underbelly. This was the scene of the murder more than a century ago, and the area was still dank and heavy with gloom and despair.

"Down here," a voice called out from below the bridge.

Sam and Kimberley carefully walked down the steep valley off the side of the road leading to the creek that cut beneath it, pushing wheatgrass out of their way as they threaded through.

Deputy Hill stood off to the side of the creek bank. An older man dressed in olive-green chest waders, a red flannel shirt, and a worn fisherman's bucket hat was sitting on a rock holding his head in his hands. When Kimberley got closer to him, he stood abruptly, and she could see the terror on his face; skin paper white, eyes darting back and forth in low-slung half-circles, like a pendulum trying to sweep away the horror he saw. Past Deputy Hill, under the bridge, the crime scene had already been sealed off, yellow tape twisting and flapping in the wind. Several deputies, including Burns, walked up and down the creek, their mag lights scanning the ground during the heavily overcast day, searching the area for God knows what.

Deputy Hill greeted Sam and Kimberley with a quick nod. "Teddy here found the body around an hour ago." He gestured to the fisherman with his hand. "Said he was out doing some fishing and just walked up on the body over yonder." Hill tilted his head back toward the yellow tape.

"It was ju-just horrible." Teddy shook his head and squeezed his eyes tightly shut, two flesh dams closing to stop the spill of water. "I've seen a lot of bad things in my life, but… nothing like that." His shoulders trembled as he began to cry, the dams unable to hold back the force any longer.

Sam patted Teddy on the shoulder to comfort him. "It's alright, you don't have to say any more right now."

The fisherman nodded, wiping his eyes with the back of his hand.

"Deputy Hill, would you kindly take Teddy away from the crime scene and get him something warm to drink and eat? Take down his official statement whenever he is calmed down and ready," Sam advised.

Hill nodded. "Come on, Teddy, my car is this way." They started walking, Hill with his slight limp, but he stopped six feet from Sherriff Walker and Chief Deputy King. Turning back, he said, "The pathologist is on the way in from Oklahoma City, should be here any minute. And one of the other deputies is with the baby down past the crime scene." Deputy Hill pointed his finger at a man in uniform crouched down by a stroller.

"The baby?" Kimberley's eyes widened.

"Yeah, did they not mention it when they rang you? The baby was discovered wrapped in blankets in her stroller a hundred yards away from the body." Deputy Hill scratched the back of his neck.

"Fucking Jesus. You guys have baby killers here?" Kimberley shook her head. The taste of iron formed on her tongue. She swallowed hard.

"The baby's alive," Hill confirmed with a nod.

"Is the child alright? Approximate age?" Kimberley asked, almost in a panic. She thought of her own daughter, and couldn't bear the thought of her sitting in a stroller alone all night outside.

"She's fine. We're guessing around a year."

Sam and Kimberley exchanged a look as they let out a sigh of relief.

Hill motioned to Teddy and the two walked away in the opposite direction of the crime scene.

"Ahh, if it isn't my favorite Custer County sheriff," Megan Grey greeted as she walked down the valley from the road.

Her hair was a deep scarlet-red with a sleek cut that fell just below her chin. Her sharp features played in her favor as they matched her bulldozer attitude. She didn't look like the other women that Kimberley had seen around town. Hell, she would have fit in walking around Greenwich Village. Megan was polished from head to toe, and like a crime scene, everything about her appearance had more to say than what was shown. She slid on a pair of white gloves as she approached Sam and Kimberley.

"Megan, so nice of you to join us." Sam tipped his head. "This is Chief Deputy Kimberley King. She just joined us four days ago."

Megan held up her hands, showing off her gloves as an excuse as to why they couldn't shake hands. Instead, they nodded at one another.

"This is Megan Grey. She's our designated pathologist from Oklahoma City when we get something that is beyond our own resources. She's not from around here as you can see," Sam explained.

"Well, you know how I feel about small towns. A bit too claustrophobic feeling for my taste." Megan shook her head. "So, what do we have here?"

"We just arrived ourselves, but from what I know we've got a dead woman and her baby found alive a hundred yards away from the body." Sam nodded.

"Let's have a look," Megan said, marching toward the crime scene, her hips swaying like a runway model as she walked toward the scene, a crime scene being her stage.

They ducked under the police tape, greeting a deputy in his late forties with a potbelly, Kimberley presumed was from the night shift, and Deputy Bearfield. They were standing guard near the body.

"I got the area sealed off right away." Bearfield stood stoic. Some of his long, black hair had come loose from his ponytail, blowing in the dry Oklahoma wind.

"Good work, Bear." Sam gave him a nod.

Kimberley circled around it and was horrified at what she saw. The woman's head had been severed from the body, a pool of blood emanating out from the open hole, like a wine bottle that had been felled on its side, left unchecked to pour its contents out in an ever-expanding pool of deep-crimson liquid. The sight was grim. Surrounding the weeping graying flesh was the exposed cervical spine and open trachea, a dark cavernous tunnel leading deeper into the once warm depths beyond. Kimberley's eyes searched the area around the corpse. No head in sight.

"Watch your step," Megan warned.

Kimberley caught Sam roll his eyes. It seemed the working relationship between Sam and Megan was rocky at best. From what Kimberley could tell so far, Megan had a high level of attitude, but if her work was as impeccable as how she presented herself, it would be worth the price.

"Where's the head?" Kimberley asked Deputy Bearfield, ignoring Megan's warning.

"Haven't located it yet. I've got men casing up and down the river in search of it."

Kimberley nodded approvingly. For being a department that didn't experience these types of severe crimes very often, they were handling it with a level of professionalism that surprised her.

Sam rubbed his chin with his hand and looked up at Kimberley. "You know what this all looks like, don't you?"

"I do. I just hoped it wasn't."

Sam and Kimberley were already on the same wavelength, almost as if they had been working together for years, not days.

"You should probably wait until I'm done investigating the crime scene before you jump to any conclusions." Megan lifted her chin.

"Why don't you stick to your job and I'll stick to mine," Sam said tensely. "What's the cause of death?"

"Well, without the head, all I can say as of now is decapitation. The body looks pretty clean otherwise." Megan bent down beside the corpse, lifting the hand of the woman carefully. She inspected the nails. "No defensive wounds on the arms or hands. I'd assume she knew her assailant, or she didn't see it coming, and her death was quick."

Megan placed the hand back in the dirt and looked over the woman's clothing. She was dressed in blue jeans and a short-sleeve cotton top. There was a bulge in the front pocket of her jeans. Megan carefully pulled the item from the pocket revealing an older iPhone, maybe a five. She clicked the button and a lock screen appeared.

"Bag and tag this," Megan said.

A deputy extended an open evidence bag toward Megan, and she dropped it in.

"Can you make that a top priority, so we can get our hands on it?" Kimberley asked, thinking the evidence they needed could be one four-digit code away.

"Of course." Megan nodded as she continued to inspect the body. One of her tennis shoes was off, just a foot away from the body.

Kimberley followed Megan's eyes, down the victim's body to the shoe and beyond. "She looks like she was dragged to this location. There are some drag marks in the dirt around three feet in length, and it seems to have been brushed away after that, like someone was trying to cover their tracks."

Sam nodded.

"That's exactly what I was going to say," Megan said, looking up at Kimberley. "Where did you come from?"

"New York City. I was an NYPD homicide detective," Kimberley replied.

Megan nodded and then her eyes widened slightly, a moment of recognition. "Wait, King. Kimberley, King... You're the detective, the one that..." She paused and her eyes became sympathetic. "I saw the headlines a while back."

Kimberley swallowed hard. She was surprised Megan would have not only heard of the case but remembered the mention of one of the lead detectives, but then again, it had become infamous, and all the major newspapers had covered it.

A slideshow of images played right in front of her eyes, like a private viewing for just Kimberley. The woman shackled to the mattress. The woman strung up by her neck in the attic. The woman in the bathtub. And the...

Kimberley blinked rapidly and swallowed hard before the slideshow continued. "Yeah, that's right."

"It's a shame you guys never caught him." Megan gave her a sympathetic glance.

A pang of guilt hit Kimberley like a punch to the gut. 'I... I,' she began.

Sam coughed, clearing his throat and the conversation. "If this is a copycat killer, we're going to need to get a log of every person that passed through town recently. This place attracts a fair number of true-crime obsessives and murder tourists attracted by the Katie DeWitt James murder, so it might be a long list."

Kimberley was grateful Sam had changed the subject. It was obvious Sam knew about her past and had given her the job anyway. A Google search of her name pulled up every news article related to the unsolved case. It wasn't a case she liked to talk about, but it was one that lived inside of her like a parasite that burrowed its way in, refusing to leave or let go.

"Fair number? How many murder tourists do you all get around here?" Kimberley asked, looking over at Sam.

He rubbed his chin. "Probably a couple dozen a month, but I don't know for sure."

Kimberley nodded. "And where do these tourists stay?"

"Motels, Airbnbs, and campsites, I presume. Many probably pass through the same day. Not a whole hell of a lot to do in Custer County."

Megan redirected her attention to the vacuous, engorged hole where the woman's head used to be. She leaned in a little closer, examining the flesh. "This is a clean cut," she said.

"And what's that mean?" Sam folded his arms across his chest.

Megan looked up at him. "It means her head was severed from the body with one blow. So, the weapon was large and sharp."

"Like an ax or a machete?" Kimberley thought out loud.

"Definite possibilities." Megan nodded.

"Well, shit. Everyone around here has both of those." Sam scratched the back of his head.

"Whoever did this has considerable strength to be able to hack straight through the spinal cord. There're no tears on the skin." Megan pointed to the edges of the neck. "If they had been stopped by the spinal cord or done multiple blows, I would expect to see tears around the neck lining, where the tendons and sinew would have pulled and given way. But this is very clean, almost like a guillotine."

"So, we're looking for a large man," Sam said.

"Or a woman. Nothing in this crime scene says it was a man," Megan said steadily.

"Sure, fine. Or a really strong woman," he obliged.

"Anything else you can tell us?" Kimberley asked.

"Not without the head or performing an autopsy. At first look, this doesn't appear to have been sexually motivated as her clothes aren't in any disarray, but I'll perform a rape kit to be sure." Megan stood up and removed her gloves. "I'll have my team do a clean sweep of the area as well and bag up all evidence."

Before Sam or Chief Deputy King could ask any more questions, Deputy Burns standing a little way down the creek yelled out. "Found the head!"

Megan raised an eyebrow, while Sam and Kimberley exchanged a glance. Immediately, the three exited the crime scene and trudged through the long wheatgrass in the direction of the deputy.

Burns stood over the object, pointing down at the head lying in the tall grass as Megan, Sam, and Kimberley approached. He was visibly upset, the color drained from his face and his hand shaking as he pointed. Kimberley gently pushed his arm down to his side, giving him a slight nod. Megan slid her white gloves back on her hands. The face was covered by the woman's long dark hair, matted to her skin by dried black blood. Tiny pieces of flesh were missing at the base of the neck, and there were a few small bite marks and scratches along the cheeks and chin. The flesh was turning pale gray as there was no blood to fill it or warm it to its regular color.

"Good work," Sam said to Burns.

Burns stood frozen, staring at the head.

"I thought you said this was a clean cut. The bottom of the neck is all mangled with chunks missing." Kimberley pointed out the battered skin.

"Looks like an animal got to it first. It must have dragged it away from the body and left it here when it realized there's not much meat on a head," Megan explained.

"You think?" Sam questioned.

"I know. Definitely a fox or a coyote." Megan bent down and pointed at the skin. "See those bite marks. Too deep and elongated to be a human."

Sam and Kimberley nodded, accepting her explanation.

Megan gently pushed the long dark hair aside, uncovering the woman's face. The vibrancy of her green eyes had faded, leaving behind a muted dullness, two emeralds submerged just below the surface in a pool of milk. In the center of her forehead, there was a small hole and a trickle of blood seeped from it, running down the side of her face into her hairline.

"There's your cause of death. Gunshot to the head," Megan said.

"How do you know the gunshot happened before the head was removed?" Sam rocked back on his heels.

Megan pointed to the dried blood. "Because of the blood trickling out of the wound, and it's darker than the blood at the main crime scene, meaning it's older."

Sam gave a slight nod.

As Kimberley's eyes scanned the face of the dead woman, recognition jarred her to the core like a hefty punch to the gut. Kimberley gasped and a look of horror washed over her. "Oh my God. I know this woman."

CHAPTER TWELVE

Kimberley took a few small steps back. Her heart began to race, and her eyes glistened, but she forced herself to take a couple of large breaths before she completely lost it. She had known this woman. She had spoken to this woman. She knew her story. She could have been there for her. Maybe she could have stopped what happened to her.

Sam closed the distance between himself and Kimberley. Megan continued examining the head, taking swabs of it with a Q-tip and bagging them.

"What do you mean you know her? How? You just moved here. Who is she?" he asked.

"Her name's Hannah. I've met her a couple of times at my daughter's daycare. The child in the stroller must be her fourteen-month-old daughter, Isobel," Kimberley explained, laying out the facts as if this were just another case… but she knew it wasn't, at least not to her. Could she have helped this woman? When she met her, had Hannah known she was in danger? Was that why she needed a friend? Kimberley's thoughts raced, trying to piece together parts of a story for a woman who would never be able to tell it.

"Okay. Do you know anything else about her?" Sam scratched at his chin.

"She works part time at the local pharmacy. Isobel's father isn't in the picture, but I'm not sure who he is or where he is. I just know Hannah was a single mom."

Kimberley rubbed her forehead as if she were trying to conjure up more details that she knew about this woman.

"The couple of times I've spoken to her, she seemed frazzled, tired, lonely," Kimberley said.

Sam nodded.

"But that's characteristic to most single moms," Kimberley thought out loud. "But she seemed nice, and she was good with her daughter. It's hard to believe she got wrapped up in a situation like this."

A couple of deputies walked toward the decapitation resting site, joining Burns who had found the severed head. They spoke quietly.

"This isn't a hen house. This is a crime scene," Kimberley snapped. "Cordon off the area."

They froze, glancing back and forth between Sam and Kimberley.

"You heard her. Get this area sealed off!" Sam commanded.

Their faces reddened and they immediately shuffled to get to work, bumping into one another at first. Finally, one of them grabbed some wooden stakes from a nearby pile that were brought to seal off where the body was. Another grabbed a hammer and pounded them into the ground while Burns unrolled the police line and wrapped it around the stakes, creating a barrier separating the surrounding area from Hannah's head.

"Thanks," Kimberley said to Sam.

She appreciated that he had backed her in front of the deputies. She knew it'd take time to garner their respect, but she didn't have time now—not with a murderer on the loose.

"Of course." He nodded at her.

Megan stood up and dusted off her pants. She handed a few bags to one of her workers, telling him to tag them and load them up.

"What's the plan?" Sam asked.

"My team will do a final sweep of the area. Clear the scene, and I'll examine the body down at the Custer County Medical

Examiner's Office. Should have toxicology, DNA, and forensic exam results in forty-eight hours." Megan removed her white gloves.

"Sounds good."

"Let me know if you need anything else," she said as she crossed over the newly erected police line.

"I trust you'll be thorough, as per usual," Sam said with a nod.

Megan walked off, leaving Sam and Kimberley standing near the severed head of Hannah.

"I'm going to make a call," Kimberley said, pulling out her phone.

"To?"

"Social services. They've got to come get Isobel, and I'll see if they can identify next of kin."

"Good thinking."

Kimberley walked out of earshot of the other deputies on the scene. She pulled her phone out, but her hand began to shake as she went to look up the number for social services. She had seen lots of murder scenes in New York; this was nothing new to her. But something about this one had her jarred. Maybe it was the proximity to Jessica. A woman who dropped her child off at the same daycare, a child who was supposed to meet her Jessica and all be one sweet and happy group together. Or maybe it was the feeling of guilt lodged deep inside her. If she had just grabbed a drink with this woman the night before, made a better effort.

"Get out of your own fucking head, Kimberley," she whispered to herself. *You can't dwell on what you can't control*, she thought. If she wanted to help this woman now, the first thing Hannah would have wanted was her daughter taken care of.

Kimberley brought her phone back up and dialed. Ten minutes later, she hung up the phone satisfied with her call. Instead of walking back to join Sam and Megan, her feet and her heart pulled her toward the stroller where a young deputy stood at attention beside it, as if he were guarding a bank vault instead of a baby. Kimberley gave him a slight nod.

"How is she?"

"She's unharmed," he said matter-of-factly. It was clear he had no experience with children.

Kimberley leaned down. Isobel's big green eyes stared up at the vast blue sky in wonderment. Her mouth was slightly open with a couple of small pearly white teeth peeking out just above her bottom lip. Her cheeks were bright red.

"Hi, Isobel. How are you, sweet girl?" Kimberley smiled, but moisture filled the corners of her eyes, cracking the façade she was trying to put on for Isobel. That everything was okay.

Isobel smiled and gurgled, kicking her legs and reaching out her arms.

Kimberley wanted so badly to pick her up and hold her, but she knew she couldn't as there might be evidence on her. They needed to reduce the number of people that would handle her.

"It's all going to be okay, sweet girl, I promise," she whispered.

Kimberley stood up straight and gave her another smile before heading back over to Sam.

"Social services are on their way here to pick up Isobel," Kimberley called out to Sam, who was chatting with Megan.

Kimberley joined them.

"Area is swept. We'll finish loading everything up. Preliminary reports will be ready this afternoon," Megan said. She walked back toward the road where her vehicle was parked, striding briskly like a woman on a mission.

Kimberley looked out. Scanning the horizon, she saw a mixture of dissimilar images. At some angles, her view revealed peace and tranquility. A steady, flowing creek under an unmoving bridge, swaying fields of wheat that would bend to the wind but not break, and a still sky that allowed for the human eye to see for miles and miles. She could also see squad cars aplenty, swirling lights, a darting and converging of tan and blue polyester, yellow police tape. The scene was both chaotic and serene. A weird blending of two worlds, like the convergence of a warm and cold front in the atmosphere, an impending storm not a possibility but an inevitability.

"I never expected something like this to happen in my town," Sam said, shaking his head.

Kimberley nodded.

"That poor girl." He looked over at her.

"I can't believe another person could do something like that, especially in front of a child. It takes a monster." Kimberley twisted up her lips.

"A real cold-hearted son of a bitch." Sam tightened his eyes and shook his head.

Kimberley let out a deep breath. She was sickened by the whole thing.

"I know Megan said not to jump to any conclusions—she always says that sort of thing—but my gut says we've got a copycat killer on our hands." Sam furrowed his brow.

"Sure looks that way. There's no denying the similarities between Hannah and Isobel, and Katie DeWitt James and her daughter," Kimberley noted.

"It happened back in 1905. I'm thinking the person responsible for this must be one of them true-crime obsessives or someone real interested in the folklore of Dead Woman Crossing." Sam rocked back on his heels.

"Someone must have found the opportunity to recreate the grisly events… but why? And why now?" Kimberley looked over at Sam.

"Sir, ma'am, social services have arrived," Deputy Burns called out from behind where Sam and Kimberley were talking.

Kimberley turned back and looked at him. Giving him a nod and a tight smile, she thanked him. He was still pale, like he had never seen such horror before. Kimberley immediately felt sorry for him as she knew he was the newest deputy on the force. She remembered the first time she had seen a dead body. She was never the same after that. The image of the young boy can still be easily recalled to the front of her mind. Kimberley shook her head slightly, trying to erase the memory like on an Etch a Sketch.

"Why don't you go back to the station and start working on Hannah's phone records? You can get her number from the daycare. When Megan's team is finished dusting her cell phone for fingerprints, I need you to pick it up and get into that device," Kimberley said, giving him some reprieve from the crime scene.

He nodded and immediately turned away, practically running from the scene back up to his car.

"You're a bit of a softie," Sam said quietly.

"He's too young for this. He looks fresh out of the academy," she said.

"He is. Started the week before you arrived."

Kimberley nodded. "I figured he'd be better off back at the station. He looked like he was going to faint or vomit, maybe both, and that's the last thing we need at an active crime scene."

Kimberley spotted the social-services worker. She was easily identifiable in a blazer, pinstripe black pants, and booties with a slight heel. Deputy Bearfield helped the woman walk down the valley on the side of the road, careful she didn't trip, toward Isobel, who was still sitting quietly in her stroller while another deputy watched over her.

Sam and Kimberley met the woman by the stroller and introduced themselves.

"Nancy Singer," she said as they shook hands. Nancy had black curly hair and a warm presence.

"Sheriff Sam Walker and this is Chief Deputy King," Sam said shaking her hand.

Nancy pulled a notepad from her messenger bag that hung on her left shoulder. She opened it up and scanned it, then looked back at Sam and Kimberley. "I was told on the phone the mother was murdered. Mother's name?"

Sam looked to Kimberley.

"Hannah. Her name is… was Hannah. I'm not sure what her last name is. Her daughter, Isobel, is fourteen months old, and she attends Happy Trails Daycare Center in Dead Woman Crossing. If you call there, they'll be able to give you a last name, I'm sure." Kimberley said it all in one breath. They were all just simple data points. That was all that Hannah would be now, a list of biographical facts. She'd have a name. A date of birth. A list of family members. A job she worked. Places she frequented. And a date of death. That was what angered Kimberley most about murder. It took a living, breathing person that had goals, dreams, quirks, flaws and boiled them down to a list of fucking facts.

The woman quickly scribbled down the pertinent information.

"They might be able to give you next of kin as well. The daycare center has parents put down emergency contacts and people authorized to pick up and drop off their child, so they should have something."

Nancy nodded.

"I need you to find her next of kin," Kimberley said, more of a command than a suggestion or a request. She needed to know Isobel would be safe and with someone that loved her, not in some foster home.

"We'll do everything in our power to locate next of kin and place the child with them. You have my word, Chief Deputy King." Nancy slid her pen and the pad of paper back into her messenger bag. "Thanks for your help. Isobel is in good hands."

"Deputy Bearfield, please help Nancy get Isobel and the stroller safely up to her car," Kimberley said.

He nodded and picked up Isobel, holding her against his chest with one arm. He picked up the stroller with his other hand. She immediately started screaming like she had become aware of everything. Like she knew her whole world had just changed, that her mother was dead, and she was all alone in it. He tried to calm her by bouncing her a little in his arm and making funny faces and talking in a soothing voice, but nothing was working. Kimberley grabbed an old worn-looking rabbit stuffed animal that had fallen from the stroller. She walked to Deputy Bearfield, sticking out the stuffed animal to the screaming child. It took her a moment to register, but as soon as she had it tucked under her arm, Isobel stopped crying.

"Good girl," Kimberley said, rubbing the child's arm. "You're going to be okay. Everything is going to be okay," Kimberley spoke softly.

"All good?" Bearfield asked, giving Kimberley a warm smile.

Kimberley nodded.

"I'll need the police report for her case file," Nancy said before turning away. "And I'll take Isobel to the hospital to be examined. The report will be sent to the station to aid in your investigation."

"Please let me know when you find her next of kin," Kimberley added, a slight plea in her voice.

Nancy nodded before turning away. Bearfield followed Nancy up the hill with Isobel and her stroller in tow.

"Bear," Sam called out.

He turned around.

"When you're finished, I need you to conduct some initial interviews with her co-workers at the pharmacy."

Bearfield nodded and turned back, following Nancy up the hill.

Kimberley's eyes, glossy and strained, bounced from Nancy to Isobel to Hannah's body to down the creek and back as if she were trying to solve the case, put all of the pieces together, right then and there.

Sam glanced down at the ground and kicked a lone stone. "We're going to find whoever did this. We'll head down to the medical examiner's office later this afternoon and see what Megan has pulled together for the preliminary report."

"I'm hoping they were sloppy. Left some fibers or fingerprints behind. But based on this scene, I don't think we're going to get that lucky," Kimberley said.

Sam nodded. "Most likely not. You're right. Too clean of a scene."

"I'm going to start by pulling whatever I can on Hannah. Who she knew, who she talked to, who Isobel's father was."

"Thinking she knew her attacker?"

"They usually do," Kimberley said.

"My gut is still saying we got ourselves a copycat killer, an outsider looking to stage some sick fantasy. But you may as well pull that information together so we have a full picture of what we're dealing with here." Sam scratched the back of his neck.

"You got it. The only thing that matters is what we can prove." Kimberley nodded as she excused herself and headed back toward the vehicle.

CHAPTER THIRTEEN

Barb walked into Sheriff Walker's office carrying a bottle of water and a piece of homemade apple pie. He was seated at his desk with hundreds of photos spread out in front of him. He looked up and then quickly tried to turn the photos over.

"No need to spare my eyes. I watch all them CSI shows."

He looked up at her and a look of despair flashed across his face.

"I've seen nothing like this, up close. Such a violent death with no regard for another human's life."

Barb shook her head. "I know. It's awful what happened to that poor girl." She set the apple pie and bottle of water down on the desk.

"I can't believe someone could do something like this, especially in my town." He ran the palms of his hands down his face and let out a breath of frustration.

"I haven't a doubt in my mind you'll find the bastard that did it," Barb said, patting him on the shoulder.

"Thanks, Barb."

"Let me know if you need anything, anything at all," she said, leaving the office.

Sam took a gulp from the water bottle and returned his attention to the photos in front of him. There were close-ups. Pictures of the surrounding area. Every detail was captured.

Kimberley knocked once and walked in carrying a pen and a pad of paper.

"Whatcha got for me?" he said, looking up at her.

She took a seat in front of his desk. "Hannah's last name is Brown. Never been married. Still trying to figure out who the father of Isobel is. Bearfield conducted an initial interview with her boss, Frank and her co-worker, Michelle. All they had to say was she went to work yesterday at the local pharmacy, she was late as usual, and neither of them noticed anything different. Bear swung over to the Happy Trails Daycare Center. He got the same thing there. Isobel's daycare teacher didn't notice anything unusual about Hannah when she picked up Isobel yesterday afternoon. Her mom, Lisa, lives in town. Nancy from social services just rang me to let me know that Isobel is with her, so I think we should head over there."

Sam steepled his hands in front of his face.

"Good. I have Hill pulling together a list of outside-town visitors as well. He's checking on motels and Airbnbs. I really have a hard time believing that a local could have done something like this."

"And why's that?" Kimberley asked, raising an eyebrow.

"Just a feeling," he said curtly.

Kimberley averted her eyes back to her pad of paper so Sam wouldn't see the look of skepticism slip across her face. She tapped her pen repeatedly on the page. She knew Sam would have a set of blinders on when it came to his locals. Small towns typically did. It's hard to criticize the trees when you're so protective of the forest. Kimberley was convinced that Hannah had to have known her attacker. With no defensive wounds and no sign of a struggle, either this killer was as stealthy as a ninja, taking her out without her ever seeing it, or she was comfortable enough to get close to them. With the exception of serial killers and terrorist attacks, murders were statistically personal. The only doubt that creeped into her mind were the similarities in the case between Katie DeWitt James and Hannah Brown. Well, more than similarities, an exact copycat.

"I was doing some research online, and I came across this." Kimberley pulled out a piece of paper from the middle of her notepad, unfolding it and handing it to Sam.

It was a printed-out advertisement for a ghost tour Kimberley had found online.

It read: *Discover Oklahoma's most terrifying ghost story! Come learn about the unsolved murder of Katie DeWitt James and how the town of Dead Woman Crossing got its name. Legend has it that Katie's restless spirit still roams the area near Deer Creek, calling out for her baby daughter. Daily tours, $20 per person.*

Sam rolled his eyes. "I'd heard about this. Old Man Kent Wills started this business nearly a decade ago."

"It's disgusting." Kimberley shook her head.

"It's how he makes his living apparently. He lives on the outskirts of Dead Woman Crossing. Mostly keeps to himself, aside from his little ghost tour business."

"Well, he must keep a record of who goes on the tour," Kimberley said connecting the dots.

"Ahh. Yes. Good thinking. I've never liked this type of thing, ya know?" Sam shook his head.

"You mean exploiting someone else's pain and suffering for financial gain? Yeah, me neither." Kimberley's tone was sarcastic.

"Add him to the list of people to talk to."

Kimberley nodded.

Sam's desk phone rang, and he quickly picked it up.

"Sam… Yep. Sounds good. We'll be right there," he said into the phone and then just as quickly put it back on the receiver.

"Don't tell me another body."

"No, preliminary results are in. Let's go."

Kimberley breathed a sigh of relief and stood from her chair. She knew and Sam knew they had nothing to go on as of yet. They needed something. A fingerprint. DNA. Just anything.

*

Megan Grey met Chief Deputy King and Sam at the front of the medical examiner's office, which was located in the same city as the sheriff's station, Arapaho. The outside was a discreet pale-yellow brick building. Inside, it was nearly all white, the most sterile of environments. It was an unwelcoming building as it was one reserved for the dead. Megan held a clipboard and wore a long white doctor's coat. She nodded at them, a tight smile on her face, before turning down the long corridor. Kimberley and Sam followed behind as she walked down the brightly lit hallway, her heels clicking along the tile.

They entered the medical examining room where Hannah's body and head lay uncovered on the embalming table. Her clothes were gone, bagged up for the sexual assault evidence kit, Kimberley presumed. There was a long incision down the center of her body, exposing everything inside of her—cracked ribs, organs that no longer functioned. Kimberley found her unrecognizable compared to the friendly, yet lonely woman she had met just a few days ago.

"Please tell me you've got something good," Sam said, taking a deep breath.

Megan walked over to the body—that's what she would be called now, Kimberley thought. A body. Not a woman. Not a mother. Not a part-time pharmacy worker. Not Hannah. She was a body. She was rotting flesh, broken bones, useless organs, because she hadn't declared herself an organ donor. Hannah Brown didn't exist anymore... but a body did.

"I retrieved this." Megan used a pair of tweezers to hold up a bullet. "It was lodged in her brain, two inches from the frontal bone. I can say with certain this was the cause of death." She set the bullet back into the Petri dish.

"What caliber?" Kimberley asked.

".38."

"Same as Katie DeWitt James," Sam said scratching his chin.

"Any fibers, fingerprints, DNA?" Kimberley looked to Megan.

"No fingerprints or foreign fibers. The cell phone we found on her only had one set of fingerprints, which matches Hannah's. One of your deputies picked it up an hour ago. I also performed the sexual assault evidence kit. I'll have the results tomorrow afternoon. However, since her body was spotless and free from any bruising, scratches, fingerprints, I'm thinking it'll come back clean." Megan furrowed her brow.

"To leave no evidence behind, this had to have been planned meticulously. It wasn't an impulsive murder," Kimberley said.

Sam nodded. "Have an idea of time of death?"

"The time of death was sometime between two and four a.m. on September eighth," Megan said confidently.

"How about Isobel?" Kimberley asked.

"No marks on her. Not even a hair out of place. The hospital where Nancy brought her took some swabs after her wellness examination and sent them over. We analyzed them to see if we could find any DNA, like, perhaps, the killer held her. Preliminary is showing several different strands of DNA though."

"What's that mean?" Sam asked.

Before Megan could speak, Kimberley cut in, "She went to daycare yesterday, so she'd have lots of DNA on her. Sounds like a dead end."

"Exactly. I can do further testing, but, like Chief Deputy King said, it's a lost cause."

Sam sighed heavily and nodded.

"Anything else you can tell us?" Kimberley asked.

"Not right now. But when the results come in, I'll keep you both posted." Megan thumbed through the papers on her clipboard.

"Thank you, Megan. We'll see ourselves out," Sam said with a tilt of his head and walked out of the room.

Kimberley paused for a moment and looked over at Megan. "What's your take on this case?"

She looked up from her clipboard, raising her eyebrows. "In my professional opinion, I think you hit it right on the head. Hannah Brown knew her attacker."

Kimberley nodded. "You know… your work is impeccable, Megan."

"You don't have to say that. I'm sure you're used to a higher standard coming from the NYPD." Megan tilted her head, looking back at her clipboard.

"By all standards, I mean." Kimberley gave a small smile.

Megan glanced up at Kimberley. "I usually hate being called out to the boonies for these one-off cases, but with you around, I'm looking forward to it. Seems like I can learn a lot from you."

"Likewise." Kimberley nodded.

Megan returned a small smile, before diving back into her work, while Kimberley left the room, catching up with Sam.

"Jack shit to go off of besides the caliber of the bullet and a time of death," Kimberley was thinking out loud as they were driving to Hannah's mother's house. "The time of death tells us something though, she definitely knew the person."

"How can you be so sure?"

"Why the hell would she be under that creepy bridge between two and four in the morning on her own? Plus, why would you bring your daughter with you? In a stroller, no less. Makes me think she was drugged or tied up somewhere else and then brought there. The killer probably even brought the stroller from her house. Maybe that's the place to start, search for signs of a struggle or anything out of place." Kimberley was on a roll in her mind. "And you heard Megan. That crime scene was clean as a whistle."

"That's all speculative and circumstantial at best. We're not rushing to any conclusions." Sam chewed on his bottom lip.

"Besides, it still don't sound like anyone I know in this community," he added.

Kimberley took a deep breath and decided not to press the issue any further.

CHAPTER FOURTEEN

Sam pulled his police-issued Ford Bronco into the gravel driveway leading up to a small ranch house in the center of Dead Woman Crossing. The home hadn't seen any upkeep in years as the painted siding was chipped and the white shutters were either partially broken or hanging off their hinges. A garden overgrown with weeds sat off to the side of the house. The owner had clearly given up caring about its appearance, and the home and property reflected this aesthetic in kind.

"Here it is," Sam said, putting the vehicle in park.

Kimberley looked up at the house. It was exactly as she had expected, given the fact that Hannah's mom, Lisa, was a grocery-store clerk living alone on minimum wage. According to what Kimberley could gather on her, Lisa had had Hannah very young and she was her only child. Hannah's father had never been in the picture and, in that sense, history had repeated itself for these two women. Kimberley hoped to learn who Isobel's father was and where he was. But most of all, she wanted to see Isobel, to ensure that she was okay.

It took several knocks on the front door before Lisa opened it. Propped on her hip, she held Isobel close. Lisa looked like an older version of Hannah—that same long dark hair and those emerald-green eyes. But time had clearly not been kind to Lisa. The lines on her face were deeper than they should have been for a woman in her early forties, making her face look like a broken vase that was somehow still intact, cracks running all over it as if it were a part of its design. Her skin was red and blotchy, with a wet sheen thanks to smeared tears that hadn't yet dried. She sniffled and wiped at her nose with a tissue.

"Did you find the person who murdered my daughter?" Her voice cracked and she began sobbing uncontrollably.

"Let's go inside," Kimberley said, placing a hand on her shoulder and helping her back into the house.

"Mama. Mama," Isobel said over and over.

"She keeps saying that…" Lisa wailed.

Kimberley took Isobel from Lisa just as she collapsed on the tattered couch, her head in her hands, her shoulders shaking.

"I'm sorry," she cried.

"It's okay. There's no need to be sorry. Take your time," Kimberley said, holding the little girl.

Kimberley looked over Isobel, but when she got to the little girl's emerald eyes, she couldn't look away. Almost like she was spellbound by them. She knew she was too young to provide any useful evidence or testimony, but she wondered what those eyes must have seen. Did she see her mother get murdered? Did she see the killer? Would the horrible memory manifest itself into something much worse when she was older? No, of course not. She was too young. She'd remember nothing… not even her own mother. Kimberley closed her eyes for a second to compose herself. Her eyes forcing tears back into their ducts at the thought of Jessica enduring the same fate.

"Mama." The child began to cry, reaching her hands out for something that would never be there again.

"Will you take her?" Kimberley asked Sam.

"Uhh, sure."

Sam held the small child in his arms, bouncing her ever so gently. Her cries stopped and she stared up at him, confused at first. He stuck out his tongue and blew out his cheeks, causing an eruption of laughter to come from Isobel. She smiled wide, reaching out for his cheeks.

Kimberley couldn't help watching Sam. She couldn't believe how good with kids he was, especially for a man that didn't have any, or so she had assumed. They had only worked together less than a week and he hadn't really told her anything about himself. But then again, she hadn't asked.

Hearing Lisa's sobs again, Kimberley pulled her attention from Sam and Isobel. She walked to the couch and took a seat next to her, not too close to invade her space, but close enough for comfort.

"We're going to do everything we can to find the person responsible for Hannah's death," Kimberley assured.

Confidence and reassurance were the most important things she needed to get across to families of victims. If they felt you could help, they'd be more helpful, Kimberley had learned. Unless of course they were involved.

Lisa's shoulders shook a couple more times before she started gaining control of her outpouring of grief and heartache. She sat up straight, grabbing a handful of random restaurant napkins from the coffee table, and wiped her face.

"You promise?" Lisa looked directly into Kimberley's eyes, a plea for her dead daughter.

Kimberley paused. She never made promises she didn't think she could keep.

"I need your help to fill in some of the gaps we're missing?" Kimberley said, changing the subject and pulling out a small notepad and a pen from the front pocket of her shirt.

"Okay." Lisa sniffled.

"Can you tell me about Isobel's father?"

She held the pencil upright against a blank page of paper.

Lisa's shoulders shuddered. "His name's Tyler Louis. He works in the oil industry out in Texas, and he's not involved at all. He didn't even have the decency to send his daughter a birthday or Christmas gift." There was an edge of spite in her voice.

Kimberley took notes as Lisa talked.

"When was the last time he had contact with Hannah?"

"Hell if I know. That boy took off as soon as Hannah got pregnant." Lisa let out a huff.

"And how long were they together?" Kimberley asked.

"Maybe a year or two. Him running out on Hannah and Isobel really caught me off guard. He seemed like a nice boy, and then one day he was just gone. Up and skipped town." Lisa shook her head.

"So, he's had no interactions with Hannah over the past fourteen months?"

"Not that I know of."

"Do you have a phone number or an address for him?" Kimberley asked.

Lisa shook her head.

"That's okay. We can get that information."

"Think he did it?" Lisa asked, looking up at Sam.

"We're looking at a number of possibilities," Sam said, looking at Lisa while flipping through the pages of a picture book for Isobel.

"The autopsy report came back with the time of death estimated between two a.m. and four a.m. Did you notice your granddaughter and daughter were missing?" Kimberley spoke a little softer, knowing she had to tread lightly.

"No…" Lisa cried out. "I should have known. I should have felt it. A mother's intuition or something, but I was asleep."

Kimberley paused in her note-taking and let Lisa sob. If there was any guilt Lisa was feeling, she needed to get it out.

"We had had a fight that morning. I was supposed to watch Isobel that day, but I got called into work. I work at the local grocery store. She was mad at me, and she stormed out of my house with Isobel. I figured she'd cool off, and I could make it up to her another day, like go out for lunch or spend a day at the zoo, just the three of us." Lisa stopped talking as she cried. "There is no 'another day' now. When I didn't hear from her for the rest of the day, I just assumed she was still mad at me. And she doesn't live here, so it's not like I knew she hadn't come home." Lisa threw her head into her hands again. "I should have known. I should have known."

Kimberley closed up her notepad and placed her hand on Lisa's back, rubbing it. "None of this is your fault, and it won't do you any good to think that way. You have a beautiful granddaughter that needs you to be strong for her."

As if Isobel knew what Lisa needed in that moment, she said, "Nana."

Lisa looked up, her face soaked with tears, her eyes red, her face crumpled. Somehow, she found the strength to smile at her granddaughter. She found the strength to stand up. She found the strength to hold Isobel and to tell her, "Nana's here."

Lisa held her close against her chest, running her hands through her granddaughter's hair, whispering words of reassurance and love into her ear.

Sam pulled a card from his pocket and handed it to her. "Mrs. Brown, please give us a call if you remember anything else that could help. No matter how small."

Lisa took it from him and nodded.

"You'll find my daughter's killer?" she asked again, a final plea for justice.

"Of course," Sam said.

Out in the car, Sam took a deep breath while turning the key in the ignition.

"I don't usually do that," he said, putting the vehicle in reverse.

"Do what?" Kimberley looked over at him, studying his face. He wrinkled his forehead and sighed.

"Make promises I don't know if I can keep."

"You didn't. We're going to find the person who did this. Unsolved cases aren't really my thing," Kimberley said confidently, although there was doubt in her mind.

Her last case that had this little to go on went unsolved. It was the case that ate away at her, shook her to the core. "Who's the King now?" written in blood across the mirror flashed to the front of her mind. The bloody sink. The bathtub. The women. One after another. She rubbed her temples and squeezed her eyes tight, forcing the images to fade just as quickly as they appeared.

Kimberley reassured herself that this was different. This was one murder, not the work of a twisted serial killer, and this wasn't New York City. This was Dead Woman Crossing, a small town, and people talked in small towns. She was certain one way or another, there'd be a break in the case.

Kimberley pulled out her phone and called the station. Barbara answered on the first ring.

"Custer County Police Department, this is Barbara. How may I direct your call?" she said.

"Hey, Barb. It's Chief Deputy King."

"Oh, yes. How are you?"

"Fine. I need you to pull up information on a Tyler Louis. Should be residing somewhere in Texas. Mid-twenties, and he works in the oil industry."

"I'm on it," Barbara said confidently. "Oh, yes. There's a piece of apple pie waiting for you on your desk when you get back."

"Thanks, Barb. You're too kind."

"I've gotta make sure you and Sam are eating. Gotta keep your energy up if y'all are gonna catch that maniac."

Kimberley could practically hear Barb smiling.

"I appreciate it. We'll see you soon."

Kimberley ended the call.

"You know you could have asked one of the deputies to do that?" Sam raised an eyebrow.

"That binder Barb put together on the town troublemakers was the most detailed research I'd ever seen. She even had their likes and dislikes listed. I trust her to dig up everything on Tyler."

Sam cracked a smile. "Yeah, Barb is something else. We're lucky to have her."

"She said there's a piece of apple pie waiting on my desk for me."

"Careful of the Barb Fifteen."

"What's that?"

"You'll gain fifteen pounds thanks to Barb's baked goods." Sam patted his stomach, despite the fact that he was fit from what Kimberley could see.

Sam turned left onto the main road into town.

"Where we heading?" she asked.

"Over to Hannah's house."

Kimberley nodded.

Kimberley looked out the window, taking in more scenery of her new fiefdom. Leaving Arapaho and finding their way onto the small two-lane county roads showed Kimberley an almost endless expanse of fields of wheat, random smatterings of cattle, antelope, and a few trees here and there. In the dry environment of Oklahoma, the dust and wind dominated; only voracious weeds and the most virile of seeding plants could hold up to the abuse. The thing that struck Kimberley was how much it all looked the same, even after only a few miles, like she had seen the whole state in one drive. She knew there must be more though. Within that vast expanse of wheat, an entire world must be thriving and moving underfoot, because Kimberley saw countless hawks circling the plains, diving from time to time.

Sam put the vehicle in park on the side of the road in front of a small blue ranch house. Unlike Lisa's home, the outside was well maintained with freshly painted white shutters and perfectly hedged bushes lining the front of the house. Kimberley and Sam got out of the vehicle and walked to the front door. He twisted the handle and the door opened.

"She doesn't lock her doors?" Kimberley questioned.

"No one does around here. This ain't New York City," Sam said, entering the small home.

Kimberley pursed her lips together. For the most part, New York City was safe. True, people didn't leave their doors unlocked, but they also didn't walk around in fear of being murdered or robbed at any moment. Like any city, there were unsafe areas, but, on the whole, it was safe. It was obvious when someone hadn't been to NYC, because they talked about it in generalities, based on what they'd seen on television. Looking at Sam in irritation, Kimberley presumed he had never set foot outside of Oklahoma.

The front door opened to a small living room and an open-concept kitchen. Inside, everything was immaculate and well kept. Not a single item was out of place. The home was sparsely furnished, the living room only having a loveseat, a coffee table, and a TV stand with a small flat-screen television. The kitchen had a square table with two chairs and a highchair. They walked through the house, down the hall, passing a bathroom that was spotless, a nursery that had nothing more than a few toys, a crib, and a rocking chair. Hannah's room was like the rest of the house: clean and sparsely decorated. Just a made full-size bed, a dresser, and an end table sat inside the room. Hannah clearly didn't have much, but she took pride in what little she had.

"She didn't leave in a hurry," Kimberley said, looking inside the closet. Her clothes were hung up and color-coded and an empty travel suitcase sat on the floor.

Sam nodded his head while pulling open some drawers of the dresser. All the clothes were folded neatly and stood up on end.

"She was tidy," he noted.

Kimberley raised an eyebrow. "A little surprising."

"Why's that?" Sam looked over to Kimberley.

"The run-ins I had with her, she was always late, flustered, and frantic, and with a young child, I'd expect an unkempt home. You should have seen my apartment in New York—toys everywhere, piles of clothes," Kimberley thought out loud.

"You're right, she's very tidy," Sam said, looking around.

"Like a type-A personality. She's a planner."

Kimberley walked over to Hannah's bed. On the wall above it was a large bulletin board covered in photos and quotes, almost like a mood board for a life she wanted and dreamed of. There were pictures of places overseas: the Caribbean, Australia, the Eiffel Tower. A pang of sadness hit Kimberley like a punch to the gut. Hannah wanted more out of life. She wanted out of Dead Woman Crossing. And she got the exact opposite. She shook her head in disgust at the person who took it all away from her.

"It's just so sad. Look at this." Kimberley pointed to the mood board.

Sam stood beside her and glanced up, scanning all the colorful images.

"She had so much she wanted to do and see, and some asshole just ripped it all away."

"It's a fucking shame." Sam shook his head. He looked over at Kimberley. "You alright?"

Kimberley pulled her eyes from the mood board and looked at Sam. "I will be once we catch this guy."

They walked back down the hallway, into the living room, giving Hannah's home a final once-over.

"I was hoping we'd find something like a planner saying, 'Meeting with so and so.'" Sam scratched at his chin.

"Well, we've got her cell phone. Burns is in touch with her provider to get the device unlocked and pull records," Kimberley said.

"How long 'til we have those?"

"A day or two."

"Why don't we head on over to Kent's place? He don't live too far from here."

"Maybe we'll have more luck with this town's only ghost tour operator than we've had with Lisa and Hannah's home."

"Don't get your hopes up—Kent Wills is a bit of a nutjob." Sam tilted his head.

CHAPTER FIFTEEN

Leaving Hannah's house, Kimberley and Sam were once again navigating back roads on their way out of town toward the outskirts where Kent Wills lived. With wide-open space and no cars in sight, the road felt like their own; a telegraphed path that their vehicle had to traverse merely for the sake of it. Looking out at the countryside, Kimberley was already starting to grow tired of the same scenery set in a seemingly continuous loop. Tree. Wheatgrass. Tree. Wheatgrass. Oh look, a cornfield. Tree. Wheatgrass.

Could this be any more drab? Kimberley thought to herself. I mean hell at least in—

SCREEEEECHHH.

Kimberley's head slammed forward, pulling her from her thoughts with a violent force.

"Jesus Christ," Sam yelled, as he just missed the tail end of a deer hopping off into the tall grass.

Kimberley could smell burned rubber as the Ford Bronco had come to an immediate halt. Kimberley looked over at Sam, who still had his hands at ten and two on the steering wheel, gripping it tightly.

"Sorry about that. I zoned out for a moment," he said, looking over at her.

Kimberley's heartbeat was just starting to come down. "Does that happen a lot around here?"

"Well, we do have a lot of wildlife. Probably never saw that in the city."

"Can't say I have. In the city you dodge pedestrians, but they don't move like that," Kimberley said with a small smile.

The same screeching noise was repeated again, this time punctuated with a sickening thud and the shattering of glass. Kimberley looked up just in time to see droplets of blood spraying into the air, clumps of fawn and white fur blowing in the wind, glass shards sprinkling the road like a fresh hail had just fallen, and chunks of plastic and metal strewn to the sides of the vehicle that had been coming from the other direction. The deer slid across the pavement, doing roll after roll until it came to a stop in the gravel side strip off the highway.

Immediately, Sam and Kimberley jumped out of the vehicle, running toward the black Ford Focus. Kimberley got to the driver's side first. The airbag had gone off, and a woman with long blond hair that looked both dry and oily sat dazed in the passenger seat. Kimberley yanked open the door.

"Are you okay?" she asked, examining the woman.

She was thin, dressed in blue jean shorts and a white tank top. Scrapes and cuts covered her bare thighs where tiny shards of glass were sprinkled all over her. The woman looked up at Kimberley, her face a mix of a blank stare and confusion. A dark bruise wrapped around her left eye like a coiled black snake. *That couldn't have formed that quickly*, Kimberley thought to herself.

Sam stood behind Kimberley. "Sarah, let's get you out of the vehicle slowly," he said.

Kimberley glanced at Sam and then at the woman in the car… Sarah. He knew her. She reached her hand out to help. Sarah hesitated, but allowed Kimberley to assist her. With one foot on the pavement, Kimberley pulled her out, so she wouldn't slide against the broken glass that had fallen between her legs. She gently brushed the remaining glass off of herself.

"Sarah, are you okay?" Sam asked.

"Yeah, I'm fine. Just rattled," she said. "I don't know how I didn't see that deer." Sarah looked out at the fields on either side and then back at Kimberley and Sam.

"We almost hit one too," Kimberley said.

Sam leaned his head toward his radio clipped on the front of his shirt and spoke into it. "Sam, here. I've got an 11-81 out on E1000, east of N2440. Send a couple of deputies, a tow truck, and an ambulance, please. Over."

"Bearfield here. Burns and I are on our way. Over."

Sarah pulled a cell phone from the back pocket of her jeans.

"Do you wanna call your husband?" Sam asked.

Sarah looked up at him and nodded.

"Go on ahead. We'll take care of the deer and wait here until the other deputies arrive." Sam nodded, walking past the damaged vehicle to the back of it.

"What do you mean we'll take care of it?" Kimberley asked, keeping pace with Sam's slow walk.

As they neared the trunk of the vehicle, she could hear a muffled moan. In the ditch lay the bloodied, broken deer. Its tongue hanging out, its head swaying side to side, and then that awful muffled groan emitting from its open mouth. Its black eyes stared at Kimberley, a shred of life still in them, begging for help.

"We can't let it suffer," Sam said, pulling his revolver from his holster.

"You're just going to shoot it? Isn't there an animal hospital you can take it to?" Kimberley asked, knowing full well her question was ridiculous.

Sam glanced over at her. "It's the compassionate thing to do." He raised his gun, aiming at the deer's swaying head. Sam squeezed the trigger. Bang. The deer's head hit the ground with a thud. Its black eyes still stared at Kimberley, but there was nothing left behind them. Shooting animals was new for her and not something she ever thought she'd get used to. At least with humans, the really bad ones, she could wrap her head around the idea that the world was better off without them, that justice was served, that they deserved it. Kimberley found humans were more like animals than animals were. She took a deep breath, inhaling the dry, dusty air. It scratched the back of her throat, causing her to cough several times.

"You alright?" Sam drew his brows together.

"Yeah." She cleared her throat and glanced over at the woman, who was in a hushed conversation on her phone, pacing back and forth on the country road. "You see the bruise on her left eye? That couldn't have happened during the car accident?" Kimberley's voice was full of concern.

"You're right. It didn't. That's Deputy Craig Lodge's wife." Sam raised an eyebrow.

Sarah ended the call, sliding her phone back in her pocket.

Kimberley shook her head and clenched her fist. She wasn't sure she'd be able to stop it from connecting with Lodge's face when he showed up.

"He's on his way," Sarah said, looking at Kimberley and Sam and then down at her feet, almost as though she was ashamed to say it.

"Looks like I'll be meeting Lodge sooner than I thought I would," Kimberley whispered to Sam.

"Be nice. We all want to clock the guy, but there's a right way to do things around here," Sam warned.

A black lifted Dodge Ram came speeding down the country road toward Sam, Kimberley, and Sarah. Dust and dirt encircled it as it kicked up everything loose on the ground. The exhaust emitted a blaring roar, which was rather annoying. Oh great, Sarah's knight in shining armor. Kimberley rolled her eyes. The truck came to a screeching, dramatic halt with Deputy Craig Lodge jumping out of the truck and running to his wife. He was dressed in ratty jeans and a wife beater, but he was shorter than Kimberley had pictured him, coming in at around five foot nine. It was clear he tried to make up for his lack of height with lifting as his arms were thick, veins wrapped around them like ropes. He sported a buzzed military cut, despite never being in the military, and a crooked nose, which suited him.

"Are you okay, sweetheart?" Craig wrapped Sarah in his beefy arms.

She nodded. "It came out of nowhere. Sam said they almost hit one too."

Sam walked toward them, and Kimberley followed behind. She raised her chin and shook out her clenched fist. Walker was right. There was a right way to do things.

"Deputy Lodge." Sam tilted his head.

"Hey, Sam." Craig released Sarah from his bear hug and stood beside her. "Thanks for being here to take care of my wife."

Kimberley expected him to be a huge dick, but he was being pleasant, nice. A wolf in sheepskin. Sam nodded.

"This here is Chief Deputy Kimberley King. She's new to the force from the NYPD, but you'll be working under her when your suspension is up." Sam gestured to Kimberley.

Craig outstretched his hand for a handshake. She noticed his knuckles were scabbed over, and it took every ounce of willpower for Kimberley to reach hers out. *Be professional*, she reminded herself. Their hands connected and Kimberley squeezed as tightly as she could. A couple of bones in his hands cracked. She could see him wince a little. His eyes narrowed for a brief second, but he didn't say a word. It wasn't a firm "nice to meet you" handshake. It was a "hello, dickwad." A warning.

"Great to meet you, Kimberley. Can't wait to get back on the force," he said with a smile.

They released hands. "It's Chief Deputy King," Kimberley corrected. "And, yes, I look forward to it."

"Ah yes. Chief Deputy King. Sorry about that," he said with a laugh. "Been off the force too long." He wiped his hand against his sweaty forehead.

"I've got Bearfield and Burns coming down to take the accident report as well as paramedics and a tow truck."

"I'm fine, really," Sarah said.

"You should still get checked out," Craig said, rubbing her shoulder.

Kimberley could see her tense up immediately upon his hand touching her body. Sarah nodded.

"What about the deer?" Craig asked, looking at Sam.

"We'll get it cleaned up."

"Mind if I take it home? I mean, it's fresh, and it'd make for some good eating." Craig punctuated his request with a smile.

Sam paused for a moment and then nodded. "Knock yourself out."

"Thanks, Sheriff," Craig said pleased.

This would be the type of guy that'd pick up dead animals off the side of the road, Kimberley thought to herself. She couldn't stand being in his presence any longer. Every second she stood there was another moment she might punch Lodge in the face.

"Should we head out?" Kimberley looked at Sam.

"Oh yeah. I heard about Hannah Brown. Such a shame." Craig shook his head. "If you need me back sooner to help out, I... I'm available."

Yes, that's what we need to crack the case, Deputy Craig 'wife beater' Lodge. Kimberley forced her eyes to stay in place.

"We're good. Finish up your suspension and mandated counseling and stay out of trouble. We'll see you back in the office next month," Sam said curtly.

Deputy Lodge nodded, acting as though he had accepted the answer, but a couple of veins in his neck had jutted out. "Of course." He grinned.

Kimberley could hear the sirens getting closer and closer.

"Alright, we're going to head out. Burns and Bearfield and the ambulance will be here momentarily. You two good?" Sam asked.

Sarah nodded.

"Yeah, thanks again. And it was good meeting you, Chief Deputy King," Craig said with a nod and a smile.

"Likewise," Kimberley forced herself to say. She walked toward Sam's Ford Bronco.

Inside the vehicle, Kimberley let out a deep breath—it was all the tension she had been holding in. Sam turned on the engine and looked in the rearview mirror. Bearfield and Burns were getting out of their vehicles and walking toward the Ford Bronco. An ambulance sped toward them in the distance, a mile or so down the country road. Sam rolled down his window as Bearfield approached.

"Afternoon, Sam," Bearfield said. "Chief Deputy King."

They both nodded at him.

"What we got?" Bearfield asked glancing at the damaged vehicle, Craig and Sarah, and back at Sam.

"Animal accident. The deer's been put down and is behind the vehicle. Sarah has some minor cuts, so make sure paramedics check her out. Deputy Lodge is taking the deer with him. No write up for animal control," Sam rattled off. "As soon as the scene is cleared, I'll need you and Burns back on the Brown case."

Bearfield nodded. "You got it."

"And don't give Lodge any details on the case," Sam added.

"Yes, sir."

Kimberley looked up ahead. Craig was no longer standing by Sarah. She couldn't see him anywhere. Her eyes focused on the wrecked Ford Focus. He wasn't inside of that either. She turned back to see if he had gone back to his truck. Not there either. When she looked forward again, she spotted him dragging the deer's body out from behind the car. The carcass left a bloody trail behind it, and he smiled widely at his newfound prize.

"Burns, help me with this," he called out.

Before Burns walked away, Kimberley stopped him. "Burns, how's it coming along with Hannah's phone?"

"I just got the device unlocked before I headed here. Phone company said it'd take twenty-four to forty-eight hours to produce phone records. But I'll start going through what's on the actual phone just as soon as I'm done here," he said.

"Good work. I need them right away. So finish up quickly here."

Burns nodded. "Of course," and then headed toward Craig and the dead deer.

"Bear, help him compile the phone data. We need all hands on deck," Sam instructed.

Bear nodded and took a step back from the vehicle as Sam put it in drive and pulled forward slowly.

Craig stared at Kimberley as they passed by. She didn't believe that people could see the future, but she could see his and it wasn't going to turn out well if she had anything to do with it.

"Let's go give Kent Wills a visit," Sam said.

"Sure, let's just get the fuck outta here."

CHAPTER SIXTEEN

Looking through the windshield of the police cruiser, Kimberley knew Sam was right about Kent Wills just from seeing the outside of his house. It was adorned with Halloween decorations despite it being the end of summer. Ghosts hung from trees. Jack-o'-lanterns lined the front porch. There were fake cobwebs stretched over everything; the windows, trees, bushes. He had really gone all out on his ghost tour business.

Kimberley and Sam stepped out of the vehicle and made their way to the front door. Sam knocked twice before he heard rustling inside.

Kent Wills, a man in his sixties with thinning gray hair and glasses opened the door. He was dressed in a graphic T-shirt that read "Ghosts are real. I've seen them." His shirt was tucked into his pants, held up by a worn brown leather belt.

"Sam, to what do I owe the pleasure?" he said sarcastically.

"Just need to ask you a few questions. This here is Chief Deputy Kimberley King." He gestured to Kimberley.

Kent Wills waggled his eyebrows slightly. "Got yourself a looker." He leered. "What's a pretty girl like you doing in a town like this?"

"Solving the murder that happened near where you put on your ghost tours. Know anything about that?" Kimberley raised her chin.

Kent coughed a few times and swallowed hard. "Of course not."

"Let's go inside and chat," Sam said. His tone was friendly, disarming.

Kent backed up, allowing Kimberley and Sam to enter his home.

The home was beyond cluttered with outdated furniture and décor. Stacks of cardboard boxes lined a wall. Another wall was covered in a hodgepodge of tacky bird clocks that Kimberley found quite disturbing. The beige carpet was worn and covered in stains. It was clear all of Kent's energy was put into his business and not his house. He walked over to the orange couch and pushed a stack of newspapers off of it.

"Here, have a seat," he said.

Kimberley was going to decline, but when Sam sat down, she figured she would too. Kent sat down in the plaid tattered chair kitty-corner to the couch.

"Do you keep records of the people that go on your ghost tours?" Kimberley asked, cutting right to the chase.

"Why you asking about my ghost tour? You trying to book a spot?" Kent lifted an eyebrow.

"No. We're just gathering some information. So, do you keep a record of your ghost tours?" Kimberley asked again.

"Of course. Got to for future marketing." He nodded.

"And tax purposes," Kimberley added, knowing full well there was no way Kent was paying taxes on the money he earned from his ghost tours. When she had learned he only accepted cash, she figured it'd be an angle she could use to force information out of him if he were uncooperative. The IRS threat worked on most people.

"Yeah, for that too," he said unconvincingly.

"How far do your records go back?" Sam asked.

"Since I started the business."

"We're going to need records for the last twelve months," Kimberley said. She figured in order to appease Sam's "gut feeling" she'd have to be thorough. Six months would have sufficed, but twelve months would allow Kimberley to see the bigger picture. How many people on average went on the tour? Were there any repeaters? Her gut told her they were barking up the wrong tree, but this was Sam's town.

Kent looked at Sam and then at Kimberley, his eyes like a pendulum. Finally, he stood up. "Let me just get that from my office then."

Kent walked slowly out of the room, shuffling his feet along the floor. Kimberley and Sam exchanged a look of disbelief. As soon as he was out of the room, Kimberley stood up and hurried over to the cardboard boxes. She opened up one. It was full of old books. Another one revealed a set of dishes.

"What are you doing?" Sam asked just above a whisper.

"Shh, just browsing," Kimberley hissed.

Kimberley opened another box. A stack of old *Penthouse* magazines sat inside. The top one was from June 1978 and on the cover appeared the naked bottom half of a woman upside down inside of a meat grinder with the text "'We will no longer hang women up like pieces of meat.' Larry Flynt."

Grimacing, she hurriedly closed the box back up and took her spot on the couch when she heard Kent's shuffling footsteps.

Kent returned with five spiral notebooks. He handed them to Kimberley before retaking his seat.

"They're all in there. Names. Email addresses. Phone numbers. Separated out by each day. I do one tour a day, three hundred and fifty-one days a year. I give myself a total of two weeks of vacation. I'm the hardest working retired man you'll ever meet," he said, raising his chin proudly.

Kimberley gave Sam a puzzled look and then looked down at the spirals, thumbing through them. Each page had the date at the top and then below it a table was drawn in pencil with three columns labeled—name, email and phone number. Like a guest book for his tours. With this type of outdated record-keeping, she wondered how reliable they actually were.

"No one is calling your work ethic into question," Sam said soothingly. "We're just trying to get a sense of people coming in and out of town. And since your ghost tour is more of a tourist attraction, we figured it'd be a good start."

Kent looked mollified. "Oh. Okay. You said someone was murdered down by where I give my tours? Think someone on one of my tours did it?"

"We're exploring a number of possibilities," Sam said carefully.

"Have you noticed anyone acting rather strange on your tour? Maybe someone a little too invested in the true-crime story you cover?" Kimberley asked, also careful not to reveal too much.

Kent scratched at his chin as if he were considering, thinking back to the people he had encountered. "Not that I can think of off the top of my head. Well, we had this one weirdo a while back. I remember because it was the hottest day of the year—over a hundred degrees outside—and he was wearing black jeans and a black hoodie. He had them big holes in his ears. I swear I could have fit one of my dinner plates inside of them."

"How long ago was this?" Kimberley tilted her head.

"Years ago."

She let out a small sigh and moved on with the questioning. Kent was an old-fashioned man, so anyone that was dressed out of the ordinary would appear to be a weirdo to him. As this person clearly had a goth or punk style and visited years ago, it wasn't of any help to the current case.

"And you're the only one that gives the tours? Your wife doesn't help out?" Kimberley asked.

"Just me. My son Kent Jr. was helping here and there when we were fully booked, but he hasn't in a while. My wife's actually the reason I even got into it. I retired early and she was tired of me sitting around watching Fox News. So, she kept harping on at me to pick up a hobby or volunteer somewhere. That's when I came up with the ghost tour idea, and I've been doing it ever since."

"What's your wife do?" Kimberley asked.

"Ruth… she works at the local pharmacy."

"Is she there now?" Kimberley asked.

"No, she's getting groceries. She works very part time, just coverage when they need it."

Kimberley nodded. Then her eyes widened for a second. Like a lightbulb went off in her head. His wife works at the pharmacy. She must have known Hannah Brown. Would Kent have known her too? Well, obviously, given how small the town is.

"Well, I think that's everything." Sam stood from his seat and pulled a card from his front pocket. "If you think of anything else, please give me a call."

Kent took the card from him. Kimberley stood and followed Sam and Kent to the front door.

"Who was it?" Kent asked.

Sam turned back toward him as he stepped outside onto the porch. "Who was what?"

"The person that was murdered."

Sam looked at Kimberley and then back at Kent.

"Hannah Brown."

Kent's mouth dropped open. "That poor girl."

"Wait, Ruth works at the pharmacy where Hannah worked at?" Kimberley raised an eyebrow.

"That's right."

"Has your wife ever mentioned Hannah?" Kimberley asked.

Kent scratched at the back of his neck. "Yeah, I'm sure. She's filled in for shifts for Hannah and Michelle, but she works alone since she's very part time and only there for coverage."

"Did you know the victim, Kent?" Kimberley took a tiny step toward him, closing some of the distance between her and him.

"Oh, yes. Hannah was a sweet girl. I didn't know her all that well, but I knew her. It's a small town." Kent nodded.

"Indeed, it is," she said. "Have a good day, Mr. Wills. And thanks for these." She held up the notebooks.

"Of course. Whatever I can do to help. Just let me know. And you'll get those back to me when you're done, right?" he asked.

"Yes," Sam replied.

"Ya know, for taxes purposes." Kent winked at Kimberley.

She turned her head and rolled her eyes. Sam nodded at him and they both headed back to the vehicle.

"Whatcha think?" Kimberley asked, fastening her seat belt.

"I think I'll have Deputy Burns call around to local inns and motels, see who's been passing through town recently and we'll get started on sorting through those log books tomorrow."

"What about Kent?"

"What about him?" Sam looked at Kimberley.

"Whatcha think about him?"

"I think we should head over to The Trophy Room. I could use a beer." Sam turned the engine on.

It was clear to Kimberley, Sam had no intention of pointing any fingers at his residents just yet. He had tunnel vision and that tunnel went straight past his precious Custer County.

"Besides, I think we can squeeze some info out of the locals there. See who's passed through town. Kill two birds with one stone, as they say."

"Right," Kimberley said, opening the first spiral.

The page was nearly filled with names, a full tour for the day, showing that Kent's business had to have been quite lucrative.

CHAPTER SEVENTEEN

Sam walked into The Trophy Room first, holding the door for Kimberley to enter behind. She looked around, noticing the bar was exactly how she had left it a few days earlier. The same old men sat at their gambling machines, permanent fixtures of the establishment. The pool tables and dartboards were in use by bikers and farm boys. A couple of regulars were spread out, bellied up to the bar, drinking their pints of cheap beer. It was like a level of a video game, the same environment and characters loaded for play the exact same way every time you booted up the scenario. As soon as people noticed Sam and Kimberley's presence, all eyes were on them. Whispers ensued. Kimberley was sure that news of Hannah's murder had traveled fast. She expected that. In a small town like Dead Woman Crossing, gossip was like an airborne virus. Difficult to contain and easily transmitted. They were all infected.

Standing behind the bar with a dirty dishrag thrown over his shoulder was Ryan, just the guy they were looking for.

"This is the town watering hole and Ryan here is at the center of it. He knows most everything about everyone," Sam said in a low voice to Kimberley.

She nodded. In New York City, the ones that had dirt were informants. Here in Dead Woman Crossing, they were creepy bartenders.

Despite what had happened in his town, there was still an arrogance to him. He gave them a smug look, never breaking eye contact. Kimberley took the lead, walking to the bar and taking a seat on one of the stools. Sam sat beside her, tipping his head at a couple of the regulars.

"Miss me?" Ryan smirked at Kimberley. He pulled the towel from his shoulder and wiped the bar top down in front of them.

"Hardly," Kimberley retorted. "Two Bud Lights," she said, holding up two fingers.

She decided to take the approach that she and Sam were just blowing steam off after a difficult workday, rather than the fact that they were there to collect information.

Ryan filled the two pints and set them in front of Sam and Kimberley. Sam immediately threw a ten-dollar bill on the bar. Ryan nodded, took the money and returned four single dollar bills.

"You look better in uniform," he said to Kimberley with a sleazy leer.

Sam took a long drink, set the pint glass down, and narrowed his eyes at Ryan.

"I think you'd look better in uniform too. Got a nice orange jumpsuit at the station with your name on it."

Ryan let out a chuckle. "Alright, I get it. She's your girl." He backed up and tended to a patron at the end of the bar.

Sam shook his head.

"Sorry about him. He's our town dipshit."

Kimberley smiled. "My first interaction with him led me to that conclusion as well." She tipped back the pint glass, consuming nearly half the beer in a couple of gulps.

After the day she'd had, the beer went down like water. Crisp and refreshing.

An old man with a belly and a bald head tapped Sam on the shoulder. He clearly took no pride in his appearance as he was wearing ratty jeans and a graphic tee with a lion on it.

"Heard about the murder, Sheriff Walker. Such a shame. Hannah was a good girl," he said, every other word slurring.

Sam nodded. "It sure is. Can't believe something like that happened in our town. Have you heard anything, Jeff?"

Jeff rubbed the top of his head. "A lot of talk goin' round town, like maybe Hannah was into something dirty. I've 'erd chatter of 'er being a sex worker."

Sam shook his head. "This town's only good for bullshit gossip. Where'd they get that idea from?"

"Ya know how people are round here. They make mountains out of mole hills. I've been tryin' to shut it down. Hannah was a good girl. Ain't no way she got tangled up in summin like that."

"Who d'you hear that from?" Kimberley quickly jumped in.

"Overheard a couple of them farm boys talking about it. Not sure on their names though."

"And you knew Hannah? How did you know her?" Kimberley asked.

"Well, I got the diabeetus, so I'm at the pharmacy a lot for my meds. She was always kind to me. Always greeted me with a smile, asked how I was."

"Thanks, Jeff. Seen any outsiders come in recently?"

"Just some bikers, travelin' through a week or so ago, two couples. Ya know the types? Middle-aged, dressed in leather from head to toe, riding Harleys. We get lots of bikers coming through though and I usually keeps to myself." He looked over at Kimberley. "You must be our new chief deputy. Heard a lot about you."

Kimberley nodded. "None of its true."

Jeff let out a deep laugh. "She funny," he said, pointing at Kimberley.

"Indeed. Let me know if you hear anything." Sam sipped his beer.

"Course."

Jeff backed away, returning to his stool in front of a slot machine.

Ryan returned from the other side of the bar. "Another one?" He gestured to the empty glass.

Kimberley nodded. "Tell me, Ryan, have you gotten any outside visitors passing through town lately?"

Ryan raised an eyebrow while refilling her pint glass. He set the beer in front of her and then scanned the bar. "Don't really have any time to be answering your questions," he said.

Kimberley looked around. There weren't that many people in the bar, and it seemed everyone had already been taken care of. Ryan was being reluctant, uncooperative and it immediately raised a red flag. Was he hiding something? Or was he just not the type to talk to the police?

Kimberley looked at her watch and then back at Ryan. "Oh, gee, I didn't even notice the time. You're right! I guess it is time to do a full inspection on all the regs for upholding a county liquor license. Sam, where do you wanna start? I would assume kick everyone out first so as to not interfere with police business?"

"Nah. I say we ID all of them first. Make sure they are all the legal age of consumption. Log each patron and then we will need receipts and inventory logs for every bottle of alcohol. Make sure they were all purchased legally and with proper documentation and definitely make sure there's nothing illegal like moonshine or any narcotics on the premises."

Ryan twisted his lips and folded his arms across his chest. "Alright, alright. Just chill the fuck out. I seen a couple in here the other day, visiting from out of town. Murder tourists as they called themselves. A bit sketch, if ya ask me. Mid-thirties, from Texas or South Carolina or something, and they were in here asking a lot of questions about Dead Woman Crossing and the story of Katie DeWitt James."

Sam gave Kimberley a puzzled look.

"You know where they were staying?" Kimberley asked.

"Nope." Ryan shrugged his shoulders.

"They just came in here asking about murder?" Kimberley raised an eyebrow.

"Yup. Like I said a bit sketch, if ya ask me."

"Sketch, how?" Kimberley asked.

"Ugly, missing teeth, ratty hair, like that kind of sketch…"

She wasn't sure if Ryan didn't know the definition of "sketch" or if this was all a load of bullshit. It seemed as though he was messing with her and Sam, and Kimberley thought the only way to get any answers out of him were in an interrogation room, not in his bar, his domain.

"When were they here?" she asked.

"I don't know. Yesterday. Could have been the day before. Could have been both days for all I know." Ryan rubbed his forehead.

"They talk to anyone else?" Sam asked.

"They could have. I don't know for sure."

Sam drained the rest of his beer and set the empty pint glass down. Without asking, Ryan refilled it, but Kimberley was sure he only did so to busy himself, to get out of this conversation. She wasn't buying his story. It was too buttoned up. Too pretty. Like a wrapped gift with a big bow. Ryan seemed to just be giving enough information to appease so he could get on with his day. But why? Why lead the police astray? Why give some false accounts of a couple of murder tourists stopping into his bar? Was Ryan hiding something? Or was he just what Sam had described him as, the town dipshit?

He set the beer down in front of Sam, telling him it was on the house.

Jeff meandered back over to the bar with his glass full of ice. "Ryan, 'nother Jack and Coke," he said.

"You got it, Jeff." Ryan collected the glass and busied himself with making a fresh drink.

"Hey, Jeff. You see a couple in their mid-thirties here talking about murder and the history of Dead Woman Crossing this week?" Sam asked. He had smelled Ryan's bullshit too.

Jeff leaned against the bar, squinting one of his eyes. "Can't say I have."

"You been in here all week?"

"Like clockwork," he said with a nod.

Kimberley couldn't tell if he was proud of that fact or not, but one thing she knew, Ryan was lying.

Ryan set the Jack and Coke in front of Jeff.

"On the tab," Jeff said, collecting his drink.

Ryan nodded.

"Where were you this morning between the hours of two a.m. and four a.m.?" Kimberley asked. She was tired of Ryan's bullshit and with Jeff saying he hadn't seen this mysterious couple and with Ryan being uncooperative, she figured it was time to push him.

Ryan tossed the dirty rag over his shoulder and looked above the heads of Kimberley and Sam. When he was ready to answer, he locked eyes with them, raising his chin defiantly.

"I was here cleaning and closing up. Around two, I went upstairs to bed. My apartment's above the bar." He folded his arms in front of his chest.

"You live alone?" Kimberley asked.

"Most nights," he said with a sleazy smile.

"Were you alone last night?"

"You seem to be very interested in my sleeping arrangements, Chief Deputy King."

"Just answer the damn question, Ryan," Sam warned.

He let out a huff. "Yeah, I was alone last night. What else you want to know? What I wore to bed?"

Kimberley raised her chin. "Nope. That'll be all... for now."

He turned on his foot and walked to the end of the bar, as far away from Sam and Chief Deputy King as he could get.

"What you make of that?" Sam asked.

"No alibi, but nothing tying him to the murder scene. I can't tell if he's guilty of anything more than being an asshole."

"He's clearly lying, but I'm not sure why." Sam scratched his brow.

"What about that comment from Jeff about Hannah being a hooker? Think there's any truth to that?" Kimberley tilted her head.

"I find it hard to believe, but we'll follow up on it." Sam nodded.

She had had enough of The Trophy Room and was ready to get home to her daughter.

Sam drank the rest of his beer. "I'll have one of the deputies keep an eye on Ryan in the meantime. Ready to head out?"

Kimberley nodded and stood from her stool.

CHAPTER EIGHTEEN

Kimberley walked the rock-lined path around the big white farmhouse to the cottage in back. She was happy to get home to her daughter, to hold her close. It was the one thing she never took for granted, holding her baby, since she had witnessed this simple joy ripped away from others far too often.

"I got something," Kimberley said, tossing a file folder on Detective Hunter's desk. Lynn closed the filing cabinet and spun around in her chair.

Her swollen belly was in the way of getting close enough to her desk that she could lean her elbows on it. Lynn grabbed the folder and opened it up.

"Whatcha got?"

"I found the connection between the three victims." Kimberley took a seat.

"Other than they were all pregnant?" Lynn raised an eyebrow.

"Yes, so we know the first victim was Jenny Roberts, a waitress from Harlem, very early on in her pregnancy. Then, victim two was Maria Velasquez, a legal secretary from the lower eastside. Victim three was Stephanie Weisman, an investment banker from Greenwich Village. The victims came from very different backgrounds, classes, etc. and it seems like they wouldn't have anything connecting them. But they all worked at the Blue Devil Diner at some point. Maria, only

a couple years back. Jenny was an employee up until she was murdered, and Stephanie worked there back when she was attending NYU."

"How come we didn't know this before?"

"The owner, Eddie Russo, pays his employees under the table, no tax records, no employment records. He's owned the place for over ten years and he's got a rap sheet. Armed robbery. Assault," Kimberley said. *"He served time for the armed robbery from age nineteen to twenty-four."*

"Motive?"

"I'm not sure. But he's the only connection we've found between the three victims. Should we bring him in?"

Detective Hunter paused for a moment, flipping through the pages once more. She nodded. "Yeah, go ahead. Let's bring him in for questioning."

Kimberley stood from her seat. "How ya feeling?" she asked.

Lynn looked down at her belly. "I'd feel much better if we could get this case solved before I go on maternity leave, but I know it's in good hands with you, Kimberley," she said with a smile.

Kimberley gave a small smile back. "I'm going to catch this guy. It'll be my gift to you and that little boy of yours."

"You know you have to actually get me a real gift." Lynn cracked a smile, rubbing a hand over her belly.

"Who says I haven't? Weren't you the one that told me not to jump to conclusions?" Kimberley said with a knowing look.

Lynn shook her head. "Jesse here is going to love his smartass Aunt Kimberley."

"Jesse?"

"Oh, shit." Lynn put her hand over her mouth. "I wasn't supposed to tell anyone his name yet. Rick and I settled on it last night."

"It's perfect, and your secret's safe with me."

*"Thanks, Kimberley. Now, go. Round up some officers, track
down Eddie, and bring that bastard in. I'll obviously be here
on desk duty waiting."*

*"You got it!" she said, ducking out of the office. Kimberley
peeked her head back into the cubicle. "Try not to give birth
until I get back."*

Opening her eyes, Kimberley was standing in front of the
cottage. This isn't the same, she told herself. She wouldn't let
another monster slip through her grasp. She couldn't live with
herself if she did, so Kimberley vowed to do everything in her
power to bring Hannah and her family justice. So far, they had
nothing to go on. Whoever did this knew what they were doing.
She hoped Megan would come back with something useful, but
Kimberley knew that wasn't looking good. All she had in terms
of suspicion was dipshit Ryan and maybe something would come
of those notebooks she collected from Kent.

She shuffled into the house. Finding the living room empty, she
walked into the dining room and as soon as she saw Jessica, all the
frustration drained from her. Jessica was seated in her highchair,
while Nicole was trying to help her hold a spoon to scoop from the
bowl of applesauce in front of her. It appeared to not be going all
that well, since both of them had smears of applesauce on them.
Kimberley walked to Jessica and kissed the top of her forehead.

"How was work?" Nicole asked, while keeping her eyes on her
granddaughter.

"Awful."

Kimberley disappeared into the kitchen, returning a moment
later with a bottle of Bud Light. She took a seat at the dining-room
table, across from Jessica and Nicole.

"I heard about Hannah Brown." Nicole raised an eyebrow.

"News travels fast around here." Kimberley took a swig of her
beer.

"It's just awful. I'm confident you and Sam will find the person responsible though, but I do worry about you."

"There's no need to worry, Mom."

"You're putting yourself in danger."

Kimberley refused to argue with her mother about the dangers of police work. If she only knew what kind of danger she had put herself in as a detective working high-profile cases.

"Did you know Hannah?"

"Yes, but not well. I just knew her from around town and at the pharmacy. Always said hi to me. She seemed like a sweet girl."

Kimberley took a swig of her beer. "Yeah, that's been the general consensus so far. Sweet girl, but no one really knew her. I can't stop thinking about her daughter Isobel, growing up without a mother." She shook her head as she rotated the bottle of beer in her hand, keeping her eyes focused on the label.

"It's just awful. That poor little girl." Nicole frowned.

"One of the locals at the bar said there's a rumor going around that Hannah slept with men for money. Have you heard that?" Kimberley asked, looking at her mom. She couldn't help but always investigate a case, whether she was on duty or not.

"That's ridiculous." Nicole pursed her lips. "I swear these people around here have nothing better to do than gossip. Hannah was a nice girl. She kept to herself mostly, but she was friendly when I saw her at the pharmacy on occasion."

Jessica dropped the spoon and dove her hand into the bowl of applesauce, giggling.

"You're such a stinker," Nicole said, pinching her cheek.

She repositioned the spoon in Jessica's hand and mimed putting it in her own mouth. "Just like that, Jessica. You got this," she cheered her on.

Jessica rammed the spoon into the bowl and lifted it, zooming it into her mouth.

"Yay. Such a smart girl," Nicole said.

Kimberley watched them closely, struck by the bond that had sprung so quickly between grandmother and granddaughter. A small pang hit her out of nowhere as she remembered her own childhood, one free from the love and closeness taking place right before her eyes. Her mother showed her love, but not like this. She was too busy fighting with her alcoholic husband, so Kimberley had spent most of her childhood in her room with the door closed and music playing, trying to drown out the arguing and screaming.

All of a sudden, Kimberley is twelve years old again, sitting on her twin-sized bed holding a stuffed teddy bear tightly against her chest. On top of her dresser sat a small CD player with Now That's What I Call Music! 5 *playing. The song "Absolutely (Story of a Girl)" by Nine Days played loudly on repeat while Kimberley sat stiffly on her bed, quietly singing along to the lyrics in order to drown out what was happening on the other side of her closed bedroom door.*

"I'll fucking kill you, Nicole. You talk to me like that one more time, it'll be the last thing you ever say," her father screamed. His words were slurred, tainted with the cheap whiskey he started drinking on his way home from work and didn't stop drinking until he passed out.

His footsteps were as loud as thunder, like there was a storm brewing in the small home. She heard them pound closer and closer to her room. Her bedroom door was unlocked. She made the mistake of locking it once and it's why the door was now cracked and splintered.

"You don't lock doors in my house," is what her father had yelled as he kicked and banged on it until she unlocked it. She had missed a week of school after that incident as he wouldn't let her go until the bruises had faded.

"*Leave her alone,*" *her mom yelled. The footsteps pounded down the hallway. Kimberley's heart raced as she squeezed her teddy bear.*

"*She's my daughter. I'll talk to the little bitch whenever I want,*" *her father screamed back.*

Three… two… one… the door swung open, banging against the drywall. There was already a hole where the handle hit. This wasn't the first time her dad had thrown open the door in a fit of rage. His hair was blond and stringy, tied back in a stubby ponytail. His face red and blotchy, thanks to his alcoholism. His eyes were a striking blue like the Hope Diamond, but there was no hope for him.

"*Why is your music so damn loud?*" *he said, stomping over to the CD player.*

Her mother stood in the doorway, tears streaming down her face. "*Stop it, Bruce,*" *she said, trying to protect her daughter. She looked over at Kimberley with forlorn eyes.*

"*This is the story of a girl who cried a river and drowned the whole world,*" *played through the speakers just as her father got to it. He slammed his fist against the top of it, opening the disc drive up. The song abruptly stopped while the CD skidded round and round. He pressed his fingers against the disc, stopping it and picked it up.*

"*Now That's What I Call Music?*" *he said with a laugh.* "*More like now that's what I call garbage.*" *He snapped the CD in half and tossed it on her dresser.* "*Next time, she'll learn to keep it down.*" *He narrowed his eyes at Kimberley and walked out of the room, pushing Nicole aside as he passed by.*

"*I'm sorry, baby,*" *Nicole whispered, closing the door.*

If she was so sorry, she'd leave him, Kimberley thought to herself as she sat there in her silent bedroom, crying a river that she hoped would be just enough to drown her father.

Kimberley took a gulp of her beer, washing down the memory.

"We have no leads on the case, but it's quite eerie Hannah was killed in the same way as Katie DeWitt James. Bullet to the head and decapitated," Kimberley said.

She was consumed by the case and all she wanted to do was talk about it, think about it, dream about it. She figured if she thought about it enough, she'd eventually solve it.

Nicole put her hands over Jessica's ears. "Don't talk about that in front of your daughter."

"Mom, she's only one. She doesn't understand what I'm saying," Kimberley argued.

"Just shush about that around her."

Kimberley rolled her eyes. "Wish you would have had that same sentiment when I was growing up," she said just above a whisper.

Nicole glanced over at Kimberley with narrowed eyes. "What did you say?" she asked, but Kimberley was sure she had heard her.

"Dad said and did worse things to me, and you didn't do anything to stop him." Kimberley raised her chin.

Nicole closed her eyes for a moment and took a deep breath. "I did everything I could to protect you."

"Except leave him." Kimberley downed the rest of her beer and stood from her seat.

"That's really unfair, Kimberley."

"You're right, it is. Sorry I brought it up."

Having enough going on in her life right now, she decided to drop it. Her focus and attention needed to be on the case, not fighting with her mom about a dysfunctional childhood long past.

"I'm going to head out for a run. Can you watch Jessica?" She looked at Nicole, waiting for an answer and trying to determine if she was mad at Kimberley for bringing up her childhood. Nicole took a couple of small, deep breaths, seeming to calm herself down.

Finally, she nodded. "Yes. Don't forget you're having dinner with Emily tonight over at the farmhouse, while I watch the grandchildren."

It had been Nicole's idea to take the grandchildren for the evening, while Wyatt and David had a boys' night and Emily and Kimberley had a girls' night. Nicole wanted both sides of her family to be close, and this was her way of forcing it to happen. Kimberley nodded and left the room to change. She was looking forward to having dinner with Emily as she wanted to bond with her as a friend and a stepsister. It would be good for Jessica to have family and good for Kimberley to have a friend. She never really had one of those.

Kimberley's Adidas tennis shoes hit the ground, spitting up gravel behind her. She ran like she was running away from something or toward something, she was never sure which it was. She was used to running on treadmills and pavement, so her speed was a little slower than usual, careful not to trip over a rock or twist her ankle in an animal's hole. She decided to run around the property, the outskirts of the farm—not too far away from Jessica.

She tried to clear her mind, focus on her breathing, her footsteps, the simple beauty of Oklahoma. The pale burn of the sun looked like it was being sucked down into a vortex, the navy and black of the sky filling in toward the exiting light, the captors following the victim as its last signs of life diminish. The bright moon like a stand-in for the burning ball that was once there, hoping to fool any onlookers who might have suspected foul play. The stars being the multitudinous set of accomplices, steadfast in their watching. The sky out here looked like nothing she had seen before. In New York, the city gave off so much ambient light that you couldn't even see the sky at night, let alone the stars. It truly was a beautiful sight.

Her mind kept spinning back to Hannah. The Hannah she had met before tragedy struck her life. A young, lonely single mom just trying to survive in a world that hadn't been all that kind to her. Regardless of her circumstances, she had still been hopeful and optimistic for her and her daughter's future. Where did it go wrong? What happened to take it all away?

"Why were you down at Deer Creek alone in the middle of the night with your baby, Hannah? Who were you meeting there?" Kimberley asked out loud as if she thought Hannah would answer her from beyond the grave.

There was silence aside from the sound of the wind. Kimberley ran past a couple of outbuildings on the property. She wasn't sure what was in each of them, but she presumed some sort of farming equipment. In a building ahead of her, Kimberley could see someone moving around, shadowlike. She slowed her running to a jog and then to a fast-paced walk, creeping closer. A door slid closed behind them as they exited a wooden structure that looked like an old shed. Kimberley got closer and closer, keeping the figure in her line of sight. She breathed a sigh of relief when she realized it was Wyatt. Dressed in a dirty white tee and torn up jeans, he looked tired.

Kimberley closed the distance between him and her, and as soon as he noticed her, his eyes widened as if he were startled. He quickly picked up his cell phone and started talking.

She waved as she approached him. Instead of returning her greeting, he pointed at his phone indicating he was on a call. Kimberley stopped in her tracks and bent over, trying to catch her breath. She was just a few yards from him and thought he'd finish up the call quickly to chat with her. Wyatt had something else in mind. He kept the phone pressed to his ear and walked away from her toward the farmhouse, leaving Kimberley standing alone.

Kimberley scrunched up her face and watched him. He looked back once, but quickly turned away as soon as their eyes met. He didn't seem like he was on a call, she thought. It looked more like an excuse to not talk to her. Wyatt had been like that with her since she arrived, and she wasn't sure why he'd been so taciturn. He almost seemed to be going out of his way to avoid her. Kimberley shook her head and walked toward the cottage, hoping she'd get answers out of Emily at dinner.

CHAPTER NINETEEN

Dressed in dark blue jeans and a black top, Kimberley walked up the steps of the oversized farmhouse. She considered going right in like she was family, and she basically was, but she didn't feel that way yet. Emily had been welcoming, but Wyatt's coldness made her wary. Instead, she knocked on the screen door. It was old and wobbly, so it banged against the door frame louder than she had intended.

"Come in," Emily yelled from inside.

Kimberley hesitated for a moment as she hadn't been in the home yet, which she found odd. After all, she'd been living on the property for nearly a week. But she did as Emily asked and walked into the farmhouse. Inside, a large wooden staircase went to the upstairs, with a hallway beside it heading back into the home. Kimberley peeked her head to the right where there was a large front room with a couple of couches and chairs all set around a wide coffee table. The design was simple, mostly whites and blues with tan hardwood walls and floors, which appeared to be original to the home's creation. Very stylish for a simple farmhouse. To the left was the living room. It looked similar to the front room, except all the furniture was facing a large-screen television in the far corner. She slipped off her shoes.

Jack and Tom came thundering down the stairs, little Jack two steps behind Tom. They were all smiles, dressed in pajamas and slippers.

"Hi, Aunt Kimberley," Tom said as he reached the bottom of the stairs.

Kimberley's eyes went wide hearing the word "Aunt" in front of her name. Emily must have told the boys to call her that.

"Aunt Kimberley, when is Jessica gonna be strong enough to stay home on the farm with us?" Jack asked, still coming down the stairs.

Tom ran to her, wrapping his arms around her waist for a hug. Jack joined in the hug as soon as his feet hit the landing. It was unexpected. Kimberley patted the boys back.

"Just a few years, and then I'm sure she'll be too strong for daycare," Kimberley said with a smile as they pulled away.

Emily peaked her head out from down the hallway. "You two be good for Grandma," she warned.

"We're always good," Tom said with a grin.

"Yeah, Mommy. I'm gooder than Tom," Jack said.

"No, I am."

"No, me."

"Neither of you are being good right now. Now get over to your grandma's. She's expecting you." Emily shooed them off.

"Bye, Mom. Bye, Aunt Kimberley," Tom said, throwing open the screen door and running down the steps of the porch.

"Bye, Mommy. Bye, Aunt Kimberley." Jack took off after him.

"Thank goodness they're gone," Emily said with a smile. "Come on." She beckoned with her hand, disappearing back into the kitchen.

Kimberley walked down the hallway, following the strong, aromatic smell of pepper and garlic. The hallway led right into the kitchen and dining room, appearing to be the only thing that had been updated in the home. It was large and spacious, with a white-tile backsplash above the wooden countertops. An island sat in the middle and a rectangle table large enough to seat ten was placed in the center of the open-concept dining room and kitchen.

Emily stood at the island counter, a floral apron wrapped around her. Her hair was tied back, and her lips were pink and had a sheen, like she had just applied lip gloss. She smiled widely at Kimberley and walked around the counter to give her a hug.

"I'm glad we could do this," Emily said, embracing Kimberley's stiff body.

She wasn't used to people hugging her, and it caught her off guard. But she still managed to give a sort of half hug, half pat on the back.

"Let me get you a drink." Emily walked to a cupboard next to the fridge and pulled out a bottle of red wine. "You like merlot?"

"I'm not picky," Kimberley said, looking around the kitchen.

There were already two place settings at the table, and she knew dinner was almost ready. She could smell it as soon as she walked in. She wasn't sure what Emily had cooked, but whatever it was, she was sure it was delicious. In the little bit of time Kimberley had known Emily, she had already picked up on the fact that Emily was a perfectionist.

Emily uncorked the bottle and poured two wine glasses, emptying the bottle between the both of them.

"Here you are." She handed the overfilled glass to Kimberley.

She took it carefully so as not to spill.

"Cheers." Emily held her glass up. "To new friends."

They clinked the glasses together and took a drink. Kimberley finished her sip, while Emily guzzled a third of the glass.

"Why don't you have a seat. Food is just about ready."

"Can I help with anything?"

"Sure, uncork another bottle of wine for the table."

Kimberley thought she was kidding for a second, but quickly realized she wasn't when Emily arched an eyebrow. She grabbed another bottle of wine from the cabinet, uncorked it and set it on the table. Emily opened the oven, pulling out a perfectly cooked roast surrounded by carrots, green beans, and cut-up potatoes. It looked as though it should have been photographed for a cookbook. Kimberley gave a small smile, expecting nothing less from this old-fashioned housewife.

Within ten minutes, they were sitting at the dining-room table with plates of warm food in front of them and freshly poured glasses of wine, already working on the second bottle.

Kimberley sliced through the roast with a butter knife. Juices pooled around it and the meat practically fell apart. Emily opting for butter knives rather than steak knives showed how confident she was in her cooking. As soon as it hit the inside of her mouth, the meat melted: a perfectly seasoned, perfectly cooked roast.

"This is really good."

Emily gave a small smile. She brought the wine glass to her lips and took another big gulp, like she was purposefully trying to drink away her façade.

"Thank you," she said humbly.

Kimberley stabbed her fork into a chunk of potato and popped it into her mouth. It was buttery with the perfect mix of seasonings—garlic, salt, pepper, parsley, and smoked paprika. She didn't know exactly what to say, so she busied herself with her food, waiting for Emily to start the conversation.

"I heard about Hannah Brown," Emily said, lifting her head cautiously.

"Everyone has."

"There are no secrets in small towns."

"So I've learned. It's one of the reasons I'm confident that we'll find the person responsible." Kimberley tossed another forkful of vegetables into her mouth.

"I know you will."

"Did you know Hannah Brown?" Kimberley asked idly.

"We went to high school together, but we weren't all that close. Any time I saw her around town, she was always pleasant, asked about the boys, and I asked about her little girl…" Emily brought her hands to her mouth with a gasp. "Her little girl. Oh my, poor Isobel. Growing up without a mother." Emily shook her head and pulled her hands away from her face.

Kimberley noticed Emily's bright eyes had a slight glaze to them, the wine going straight to her head, and the realization of Isobel growing up motherless washed a sadness over her.

Kimberley glanced around the kitchen and dining room again, taking in the surroundings. This amount of space was unheard of in the city, and she envied it, hoping one day, she'd be able to provide a home like this for her and Jessica.

"I just love this house."

She gave a tight smile. "It keeps me busy."

"It must. It's huge. Plus, your two boys, your husband, a thriving business. You have it all."

Emily took another sip of wine and laughed... bitterly, looking over the top of her glass at Kimberley. "Appearances can be deceiving," she said quietly, but Kimberley heard it.

She raised an eyebrow, carefully cataloging that bit of information to ask Emily about later. Perhaps after she had a little more wine, she'd be primed to open up a bit more.

Emily took only a few bites of her food, drinking more than she was eating. The uptight, old-fashioned version of her started to disappear midway through dinner.

Kimberley stabbed her fork into a carrot and popped it in her mouth, also cooked to perfection. She couldn't help but make a pleasurable sound.

"Are these fresh from the farm?"

She nodded. "My garden is the only thing of value here."

She puffed out her bottom lip slightly, taken aback by Emily's comment. "What do you mean by that?"

Emily sat up a little bit taller, splashing more liquid courage down her throat before speaking. "Wyatt sells our vegetables down at the farmers' market—brings in more money than the wheat does. Something about agricultural commodities prices falling. Interest rates rising. Something like that. Wyatt likes to act like financial stuff is over my head. Foolish man." She shook her head.

Kimberley nodded, agreeing with her, trying to encourage her to keep talking.

"Wyatt thinks he's so smart. Ha. He bought some really expensive farm equipment we don't even need. Put it all on credit and now we can't even afford to pay for it." She took another drink of her wine, setting the glass down with force.

"Have you talked to him about it?"

"Yes. Obviously, I don't think the business being bad is entirely his fault. He's under a lot of pressure from my dad. He's not an easy man to please."

"I've kind of gathered that," Kimberley said carefully.

"Don't take it personally. That's how he is with everyone." She rolled her eyes. "Patriarchy at its finest."

Kimberley couldn't help but smile. Emily was surprising her in more ways than one, and there was nothing better than spilling your guts while filling them with a little booze.

"Glad to hear I'm not the only one he's not entirely fond of." She took another bite of her food. "How'd you and Wyatt meet?"

"High-school sweethearts. I know, how cliché," Emily said with a laugh.

"And David didn't like him when you two first got together?"

"My dad didn't like any boy I dated. You know how dads are." Emily shrugged her shoulders.

Kimberley swallowed hard. No, she didn't know how dads were. She knew how her dad was.

"It took him a long, long time to warm up to Wyatt. But now, it's like they've gone back to square one. I feel bad for my husband, because he's doing his best to appease my dad and save this farm. But he's still coming up short. I don't know what to do. All I can do is put on a brave face in front of my kids, especially since Wyatt rarely shows his face around here now. He's always at the damn Trophy Room." She huffed, then drank the rest of her wine.

On the outside, the farm seemed like it was doing well and Kimberley assumed David had money as he had retired early. If he did, why wasn't he helping out? Emily walked into the kitchen and grabbed another bottle, uncorking it and bringing it back to the table. She refilled both glasses.

Wyatt's been at The Trophy Room a lot lately. The information finally registered with Kimberley. She'd been drinking more than she usually did, but something clicked there. Wyatt. Ryan. The Trophy Room. The whispered conversation she had seen Wyatt and Ryan having just a few days earlier. Ryan not having an alibi for the night of Hannah's murder.

"The Trophy Room? I've been there a couple of times. David warned me it was a place for men." She shook her head.

"Of course he did." Emily rolled her eyes. "Maybe that's why Wyatt's been spending so much time there. Thinking it'll turn him into a real man or something," she said with a laugh. She covered her mouth with her hand. "Oh my. I don't know what's gotten into me. That was so mean."

"Nothing wrong with venting."

"You're right about that. He's been coming home so late too. Far after closing time. Smelling like booze. Just drinking his troubles away, while I'm here in this big, dumb house raising our kids and holding the pieces of our life together." She blew out her cheeks after her rant and filled them back up with a gulp of wine.

Spending lots of time at The Trophy Room. Coming home late. Later than bar close. Kimberley started piecing everything Emily had said together. She was on red alert.

Kimberley refilled their glasses again. "Has this been going on for a while?"

"Kinda." Emily hiccupped. "Oh, excuse me," she said with a giggle.

"Will he get home late tonight even with David with him?"

"I'm sure he'll stay there even after my dad leaves. He'll come clabbering to bed around three or four in the morning just like last night." She took another drink of her wine.

"He got home after three a.m. this morning?"

"Oh yeah. He thinks he's being discreet. But he's as quiet as a buffalo."

Wyatt had been acting strange since she arrived. She knew something was off. He had money problems. His marriage was falling apart. His business was failing.

"Did Wyatt know Hannah too?" Kimberley asked. She feared it was too forward, that Emily would realize what she was getting at.

"From high school. They ran in different crowds though. Wyatt was popular, all-star quarterback, and Hannah was more of a loner." She shrugged her shoulders and took another gulp of wine. "Enough about Wyatt and me." She flicked her hand. "Tell me about you."

Kimberley filled her mouth with food to delay having to talk about herself. She chewed methodically. She didn't really like talking about herself. Her life at home had been her deep, dark secret growing up. She had learned to never go into detail about herself, to never tell the truth about what happened behind their closed doors. But she wasn't a little girl anymore. There wasn't a monster sleeping two rooms away. She'd have to learn to open up if she was ever going to make friends and make a better life for Jessica.

"There's not a lot to tell, I guess. You know we came from New York City. My life has been all work up until sixteen months ago, when it became all Jessica and also all work." Kimberley shrugged her shoulders. She purposefully left out any mention of Aaron. Thinking or talking about him always put her in a foul mood, so it was best to be avoided.

"There's got to be more than that. Tell me what you like to do for fun." Emily smiled.

"I like to run, but most people don't find that fun. Hallmark and Lifetime movies are my guilty pleasure, but I'll deny it if you tell anyone." Kimberley laughed.

"Well, I'll be." Emily slapped her knee. "I would not have expected that. You seem more like a History Channel buff or maybe something serious like *The Sopranos* or *The Wire*." Emily raised an eyebrow.

"Nope, I like my entertainment to be predictable, maybe because my line of work has never been. I also want it to do go down like a piece of pizza, extra cheesy. If I know what the ending is going to be in the first few minutes, I'm hooked."

Emily let out a big grin. "You are something else, Kimberley," she said in the most endearing way, lifting her glass to her lips for another sip.

Kimberley smiled back. It felt good to open up, even if it was about something as trivial as to what she liked to watch on television. It wasn't much, but it was something to Kimberley. A small door slightly ajar.

"This was so fun," Emily said as she walked Kimberley to the front door. There was a lightness in her voice, and she swayed a little as she walked.

They were both rather drunk after consuming three bottles of wine with dinner.

"It was. We should do it again sometime." Kimberley pushed open the screen door and tripped out onto the porch into the warm Oklahoma air.

"Definitely," Emily said with a smile. "Go ahead and send the boys back over. I'm hoping they go straight to bed. I'm too drunk to parent." She laughed.

This was clearly out of the norm for Emily, to let loose and it was a breath of fresh air to see.

"I'll send them back in twenty minutes to give you a little time to yourself."

"You're a lifesaver. Thank you!" Emily held out her arms and hugged Kimberley.

She was stiff for a mere second, but then loosened up, hugging her back.

"Good night. Thanks for dinner and of course the wine." She took a step back and headed down the stairs of the front porch.

"Anytime," Emily said with a wave.

Kimberley turned the corner, heading down the stone path to the cottage. She had thoroughly enjoyed the evening with Emily, but there was still something lingering, something she couldn't get her mind off of… Wyatt.

CHAPTER TWENTY

The pounding in her head woke Kimberley before the alarm on her phone did. She pressed her hand against her temple, trying to push away the throbbing, but it didn't help at all. Wine headaches were the worst headaches. She swallowed a couple of times, trying to bring some moisture back into her parched mouth; another failed attempt. Swinging her legs out of bed, she got up, rubbed at her eyes and made her way out of the bedroom, down the hall, but stopped in the living room as Nicole and Jessica were sitting on the floor between the coffee table and the television playing with a dozen random colorful toys. Jessica kept sticking them in her mouth, and Nicole kept pulling them out, trying to show her all the things each of them could do. A colorful truck that rolled over the shaggy green carpet. A stack and learn. A magnetic drawing board. And a set of foam blocks with numbers and letters on them.

"Morning," Nicole said. "That's for you." She gestured with her hand to the coffee table where a glass of water, two ibuprofens, and a cup of coffee sat.

Kimberley walked around the coffee table and kissed the top of Jessica's head. "Thank you," she mouthed to her mom. She plopped down on the couch, tossing the pills in her mouth and washing them down with the entire glass of water.

"How ya feeling?" Nicole asked, leaning against the counter.

"Like I got hit by a bus." Kimberley took a sip of coffee.

"But you had a good time?" Nicole gave a small hopeful smile.

"I did. Emily's a lot of fun."

"She is. What d'you two talk about?" Nicole pulled another toy from Jessica's mouth. "No, sweetie. You don't eat the toys. You play with the toys."

Jessica's face crumpled. Toddlers did not like being told what they could and could not do. Before she full-on erupted, Nicole handed her a green, gummy-like teething toy. She immediately stuck it in her mouth, her face uncrumpling.

"Actually, we talked about Wyatt a lot. Did you know he's been hanging out at The Trophy Room, staying out later than it's even open?" Kimberley took a sip of her coffee.

Nicole's eyes widened. "What? No. Emily doesn't think he's cheating, does she? They seem so happy."

Kimberley sat forward. She hadn't even thought of that. Maybe he had nothing to do with Hannah's murder. Maybe he was cheating. But still, the fact that Emily had said he didn't come home until after 3 a.m. the morning Hannah was murdered didn't sit right with Kimberley. It was worth looking into.

"Want something to eat?"

"No. I'm not hungry."

"You have to eat."

"I couldn't even if I wanted to," Kimberley said, groaning and resting her head in her hands.

The pieces of the night before started falling back into place slowly. Some of them sticking out more than the others. One in particular brought on a bit of anger. The farm was in trouble financially and her mother hadn't mentioned it to her. Why wouldn't she tell her about that?

Kimberley picked up her head. "Emily mentioned the farm's in trouble. Did you know that?" She raised an eyebrow over the top of her coffee mug as she took a drink.

"I knew it wasn't doing all that well. But I try to stay out of it. That's between Wyatt and David." She pushed a button on the truck that made a sound like an engine turning on.

"Where *is* David?" Kimberley looked over into the dining room.

"Somewhere on the farm, working on something," Nicole said not looking at Kimberley.

"I'm going to take Jessica to daycare."

"I thought I was going to." There was a tinge of annoyance in Nicole's voice.

"I got it. Can you get her dressed? I'm running late and gotta get going." Kimberley punctuated her impatience by drinking the rest of her coffee in two big gulps.

"If you're running late, then I can take her to daycare."

Kimberley walked back to her bedroom, her mouth dry and her head pounding as she got dressed as quickly as possible into her uniform. She was pissed her mom hadn't told her that the farm was in financial trouble and that she once again was using a passive approach when it came to issues in her household. She had done that her whole childhood, letting her father get away with anything and everything. She pulled her hair back into a low ponytail and smeared a tinted moisturizer all over her face. Kimberley came back out into the living room, expecting Jessica to be ready to go, but she was still sitting on the floor playing with toys, while Nicole sat with her.

"I thought you were getting her ready," Kimberley said, pressing her lips firmly together.

"What is your problem, Kimberley Ann?"

"Why didn't you tell me how much financial trouble the farm was in?" She folded her arms in front of her chest.

Nicole opened her mouth to answer.

"Because it's none of your goddamn business." David stood in the door frame of the dining room.

Jessica began crying, clearly scared from the raised voices and the tension that felt heavy like a thick fog.

She turned to face him. "It is my—"

"Kimberley, just stop. I don't need you two arguing, especially in front of Jessica," Nicole warned. She pulled her granddaughter into her lap, running her hand over her head, trying to soothe her. "You just go on into work. I'll get Jessica ready and take her to daycare." Jessica's crying faded, turning to sniffles.

Kimberley narrowed her eyes at David and then at her mother.

"*Fine*, Mom. You handle things the way you've always handled them by sweeping them under the rug."

Kimberley turned around, storming out of the house.

"Fuck this," Kimberley whispered to herself when she was outside of the cottage. She started walking briskly along the path toward the front of the property when it hit her. The sour taste in the pit of your stomach, like her intestines were slowly twisting in on themselves, and then the release, shooting up like an elevator whose cables have snapped, but in reverse. Kimberley vomited the better part of a bottle of wine into the grass along the side of the pathway.

CHAPTER TWENTY-ONE

Kimberley hustled into Custer County Sheriff's Office, eager to tell Sam what she learned the night before about Wyatt. Barbara sat at the front desk with a smile on her face. It immediately faltered when she saw how terrible Kimberley looked; she was pale with messy hair and bloodshot eyes. Her uniform was wrinkled, and her shoes were caked in dried mud.

"Are you alright? You look terrible," Barbara said, standing up from her desk.

Kimberley looked down at herself and attempted to smooth out her wrinkly shirt, but there was no use. She rubbed the palms of her hands over her head, flattening the flyaways.

"Yeah, I'm fine. Just didn't get much sleep," Kimberley lied.

It wasn't a good look to say she had drunk two bottles of wine the night before.

"I'll have to bring you in some coffee and a chocolate croissant," Barbara said with a smile. "Chocolate always makes me feel better."

Kimberley nodded and thanked her, even though her stomach heaved at the thought of it.

Barbara walked around her desk, carrying a binder. "By the way, I pulled everything on Tyler Louis. It took me longer than usual. He's pretty elusive and it's such a common name."

"Perfect. Let's walk and talk. What can you tell me about him?" Kimberley said, walking through the first set of doors.

Barb followed behind, keeping up with her quickened pace.

"He's twenty-nine. Grew up in Dead Woman Crossing but relocated to Houston, Texas thirteen months ago. He works in the oil industry as a driller on an oil rig. He's an avid Texas Longhorns fan. Traitor. He's an Aquarius, which explains a lot. They're total chameleons, inconsistent and unpredictable—"

"Okay, Barb. I need more facts and less astrology," Kimberley said as they passed through the second set of doors entering the open floor office area.

Passing by the desks, several deputies gave her second looks, surprised by her disheveled appearance.

"Wooo, someone had a late night," Deputy Bearfield commented as she walked by.

Kimberley gave him a tight smile.

"Who's the lucky guy?" Hill asked.

Kimberley ignored the comments and the looks. She was used to that type of banter back in New York. It was typical of fellow officers to give each other shit, but between the throbbing headache and the news she had to share with Sam, she didn't have the time or energy to tease back. Barbara gave them a disapproving look and they quickly quieted down. Sam wasn't in his office. Kimberley ducked into hers with Barbara following closely behind.

Barbara nodded and flipped several pages, which Kimberley presumed all had to do with Tyler's astrological sign or other non-pertinent information. "Let's see here. Both his parents live over in Weatherford. I have a phone number for them and a cell phone number for Tyler. I couldn't find an exact address in Texas, but I have the parents' address."

Kimberley entered her office, setting her tote bag on the floor beside her desk.

"Perfect. Let's call Tyler first." Kimberley handed Barb her cell phone.

She quickly punched in the numbers and handed it back to Kimberley with a smile. Kimberley held the phone to her ear. It went straight to voicemail.

"Tyler Louis, this is Chief Deputy Kimberley King of Custer County. I need you to give me a call back to answer a few questions in relation to an investigation I'm conducting. Thanks."

"Do you want to try his parents?" Barb asked.

"No, I'll give him a day before I contact them," Kimberley said, thinking she had more promising leads to chase down and some damning information she needed to tell Sam. Besides, Hannah's ex lived over five hundred miles away.

"Well, I'll let you get…" Barb looked Kimberley up and down, taking in her unkempt appearance, but not judging her "… Settled."

"Thanks, Barb," Kimberley said with a small smile.

Barb nodded. "I'll be back with coffee and a chocolate croissant. You'll be right as rain then," she said, closing the door behind her as she left Kimberley's office.

Kimberley closed the blinds that looked out onto the deputies' floor and walked to her wardrobe. She looked at herself in the mirror. "Real professional," she said out loud. Kimberley didn't want Sam to see her like this. Showing up on her fifth day of work hungover and looking disheveled wasn't the look she was going for. She immediately retied her ponytail, ensuring her hair was in place. She swiped on some lip balm and massaged the color back into her cheeks. Kimberley kicked off her dirty shoes and unbuttoned her pants and shirt, pulling off her wrinkly clothes.

She grabbed a fresh-pressed outfit hanging from the closet and laid it on her desk.

"Knock, knock," Sam said, opening the door.

Kimberley tried to cover herself with her hands and arms, twisting her body to the side, but her white underwear and bra were on full display.

Sam didn't notice right away as he was looking down at an opened folder. But when he looked up, his eyes widened, eyebrows raised, mouth dropped open.

"Oh, God. Sorry," he stammered, stepping back out of the office and closing the door behind him.

Kimberley brought her hands to her flushed face. "Could this day get any worse?"

Less than ten minutes later, she put her hand on the door handle and took a deep breath. *It's fine*, she thought to herself. *It's just like a bikini. It's not that big of a deal.* If anything, *he* should be the one embarrassed. Who says "Knock, knock" rather than actually knocking? She opened the door and headed straight into Sam's office, holding her head up high with her shoulders pressed back.

He was seated at his desk, poring over several case files.

"Hey," Kimberley said, trying to be as nonchalant as possible, ignoring the fact that her boss had just seen her in her bra and underwear, in the office no less.

Sam looked up at her. His cheeks slightly red.

"Good morning," he said. "Sorry about that. Didn't realize you used your office as a changing room." The corner of his lip twitched.

"Didn't realize you didn't know how to knock," Kimberley said crossly, taking a seat across from him.

"There you are," Barbara said.

Kimberley turned back to find Barb standing in the doorway, holding a mug of coffee and a small plate with a chocolate croissant. She walked in the office and set them down on the desk in front of Kimberley.

"Thanks, Barb," Kimberley said.

"Of course. Hope this helps you feel a little better." Barb gave a warm smile and left the office.

Sam raised an eyebrow. "You're not feeling well? You know you can take the day off?"

"I'm fine, and I don't take days off of work," Kimberley said, picking up her mug and taking a huge gulp of coffee.

"What's wrong with you?" he asked.

"Just caught one of them pounding headaches," Kimberley said.

Sam leaned back in his chair. "Hope it's not contagious."

"I'm sure you'll be fine," Kimberley said crisply, setting down her mug. "I think I got a break on the Hannah Brown case."

Sam instantly leaned forward in his chair, placing his elbows on his desk, all ears. Kimberley bounced her foot, nerves creeping up for what she was about to do to her family, well, her mother's family.

"Last night, I went over to Emily's place for a girls' dinner-type thing," Kimberley explained. "And I found out some things about Wyatt. Apparently, the farm is in trouble, their marriage is on the rocks, and he's been spending his evenings at The Trophy Room."

"Okay," Sam said carefully.

"On the night of Hannah's murder, he didn't come home until after three a.m. because he was drinking at the bar. Ryan said he closed up at two and went to bed after that. The timing and the stories aren't adding up. Wyatt or Ryan are lying. Maybe they're both lying, but they don't have a concrete alibi for when Hannah was killed." Kimberley rattled off everything she knew.

"That's not enough to arrest someone." Sam tilted his head.

"I know. But it's enough to ask *questions*."

"Sam. Chief Deputy King." Burns stood in the doorway holding a file. Kimberley turned back in her chair.

"Come in, Burns," Sam said, beckoning with his hand.

He walked into the office to the side of the desk and handed the file over to Sam. He opened it and started flipping through the pages covered in text.

"What am I looking at?"

"Hannah Brown's phone records."

Kimberley sat forward in her chair, trying to get a good view of it.

"Give me the highlights," Sam said.

"Nothing discerning about her text messages. She only ever texted her mom and her co-worker. Either she wasn't a big texter or she didn't have a lot of friends. There's an unsaved number on the phone that she receives and makes calls to several times a week, going back at least a year. That's as far back as we could pull. The calls occur late at night or in the wee hours of the morning."

"Who's the number belong to?" Kimberley asked.

"We're still trying to determine that. Bear called it himself and it went straight to the standard preset voicemail. We're in contact with several cell phone providers to determine the owner of the number. But we're thinking it's unregistered, a burner phone."

Sam nodded.

"What about her photo album? Social media?" Kimberley asked.

"Nothing strange about her photos, mostly pics of her daughter. She has the Facebook app on her phone and we checked that. She rarely posted," Burns explained.

"Anything else?" Sam asked, thumbing through the papers.

"Yeah, she made a phone call at three a.m. on September eighth."

Kimberley's eyes went wide. "That's smack-dab in the middle of the estimated time of death when she was murdered?"

"Why the hell didn't you start with that?" Sam closed up the folder and tossed it on his desk.

"Who'd she call?" Kimberley asked.

"Wyatt Miller."

Kimberley looked over at a now wide-eyed Sam. "Is that enough to bring him in for formal questioning?"

"Abso-fucking-lutely," he said, standing from his seat.

"How long did they talk for?" Kimberley looked to Burns.

"They didn't. Outgoing call. Less than ten seconds. Looks like he didn't pick up."

"Was his number saved in her phone?"

"Yep. Under Wyatt Miller. We verified with the cell provider to make sure it belonged to him. It does." Burns nodded.

"Why the hell would Hannah call Wyatt?" Kimberley thought out loud.

"I don't know. But we're sure as hell going to find out." Sam grabbed the folder from his desk. "Good work, Burns. Work on finding out who that other unsaved number belongs to."

"You got it." He nodded and ducked out, heading back to his desk.

"Let's go, King," Sam said, marching out of his office.

Kimberley followed behind. She didn't relish the prospect of bringing in her stepbrother-in-law, but she knew it had to be done. They had cause to bring in Wyatt. No alibi and the last phone call Hannah made was to Wyatt. It was the right thing to do, regardless of how it would affect the already fragile family relations.

Sam looked at Kimberley as they walked across the parking lot to his Ford Bronco, lips pressed together, like he was mulling it all over, deciding the best course of action. They were more alike than either of them knew. Thinking of one hundred different ways this could go right or wrong.

"This is your family, so I can take care of it, if you want?" Sam offered.

Kimberley looked back at him squarely. "You're right. This is my family... so I'll handle it."

She hopped in the passenger seat and Sam in the driver's seat. Before starting up the engine, he looked over at her. Her eyes were strained and bloodshot. Her jaw clenched. Her chin slightly raised. Her lips pressed firmly together, defiant. He opened his mouth, but then closed it as if he were about to protest but decided not to.

Kimberley was dead set on doing this, with or without Sam's permission.

CHAPTER TWENTY-TWO

Sam glanced over at Kimberley as he put the vehicle in park. She was looking out the passenger-side window, staring at the golden rolling fields surrounding the family farm. Her brows pinched together as she remembered what it was she was here to do.

"You sure you want to do this?" Sam asked.

Kimberley turned her head toward him. "I don't want to. I *have* to."

"We're going to pick up Ryan too, since, from what you told me Emily said, their alibies are dependent on one another and conflicting. Ryan claims he closed up at two a.m. and went to bed and Emily said Wyatt was at the bar until after three a.m."

Kimberley nodded.

They sat there for a few more silent moments.

"You know how Jeff, the drunk at the bar, said there were rumors that Hannah was a prostitute?" Kimberley thought out loud.

"Yeah."

"You think that's why she called Wyatt? Maybe he was paying her for sex." Kimberley raised an eyebrow.

"I don't know. You notice anything odd about Emily and Wyatt's relationship?"

"They seemed like a normal married couple. Wyatt's a bit distant, so I don't have much of a read on him. I honestly didn't really see them around each other much," Kimberley said.

She stepped out of the SUV before she changed her mind. She hoped she wouldn't have to search the whole farm to find

Wyatt, because her legs felt heavy, like she was walking through wet cement. Sam stayed a few feet behind her, letting her take the lead. Kimberley walked around the big white farmhouse toward the outbuildings, where she figured she'd find her step-brother-in-law.

"Fuck," she said out loud when she spotted Wyatt up ahead near the barn.

He was sitting on a bale of hay beside David, drinking glasses of lemonade. Emily and Nicole stood beside them with Emily holding a pitcher of the freshly squeezed drink. It was a picture-perfect scene, and Kimberley was about to destroy it. Why couldn't Nicole be in her cottage? Why couldn't Emily be cleaning that massive farmhouse? She glanced back at Sam.

"I can still take the lead if ya want," he offered.

She turned her head away, shaking it. This was her responsibility.

David tapped Wyatt on the shoulder, pointing at Kimberley and Sam. They were just thirty yards away. Emily and Nicole turned around and waved. But when they saw the stern look on their faces, they slowly dropped their hands and their smiles.

"Morning," David called out.

Kimberley and Sam nodded as they closed in, joining in the half circle.

"What's going on?" Nicole's eyes widened, bouncing from Kimberley to David and back again.

Kimberley took a wide stance, asserting her authority in this situation.

"Wyatt Miller, we need you to come down to the sheriff's station for formal questioning in regard to the murder of Hannah Brown." Kimberley raised her chin slightly.

"You've got to be fucking kidding." David rose from his seat. Anger attached to his voice, while red creeped up his neck like a curtain being drawn. Kimberley noticed his hands clench into stiff fists, so instinctively her hand hovered near her trusty Glock.

Emily's mouth dropped open.

"Kimberley, what are you doing?" Nicole asked, her voice as tight as a drum.

"My job, Mom."

Kimberley redirected her attention back to Wyatt. "You can come with us voluntarily or we can come back with an arrest warrant. Your choice."

Wyatt let out a deep breath and stood from his seat. He drained the rest of his lemonade and handed the empty glass to Emily, who already had tears in her eyes.

"It'll be fine," he whispered to her.

Before Wyatt could take a step forward, David's hand shot up to his shoulder, holding him in place. "Don't. You don't have to go with them."

"I've got nothing to hide." Wyatt pushed past David.

Nicole shook her head sadly at Kimberley as Wyatt walked past her and Sam, heading toward the vehicle.

"I…" Kimberley stopped herself before she apologized. She had nothing to apologize for. She was doing her job. "I'll be home late. Could you pick up, Jessica?"

Nicole pressed her lips firmly together. After a few moments, she nodded.

"Thanks." Kimberley turned away.

"I can't believe you're doing this! We're supposed to be friends, stepsisters, you bitch," Emily yelled out.

Kimberley flinched, pausing for a second. Without looking back, she followed Sam to the car. Emily's anger had turned to sadness as her cries traveled across the field, stalking Kimberley all the way to the vehicle.

Sam put Wyatt in the back of the SUV.

"Now, let's go get your friend," Sam said, closing the car door.

CHAPTER TWENTY-THREE

"Go ahead and stay in the car." Sam killed the engine. "I'll go and fetch the town dipshit." He strolled into The Trophy Room, acknowledging several patrons outside with a tip of his head.

Kimberley sat in the front, looking out the windshield and glancing back in the rearview mirror at Wyatt. He hadn't said a word on their drive over. His head was lolled to the side as if he were too tired to hold it up. His eyes were bloodshot. Heavy bags hung below them. Kimberley could see how exhausted and rundown he was. She figured he wouldn't last long under her line of questioning.

A loud bang startled Kimberley and she almost sprung out of the vehicle, before she realized it was the door to The Trophy Room being kicked open by Sam. He had Ryan by the collar of his shirt. Ryan wasn't so much fighting as he just couldn't get his footing. Sam's impatience had worn thin, and he was clearly taking it out on Ryan.

Sam tossed Ryan in the backseat of the vehicle, slamming the door closed.

"What the fuck? I gotta close up the bar. My old man isn't here," Ryan yelled.

Sam got in the driver's seat. "I'll give him a call when we get to the station," he said.

"Shit. My dad's gonna be pissed."

Ryan kicked Kimberley's seat.

"Do it again, and you'll be riding in the trunk," Kimberley warned, turning back and narrowing her eyes at him.

Ryan crossed his arms in front of his chest and slumped down into his seat. He looked over at Wyatt. "They got you too, bro. Damn."

Wyatt didn't say a word. His eyes frozen forward, as if attached by a pair of strings to an object that no one else could see, and his body still, save for the rising and falling of his chest.

Standing in the hallway outside of the interrogation room, Sam scratched at his chin. "Who should we start with?"

"Wyatt already looked like he was going to collapse in on himself like a dying star," Kimberley said.

"Then let's start with Ryan. I like a challenge. And the longer wait will only fatigue Wyatt more," Sam said.

Kimberley nodded. "I had Bearfield pull them from the holding cell. Wyatt's in the interrogation room, and Ryan's in that empty office next door to it."

"Good."

"Here you both are," Barb said, holding out two mugs of coffee.

Kimberley thanked Barbara.

"Could you bring a cup of coffee to Wyatt? He's in the inter-rogation room."

"Of course. But he's not getting any baked goods. I don't bake for murder suspects." Barb twisted up her face and scurried off.

Sam and Kimberley entered the empty office. Ryan sat in a chair in the dimly lit room with his head in his hands.

"Did you call my dad?" he asked without raising his head.

Sam rolled his eyes. "Sit up, Ryan."

Ryan sat up with a sigh, pushing his hands into the front pockets of his jeans, while he slid forward in his chair.

"Your dad is taking care of The Trophy Room. So, your worry should be about why *you're* here." Sam sat on a chair on the other side of the small room.

Kimberley sat next to him. She pulled a folder from underneath her arm and placed it on her lap.

"Why am I here?" Ryan asked.

"Because your alibi the night Hannah was murdered is a load of bullshit." Sam leaned forward in his chair.

Ryan let out a chuckle and shook his head. "I didn't have anything to do with Hannah's murder."

"Your story doesn't add up. You said you closed up the bar at two a.m. and went to sleep, but we have a witness saying Wyatt Miller was at The Trophy Room until three a.m. So, was Wyatt with you?" Kimberley said, leaning back in her chair.

"Listen, I told ya, I was closing up the bar and then I went to bed. I don't know the exact time. Could have been three a.m. Sometimes, Wyatt stays late and we just shoot the shit."

"So, you're saying you were with Wyatt?" Kimberley raised an eyebrow.

Ryan shook his head. "Yeah, but we didn't have anything to do with Hannah's murder. I hardly knew her."

"Did Wyatt know her?" Sam leaned a little forward in his chair.

"Sure. I don't know how well. We all went to high school together, but that was more than a decade ago." Ryan scratched the back of his neck.

"Do you recall Wyatt receiving a call around three a.m.?" Kimberley stared at Ryan, looking for any tells of a lie.

"I don't know. Maybe. If he did, he didn't answer it." Ryan shrugged his shoulders.

"Says here in this file of yours, you've had a couple of disorderly conduct charges as well as a DUI." Kimberley scanned the file and looked up at Ryan.

"Yeah, so?"

"It seems like you are quick to anger, like you don't make the most sound decisions, especially under the influence. Would you say that's an accurate assumption?" Kimberley raised her chin.

"I know what you're getting at." He twisted up his lips. "Like I said, I didn't have anything to do with Hannah's murder."

"You mentioned previously, you don't sleep alone most nights." Kimberley made quotes with her fingers. "Ever sleep with Hannah Brown?"

Ryan let out a groan. "No."

"Ever pay Hannah Brown for any sexual favors?"

"What? No! You think I need to pay for sex?" Ryan let out a sarcastic laugh. "I think you two have nothing to go on and you're reaching, barking up the wrong goddamn tree."

"You know what I think?" Kimberley closed up her folder. "I think you're spitting a load of bullshit, Ryan. First, you tell us you closed up the bar and went to bed at two a.m., now you're saying you closed up but hung out with Wyatt until three a.m. Which is it?"

Ryan resituated himself in his chair, bringing his foot up to rest on his knee. He folded his arms in front of his chest and let out a deep breath, as if he were annoyed, refusing to answer the question.

"You know, whichever one of you talks first gets the better deal." Sam looked directly at Ryan.

"I don't need a deal. Didn't do nothing wrong."

"Think Wyatt will say the same?" Kimberley asked.

Ryan looked down at his lap and then back at Kimberley. "Yeah, I think so."

Kimberley stood from her chair, sliding the folder back under her arm again. "I think you're wrong," she said over her shoulder as she left the room, letting the door close behind her.

Sam caught up to Kimberley outside. "What was that about? We were just getting started."

"I'm tired of that asshole wasting our time. I want to interview Wyatt now."

Without waiting for Sam's approval, she turned away from him and walked into the interrogation room. Wyatt was seated in a chair and an empty mug of coffee sat on the table in front of him. He had his head propped up with his hand.

Kimberley took a seat across from him.

"Let's cut the shit, Wyatt. Where were you the night of Hannah's murder?"

Sam entered the room, closing the door behind him. He leaned up against the wall, one leg crossed over the other, his arms folded across his chest. Kimberley turned back and looked at him. He nodded approvingly. She gave a tight smile and redirected her attention back to Wyatt.

He picked his head up, his dead eyes locking with Kimberley's.

"What is it that you want, Kimberley?" he asked.

"Tell me about you and Emily." Kimberley leaned back in her chair, settling in for story time. She was going to drag this out until Wyatt was blue in the face.

"What do you want to know?"

"How's your marriage?"

"Like any other. It's fine." Wyatt scratched at his chin.

"Is that why you've been coming home later and later? Because it's *fine*?" Kimberley tilted her head.

"Is that why you've dragged me in here? Because I'm breaking curfew." His voice was laced with sarcasm and annoyance.

"Sure, Wyatt. Your wife says you didn't come home until after three a.m. the night of Hannah's murder." It wasn't a question, just a statement for Wyatt to chew on.

He rubbed at his forehead.

"Emily doesn't know what she's talkin' about." His skin flushed, like all the blood in his body had settled to his face and neck. Kimberley wasn't sure if it was because he was angry, or because he'd been caught in a lie. Either way, his body was telling a different story than his mouth was.

"Were you sleeping with Hannah Brown?" Kimberley asked.

"Hell, no! Is that what Emily said? Is that what she thinks? I would never," Wyatt said in a panic. His eyes became glossy. Kimberley had found his weak spot.

"Did you ever pay Hannah for sexual favors?"

Wyatt's shoulders shook slightly. He rubbed his hands down his head, letting out a deep breath. "No."

"Were you close with Hannah Brown?" Kimberley leaned forward, resting her elbows on the table.

"No." He shook his head vehemently.

"Then why did she call you on the night of her murder?"

Wyatt's eyes went wide. Kimberley couldn't tell if it was due to shock or because he had been caught.

"She *didn't* call me," he protested.

Kimberley opened the folder in front of her, flicking through several pages. She pulled out a sheet full of Hannah Brown's phone records. Halfway down, one line was highlighted. She pushed the piece of paper in front of Wyatt.

"Does that highlighted phone number belong to you?"

Wyatt looked at the sheet of paper, squinting his eyes as he brought it up to his line of sight. His mouth dropped open and he nodded.

"Tell me, Wyatt, why did Hannah Brown call you just before she was murdered? For someone you claim you didn't know all that well, isn't it strange she'd call you? That you'd be the last person she reached out to before someone put a bullet in her head? We know she was murdered now between three and four in the morning. That gave you an hour to get to her after that call was made. And you can get anywhere in this goddamn county in twenty minutes. I want you to tell me what happened the night of Hannah's murder. I want you to tell me what you and Ryan did to her. Or did you do it alone, after you left The Trophy Room? I want you to tell me why you did it, how you could do it." Kimberley's voice had an edge to it, sharp like the blade of a butcher's knife.

"Alright. Fuck. Goddamnit…" Wyatt slammed his fist against the table.

Kimberley watched him, waiting for the confession. He was cracking right before her. His confidence had faded away throughout the interview. Now, he was a puddle of a man sitting in front of her.

"You think I killed Hannah Brown? You think I'm capable of something like that?" He shook his head. "You're way off."

"Am I?" Kimberley tilted her head. "Because I don't think I am. Was she calling you for sex? Did she have something on you? Was she going to tell Emily about the affair?"

"No. I have no fucking clue why she called me. I don't even have her number saved in my phone. You can check it. So, if Hannah called, I didn't even know she did." Wyatt let out a huff, looking off into the corner, shaking his head as if he couldn't believe he had gotten wrapped up in this situation.

"How would she get your number then? Did she just guess it?" Kimberley was being full-on sarcastic.

"I don't know. My number is plastered everywhere down at the farmers' market. It's on the farm's business cards. Most of the town has my number, I'm sure," he said, looking back at Kimberley.

The explanation was reasonable. Kimberley herself had seen the farm business signs plastered on community boards throughout town. She hadn't been to the farmers' market yet, but it made sense. The Turner Farm sold vegetables, wheat and chicken eggs. She knew Wyatt was still lying about something though. His and Ryan's initial alibis weren't aligned.

"You didn't get home until after three a.m. the night Hannah was murdered. Ryan initially said he closed up The Trophy Room at two, so you tell me, what were you and Ryan doing between two and four in the morning? Ryan claims he was in bed. Were you in bed with him?" Kimberley raised her chin. "Is that your alibi?"

Wyatt blew out his cheeks, rubbing his face with his hands. "I can't do this anymore."

"Do what?" Sam piped in.

"Lie."

"Lie about what?" Sam took a couple of steps forward, standing right behind Kimberley.

Wyatt let out the deepest breath he could conjure up. "Ryan and I didn't kill Hannah Brown."

"Then what were you doing? Where were you?" Kimberley sat up a little straighter.

She knew Wyatt was cracking, caving under the pressure just as she thought he would. Lack of sleep and a guilty conscience will do that to a person.

"We were... making moonshine." He lowered his head.

Kimberley looked up at Sam. She drew her brows together, then refocused her attention back on Wyatt.

"What? Where?" she asked.

"We make it out on the farm in one the outbuildings. Use the wheat from the farm and sell the moonshine at The Trophy Room." He kept his head down and his eyes on the table as if he were ashamed.

Kimberley suddenly remembered the noises she heard out on the farm. The breaking glass. It must have been Wyatt and Ryan.

Wyatt looked up at Kimberley. "I needed the money. The farm's going under. We've mortgaged the house twice. There ain't no money in wheat."

Kimberley stared back at him. She believed him. She could see it in his broken face, his bloodshot, glazed over eyes, his dull, tired skin.

"I'm not a murderer, Kimberley. I swear to you I'm not. I'm just a desperate man trying to provide for his family. Wouldn't you do the same for your daughter?"

"Illegally make and sell moonshine?" Kimberley asked, cocking her head.

"No… anything you could."

"You know I would."

"Then that's all you need to know." Wyatt shrugged his shoulders again.

"Did Emily know anything about this?"

"Absolutely not. She wasn't involved at all." Wyatt sharpened his eyes and stared directly at Kimberley.

She kept her lips pressed firmly together, folding her arms in front of her chest.

"Appreciate your honesty and cooperation, Wyatt," Sam said. "I'll be sure Judge Withers knows it too. A deputy will be in shortly to read you your rights and book you as you'll be charged with illegally manufacturing and selling alcoholic beverages, pursuant to code 37-505, pending an investigation. Do you understand?"

Wyatt nodded.

"Sorry, but I need it to be verbal."

"Yes… I understand."

Sam nodded and walked out of the room.

Kimberly stood from her seat, following Sam. She looked back once more at Wyatt, who was practically folded over in his chair. She felt sorry for him even though he had broken the law. But then again, was right and wrong that black and white when it came to providing and caring for your own flesh and blood? Kimberley couldn't be so sure anymore.

"Bearfield and Burns," Sam called out. Both deputies rose from their desks immediately. "I need you to process Ryan and Wyatt, and then I need you to go out to the Turner Farm and search the outbuildings on the property for evidence pertaining to the illegal manufacturing of moonshine. Confiscate any alcohol at The Trophy Room that doesn't have proof of purchase as well."

The deputies nodded.

"I want to see my husband," a voice yelled, echoing through the sheriff's station.

Moments later, Emily emerged through a set of doors from the front with Barbara in tow, trying to stop her. She looked different from earlier, stronger, and she wasn't in her typical old-fashioned looking dresses. Emily was wearing blue jeans and a T-shirt. Her hair was a little messy, not perfectly in place as Kimberley had always seen it. Her face was red and blotchy like she had been crying, but it was clear now that her sadness had turned to anger. Her eyes were narrowed, her jaw clenched, and her lips tight. She marched right up to Sam and Kimberley, staring them both down. Barbara only half followed her, stopping in the middle of the room.

"I demand to see my husband," Emily said, raising her chin.

"You can't. He hasn't been processed yet," Kimberley said, trying to reason with her.

"Oh, piss off! Processed for what?"

"Illegal manufacturing and distribution of spirits. He confessed of his own volition."

Emily looked daggers at Kimberley. "How dare you come into my house, eat my food, drink my wine, and then you do this to us. You have ruined my family."

"Your husband..." Kimberley stopped herself. There was no point in arguing with Emily. Her world now had a patina of filth over it and until it was cleaned up, she'd only see the ugly in everyone and everything.

"You've got five minutes, Emily," Sam said softly. "He's in there. Go on. But don't do anything stupid or make a scene and make me regret this." He motioned to the interrogation room where Wyatt was.

Emily nodded, and walked right in, not saying another word to anyone else.

As soon as the door to the interrogation room closed, Sam and Kimberley walked to the viewing room.

"Hi, Em," Wyatt said, lifting his head.

"Don't 'Hi, Em,' me." She slammed her tote bag on the table. "I can't believe you did this to us." Emily shook her head.

"I did this *for* us."

"Bullshit. Right when things got tough, you turned to crime to solve your problems. You have ruined us."

"I'll fix this, Emily. I swear, I'll fix everything," Wyatt pleaded.

"No. You are done 'fixing' things. You've had your shot. You clearly don't know what you're doing, so from now on, I'll be making the decisions. Handling the finances and cleaning up the mess you've made is my new job." Emily threw her hands on her hips.

Wyatt didn't argue. He wasn't in the position to disagree with her.

"What am I supposed to tell the boys? Did you even think about them when you were out there breaking the goddamn law?" Emily slammed her dainty fist against the table, startling Wyatt.

"Of course I thought about them. It's why I did it, so I could provide for my family."

"There are other ways, legal ones."

Wyatt lowered his head, dropping eye contact with his wife.

"After you're processed and the judge sets bail, I'll figure out a way to come up with the money. But know this, Wyatt. You're not coming back to your house. You're coming back to mine." Emily picked up her tote and left the room, slamming the door behind her.

Sam gave a slight nod and left the viewing room, walking through the station back to his office. Kimberley followed behind, unsure of what was next. They'd hit a dead end in the case again. She sat down across from him while he leaned back in his chair, putting his feet up on his desk. He crossed one foot over the other, looking up at the ceiling. Kimberley knew that look. It was the "maybe if I stare off at nothing for long enough, I'll catch a fucking break in this case" look. She had had it many times.

*

Sam's phone rang, and he quickly pulled it from his belt.

"Sheriff Walker."

"It's Megan Grey. Results are in for the forensic exam."

"And?"

"We've got nothing. Body was clean. Not a shred of DNA. Rape kit came back clean as well. There's literally nothing to go on."

"Fuck."

Kimberley stiffened.

"Sorry I didn't have better news for you. I went over everything with a microscope. I can't find something that's not there."

Sam briefly closed his eyes. "I know you did. Thanks for your help." He ended the call, tossing his phone on his desk.

"What's up?" she asked.

Sam rubbed his face. "Forensics came back. Everything was clean. Not a shred of evidence."

"Fucking fuck," Kimberley said, clenching her fists. "So, we've got *nothing.*"

Sam took a deep breath and slightly nodded, unwilling to fully admit how completely fucked they were on this case.

"We got a decapitated body left by a creek with a single bullet to the head. A fourteen-month-old girl as our only witness. No DNA evidence. Phone calls to a presumably unregistered number, but no texts that would indicate any sort of a relationship," Sam thought out loud.

Kimberley said nothing.

"Hill," Sam yelled.

Moments later, Hill appeared in the doorway.

"What have you got on outside-town visitors?"

Hill cleared his throat. "Not much. Motel guests came back clean. A family on a cross-country road trip. A couple of elderly couples. No criminal histories. Nothing out of the ordinary. I talked with a motel maid and a front-desk worker. They noted nothing unusual. I'm still checking on Airbnb guests."

Sam rubbed his hand over his face. "Alright. I want all of that compiled and on my desk by tomorrow afternoon."

"You got it." Hill nodded and left the office with a slight limp.

Kimberley crossed her legs, tapping her fingers on her knee. She'd had cases like this before. Cases where there was nothing to go off on. And that was in New York City, a place with nearly nine million people, and she still somehow figured out the single person responsible, nearly every time. But this was different. This was one murder, not five, and this was Dead Woman Crossing, a town so small, they didn't even bother counting how many people were in it. The odds were better here. She had learned as a detective that people can't hide, and secrets don't stay secrets forever. She was going to catch Hannah Brown's murderer.

CHAPTER TWENTY-FOUR

Kimberley drove through town in her newly assigned police vehicle, a Ford Explorer, with "Sheriff Custer County" plastered along the sides of the vehicle. She had stayed at the office later than usual, the last to leave, mulling over anything and everything pertaining to the case. When her stomach started to rumble and she noticed dusk had fallen, she packed up her tote bag with files to bring home with her. When she left New York, she promised herself that she would never take her work home with her again. Less than a week in, and she had already broken that promise.

The town of Dead Woman Crossing was quieter than usual. At the four-way stop, she noticed The Trophy Room was closed. All the lights were off, it was silent, and the men that typically hung outside smoking were nowhere to be seen. It was like a quarantine had been put over the town; no traffic, no one outside. Not only had she alienated herself from her family, but she was sure she had done the same with the whole town. With their beloved bar closed for the night, what would the townies do? Plot her demise? Or just drink cheap beer in their own homes without the comfort of their comrades. Were they scared? After all, one of their own was murdered and there was still a killer out on the loose.

Kimberley pulled into the long gravel driveway. Her headlights lit up the large white farmhouse, and she quickly turned them off. Wyatt was spending the night in jail, so Emily would be home alone with her two boys. Kimberley parked the vehicle off to the side and grabbed her bag from the passenger seat before getting out. She looked up at the farmhouse. A light was on in a room off to the left, which Kimberley knew to be the living room.

She stood there for a few moments, deciding whether or not to check in on Emily. Before her brain could decide, her feet were already pulling her toward the wraparound porch, and her knuckles were rapping softly on the door.

"Just a minute," Emily called out.

Moments passed before she heard footsteps, the click of the lock, and the turn of the handle. Emily's face immediately went sour when she saw Kimberley. The corners of her lips turned downward. Her eyes so narrowed you couldn't slip a dollar bill between her lids. She didn't bother to open the screen door for a proper greeting either. Kimberley looked at Emily through the screen, her face split up by a thousand tiny squares of aluminum, each one displeased with her presence.

"What do you want?" Emily's voice was laced with anger and annoyance.

"I just wanted to make sure you were okay. See if you needed anything?"

"Yeah, I need you to get off my front porch."

"Emily, I'm not the enemy."

Emily shook her head, wiping the side of her face against her shoulder. "And you're not a friend either."

"You have every right to feel that way, but your husband broke the law, and I'm just doing my job."

"You couldn't have come to us in private first? Asked him to stop? He would have listened. He would have done the right thing." Her voice cracked as she forced out the words.

"I didn't know about the moonshine, Emily. I was simply trying to line up Wyatt and Ryan's stories on where they were when Hannah was murdered. He fessed up to the moonshine on his own, we didn't even have to press him." Kimberley paused, seeing the words stringing themselves heavy around Emily's neck. "Look, for what it's worth, I have seen a lot of scumbags in my career in rooms just like that, lying through their teeth, showing no remorse. This was weighing on Wyatt, and he didn't hesitate to want that burden off of him. Your husband is a good man who was trying to do right by his family but just went about it the wrong way."

Emily wiped the tears from her eyes and stared at Kimberley, waiting for her to go on.

"What he did isn't that big of a deal, and him being cooperative really helps. He will probably just get a fine and some community service and life will go on as usual."

"But we couldn't afford nothin' before. How are we supposed to pay off a fine?"

"I'm sure you will find a way. Maybe sell that equipment he bought and never used. Or take out a loan and collateralize the farmhouse. Talk to your dad—he might have some money hidden away. That'll be for you guys to decide as a family."

Emily stood silently, weighing her options.

"I really didn't mean to cause your family harm. I didn't even know about the moonshine; I just had some questions for him. That's all."

"Your family too, Kimberley." Emily slowly closed the door on her, ending the conversation.

Her words cut through Kimberley, right to the center of her chest. She slumped her shoulders and shook her head. Kimberley hadn't thought of herself as family. To her, she was a temporary guest. Her mother was family. She and Jessica were just her baggage. She walked across the porch and down the steps, cutting across the lawn to the rock-lined path that led to the cottage. She hoped with time things would straighten out between her and Emily, but she couldn't focus on that now.

At the front door of the cottage, Kimberley hesitated, her hand hovering just above the door handle. She was excited to see Jessica, but her excitement ended there as she was sure the reception from

David and Nicole would be cold. Taking a deep breath, she opened the door. The living room was empty—a small sigh of relief. She walked through it and into the dining room. David was seated at the table drinking a Bud Light, waiting for his food to be served. He didn't look up at Kimberley, his eyes forward, staring at the wall on the other side of the room as if there was something there to look at. Kimberley followed his line of vision to a blank wall, not even a splotch or a crack of paint to focus on. Her eyes went back to him, from his hands to his tense shoulders to the prominent vein in the side of his neck illustrating how infuriated he was.

Kimberley said, "Hi, David," with a nod as she walked by.

He didn't move, didn't acknowledge her. He was just still, like a statue, aside from that beating vein.

In the kitchen, her mother was at the stove stirring a pot with a wooden spoon.

"Hey, Mom," she said, trying to be nonchalant, like everything was normal and she hadn't just had her stepbrother-in-law thrown in jail.

"Kimberley," her mother said, not looking at her. It wasn't exactly a greeting, more so like she was stating who else was in the room with her.

"Where's Jessica?"

"I put her to bed."

"Before I got home?" Kimberley twisted her lips, upset that she didn't even get to say good night to her daughter, nor tuck her in.

"She was tired, Kimberley," Nicole said curtly, looking over her shoulder at Kimberley for a brief second and then refocusing her attention to the meal she was preparing.

Kimberley knew her mom was mad, but she couldn't stay mad forever. "Can I help with anything?"

Nicole shook her head. "Just pour yourself a glass of wine and have a seat."

Kimberley did as she was told, uncorking a bottle of wine and pouring two glasses, one for her and one for her mom. She took a seat at the counter, spinning her glass slowly in her hand as if she were examining the red liquid.

"Whatcha cooking?" Kimberley attempted small talk, anything to get her mom to speak to her.

"Beef stew with potatoes, carrots, and onions." Nicole took a swig of her wine and went back to stirring the pot.

"I'm sure you heard about Wyatt."

Nicole nodded. "The whole goddamn town has." She clenched her jaw, trying to compose herself.

"He fully cooperated, so the judge should go easy on him," she explained.

"They're going to lose the farm," Nicole said just above a whisper.

"What was that?"

"She said… they're going to lose the *farm!*" David yelled, slamming his Bud Light on the table, liquid shooting out the top like a volcano. The statue had woken up, his stone exterior crumbling around him. He got up from the table and with two big, thundering steps he was standing in the doorway of the kitchen. The vein in his neck bounced up and down, up and down.

Kimberley wasn't afraid of David, regardless of how large or how mad he was. She looked him straight in the eye, laser focused, and said, "Now why would a perfectly prospering and legal farm go under from a small fine?"

"Don't play fuckin' smart with me. You know damn well it wasn't any of those things." Another vein made an appearance in the center of his forehead. It looked even angrier than the one in his neck. Was it the same vein, Kimberley wondered? She pictured the rod-shaped tissue emerging from his forehead, skin splitting, blood oozing, like a scene out of *Alien*.

"David, I don't make the laws, I just enforce them. I didn't make Wyatt illegally manufacture and sell moonshine." Kimberley raised her glass of wine to her lips and took a sip.

His hands clenched the trim on the doorway, turning his fingers white. He glared at Kimberley like they were about to take part in a duel. Who would raise their gun first? David shook his head, let out a huff, and dropped his hands from the doorway. Immediately, he turned around, walking away, his heavy footsteps traveling through the dining room, the living room and then crossing the threshold of the front door, which slammed behind him.

Nicole stood silently in the kitchen holding the wooden spoon. Her mouth slightly open. She didn't know what to say. Kimberley looked over at her mom, shook her head, grabbed her tote bag and walked out of the kitchen, retiring to her bedroom for the evening. She'd had enough of the Wyatt/moonshine situation.

Kimberley closed the door behind her and felt her way in the dark. She turned on the bedside light and quietly walked toward the crib.

"Good night, sweet girl," Kimberley said softly, pushing Jessica's hair out of her face and pulling her blanket up a little higher.

She tucked her stuffed elephant under her arm, careful not to wake her.

Kimberley changed into a pair of cotton shorts and a tank top and climbed into her bed. Pulling the files out of her bag, she turned her bed into her office. The pictures of the crime scene splayed out in front of her. Reports from first responding deputies, from the fisherman. The results of Megan's forensics exams. It was all here. But when she looked at it, she realized how little they had to go on.

She read over each report carefully, looking for something to stand out, but nothing did. She looked closely at the crime scene photographs. Kimberley strained her eyes to focus on every detail. The strands of grass. The specks of dirt. The freckles on Hannah

Brown's arms. She reread the few witness statements they had, from Hannah's mom, her co-worker, her boss, her daycare, the fisherman at the scene. All the fisherman could tell them was when and where he found the body. Everything else in the report was a blubbering mess. The first deputies on the scene could only verify how they found the body. Hannah's mother couldn't tell them anything about the night that her daughter was murdered aside from the fact they fought that day. Her co-worker, her boss, and Isobel's daycare teacher said Hannah was normal on the day she was murdered. Kimberley still hadn't gotten in touch with Isobel's father, Tyler Louis. It was a loose end that needed to be tied up. She wrote his name down on a pad of paper, circling it twice. Bearfield had verified that Hannah had worked at the pharmacy earlier that day and that there was nothing unusual, but what did her co-workers know about her? She wrote down "co-workers." How often did Lisa watch Isobel? She wrote down "Lisa." Was Hannah dating anyone? Nothing in her apartment indicated that she was, nor in her cell phone records, aside from the unregistered number. What about the daycare center? Sure, as Bearfield noted in his interview, Hannah was fine on the day of her murder, but what about before that? What could they tell Kimberley about Hannah? They interacted with her several days a week. Kimberley wrote down "Happy Trails Daycare."

She tossed down the pad of paper and pen and let out a sigh. Maybe Sam was right. It was a true-crime obsessive, an out-of-towner, responsible for the gruesome murder. After all, the sheriff knew Dead Woman Crossing better than anyone, well, aside from Barb. She pushed everything back into her tote bag and laid her head on the pillow.

Kimberley told herself that she had a few things to follow up on tomorrow, as weak as leads as they may be, they were still something to get her started. That was enough to ease her slowly to sleep.

*

Kimberley's eyes shot open. A pressure had built up in her pelvic region, calling her back into consciousness. The bedroom was dark and dead silent, save for the soft breathing of her sleeping daughter in the crib. She glanced over at the clock on her bed stand. 3 a.m. She closed her eyes again, trying to fall back asleep, but the pain was too much, and duty called. She groaned to herself, sliding out of bed. Holding her hands out in front of her, she felt her way to the door. An uncomfortable sharpness met both of her palms as the popcorn walls once again jutted into her flesh, its bloodlust still not quenched. Kimberley stepped to the left and felt down for the doorknob. She pulled it open slowly and tiptoed out into the dark hallway. The house was eerily silent. The floor creaked under her. She paused, hoping she hadn't woken anyone. Silence. Not even the ambient sounds of crickets outside or the wind blowing through the vegetation. Nothing. It took her a few steps to reach the bathroom and before flicking on the light, she closed the door behind her, so as not to illuminate the main area of the house and possibly disturb David or Nicole. Kimberley felt the wall for the switch. When her hand found it, she flicked it on. She squeezed her eyes tightly shut, rubbing them for a moment, trying to let her pupils contract back to normal and dampen the amount of light coming in. Her eyes opened just a squint and there on the mirror written in blood, "Who's the King now?"

Kimberley screamed, punching the mirror with an instinctual reflex. She looked down at her hand; it was pouring blood as clunks of glass shot out of her skin like needles from a cactus. She reached for the faucet to rinse the blood, but instead of water, more blood poured from the faucet. She quickly twisted the handle back to close the valve, but it wouldn't stop. She tried to leave, get David to help with the plumbing emergency, but the door was locked from the other side. She screamed back into the pieces of the mirror that still hung in place, but two arms shot out and massive gloved hands squeezed Kimberley's throat, the air immediately cut off mid scream. She looked closer and there he was; she could finally see him, after all these years. The light began to fade from her eyes and the room went dark, no oxygen getting to her brain. This was finally it. Kimberley made a last-ditch effort and dove forward into the mirror, her face just about to make contact with whatever was on the other side—

"NO!" Kimberley yelled out loud, sitting up in her bed. Her breath was ragged. Her heart raced. Sweat was dripping from her forehead and the sheets were damp where her body had been lying. *Fuck, it was just a dream.* She held her breath, listening for her daughter, and when she heard her soft breathing, Kimberley exhaled a sigh of relief. She laid back down in bed, pulling the covers up around her.

CHAPTER TWENTY-FIVE

Dressed in her uniform with her tote bag over her shoulder, Kimberley carried Jessica out to the kitchen, setting her in her highchair. Nicole was already up, sipping on a cup of coffee while slicing up a banana. She was sure the banana was for Jessica because Kimberley still had yet to see her mother consume anything substantial. It seemed something was eating at Nicole.

Nicole placed half of the cut-up banana on a plate and put it on Jessica's tray. "Good morning, sweetie," she said, pinching at her cheeks.

"Nana," Jessica said all smiley and sleepy while she put a piece of banana in her mouth.

Nicole filled a sippy cup with water and handed it to her granddaughter. "Take a big drink."

Jessica did as she was told, taking a drink and then another piece of banana. Kimberley was grateful Jessica had always been such a good baby. Nicole poured a cup of coffee and handed it to Kimberley.

"Thanks," Kimberley said, hoping her mother's displeasure with her had faded.

Nicole gave a small nod. "David went to bail Wyatt out."

"That's good." Kimberley leaned against the counter.

Nicole pretended to be busy with emptying the used coffee beans from the pot and wiping down the counters, but Kimberley could tell she wanted to say more.

"Did you know about the moonshine?" Kimberley pried.

Nicole stopped what she was doing and looked at Kimberley. "No, of course not."

"Did David?"

"I don't think so."

Kimberley took a sip of coffee. "Did you ask him?"

"No. Why would I do that?" Nicole put a hand on her hip.

"Because it's illegal. Wouldn't you want to know if he was involved?"

"I'm not the bad guy here, Kimberley."

"I didn't say you were, but neither am I. Yet people seem to forget that." Kimberley drained the rest of her mug.

"No one thinks you're the bad guy."

"Okay, Mom," she said sarcastically, smoothing out her shirt. "I've got to get to work."

Nicole nodded. "Can I drop Jessica off for you?"

There was a pleading in her voice and eyes, so Kimberley agreed with a nod. She knew her mother wanted as much time with Jessica as she could get, so she decided to throw a bone to sweeten the deal. "Mind picking her up too? I'm sure I'll be working late."

Nicole's eyes lit up. "Of course. I'd love to."

Kimberley walked over to Jessica and leaned down, planting a kiss on her rosy cheek. "Bye, sweetie. Mommy loves you."

Jessica giggled. "Love you, Ma-meee," she sounded out.

"We've been working on that," Nicole said with a wink.

"Good morning, Barb," Kimberley greeted as she walked into the front area of Custer County Sheriff's Office. "Can you get me the number for Houston Police Department?"

"Of course. Right away!" Barb said eagerly. Her fingers tapped away on the keyboard.

Kimberley stood there, watching Barb. She couldn't help but let on a small smile. She had been thoroughly impressed by her.

"Got it!"

"Perfect. Walk with me."

Barb quickly scribbled down the number and came out from behind her desk, following Kimberley through the set of doors, out onto the deputies' floor.

Hill, Burns, and Bearfield sat at their desks, each of them working on some aspect of the Hannah Brown case. All eyes were on Kimberley as soon as she entered, as if they thought she had news to deliver. When she didn't make eye contact with any of them and kept walking, there was an almost audible groan as they got back to work. Everyone wanted to solve this case.

Kimberley entered her office, setting her tote bag on the floor beside her desk. Barbara followed behind.

Kimberley handed Barb her cell phone. "Go ahead and patch me through."

She quickly punched in the numbers and handed it back to Kimberley with a smile. Kimberley held the phone to her ear as it rang over and over again.

"Houston Police Department, this is Officer Cariello speaking."

"Hi, Officer Cariello. This is Chief Deputy Kimberley King of Custer County Sheriff's Office over in Oklahoma. I'm conducting a murder investigation, and I'm trying to get ahold of one of your residents. I'd like some Houston PD assistance locating and making contact with a Tyler Louis, born on May sixteenth, 1991."

"Is he a suspect?"

"He's a person of interest."

"Alright, you said Tyler Louis, May sixteenth, 1991?"

"That's correct."

"I'll have an officer locate Mr. Louis and give you a call back as soon as we know something."

"Thanks. I appreciate it," Kimberley said, ending the call.

Barb smiled. "Well, let me get you some coffee and a snack. You'll need all the energy and brain power for this case."

"That'd be great. But why don't you go ahead and join Sheriff Walker and I in the conference room in say fifteen minutes. Have Burns cover the front desk," Kimberley said, gathering a stack of files, binders, and notebooks into a box.

Barb's eyes lit up. "Of course." She smiled and nearly skipped out of the room.

Kimberley carried the box next door to Sam's office. He was sitting at his computer, sipping coffee.

"I think it's time we set up the burn room," Kimberley said.

She immediately walked away toward the lone conference room that rarely seemed to be in use. It had a long table with chairs all around it, fit for fourteen, six on each side and one on each end. There was a massive dry-erase board on the left wall and a bulletin board on the right wall. Kimberley dropped the box on the table.

"Burn room?" Sam stood in the door frame behind her, holding his cup of coffee.

"If you don't want a case to run cold, you set up a burn room. It's a dumb homicide joke, but essentially it's a place where everyone working the case gathers and where we can lay out what we know and what we don't know."

Sam looked out at the deputy floor. Bearfield and Hill were sitting at their desks. "Bear and Hill. Get in here. We're setting up a burn room," Sam said.

Bearfield and Hill gave each other a quizzical look, but started packing up their things to join Sam and Kimberley.

Kimberley started pulling everything out of her box, hanging up photos of the crime scene on the bulletin board, writing on the whiteboard.

Kimberley wrote "Hannah" on the board and started writing all the names of people connected to her around it, alongside how those people were connected, forming a type of spiderweb by linking the names with lines.

"What's that?"

"Her web… that we know of. Who she's connected to and how those people are connected to one another," Kimberley explained while she wrote her own name on the board, drawing a single line to Hannah's name. It was a small connection as they had only met a few times, but it was still a connection.

Sam took a sip of his coffee and set the mug down on the table. He reached inside the box and pulled out the stack of notebooks that ghost tour Kent had given them.

"Have you gone through these?" he asked.

Kimberley turned her head and looked over at Sam. She nodded. "Skimmed."

"I think we need to start here." He set the notebooks on the table.

Kimberley capped her dry-erase marker and set it on the metal lip of the whiteboard.

"Why?"

"Just a hunch."

"Does this hunch have anything to do with the fact that you don't think one of your own could have committed murder?" Kimberley raised an eyebrow.

"Not at all."

"You know the stats on homicide, right?"

"Yeah, Kimberley, I do. Eleven percent committed by strangers. You may think I'm some hillbilly sheriff, but regardless, I am the sheriff." He raised his chin in a challenging way. "You can either fall in line or you can step out of it. Your choice."

Kimberley crossed her arms in front of her chest. She had no idea where this was coming from. Sam had been so agreeable with her, respectful of her, but now he was challenging her as if they weren't on the same team. She studied his face. He didn't have the same sternness mixed with a jovial look. His eyes were strained, bloodshot like he hadn't slept. Her eyes dropped to his shoulders, which were slightly raised, tense. His chest puffed out. Kimberley tapped her foot on the ground steadily, like it was the heartbeat of her burn room. She considered arguing with him, but he seemed like he was already in a battle with himself.

Bearfield and Hill entered the room, taking seats around the conference table. They dropped their laptops and files on the table, looking at Sam and then Kimberley who were in a tense stare-down with one another.

"I've got snacks and coffee," Barb said, walking in with a tray full of donuts, napkins, a carafe of coffee and five mugs. She smiled at Kimberley, then at Sam and then Bear and Hill.

"I've asked Barb to sit in with us." Kimberley slightly raised her chin.

Sam chewed on her words for a moment.

"Alright." He nodded, letting Kimberley win this one, but he wasn't backing down just yet when it came to suspects.

Barb set the tray down and passed out donuts and cups of coffee. Sam took a seat at the head of the table while Kimberley and Barb sat on either side.

"Who's watching the front desk?" Sam raised an eyebrow.

"Oh, Deputy Burns. He's been a pain in my ass," Barb said.

Sam gave a small grin.

"Let's start with the notebooks," Kimberley said, entertaining Sam. She handed one to each person.

"What are we looking for?" Sam asked.

"You tell me. This was your idea. Your hunch." Kimberley smirked.

Sam leaned back in his chair and rubbed his chin. "Well, I'd say we look at the last six months. See if any of the people in here have criminal records, something that'd look suspicious." He patted his hand on the spiral notebook. "Maybe a history of violence, something like that. But first, Hill, you got the information compiled on motels and Airbnbs?"

Hill nodded, pulling a file folder from the stack in front of him. He slid it down the table to Sam. "It's all in there. Anyone that's stayed in the area for the last six months."

"Anything suspicious?" Sam opened the folder.

"Nothing that stuck out."

"We'll cross-reference the information in Kent's ghost tour spirals with this then." Sam flipped through the pages.

Kimberley nodded. "Alright, then." She pulled her laptop out of the box and opened it up. "Kent said these notebooks account for the last twelve months, so you just want to look at the last six?" she confirmed.

"Yeah, we'll start there. I'm especially curious about the last six to twelve weeks." Sam took a sip of his coffee.

Kimberley reached for the other notebooks and began flipping through them, looking at the dates starting six months prior and quickly making her way to recent weeks and months. She noticed the pages were full six months ago, but at four months there were half-pages of names. At three months, only a quarter of the page was filled on average. At two months, only a few names. And in the last month, the pages were all blank.

"Look at this, the month leading up to Hannah Brown's murder, there's nothing. Not a single person took the tour." Kimberley flipped the blank pages quickly, showing Sam.

"Did he just stop having people signing in?" Bearfield asked, flipping through his own spiral.

"I'm not sure, but I suggest we find out. Because if that's the case, this is pretty pointless."

Sam pulled out his phone from his utility belt and scrolled through it. He clicked a couple of buttons and put it on speaker as it began to ring.

"Hey, Kent. Sam here. We're going through those notebooks you provided, and we seem to be missing some information," he said.

Sam was silent for a moment.

"What's that? I gave y'all everything," Kent said.

"The last four weeks, you've got no names. Not a single person."

"Yeah, it's been rough. Business slowed way down. Has been slowing down for months."

"You're telling me you didn't give a tour to a single person the four weeks leading up to the murder?"

"I reckon that's correct. It's been brutal."

"And why didn't you mention this when we were there?"

Kent let out a sigh. "I don't know. It's embarrassing and I didn't think it was important. Plus, that's my business."

"Alright. Thanks for taking my call, Kent."

Sam set the phone down and took a deep breath.

"So, business had been slow," Kimberley said. She had picked up enough from the call on Sam's end to put two and two together.

"No, it had been nonexistent." Sam rubbed his face as if he were trying to rub life back into it.

"You still want to go through these notebooks?" Kimberley tossed hers on the table.

"Yeah, may as well. We don't have anything else to go on."

"Bearfield and Hill, will you take the first six months of notebooks and run all the names through our criminal database? Anything that pulls, I want to see it right away."

The deputies nodded, opening up their laptops and flipping through the spirals.

Kimberley didn't see the point in any of this. This was supposed to be the burn room, but with Sam's shortness and abrasiveness, it was becoming like a walk-in freezer to Kimberley.

She opened up a notebook, logged into the criminal database on her laptop, and started running the names through it too. The sooner she got Sam's wild-goose chase done, the sooner she could focus on actually solving Hannah Brown's murder.

Sam stood up and left the room without a word. Kimberley was unsure if he'd return and with the way he'd been acting, she hoped he wouldn't. But less than five minutes later, he reentered the room with his laptop. He got to work running the names through the criminal database on his computer as well, not saying a word.

"How do we know these people wrote down their real names?" Kimberley asked.

"We don't." He didn't look up at her. His response was curt.

"What can I help with?" Barb asked.

"Coffee," Sam said, pushing his cup toward her.

Barb pursed her lips but picked up the carafe and filled his cup anyway.

Kimberley looked over at Barb and then at Sam. Something was wrong, because he wasn't just being rude and short with Kimberley. He was doing it to Barb too.

An hour or so in, all the notebooks combined had produced a decent quantity of hits, but none so far that would suggest murder. Almost everything had related to speeding, drunk driving, late child-support payments, and petty theft. The most severe cases of battery and domestic abuse cases were often spurred on by fits of drunken stupor and were messy and loud ordeals, nothing like the calculated cleanliness of the scene at hand. Bearfield and Hill had packed up to go and patrol as there wasn't much else for them to do here.

Sam leaned back in his chair. Kimberley matched his stance, leaning back in hers. Barbara was still combing through the notebooks. She wanted to double-check everything, although Kimberley didn't know exactly what she was double-checking, but she appreciated the effort.

"Alright, I'm going to head out. I'll pick this back up tomorrow," Sam said, standing up from his chair.

Kimberley looked at her watch. It was a little after three in the afternoon, quite early for Sam to be leaving work, especially since there was an unsolved murder in his town. Kimberley shook her head, trying to shake Sam and the day off of her. He had been rude all afternoon, so she was glad to see him go. Maybe he'd be better tomorrow.

"I'm surprised he came in at all," Barb said, looking up from the notebook.

"What do you mean? Is he sick?" Kimberley leaned forward in her chair, tilting her head.

He hadn't seemed sick, but maybe Sam was one of those tough guys that didn't look sick, injured, or hurt, even when they were.

"It's just a tough day for him," Barb said, flipping a page.

Kimberley furrowed her brow.

"Why? What's today?" she pried.

"It's not my story to tell. I'll pass out the cookies, but not the tea. Isn't that what them younglings call it these days?" she said with a laugh.

Kimberley pursed her lips together.

"Oh, I've gotta go pick up my grandson. I'll come in early tomorrow to go over these again." Barbara said, rising from her chair.

Kimberley was too wrapped up in thinking about Sam and her case to say anything other than, "Sure."

Barb told Kimberley to have a good night before collecting her things and leaving.

She turned her chair around, facing the whiteboard. Hannah's name was in the center and her web of people around her—co-workers, Kimberley, Isobel, Tyler, daycare center staff, her mom Lisa. She could see the problem right in front of her. They knew nothing about Hannah Brown.

Her cell phone rang and she quickly answered it.

"Chief Deputy King."

"Hey, this is Officer Cariello from Houston Police Department. Apologies for the delay. Took a while to track down Mr. Tyler Louis. We spoke to one of his neighbors. Tyler's out on an offshore oil platform, thirty miles off the coast. He's completely unreachable."

"Shit. When will he be reachable?"

"He's due back on land tomorrow afternoon."

Kimberley breathed a sigh of relief.

"Good. Can you make sure he calls me?"

"Sure thing."

"I appreciate it, Officer Cariello. You have a good night," Kimberley said, ending the call.

She looked down at her watch. Somehow, she had gotten so caught up in the case and Sam that it was now after five. There was nothing more she was going to accomplish tonight. She was just going around and around in circles, like she was on a merry-go-round that never stopped. Everything was a blur and just out of reach. She packed up her stuff and headed out of the office to her Ford.

CHAPTER TWENTY-SIX

At the four-way stop, Kimberley glanced over at The Trophy Room. It had reopened, which she figured it would, since Ryan had made bail earlier in the day. There were a few men standing outside—the same men that were there every night, their faces engulfed in puffs of smoke. Kimberley glanced at the parking lot, spotting Sam's vehicle. What in the hell was he doing at The Trophy Room? She put her foot on the gas, but at the last minute, jerked her car left, pulling into the lot. Kimberley parked her car right beside Sam's vehicle. She wasn't sure what it was he was doing here, but she was going to find out.

Kimberley stared down the men as she walked past them into the bar. Two of them averted their eyes, the others stood their ground, puffing out their chests, raising their chins, and narrowing their eyes. They knew who she was, and Kimberley was sure they held her responsible for having their precious watering hole closed for one night.

Entering the bar was the same as the past couple of times. These places never changed. The same townies frequented them. They sat in their same spots. Country music played on the jukebox, the same musicians from Alan Jackson to Garth Brooks. The same poker machine was still broken. The same men played a game of pool. The same women lingered nearby. The same dipshit Ryan tended bar. There was only one thing different, out of place, and that was Sam, who was bellied up to the bar with a glass of whiskey that was half full.

Kimberley walked over to him cautiously. She wasn't sure what kind of reaction she'd get out of him. Would he be the ornery dick bag from earlier today or would he be the kind, respectful man she had come to know? She glanced over at Ryan who gave her a scowl mixed with a leer as if his dick and brain were crossing wires and didn't know how to respond to her.

"Sam," Kimberley said, taking a seat beside him.

He looked over at her and nodded.

"Thought you said only the town troublemakers drink here," she teased, trying to open him up, put him in a better mood.

"You spend enough time being a cop, you get more comfortable being around the troublemakers than the normal people," he said, taking a drink of his whiskey. He didn't react to the taste of it, so she assumed he had had a couple already.

"I can't argue with that."

"To what do I owe the pleasure today?" Ryan asked.

"Cut the shit, Ryan. She'll have what I'm having and without any of your grimy come-ons or flirty wanna-be hard-ass bullshit," Sam cut in.

Ryan nodded, taken aback, and immediately poured a neat scotch, placing it in front of Kimberley without a word.

"Thanks," Kimberley said to Sam as she picked up the glass and took a sip.

"Yep," was all he managed to say.

"How is he even working?" Kimberley glared at Ryan.

"Innocent until proven guilty."

They sat there in silence for several minutes, drinking their whiskey, fiddling with their glasses, and occasionally glancing over at one another. Kimberley couldn't tell if Sam wanted her there or not. But on some level, she thought he needed her there right now, next to him, quiet, just her presence. He hadn't asked her to leave. He hadn't been rude.

"How's Jessica been?" Sam asked, looking over at Kimberley.

She hadn't seen it before, but there was a sadness in his eyes—glossy, red around the rims, strained.

"She's been real good. Spending a lot of time with my mom, and they seem to be bonding."

Kimberley took another sip of her whiskey. They hadn't really talked much about their personal lives, aside from their first introduction, which was rather surface level. But this was probably good for their working relationship, to at least know some things about the other person's life when not in uniform.

"I know you moved here, just the two of you, what's the story with Jessica's father? If you don't mind saying, of course."

Any other time, Kimberley might have thought the question was too personal, but she knew Sam was going somewhere. There was something he wanted to talk about, something he wanted to tell her, and he was just going about it in a roundabout way.

"Yeah, well, we broke up. And he didn't have an interest in being in Jessica's life."

Sam clenched his fist and then brought the glass of whiskey up to his mouth with his other hand, downing the whole thing in one gulp. He set the empty glass down with such force, it made a loud thud, gaining Ryan's attention from the other side of the bar. Without Sam asking, Ryan made his way over and refilled his drink, not saying a word.

"He's an asshole," Sam said, gritting his teeth.

Kimberley nodded. "Yes, he is. He didn't even want to me to have her. Pushed for an abortion all the way up until I was twenty-four weeks along. It's not legal to have one after that, so he stopped pushing, but I always felt like he was secretly wishing I'd fall down a flight of stairs or miscarry." Kimberley washed the sour taste that had formed in her mouth with a sip of whiskey.

"I'm sorry. That's fucking awful."

"After she was born, he did a one-eighty. I thought he had changed. He was super attentive. But a few weeks in, I found

Jessica lying on the living-room floor in the middle of the night. He just left her there. Decided it was too much and didn't have the fucking common courtesy to put her back in her crib or wake me up." Kimberley took a gulp of her whiskey, thankful for the burn it provided.

"What I wouldn't give to be able to be in my kid's life," Sam said under his breath, loud enough for Kimberley to hear it, but it took her a few seconds to register exactly what he said. He took another sip of his whiskey and lowered his head, slightly shaking it. His shoulders dropped.

"What do you mean?" Kimberley asked carefully.

"Nothing. I don't know what I'm saying," he said, sipping his whiskey, staring straight ahead at the shelves filled with bottles of liquor.

Kimberley didn't press. She let Sam sit beside her, working through whatever it was he was working through. Something had happened. Maybe not today, but it had. It had changed his whole mood, made him abrasive and rude when she had known him to be kind and welcoming, a little rough around the edges, but overall a good person who meant no harm to others.

He took another sip of his drink, and Kimberley hoped the alcohol would give him the courage to get whatever was on his chest off of it. She pushed her empty glass forward. Ryan immediately refilled it, holding back the smartass comment, which surprised her. But perhaps he knew about whatever it was Sam was going through, and he knew now wasn't the time to push any buttons.

"Sorry about my behavior today," Sam finally said.

"No need to apologize. We all have bad days." Kimberley picked up her freshly filled drink and took a sip.

"It's not an excuse, but…" He paused, taking another drink of his whiskey, his words hanging in the air. "It's the two-year anniversary of my wife and son's death."

Kimberley gasped, her eyes widening.

"I'm so sorry, Sam," Kimberley started, but Sam cut in, putting his hand up.

"I didn't tell you in order to gain your sympathies."

"Why did you tell me then?"

Sam looked over at her. His eyes scanned her face, then locked with hers. "I don't know. I just... wanted you to know."

Kimberley nodded, unsure of what to say. Why did he want her to know this? Did he just want someone to confide in? Someone to understand him?

"How'd it happen?" Kimberley gave him a sympathetic look, although she didn't mean to. She knew that wasn't what he wanted, but she couldn't help herself.

"Don't look at me like that," he said, shaking his head and taking another sip of his whiskey.

"Like what?" She feigned ignorance.

"Like you feel sorry for me. Like I'm some wounded animal on the side of the road," he said.

"I don't feel sorry for you."

"Don't lie. It's written all over your face." He bumped his shoulder against hers.

Kimberley tried to make her face look mad, furrowing her brow, pursing her lips, but her eyes gave it away. They were big pools of sympathy.

"I'm sorry," she said, lowering her head, looking down at the brown whiskey in her glass.

"Car accident. A drunk driver hit them. Someone from this very town. So, when you said that I couldn't wrap my head around one of my own committing murder, that was wrong. My head is too wrapped around it." He looked around the bar at the patrons and then back at his glass of whiskey. "I think anyone is capable of anything," he added.

The last line hit Kimberley with a pang of guilt. This whole time she thought Sam had blinkers on when it came to his town, tunnel vision staring right out of Dead Woman Crossing, but it seemed he was doing that to protect his own conflicting feelings, his own biases.

"I know you don't want to hear it. But I'm sorry for what happened to your wife and son." Kimberley placed her hand on Sam's.

He looked over at her and said, "Thanks, Detective King," with a nod.

She let her hand stay on his for a moment before pulling it away. Sam drained the rest of his whiskey and threw down a twenty-dollar bill.

"I should get going," he said, standing up from his stool.

"Let me drive you home," Kimberley offered, pushing her half-empty drink toward the edge of the bar and dropping a ten-dollar bill down.

Sam rubbed his head. "Actually, maybe that'd be a good idea." He gave a small grin.

Kimberley nodded and walked out of the bar with Sam stumbling behind.

"You good?" she asked, turning back.

"Yeah, parking lot is a little uneven."

"I'm thinking you're a little uneven." Kimberley smirked. She stopped, letting Sam catch up, then put her arm around him, fitting into the crux of his shoulder, holding him up and stabling out his walk.

"How many did you have?" she asked.

"A few... too many."

Parked in front of his small ranch house, Kimberley got out of the vehicle and helped Sam inside. The lawn was well maintained, grass cut, hedges trimmed. She expected that out of Walker. He seemed like the type of guy that would take pride in his landscaping.

The front door opened to the living room, which was typically furnished like every other one; coffee table, television, couch, loveseat, recliner. But it differed in its décor, which was sparse. She could see rings of dust where things used to be. Outlines on the wall where things used to hang. It looked as though he had been slowly getting rid of items around the house, working through his grief, trying to let go of the past.

At the front door, Sam struggled to get his boots off. Kimberley took it upon herself to walk further into the house. A single framed photo hung on the far wall. As she got closer, she realized it was a family picture. His wife was blond and beautiful. His son had to have only been three years old. Then, there was Sam. She had never seen him look like that, a griefless face—pure and utter joy and elation. He was a little more worn now, but loss would do that to a person. Kimberley realized the photo had to have been taken shortly before his family passed.

"This is my humble abode," Sam said, standing upright now that his shoes were finally off.

Kimberley turned to look at him so he wouldn't notice that she had seen the photo. "Let's get you to bed."

Sam flicked on the hallway light, then walked to the end of the hall, flicking on his bedroom light. He stumbled to the side of his queen-sized bed and began unbuttoning his shirt.

"I'll get you a glass of water and some Tylenol," Kimberley said, averting her eyes as he started to undress.

She walked back down the hallway passing a bathroom, a guest room and another room with its door closed. In the kitchen, she rummaged through the cabinets until she found a glass and Tylenol. She filled the glass with water from the sink and walked back toward the bedroom where she found Sam standing with his shirt off. She swallowed hard as her eyes ran over his toned and sculpted body. She hadn't expected him to look like that underneath his sheriff uniform, and she also hadn't expected the way it would make her physically react. Cheeks reddened. Heart rate quickened. Eyes widened.

"Here you are." Kimberley cleared her throat, holding out the glass of water and three Tylenols.

Sam looked at her with a drunken smile, taking the glass and medicine.

"I guess now we're even," he said with a grin.

He tossed the pills in his mouth and drank nearly the whole glass.

"Even?" Kimberley raised an eyebrow.

"Walking in on one another changing." He tried to wink, but instead he drunkenly closed both his eyes.

"Not quite. You knew I was coming back in here," she teased.

Setting the glass on the bedside table, he pulled the covers up and slid into bed. She took his phone from his utility belt that was sitting on the floor and plugged it into the cord next to his alarm clock.

"Need a ride in the morning?" she asked.

Sam's eyes appeared heavy as they closed for longer than a blink and then reopened. He rubbed his hands over his face.

"No, Barb will come get me. She lives a couple blocks from The Trophy Room, and she's got a spare key to my truck. Barb takes care of me from time to time," he said with a grin.

"So, this isn't your first drunken escapade?"

Sam propped himself on his forearms and looked at Kimberley. His face became serious.

"Thanks for getting me home. You're a good person, Detective King, regardless if you came from New York or not," he said with a smile.

Kimberley laughed, playfully pushing him so he was no longer propped up.

"Need anything else?"

"Just for you to know I'm sorry for today and tonight." He let his eyes close.

"Don't worry about it, Sam." She backed away from the bed toward the door and turned off the lights.

Before she could close the door, Sam whispered, "Night, Kimberley."

She smiled.

CHAPTER TWENTY-SEVEN

Kimberley closed the door of her Ford and turned her shoulders side to side, cracking her back. The bed at Nicole and David's wasn't ideal. She could feel popped springs at night, and it creaked and squeaked when she moved around. She walked into the sheriff's station and was expecting to see Barbara at the front desk, but instead Deputy Burns was seated in her spot. He was tall and lanky like a teenage boy that hit a growth spurt and never filled out.

"Morning, Chief Deputy King," he said with a nod.

"Burns. Is Barb not in today?"

"She is. She's in the conference room. By the way, I got confirmation of the phone number on Hannah's phone. The one she had been calling and receiving calls from a few times a week for at least the past year. It's unregistered."

"So, a burner phone?"

"Exactly."

Kimberley took a deep breath. This case was one big dead end.

"That's useless then. Can't track it. Can't see who it's belongs to."

"Sorry, I don't have better news,' Burns said.

"Not your fault. Good work, Deputy," Kimberly said, leaving the front area and entering through the set of doors.

As she walked through the office area, Bearfield and Hill greeted her. They were all now working on the Hannah Brown case in some capacity; reviewing interviews, crime scene photos, fielding calls from locals who had "tips" or wanted to know what was happening with the case, if they were in danger.

"How's it going?" Kimberley asked.

Hill leaned back in his chair, rubbing his hand over his clean-shaven face. "I've got nothing."

Bearfield took a sip of his coffee. "I had a couple of calls refuting the rumors that Hannah Brown was a prostitute, other than that same as Hill: nada." He reached back behind his head, looping his ponytail holder one more time around his hair to tighten it.

Kimberley nodded. "Alright. Hill, why don't you go out and do some patrolling then? Keep an eye on anyone acting suspiciously. Bear, stay on the case. Review everything."

"Anyone in particular you want me to keep an eye on?" Hill tilted his head as he rose from his chair.

She thought for a moment. "Everyone. Until we find the person responsible, they're all suspects in my book."

Hill nodded, collecting his things and quickly heading toward the set of doors that led to the front.

Bearfield finished his coffee. "Don't worry. We're going to find this guy," he said to Kimberley and immediately went back to flipping through the crime scene photos.

She nodded. "I know we are," she said, her voice just above a whisper.

Kimberley walked to the conference room. She hoped with Sam's ghost tour hunch behind him, they'd be able to really dig into this case. As soon as she thought of Sam, she remembered the night before. Sweat beads formed at her hairline. Would he remember last night? Would he regret confiding in her? Had their working relationship changed? She wiped her forehead, trying to wipe away her thoughts. But all this did was lead her to thinking about his family, his wife, his son. How did he survive every day with that type of loss and grief? She took a deep breath just in front of the conference room, and when she felt composed enough, she entered.

Barbara was the only one in the room. When she saw Kimberley, a smile spread across her face. A mug of coffee and a Danish sat in front of Kimberley's seat.

"I assume this was you, Barb," Kimberley said, picking up the Danish and taking a bite out of it before sitting down.

"Guilty as charged."

"Where's Sam?"

"He's running a little late. Not feeling too hot today."

"I assumed he wouldn't be." Kimberley pulled out her laptop from her messenger bag.

"I found something peculiar." Barbara slid one of the ghost tour notebooks across the table.

A single name was highlighted in yellow marker. The date on the top of the page was five weeks before Hannah's murder. Kimberley read the name over and over, but nothing was clicking. Why did this one stand out? Why was it peculiar?

Henry Colton.

Henry Colton.

Henry Colton.

She knew that name, but why? And where did she know it from? Finally, she looked up at Barbara for the answers. Her face was lit up, pleased with herself, the same look she had when she completed her morning crossword puzzles or when she finished a knitting project.

"I ran through all the names this morning like I said I would, just wanted to double-check some things. I'm quite good at puzzles, you know." She raised an eyebrow.

Kimberley could see she was dragging this story out, relishing in it, but she allowed it. She could see it made Barbara happy to feel like she was a part of the team, like she was contributing more than baked goods and coffee, like she was making a difference. What Barbara didn't realize was she made the most difference, regardless.

"Well, I knew we were looking for past crimes and it was all run-of-the-mill stuff, so I started thinking about it in different ways. I decided to see where these people are from, and that name, Henry Colton, is the only person from Dead Woman Crossing. Every other person is an out-of-towner."

"You're a genius, Barb. Of course. Why would a local go to a tourist attraction?"

"Exactly." Barbara gave a pleased smile.

"Exactly, what?" Sam asked, entering the room.

His eyes were puffy and red. His skin didn't have its usual tan color, more like the shade of an eggshell. Sam was clearly nursing a hangover. He held a cup of coffee in his hand and a bagel sandwich in the other.

"We've got a lead, thanks to Barbara's skills."

Sam sat down, setting his bagel sandwich and coffee on the table. As soon as he was comfortable in his chair, he immediately dove into his food. There was leftover alcohol to be soaked up.

"Let's hear it," he said, in between chewing. He couldn't eat the sandwich fast enough.

Kimberley knew his suffering. She slid the notebook over to Sam. He looked at the open page, his eyes going straight to the highlighted name: "Henry Colton." He glanced back up at Chief Deputy King while he took another big bite of his sandwich, waiting for an explanation.

"Out of all the names in these notebooks, Henry Colton is the only person that's a local." Kimberley's eyes were wide with excitement.

"So…?" Sam shrugged his shoulders, stuffing the last of his sandwich in his mouth and washing it down with a gulp of coffee.

"What kind of local goes to a tourist attraction in their own town? That'd be like a New Yorker going to Times Square. You just don't do it."

Sam leaned back in his chair, putting his hands in front of his face, all of his fingertips touching. He looked at Barbara and then at Kimberley, mulling it over in his mind.

"Bear," he called over his shoulder.

Seconds later, Deputy Bearfield stood in the doorway. "Yeah, Sheriff."

"Pull everything we've got on Henry Colton. I mean everything."

"You got it." Bear nodded and hurried back to his desk.

"Good work, Barbara," Sam said, leaning forward in his chair. "We need a gal like you on the force."

Barbara blushed, flicking her hand at him. "Oh, it was nothing."

"No. It was something. I mean it, Barb, good work." A look of genuine admiration plastered on his grim and pained face. "You going to eat the rest of that?" Sam pointed at Kimberley's half-eaten Danish.

She pushed it toward him. "Have at it."

He ripped off a chunk and tossed it in his mouth.

"Thanks, Detective," he said.

First names were off the table. Everything seemed to be back to normal, Kimberley thought to herself. There was no awkwardness. They were back to being comrades, work partners.

"Once we have everything we know on Mr. Colton—"

"That's where I know him from," Kimberley interrupted, snapping her fingers as if she just snapped the memory back in her brain.

"Know who from?" Sam gave her a quizzical look.

"Henry… Henry Colton. He hit on me at The Trophy Room. He's a real creep," Kimberley explained. "I knew that name sounded familiar."

"Henry Colton is a dickwad. His name stuck out like a mule in a dress," Barbara said, crossing her arms in front of her chest and twisting up her lips. "When he was a teenager, him and his little goober friend destroyed my flowers in front of my house. Didn't even apologize or offer to fix them. I could definitely see him doing something like this."

"Okay…" Sam said carefully. "And Barb here has a personal vendetta against our potential suspect. From deflowering to murder. I suppose I can see the leap, Barb."

"I'm just saying, character-wise, he doesn't have any good points," Barbara said with a nod.

"Duly noted."

"Well, I guess it wouldn't hurt to swing by The Trophy Room later then to ask our dear old floral destructor what his interest was in the tour and what his alibi was the night of Hannah's death," Kimberley added.

"I reckon you're right about that." Sam nodded.

Just after 4 p.m., Sam and Kimberley pulled into the parking lot of The Trophy Room. They knew Henry Colton was inside, starting his daily ritual of getting blackout drunk and attempting to take home a woman.

Kimberley scanned the room, spotting some of the regulars, the gamblers, Ryan the bartender, a couple of bikers, and then there he was—Henry and his friend were at the dartboard drinking pints of Bud Light. She recognized the friend from her first run-in with him. Henry sported his full beard and messy, ash-brown hair. His hair was matted and greasy, and his skin was covered in a patina of farm shit and grime. He clearly hadn't gone home to shower after his shift.

"There he is." Kimberley pointed a finger at him.

Sam nodded and they walked in step across the bar over to Henry.

"Chief Deputy King, coming back for a little more?" Henry said with a slimy grin.

He looked over at his friend, waggling his eyebrows and smirking. His friend laughed.

"I'd walk away if I were you." Sam tightened his jaw, locking eyes with the friend.

The friend coughed awkwardly, grabbed his beer, and walked to the other end of the bar. Another man standing near them quickly cleared out too, leaving Kimberley, Sam, and Henry standing in the corner of the bar alone. The music from the jukebox and the sounds from the gambling machines made their conversation private from everyone else in the bar. Henry's face turned serious.

"Okay, what's this about?" He shuffled his feet and fiddled with his fingers like he couldn't hold still. A tell of a liar.

"Let's go outside," Sam said. There was a firmness to his voice that no one could argue with.

Henry's eyes bounced from Sam to Kimberley and then back to Sam again.

"Or we can haul you down to the station?" Kimberley said, raising her chin.

Henry gave a slight nod and headed toward the door. People stared and whispered as Kimberley and Sam walked behind him like he was a dog on a leash.

Outside, Sam pointed to an empty picnic table at the far end toward the back of the bar. Henry shuffled his feet, kicking up loose rocks as he walked. Sam and Kimberley sat on one side and Henry sat on the other, slightly slumped over.

"So, what's this about?" he asked again.

Kimberley looked at Sam and then back at Henry. "Do you know Hannah Brown?"

Henry drew his brows together. "Yeah. Went to high school with her. But haven't talked to her in years." He scratched the back of his neck. "We were close for a couple years after we graduated. But not once she started dating Tyler. He was her whole life until he split. Then her baby was her whole life, I guess."

Kimberley let out a deep breath. Everyone in this damn town went to high school together and, apparently, that was their only connection to Hannah.

Before Kimberley could ask another question, Henry was talking again. "I mean, it's sad what happened to her." He shrugged his shoulders. "But like I said, I don't really know her no more."

"Were you upset that you two weren't close anymore?" Sam raised an eyebrow.

"No, not at all. I've got my life and she… had hers." The corners of his mouth dropped.

Kimberley couldn't tell if he was sad, dumb or guilty.

"It's come to our attention that you were on Old Man Kent's Deer Creek ghost tour a little over five weeks ago," Kimberley said, raising her shoulders.

"That's why y'all are asking me about Hannah? Because of a ghost tour?" His brow furrowed.

"That's correct. Why were you on the ghost tour?" Sam cocked his head.

"I don't know. Something to do." He shrugged his shoulders.

"You have any sort of fascination with true crime?" Kimberley asked.

"True crime? Like murders?"

"That would be one example. Sure."

"Not really. I've seen some true-crime docs on Netflix, but that's about it." Henry shuffled around on the bench.

"So, you're telling us that you went on that ghost tour alone because it was something to do?" Sam raised an eyebrow.

"Yeah, that's what I'm telling you."

"What do you do for a living?" Kimberley asked.

"Farming."

"So, you regularly use things like machetes, axes, maybe a scythe?"

"Yeah."

"You're aware that Hannah was murdered down by Big Deer Creek?" Sam asked.

Henry nodded.

"And she was killed in the exact same way at Katie DeWitt James?" Sam asked, raising an eyebrow.

Henry swallowed hard. Kimberley could see his Adam's apple move up and down. He looked out at the parking lot and then back at Sam.

"You must be aware. After all, you went on Kent's ghost tour. The one that tells the story of Katie's murder." Kimberley cocked her head.

Henry fiddled with his fingers and bit at the inside of his lower lip. Once again, she couldn't tell if he was guilty or dumb, like he was still trying to put the pieces together or he had been caught. Stupid and guilty were often confused for one another in this line of work.

"Where were you on September eighth between the hours of two a.m. and four a.m.?" Kimberley asked. The blueness in her eyes intensified as she stared at Henry.

Henry looked up. He started counting on his fingers. One of his eyes closed.

"That was two days ago," Sam said, shaking his head. "Where were you two days ago between two and four in the morning?"

"Passed out, I'm sure. I work early." Henry looked at Sam, then at Kimberley, then back at Sam.

"You're sure?" Kimberley asked.

Henry gave a slight nod. "Yeah, I think so."

"Was anyone with you? Can anyone verify your whereabouts?" Sam asked.

"I was alone."

"Where?"

"At home."

"You live alone?" Sam asked.

Henry nodded.

"No girlfriend. No one slept over?" Kimberley asked.

"No, I was home alone in bed."

Kimberley looked at Sam. They made eye contact. She slightly shook her head.

"Okay." Sam stood up from the picnic table, stepping over the bench.

"That's it?" Henry asked.

"For now. Just… don't leave town," Kimberley said. She stood up and stepped over the bench, following Sam back to the vehicle. Another fucking dead end.

Inside the vehicle, Sam turned on the engine, still staring at Henry through the windshield. He stood up and watched Kimberley and Sam until he disappeared inside the bar.

Sam looked over at Kimberley. "What do you think?"

"I can't tell if he's dumb or guilty."

Sam nodded. "I was thinking the same thing. Since he doesn't have an alibi anyone can verify and the whole tour thing is odd, I'll have one of the deputies tail him, see if anything comes up."

"He was probably passed out drunk that night, but it doesn't hurt to look into it. It's not like we have anything else to go on currently." Kimberley looked around; the lone stop-signed intersection in town didn't even appear to warrant this need as the roads were empty.

The land gave shape to open fields of dirt and sand with random shoots of wheat grass and sorghum fighting a battle to hold root against a mild western wind pushing through. At the edge of the sky, the clouds were rolling up under themselves, the last vestige of sunlight painting the bottoms a pure white, while the tops loomed dark gray as the moon arose. Like a great tug-of-war trying to paint the ends in on each other. This bar seemed like an out-of-place sore on an otherwise untamed and untouched land. This land was unforgiving and prone to the extremes of the elements, the tracks of deer and rabbits and the nests of hawks, liable to be washed away in a violent storm any given day, just like Hannah's murderer seemed to storm through and remove the traces of her life within an instant, gone the very next, no sign of their coming or going.

"Wanna grab a bite to eat?" Sam asked.

"I never turn down food." Kimberley nodded.

CHAPTER TWENTY-EIGHT

"Here you are. One BLT with fries and one medium rare cheese-burger with fries." A waitress with a name tag that said "Sandy" placed a plate in front of Kimberley and one in front of Sam. "Anything else I can get you two?" She gave a toothy grin.

"Nope. All good. Thanks, Sandy," Sam said while picking up his BLT sandwich.

Sandy nodded and walked away. Sam and Kimberley were seated in a booth across from one another in Andrea's Café, Dead Woman Crossing's local diner. It had a fifties feel to it with big red cushioned booths, white tables, and black flooring. It appeared to only have a couple employees, the cook and Sandy, the waitress. Kimberley took a big bite of her burger and squirted a pool of ketchup on her plate for her French fries.

"You want some fries with that ketchup?" Sam teased.

Kimberley tilted her head with a slight grin. "Ketchup is its own food group."

"So how is it? Live up to your New York standards?"

"I mean, it's no Shake Shack, or an Emily burger, or Raoul's or Minetta Tavern or—"

"Alright! I get it." Sam put up his hands.

Kimberley shot him a small smirk. "No, it's good. A greasy-spoon burger is sometimes just what the doctor ordered."

"If you say so." Sam popped a few fries in his mouth, glancing over at Kimberley. "Detective, this case, where's your head at?"

Kimberley paused her eating and sat up straight in her seat, taking a drink of water to clear her throat.

"I still don't think it was an outsider."

"Why?" Sam wiped his mouth with a napkin.

"The scene was too clean. This person knew the area. They knew what they were doing. Her murder was swift. She never saw it coming, and she trusted this person enough to meet them down by a bridge in the middle of the night."

Sam nodded.

"Then there's the mysterious unregistered phone number. She talked to that person several times a week for at least a year. Why wasn't the number saved? Why did they only call each other? No texts. No voicemails. I think that the phone is the key, and I think we're going about this whole investigation the wrong way."

"What's the right way?" Sam cocked his head.

"I think we need to take a step back. Instead of looking for the murderer, let's look at the victim. Who was Hannah Brown?" Kimberley raised an eyebrow.

Sam scratched his chin, and when he didn't speak, Kimberley continued.

"What do we know about her? Aside from where she worked and that she was a single mother, we know nothing. Megan said no DNA evidence, so this was planned. Someone she knew did this, but why?"

"Isobel's father?" Sam said, throwing out a name. "Maybe she wanted child support."

"Maybe. I'm still trying to gather that information. I contacted Houston Police Department for help locating him. He's been out on an oil rig in the Gulf the past couple days, but I'm expecting a call from him this afternoon."

Sam nodded approvingly.

"There's also her co-workers. I know Bearfield talked to them, but the reports were minimal, more so about her state of mind the day of her murder. We need to find out what they knew about Hannah. I'd like to interview them again."

Sam nodded again.

"I want to talk to her mom again too. Find out how often she watched Isobel. Did Hannah frequently go out at night? If so, who was she meeting?"

He nodded again.

"And the daycare workers. Perhaps they know something we don't know about Hannah. She interacted with them several times a week."

Kimberley was practically manic as she went on and on about all angles of the case. Her excitement couldn't be contained. She felt like she was herself again, the New York City detective; the one that asked all the questions, even the hard ones. The one that looked at a case like it was under a microscope. She knew getting to know Hannah Brown on an intimate level would lead them to the murderer.

Before Sam could speak, Kimberley's phone rang. She pulled it from her utility belt.

"Chief Deputy King," she answered.

"Hi, this is Tyler Louis returning your call. I got a voicemail from you the other day and a police officer waiting at my door when I arrived home a few minutes ago, telling me to call you," he said. His voice was deep.

"Thanks for returning my call."

"What's this about?" he asked cutting Kimberley off.

"I'm assuming you haven't heard the news about Hannah Brown."

"No. Did something happen to her? Is she alright?" The concern in his voice was evident as he spoke a little louder.

"She's dead, Tyler. I'm sorry to tell you she was murdered."

Sam watched Kimberley deliver the news to the man on the other end of the phone. His heart broke a little and the memory of him discovering his deceased child and wife flooded his brain. He had arrived on the scene of the accident not realizing his own family was involved until he stumbled upon their broken bodies, bloody faces and motionless eyes, frozen forever. He blinked a few times, wiping away the memory. He never had control over when those images would appear right in front of him but he had learned how to rid them from his mind.

He focused on Kimberley, her lips moving as she spoke—her eyes darting back and forth, her fingers tapping on the table.

Tyler gasped. "Do you know who did it?"

"Not yet."

"Well, thank you for letting me know, Chief Deputy King," he said.

"Can I ask where you were September eighth between the hours of two and four a.m.?" Kimberley asked.

"Wait, what? You think I had something to do with this? Why would I do something like that?"

"I don't think that, I just need to know where you were is all. Just facilitates us ruling people out. Merely a formality, I'm sure you understand. Plus, it helps get Hannah justice."

Tyler let out a huff. "Working offshore with my crew. I have six guys and a manager who can tell you the same. I haven't been back to Dead Woman Crossing since last Christmas."

Kimberley nodded. "Alright. I'll be sure to confirm your alibi."

"Seriously though. Why would you think I had anything to do with it?"

"I didn't say you did, but nearly ninety percent of murders are committed by friends, loved ones, or acquaintances. Since you're Isobel's father and a former loved one, you fall into that category. We're just covering our bases," Kimberley explained.

"Wait. Did you say Isobel's father? I'm not Isobel's father."

Kimberley's brow furrowed. "What do you mean?"

"I'm not her father."

"I know you're not involved in Isobel's life, but you're still her father."

Sam shook his head.

"I don't think you understand. Biologically, I am not her father. I traveled a lot for work, and when Hannah got pregnant, the dates didn't line up. Plus, Isobel looks nothing like me. It's why we broke up," he explained.

"Are you sure about this?" Kimberley lowered her chin slightly, realizing if it was true, it was huge for the case.

"One hundred percent."

"Would you be willing to submit to a DNA test?"

"Yes."

"We'll have to get Lisa to consent, but I'm sure I can convince her."

"Good. I don't want people thinking I'm some sort of deadbeat dad. If Isobel was mine, I'd be there for her. But she's not," Tyler said, his voice cracking at the end.

Kimberley didn't know him, but she could tell there was a deep sadness there. This man wanted to be Isobel's dad and was most likely devastated when he found out he wasn't.

"I'm sorry to ask this, Tyler. But do you know who Isobel's father is?" Kimberley said the words slowly and carefully.

There was silence.

"Tyler?"

"No, I don't. She never told me."

"I'll have one of my deputies reach out to you regarding next steps for the paternity test. You'll be able to do it locally and we'll have the results sent to us. I appreciate your cooperation. Take care, Tyler," Kimberley said, ending the call and setting the phone down on the table.

"He says he's not the father." She looked at Sam with wide eyes.

"Do you believe him?"

"I do. He's agreed to a paternity test too."

Sam leaned back in his seat, glancing out the window beside him, taking in the view while he took in the new information. A nearly empty gravel parking lot edged out to the road. Beyond into the Oklahoma plains, the wind continued on, shifting everything little by little.

"If he's not the father, there's someone out there that is. Someone with motive," Kimberley said, her eyes scanned Sam's face.

Sam nodded.

"It was well known that Isobel's father was a man who left town—Tyler. Whoever the father really is clearly didn't want people to know."

"Why do you think that is?" Sam turned his head, his eyes connected with Kimberley's.

"Maybe he's married."

"Maybe. But you're right about one thing for sure."

"About what?" Kimberley asked.

"We have to find out who Hannah Brown was. She's the key to finding who murdered her."

CHAPTER TWENTY-NINE

"Alright, I'm gonna leave you to it, Detective," Sam said to Kimberley as they exited the local diner.

Kimberley gave Sam a peculiar look. "What do you mean leave me to it?"

"All those things you said you wanted to do, I want you to do them. Reinterview her co-workers, Hannah's mom, and the daycare teacher. You got this."

"And what are you going to do?" Kimberley lifted her chin.

"Well, since I'm an elected official, I get to do some of the fun stuff," he said sarcastically. "We've got press clamoring for details, locally and from some of the surrounding areas, so I've gotta hold a public information session. And since it's getting picked up, I've got to attend the county board meeting to ask for and justify some overtime pay. All the fun stuff." He sighed dramatically. "Unless you'd like to act on my behalf?"

Kimberley shook her head. "Not a chance."

"I thought you'd say that. Pharmacy is down the street. I'll have one of the deputies drop your vehicle off and work with you on the interviews."

"I prefer to work alone."

"Ouch." Sam grabbed his chest dramatically.

Kimberley put her hand on her hip. "Oh, not you."

"Yeah, sure." Sam waved a hand. "Regardless, I'll have your vehicle dropped off. We'll reconvene in the morning. If you have anything pressing though, give me a ring right away."

Chief Deputy King nodded. "You got it."

Sam tipped his head and walked to his vehicle. His eyes meeting hers again as he backed out of his spot. He gave a friendly wave as he drove off. Kimberley looked down the street lined with small businesses, no more than ten of them. It was the equivalent of a downtown, but judging by how barren it was, it sure put the "Dead" in Dead Woman Crossing.

Chief Deputy King walked down the sidewalk, passing by a hair salon big enough to take two clients at a time. There was a small coffee shop—just one, not like New York City where a Starbucks sat on every block, sometimes across the street from one another. She walked past a laundromat and a convenience store. All the essentials of a small American town, nothing more—no frills, just the basics. Beside the convenience store was the pharmacy.

She noted the hours that hung on the sign hanging from the glass door. "Open Monday–Saturday, 8 a.m. to 6 p.m. and Sundays, Closed." A bunch of local postings were stuck on the inside of the storefront window, including a poster for the Turner Farm with information on purchasing wheat and vegetables. At the bottom was Wyatt's contact information. Kimberley entered the small store that had several aisles stocked with a variety of medications, covering everything from heartburn to the flu. At the back wall was a pharmacist's window and at the front a cash register with a woman leaning against the counter filing her nails. The only reason Kimberley knew she worked there was from the name tag pinned to her cotton shirt that read "Michelle." When she noticed Kimberley, the girl stood up straight and set her nail file down. Her brunette hair was pulled in a ponytail on top of her head, making her look even younger than she actually was.

"Can I help you?" she asked, her voice delivering the right customer-service tone, warm and inviting.

"Yes. I'm Chief Deputy King," Kimberley said, walking up to the register. "I'm here to ask a few questions about Hannah Brown. Do you have a moment?"

The girl glanced around the empty store. "Yeah, but another deputy already came around asking questions about her a few days ago," she said, chewing on a piece of bubble gum that seemed to have appeared from nowhere.

"I know." Kimberley pulled a notepad and a pen out from the front pocket of her shirt. She flipped it open, noting the date, time and the interviewee's name at the top. "Were you close with Hannah?"

"Not really. We talked when we worked together. There's an overlap in shifts by like an hour. We never hung out outside of work."

"Anyone else work here?"

"Just the boss, Frank. He's the pharmacist and owner. He's in the back. Otherwise, it's just me full time and it was Hannah part time."

"No one else? What about Ruth Wills?" Kimberley tilted her head.

"Oh yeah. She's technically just on call as she's retired. But she covers shifts here and there. More so recently, after Hannah, ya know?" She dragged her finger across her neck.

Kimberley pressed her lips firmly together. "Did Hannah ever work nights?"

"No, we close at six and then clean up and restock 'til seven. Once a quarter, we do inventory later into the night, but Frank and I usually handle that."

"Just mornings?"

"Yeah, Monday through Friday for four or five hours. Occasional Saturdays if I need one off and Ruth can't cover." Michelle blew a bubble with her gum, popped it and sucked it back in.

"Anyone ever come in here to visit her?"

"Not that I saw."

Kimberley scribbled down a few more notes, realizing this follow-up interview was rather pointless. Nothing new was coming out of it, because it seemed no one really knew Hannah Brown.

"Do you know if she was seeing anyone?" Kimberley raised an eyebrow.

Michelle twisted her lips like she was considering what to say. Her eyes bounced all around Kimberley and then on her. Kimberley noted her unusual behavior.

"I ain't one to gossip," Michelle said. "But I think she was."

Kimberley tilted her head. "Why do you think that?"

"I seen her purchase a box of condoms from here and a Plan B pill."

Bingo. That was what Kimberley needed. Something that tied Hannah Brown to another person. Even though the tie was small, and she didn't know who the man was, at least it was something to go on.

"Did she say anything when she purchased the Plan B?"

"Nope, I pretended not to see her. She was nice and all, but she didn't talk about herself all that much. Once in a while, she'd talk about her daughter. But we mostly chatted about work or joked around about what medications and ointments customers were buying, who was constipated, who had hemorrhoids, which men couldn't get it up and were in here buying Viagra." Michelle laughed. "Just silly stuff like that, nothing serious."

"How long ago did she buy the Plan B?"

"Plan B, a few weeks ago. Condoms, there's been multiple purchases. She thought I didn't notice, but I did. We aren't ever supposed to ring ourselves out if we can help it, but when I saw what she was buying, I just left her to it."

Kimberley nodded, jotting down notes on her notepad.

"And you're sure?"

"Absolutely. I mean she could have been buying it for someone else I s'pose, but who does that? She never talked about having a man."

"Hello. Can I help you?" A voice called from behind her.

Kimberley turned around to find a small elderly man with a bald head and glasses lingering at the tip of his nose. He was dressed in a doctor's coat with a name tag pinned to his chest that read "Frank."

"I'm Chief Deputy King. I was just interviewing your employee about Hannah Brown. Mind if I ask you a few questions, while I've got you here?"

"Oh, of course." Frank walked slowly up the aisle. He stopped just a few feet shy of Kimberley. "It's just awful what happened to her. Hannah was a sweet girl, dependable too, aside from always being ten minutes late. I was never mad about that though. I knew she had a young daughter and she was raising her on her own, so I gave her some slack. I used to joke around with her, telling her she was on Hannah time and she needed to be on Frank time. See, I'm always early. Been that way my whole life. Such a shame. It's going to be impossible to replace her. I haven't even posted a job opening yet." He pulled his glasses from his face and wiped his eyes. "It's just too soon. You know? So, I'm doing what I can to cover in the mornings. It's tough, but my customers have been patient with me."

"Frank," Kimberley finally found a moment to interrupt. He reminded her of her grandfather when he was still alive. He would go on and on when he started talking, as if he had saved up all his words for you.

"Yes, Chief Deputy King," Frank said, looking up at Kimberley, returning his glasses to their position at the tip of his nose.

"Thank you for your time. I appreciate you talking with me today." There was no point asking him any questions as she felt sure he knew nothing more about Hannah than he had already told her.

Frank nodded. "Oh, of course. Anytime."

Kimberley closed up her notepad and put it back in her pocket. She pulled two business cards from her utility belt and handed one to Frank and one to Michelle. "If you think of anything else, please give me a call."

Michelle nodded pocketing the business card. "Have a nice day, Chief Deputy."

Frank brought the business card close to his eyes, squinting at it. "So, I just call this number?"

"Yes," Kimberley said, immediately regretting giving him her card. He was a nice old man, but she was sure he had nothing of substance to add. He was just a lonely old-timer.

"Have a good one," Kimberley said to both of them as she left the pharmacy.

"Perfect timing," Deputy Hill said, getting out of Kimberley's Ford Explorer. He tossed the keys to her.

"Thanks, Hill. You got a ride back?"

"Bear is gonna scoop me. Sheriff Walker mentioned you potentially wanting some company?"

Kimberley smirked. "All good here. Thanks, though," she said, walking past him and getting into the vehicle. Deputy Hill nodded and disappeared into the coffee shop.

One down, two to go. Up next was Hannah's mom, Lisa.

Kimberley knocked on the door. It took nearly a minute for it to open, and when it finally did Lisa stood on the other side, looking worse than she had before.

"Did you find my daughter's killer?" she asked, her eyes pleading for a yes.

Kimberley shook her head. "Can we talk?"

Lisa deflated like a balloon, but nodded her head, opening the door for Kimberley to enter. The house was messy with dirty dishes and used Kleenexes covering the coffee table. An empty wine bottle sat next to a dish with a half-eaten pizza slice on it. The television had *Judge Judy* on, but was muted so she couldn't hear the clever quips. The couch had bed pillows and a comforter on it. Lisa was clearly sleeping out here, drowning her sorrows in wine and television. The floor was covered in baby toys. A Pack 'n Play sat empty in the corner.

"Come sit," Lisa said as she quickly cleared the couch, tossing the blanket and pillows into a ball in the corner and attempting to pick up all the garbage from the coffee table. "I wasn't expecting company. Sorry."

"No need to apologize." Kimberley took a seat on the couch.

Lisa disappeared with a handful of dirty dishes, tissues, and the empty wine bottle.

"Where's Isobel?" Kimberley asked, concerned for the child.

"I have her crib set up in my bedroom. She's asleep in there," she called out from the kitchen.

"Can I get you something to drink?" Lisa asked, entering the living room, her hands now free of garbage.

Kimberley shook her head. "This will just take a few minutes."

"Okay." There was hesitation in Lisa's voice as she took a seat next to Kimberley.

Chief Deputy King pulled her notepad and pen from her pocket again, readying herself to take notes.

"I talked to Tyler Louis earlier today."

"And what did that slimeball have to say?" Lisa twisted up her face and folded her arms in front of her chest.

"Lisa, I'm sorry to say this, but Tyler said he's not the father of Isobel."

Her mouth dropped open in complete shock. "He said what?"

"That he's not the biological father of Isobel."

"How fucking dare he…"

"Lisa, getting upset over this isn't going to help. I understand this is difficult. He has agreed to submit to a paternity test, and as you're the guardian of Isobel, I need your permission for her to also submit." Kimberley tried to convey how important this was to the case. She tilted her chin, held eye contact, spoke in her most direct and soothing voice.

"Absolutely not. I will not have him tarnish my daughter's reputation." Lisa shook her head adamantly.

"Lisa, I need you to listen to me." Kimberley waited until she looked at her. "Tyler seemed very sincere, and he agreed to a paternity test. He also disclosed that that was the reason they had broken up. That when Hannah got pregnant, he was traveling for work, so he couldn't be the father."

A single tear rolled down Lisa's cheek. "Why is he doing this now?"

"He's not doing this to hurt you or Hannah. He's doing it to help us."

"Why didn't Hannah tell me? I'm her mother."

Kimberley didn't answer. It wasn't a question for her.

Lisa's eyes went wide. "If Tyler's not the father, then who is?"

"We don't know yet. But if Tyler's not Isobel's father, then Hannah was clearly hiding this for a reason. Maybe it went sour, maybe she wanted more out of him, a relationship, child support, maybe he's married. I'm not sure. But it's a hunch I have to see through."

Lisa turned her head, staring off into the corner of the living room. She wasn't looking at anything in particular. She was processing everything, trying to understand it, trying to make sense of it.

"Okay. I'll agree to the paternity test." Lisa nodded, still staring off into the corner.

"Good. I do have a few questions for you as well. Are you up for them?"

Lisa blinked back tears and nodded.

"Did you ever watch Isobel at night?" Kimberley held her pen to the pad of paper ready to take notes.

"Yeah, we did a standing overnight once a week, Fridays or Saturdays. It changed depending on my work schedule. On average, I'd say I watched her two nights a week, one overnight."

"Did she ever tell you what she was doing on those evenings she didn't have Isobel?"

Lisa tilted her head. "Just that she was running errands or hanging out with friends or something like that."

Kimberley moved her pen quickly.

"And she never mentioned seeing anyone?" Kimberley paused her note-taking to study Lisa's face.

She shook her head. "Why wouldn't she tell me? We were close. I'm her mother. She could have come to me about anything." Lisa leaned forward, crying into her own lap.

Kimberley put a hand on her shoulder in an attempt to comfort her, but she knew it wasn't possible. The only person that could do that for Lisa right now was her daughter.

She stood up from the couch. "I'll have a deputy get in touch with you tomorrow regarding the paternity test."

Lisa unfolded herself, looking up at Kimberley, her face wet with tears.

"How's Isobel been doing?" she asked, hoping to leave Lisa in a better mood.

"She's still calling out for her mom, but other than that, she's been sleeping and eating good. I just wish I could do more for her. Wish I could give her what she needs... her mom." Lisa's eyes swam with tears again.

"I'm going to find the person that did this. Just hold on a little bit longer. Your daughter will have her justice."

Lisa nodded. "Thank you, Chief Deputy King."

Kimberley nodded and saw herself out.

CHAPTER THIRTY

Kimberley parked her car on the side of the road just before the bridge that crossed over Deer Creek. She hadn't been back here since the day Hannah's body was discovered, and she wasn't sure what exactly brought her here. Perhaps she was looking for another clue or just clarity. She felt good about where the investigation was going, like it was finally heading in the right direction. Her gut told her it was.

Before she could step out of the vehicle, a black lifted Dodge Ram pulled up slowly beside her and stopped. Deputy Craig Lodge rolled down his window. He was wearing a pair of aviators, a crooked smile and his signature wife beater. A fat wad of dip sat behind his lower lip.

"Chief Deputy King," he said with a tip of his head.

Kimberley took a deep breath. This was the last person she wanted to deal with right now. *Be professional. Be professional.* She repeated to herself.

"Lodge," she said, withholding the "Deputy." In her book, he did not deserve the title. "What are you doing here?"

"Just checking out the area so I'm up to speed when I get back on the Brown case."

"From my understanding, your suspension isn't up for another four weeks." Kimberley raised an eyebrow.

"That's true, but I'm sure this case won't be solved by then. From what I've heard round town, y'all are running around in circles, got zilch to go on."

Fucking asshole. Kimberley got out of her vehicle, closing the door behind her. She stood a few feet from Craig in his stupid lifted truck. "I think your time is best spent focusing on completing your therapy and your AA classes, Lodge. We've got it covered here." She narrowed her eyes at him.

He twisted up his lips and repositioned the wad of dip in his mouth. "Alright then, King. See ya around."

"When you're back on the force, you better have learned to address me properly," she warned.

"Apologies, Chief Deputy King."

Kimberley turned on her foot and walked away toward the bridge. Craig revved his engine and stepped on the gas pedal, taking off at full speed, kicking up dirt and loose rocks. Jackass.

Kimberley carefully trekked down the side of the hill, brushing past the long blowing wheat. The sun was peaking behind the horizon, one last look for the day, before it fell completely. Kimberley glanced up and down the creek, listening to the water babble its way past rocks. She walked to the spot where Hannah's body had been discovered. It was now just an area where the wheat had been flattened and the dirt was out of place. There was no indication that death had been there. Death always left a mark.

"What were you doing down here, Hannah?" Kimberley whispered as if hoping the wind would answer back. "Why were you here with your baby?"

Kimberley's eyes ran over the flattened wheat. It was like a crop circle indicating life lost rather than new life. She walked around Hannah's spot, down the creek to where the head was discovered. There was nothing to indicate a body part once laid there. No blood. No flattened wheat. No kicked-up dirt. Nothing. But she remembered exactly where it was. The memory of Hannah's emerald-green eyes submerged just beneath a pool of milk would never leave her mind. Another tattoo for the brain.

The sound of a vehicle and a loud voice caught Kimberley's attention. She put her hand over her eyes and looked up at the side of the road. She shook her head when she saw Kent Wills, a younger man that looked just like Kent, and a group of people behind them.

"The story of Dead Woman Crossing began over one hundred years, but it's one that continues to this very day, taking the life of Katie DeWitt James back in 1905 and now Hannah Brown, both slain in the exact same way: a bullet to the head and decapitation right in front of their infant daughters. Some say you can still hear Katie calling out for help around here late at night, and recent sightings say they've heard Hannah calling out for her baby Isobel. 'Where are you, Isobel?' she yells all throughout the night," Kent said, guiding his tour group down the valley.

Kimberley shook her head in disgust and rolled her eyes.

Kent tipped his head at Kimberley. "See if you can feel them. See if you can hear them. Go wander," he instructed.

His tour group of ten spread out, walking up and down the bank of Deer Creek, traipsing over the place that should be seen as sacred rather than some tourist attraction for the morbid. Kent walked toward Kimberley, side by side with the younger-looking Kent that she presumed to be his son. He looked around thirty with a full beard and blue eyes that contrasted with his dark brown hair.

"Chief Deputy King, I thought this scene was cleared yesterday," Kent said.

"It was."

"Well, then, what brings you down here?" he asked, rocking back on his heels.

"Just covering my bases."

"Alright… this here's my boy, Kent Jr." He patted his son on the back. Kimberley should have known that Kent was the type of man to name another human being after him as if there were some legacy he was leaving behind and ensuring it was carried on.

The son held out his hand for a handshake.

Kimberley looked down at his hand, ignoring it. She looked back at Kent and Kent Jr. She wasn't interested in pleasantries with either of them. "You got a whole part in your ghost tour about Hannah Brown already?"

"Gotta seize every opportunity you can," Kent said with a "what can you do" shrug.

"I wouldn't call the death of a young girl an opportunity." Kimberley's tone was icy.

"And that is where we differ." He tilted his head, an edge to his voice.

"Looks like your profiting quite nicely from this tragedy. Is that a full tour you got?" Kimberley looked past them at the people milling about the former crime scene.

"Murder has been good for business." Kent Jr. smirked.

Kimberley clenched her fist. *Don't deck him. Don't deck him. Don't deck him.* She repeated to herself. She wiggled life back into her fingers, composing herself. She wasn't sure she'd be able to do it again. The smugness on his face infuriated her.

"What my boy meant to say is, although it was devastating what happened to Hannah, it's provided our family with so much, like reincarnation of a sort. I'm getting bookings again, lots of them. So much business, I had to bring Kent Jr. in on it just to help me manage, which was lucky since he lost his job a while back. We plan to do it all—merchandise, a documentary and a book," Kent said, overjoyed by his own success.

Kimberley tasted bile in the back of her throat.

"Hannah hasn't even been buried yet. Seems sick, don't you think?" She tried to remain cool, calm, and collected.

"Nothing sick about capitalism," Kent Jr., said, raising his chin.

Nope. She couldn't do it. Not the second time. Her hand clenched again forming a fist, but this time rather than staying by her side, she reeled it back and slammed it into Kent Jr. fuckface's nose. She heard a crunch, like stepping on a gravel driveway. Blood instantly poured from his nose like a faucet in his head had been turned on. Kimberley pulled her fist back just as he fell backward, his ass hitting the ground in the exact spot that Hannah's head laid just a few days before.

"What the *fuck*?" he yelled, trying to tip his head back while holding his nose that Kimberley knew for sure was broken.

She shook out her hand and took a step back.

"What the hell did you do that for?" Kent spit, while attempting to help his son.

"Just seizing an opportunity," she said sarcastically. But in her head, Kimberley was kicking herself for what she had done.

"I'm reporting this to Sam," Kent yelled out as Kimberley walked away, passing by the tour guests. Those that saw what happened stared and whispered.

"No need. I'll do it myself," Kimberley called over her shoulder.

"Fucking bitch," Kent Jr. yelled, but the blood pouring from his nose made him sound gurgly, rather than threatening.

Kimberley shook out her hand a couple more times as she walked up to the road. Regardless of how pissed off Sam would be, she would never regret hitting that prick. She looked down at her knuckles, a blue tint already spreading over them. She liked the way it looked. A small blemish of justice.

Kimberley hopped out of her vehicle and sprinted toward the Happy Trails Daycare Center. She was ten minutes late thanks to her run-in with Dipshit Senior and Junior. Nicole had offered to pick up Jessica, but Kimberley needed to speak with the daycare teacher anyway, and she hadn't gotten to pick up Jessica all week. The point of moving to Dead Woman Crossing was to spend more time with her daughter, but it wasn't happening as of yet. At least, she was making it home for dinner, which she rarely did in the city. She threw open the doors and there, sitting on the floor playing with a stack of colored blocks, was Jessica.

Jessica looked up, her face instantly brightening when she saw her mother. She stood and ran toward her clumsily. Kimberley bent down, reaching out her arms, and as soon as Jessica was safely in them, she lifted her into the air, twirling her around.

"I missed you so much, baby," Kimberley said, kissing both sides of her cheeks.

Jessica wiped at her face giggling. "Ma-ma. Missed... you," she said.

Kimberley smiled so wide she thought her lip might split. "Such a smart girl, you are."

It was important to Kimberley to always tell her daughter how smart, strong, and clever she was. She wanted Jessica to grow up valuing strength and intelligence over looks.

"Next time you're late, I'll have to charge you for the after-school program," Margaret said, standing from a chair.

Kimberley hadn't even noticed her sitting there.

She set Jessica down, careful to not get her legs caught up on her utility belt. "Play with your blocks, sweetie," she said.

Jessica ran back to her stack of blocks, sitting back down beside them.

"Sorry about that, Margaret. I got held up at work."

"It's okay. I understand you're under a lot of pressure with the Hannah Brown case. I appreciate your efforts, and I hope you catch the person responsible, so we can all rest a little easier at night," Margaret said. Her stern face had become soft and sympathetic.

"Thanks. Actually, I had a couple of questions for you about that. Do you have time to speak now?"

"Certainly. Anything I can do to help."

Margaret took a seat and motioned for Kimberley to sit in the chair across from her. She walked to the chair, taking the seat she'd indicated, and pulled out her notepad and pen.

"You were Isobel's daycare teacher, correct?"

"Yes, since she turned twelve months old and moved up to toddler care around two months ago." Margaret nodded as she spoke.

"Did anyone ever drop or pick Isobel up beside Hannah or her mother?"

"Not that I can think of. I can check her emergency contact sheet to see if she had anyone else down."

"That'd be great." Kimberley smiled.

Margaret rose from her seat and disappeared down the hallway. Kimberley glanced over at her daughter as she held up a blue block.

"What color is that, Jessica?"

Jessica looked at the block, turning it over in her tiny hands, then looked back at her mother. "Boo."

"Bl-ue. That's right. Such a smart girl," Kimberley gushed.

"Here you are," Margaret said, entering the room and extending out a yellow file folder. "All of the information Hannah put down is in there."

Kimberley took the folder and opened it up. The page was filled in with Hannah's handwriting. Kimberley saw the contact information for the pharmacy, her mom, Hannah's cell phone, and there was one number without a name.

"What's this?" Kimberley asked. "There's a phone number with no name or address."

"Ah shoot. She must have forgot to fill that part in."

"Mind if I take a picture of it?"

"Be my guest."

Kimberley pulled out her phone and snapped a photo of the contact form, focusing on the lone number with no other details, just ten digits in a row that may or may not have belonged to the murderer. It could just be a friend of Hannah's, a co-worker, a house phone, but the way it was written just seemed odd. The first number was a four. A heavy dot of ink was at the top of it, like

Hannah had held her pen down for too long, hesitating whether or not to write the number. The rest of it is a scribble, like a chicken scratch, as if she had made the decision as soon as she wrote the number four. Maybe Kimberley was looking too much into it. Maybe she had forgotten the number, held her pen down and then suddenly it came to her. Perhaps Kimberley was looking for something that wasn't there. She closed up the folder before she started analyzing every letter and number Hannah had written down. Handing it back to Margaret, she thanked her.

"Anything else you can tell me about Hannah?"

"Well, she ran late dropping off Isobel in the mornings, and she just always looked tired. But she was a single working mom. So, that's not unusual. She was never late picking Isobel up in the afternoon." Margaret paused for a moment. "There's not much I can really tell you. Hannah was a very nice woman and clearly a good mom who loved her daughter dearly. I've had Isobel in toddler care for two months and she's an absolute joy." Her eyes became a little misty.

"Thank you, Margaret. I appreciate your time."

Margaret wiped her eyes. "No problem. Anything else I can help you with?"

"I think that's everything for now." Kimberley put away her notepad, pen, and phone. Standing up from her chair, she scooped up Jessica.

"I really hope you catch the person that did this," Margaret said as Kimberley walked away. There was a sadness in her voice.

Kimberley turned back. "I will, Margaret. Have a good night," she said, leaving the daycare center.

CHAPTER THIRTY-ONE

"Hey, Mom," Kimberley said as she carried Jessica into the living room. Nicole sat on the couch reading a book with a half-naked cowboy on the cover. The smell of some sort of roast wafted through the home. On the coffee table sat a plate of grapes and cut-up cheese, a bottle of wine, Jessica's sippy cup, and two glasses of wine, as if Nicole were waiting for Kimberley to join her.

"Hey." Nicole closed up her book and placed it on the coffee table, exchanging it for a glass of wine. Her attention immediately went to Jessica. "Hi, sweetie." Her voice increased a couple of octaves. Kimberley sat down beside her mom with Jessica on her lap.

Kimberley handed Jessica her sippy cup. She gripped the handles with both hands and took a drink while Kimberley popped a piece of cheese in her mouth and grabbed her glass of wine. The whole setup was clearly Nicole's peace offering.

"Food won't be ready for a while. I'm running late due to my hair appointment."

Mid popping a grape in her mouth, Kimberley stopped and looked over at her mother. The gray that speckled and streaked her hair had been replaced by a deep chestnut color. She hadn't even noticed how vibrant and shiny it looked.

"Mom, your hair looks stunning. I haven't seen it look like that in years," Kimberley gushed.

Nicole couldn't help but smile. "Thanks. I figured I needed to change it up. Jessica learned the word 'gray' the other day, and she started pointing at my hair, saying 'gray' over and over again."

Kimberley laughed, handing a sliced grape to Jessica.

"She has your honesty. There's no doubt about that."

"Yu... mmy," Jessica said as she popped it in her mouth.

"That's right. Can you say 'grape'?" Nicole leaned into her granddaughter, sounding the word out.

"Gape," Jessica squealed. Then she repeated it over and over until it sounded more like 'grape.'

"Good girl." Nicole ran her hand down the side of her head.

"Is everyone still mad at me?" Kimberley asked, taking more than a sip of wine.

"Mad? No. Unsettled? Absolutely."

"Mommmm," Kimberley groaned. She ate a piece of cheese and then a grape and then a piece of cheese.

"I think Wyatt is more embarrassed than anything. I don't think he's upset with you. He's been keeping busy on the farm, trying to double up wheat orders and expanding Emily's garden. Emily is looking at refinancing their mortgage again, and David is helping them sell off some of the farm equipment they don't use or need," Nicole explained.

"Well, that's good then. Right?"

Nicole shrugged her shoulders. "It might be enough to keep them afloat. David said he'll take a chunk out of his retirement to keep the farm going."

"Admirable." Kimberley nodded.

"This is his family's legacy. He'll do anything to keep it going." Nicole stared off at the wall as she fiddled with her wine glass. "But I think you should try to stay clear of David and Emily, or at the least not antagonize them until they cool off."

"Noted."

"I heard you have a lead in your case."

Kimberley's eyes went wide. "Who said that?"

"My hairstylist's daughter, Michelle. She works at the pharmacy, said you were asking about Hannah's secret boyfriend." Nicole raised an eyebrow.

Heavy footsteps pounded against the floor, across the kitchen, through the dining room, and into the living room. David stood in the doorway covered in mud and sweat and dressed in overalls. He gave Nicole a small smile.

"She said she wasn't one for gossip." Kimberley rolled her eyes. "It's just a hunch."

David looked at Kimberley, his face not as tense and angry as it was the night before. The vein in his neck and forehead had retreated. "Kimberley," he said with a nod.

"David." Kimberley nodded back while popping a piece of cheese in her mouth.

It seemed they were progressing into neutral territory, almost an indifference toward one another. Like they were neighbors that just happened to reside in the same house. He wasn't yelling at Kimberley, and she wasn't tossing around sarcasm and insult, so that was progress. A small amount. But as they say, progress is progress.

David walked to the coffee table with one step, and bent down, grabbing a handful of cheese and a vine of grapes.

"You look different." He ran his eyes over Nicole's face, popping several chunks of cheese into his mouth.

"She got her hair dyed. Isn't is obvious?"

Nicole smiled, pushing up the ends with her hand like she was showing it off.

"Looks nice," David said, pulling a grape from the vine with his teeth. He chomped down, popping the fruit in his mouth. "When's dinner going to be ready?"

Nicole pressed her lips together for a moment. "About an hour."

"I think it looks amazing, Mom," Kimberley said, her eyes peering over the rim of her wine glass.

"Thank you. Now what were you saying about this hunch?"

David stood there, switching between eating a piece of cheese and a grape.

"I really shouldn't be talking about an ongoing case."

Jessica swatted Kimberley in the face. "More," she demanded.

"Ouch. Don't hit Mommy," Kimberley said, handing her a piece of cheese. She immediately put it in her mouth.

"From what Michelle's mom said, it sounded like this mystery man may be Isobel's father," Nicole said.

"Mom, stop." Kimberley rolled her eyes.

"What? You're not talking about the case. I am," Nicole said lightly. "I thought Hannah's ex, the boy who moved out to Texas was the dad. What was his name?" She scratched her head, trying to conjure it up.

"Nicole, Kimberley said she wasn't allowed to talk about the case, so don't put her in a position to jeopardize it." David looked at Nicole firmly.

"Okay. Sorry." Nicole dropped her shoulders.

David tossed the stripped grape vine on the plate and left the living room, heading down the hallway to his bedroom. If she hadn't known it already, that interaction right there would have told Kimberley that David was former military or police. He put a heavy importance on confidentiality and tight lips, and Kimberley realized she hadn't been doing the best job when it came to nondisclosure. In a city like New York, where there were thousands of cases going on, no one cared about chatter, but in this town, the town of Dead Woman Crossing, this was *the case*. Small towns brought out lots of talk and Kimberley wasn't immune to it.

"Sorry, Kimberley," Nicole apologized again.

"It's fine, Mom. I wish I could tell you everything, but he's right, I really shouldn't be discussing an active case."

Nicole nodded, topping off her wine glass.

It was true, Kimberley wished she could tell her mom every-thing, like how Hannah's murder had brought up old wounds, how it had rattled her and made her sleep less... but it was like a slight tremor in comparison to the earthquake of a case that still haunted her every moment, whether she was asleep or not.

"Hey, Lynn. We finally tracked down Eddie Russo. We had no luck last night but got a tip today from the cook, Mario, and found out he was hiding at a friend's house in the Bronx. We've got a patrol car bringing him in, and I'm not far behind with Shake Shack, your favorite. See ya soon," Kimberley said, ending the call.

It was noon on a Friday, an absolute nightmare to drive in New York City, but she didn't mind the traffic today. This case had haunted her for the past year and a half, and Kimberley felt like she was finally close to solving it, to finally getting justice for Jenny, Maria, Stephanie, and their unborn children. She drummed her fingers against the steering wheel to the beat of a catchy pop song that played quietly on the stereo.

"Dispatch. All units, 10-18 to 1058 White Plains Rd. Bronx, NY for a 187," played over her police radio.

Kimberley looked at the sign, realizing she was just a couple of blocks away. She clicked the radio. "Dispatch. This is Detective King. I'm in route. 10-4." She pulled up to an abandoned two-story brick house. The windows were boarded up with plywood and the front door was busted open. Nothing about it stood out as it looked like many of the other houses in the neighborhood. It was the perfect place to carry out a murder.

The open staircase creaked as she made her way down to the unfinished basement of an abandoned house. The musty, mildew scent invaded her nose before her boots touched the dirt floor. Her flashlight was the only light source.

"Careful, the last step is rickety," an officer at the top of the stairs called out. He and his partner had been the first to arrive on the scene.

She skipped the bottom step, planting her feet firmly on the ground. A thick, black rat scurried across her boot. She was used to vermin, so Kimberley didn't react. Her feet followed the illumination of the flashlight she was holding. Sticky cobwebs grabbed hold of her face, and she quickly pulled them off. In the far right corner of the basement, she shone her light, starting at the floor and working up slowly. First, she saw the feet covered in small burns and cuts. Her feet dangled above the ground as she was seated in a tattered chair. Her legs were equally inflicted with similar cuts, hundreds of them as though he had scored her flesh like a chef would with a piece of pork or chicken. She was stripped bare, no clothing, no jewelry, nothing, except for a paper bag that covered her head.

Kimberley walked closer, tucking the flashlight under her arm, while she slid on a pair of gloves. She heard footsteps upstairs as more officers arrived on scene. Stopping just in front of the woman, Kimberley slowly slid the bag from her head. Time froze. The bag floated to the ground as her fingers must have let loose. Kimberley began slowly falling away from the body, but she could feel no weight, like an object just being pushed away in space, two magnets with the same polarity. Her face caved in on itself, all of the muscles contracting as her heart beat at triple its speed and the pit of her stomach began doing backflips. Tears streamed down her face in a torrent. She must have finally made contact with the ground because she was now sitting and threw her head back as she wailed. Bile burned her throat and she vomited onto the dirt floor, screaming and crying, eruptions of emotion coming out in all forms.

*

Kimberley was pulled off the case after Detective Lynn Hunter was murdered. She didn't know if that made it worse. Eddie Russo wasn't the serial killer. He had solid alibis for three of the four murders. As he was on parole, his parole officer had verified his whereabouts. There weren't any murders after that. He went inactive, as many serial killers do, as if taking lives was their job and they needed time off. Kimberley knew she would live with it for the rest of her life, losing her partner, her mentor, her best friend, and she would always blame herself for not protecting Lynn and her unborn child, Jesse.

CHAPTER THIRTY-TWO

"Hey, Barb," Kimberley greeted, carrying in three cups of coffee in a carry tray and a bag that contained a large chocolate muffin.

She walked to the desk, setting down the brown paper bag and a cup of coffee. "I figured I'd bring you the coffee and baked good today," Kimberley said with a smile.

Barb's face lit up. "Oh my. You didn't have to do that."

She opened the bag, pulling out the oversized chocolate muffin. "No one's ever brought me coffee or treats." Her eyes moistened. "Oh, I hope you got something for Sam. It might make him a little less angry with you."

"So, he's heard?" Kimberley tilted her head.

"Everyone has. I don't blame you. If I had the strength, I would have done the same," Barb said.

"Thanks for the heads up."

"Oh, wait!" She bent down beside her desk, pulling a butter knife out from a drawer. She sliced the muffin in half and wrapped part of it back up, putting it in the bag. "This will help." She smiled. "Sam has a sweet tooth and chocolate will sweeten him up for you."

Kimberley took the bag from Barbara, thanking her again. She walked through the set of double doors into the belly of the sheriff's station.

"Hey, slugger," Deputy Hill said with a smirk, shuffling papers at his desk.

Bearfield emerged from the break room, pretending to box with his hands. "Heard you been out there rolling with the punches."

"Ha-ha," Kimberley said sarcastically, walking past them.

"You got quite the punch. Heard you broke his nose," Hill said.

"He's lucky that's all I did," Kimberley called out over her shoulder as she made her way into Sam's office.

He was sitting at his desk, squeezing a stress ball. It looked new, like he had purchased it solely on Kimberley's behalf. His lips were pressed firmly together, and his gaze was locked forward, like a laser.

"Hey, Sheriff," Kimberley said nonchalantly. "I gotcha a coffee and a chocolate muffin." She sat the cup and the bag in front of him, tossing the carrying tray in the garbage can, and taking a sip from her own coffee.

"Don't fucking 'Hey, Sheriff' me. Sit down," Sam said without looking at her.

Kimberley sat down, her eyes meeting his. "What's up?"

"You know what's up. Kent filed a complaint with me that you assaulted his son. Is that true?" He leaned forward in his chair, taking a sip of the coffee. His eyes glanced at the paper bag, like he wanted to pull out the muffin and eat it but had to get his reprimand over with first. Barbara was right about his sweet tooth.

"Yes, it's true. I lost my temper."

Sam let out a sigh. "I don't know what you got away with in the city, but this can't fly around here. It's a small town. People talk, and it's not a good look for any of us."

"I know. I'm sorry for that, but I'm not sorry I did it." Kimberley crossed one leg over the other.

"Look, I know the Kents are creeps, and what they're doing right now is awful. Between you and me, I would have had a hard time not clocking the guy too, but that doesn't make it right."

Sam glanced at the paper bag again.

"I should suspend you. Kent wanted to press charges, but I was able to sway him not to."

Kimberley nodded.

"Just don't let it happen again."

"I'll try not to."

Sam squeezed his stress ball harder and shook his head. He glanced at the paper bag again.

"Just eat the muffin," Kimberley teased.

Sam opened the bag, pulling out half a muffin.

"Where's the other half?" he asked, setting it down on a napkin.

"Barb has it."

Sam ripped off a piece and shoved it in his mouth, his face instantly brightening from the sweet, chocolatiness. "She told you I had a sweet tooth, didn't she?"

"Yep."

"And she told you I was mad, and this would help, didn't she?"

"Yep again. So, is my reprimand over?"

Sam placed another piece in his mouth. "For now... Now, what you got for me? Were you able to interview all the people you discussed yesterday?"

Kimberley pulled her notepad from her front pocket, flipping through several pages. "Michelle from the pharmacy said she witnessed Hannah purchase boxes of condoms several times and a Plan B pill a couple weeks before her murder."

Sam leaned back in his chair, nodding.

"Lisa agreed to submit Isobel to a paternity test, which will happen today. Tyler's sample was overnighted, and I fast-tracked the testing, so we'll have it by end of day."

Sam nodded again as he put the last of the muffin in his mouth.

"I spoke with Margaret, the daycare teacher at Happy Trails. She provided me with Isobel's file." Kimberley pulled out her phone, bringing up the photo she had taken of the contact sheet. She zoomed into the phone number with the heavy ink spot and handed the phone over to Sam. "That number that's on the contact form didn't have a name or an address to go along with it. That same number is the unregistered one in Hannah's phone, the one that she's been talking to several times a week for at least a year."

Kimberley closed up her notepad, sliding it back in her pocket.

"So, what you're saying is whoever killed Hannah was sleeping with her and is most likely Isobel's father?" Sam said.

"Yes, pending the paternity test."

He scratched his chin. "And we have no idea who she could have been seeing?"

"None. No one could give me anything. Not her mom, not her co-workers, not the daycare, no one. This relationship was in secret, which leads me to believe the man is probably taken, married or at the very least in a serious relationship."

Sam nodded. "Any other reason someone would keep a relationship with a single woman a secret?"

"Not that I can think of." Kimberley leaned back in her chair, bringing her coffee to her lips and taking a drink.

"Sam. Chief Deputy King," Deputy Bearfield called out as he rapped on the door frame with his knuckles twice. Kimberley turned to look at him.

"Bear," Sam greeted.

"You know the guy you have me tailing, Henry Colton?"

Kimberley and Sam nodded.

"Well, I just got a phone call on our tip line. He dated Hannah Brown after high school."

Sam leaned forward in his chair, showing interest.

"Apparently, their breakup was ugly, as was their relationship. Word is he cheated on her. There was a spat of domestic violence throughout the relationship too. Police were called once, but she chose not to press charges, so they were just separated for the night," the deputy explained.

"Why didn't we know this before?"

Kimberley turned back toward Sam. "Because we've been chasing down Kent's ghost tour and Henry wasn't all that forthcoming. Apparently, he's dumb and guilty."

Sam let out a deep breath.

Kimberley looked over her shoulder at Deputy Bearfield. "How long were they together, and when did they break up?"

"From what I gathered around two years. They broke up right before she started dating Tyler Louis."

Kimberley nodded. "Who called this in?"

Bearfield shrugged his shoulders. "Not sure. They wouldn't give their name. But it was a male voice."

"Would she hide a relationship with Henry Colton?" Sam pondered.

"Maybe out of shame. She dated him before. He cheated on her, was abusive to her. And you saw him, he's a drunk idiot—I'd lie about dating him too," Kimberley said pointedly.

Bear chuckled.

"Do we have enough to bring him in for questioning?" Deputy Bearfield asked.

"He did have a past relationship with the victim, and he has a violent record." Kimberley raised an eyebrow.

Sam took a sip of his coffee, considering for a moment. "I've got the press and the locals' eyes on me, so I don't want to just keep pulling in people without more to go on. Bear, tail him for the next twenty-four hours, make our police presence known. Let's see if we can shake something loose. Regardless, we'll pull him in for questioning tomorrow."

Deputy Bearfield nodded and left the room.

"Why not pull him in now?" Kimberley cocked her head.

She didn't understand this pussyfooting Sam partook in. Why was he being so careful? If it was up to Kimberley, Henry would be sitting in her interrogation room in about five minutes. She'd have him confessing everything he's ever done, even something as miniscule as jaywalking.

"Like I said, we've got a lot of eyes on us. Murder might be typical in the city, but it's not around here."

"Your town is literally named after an unsolved murder." Kimberley rolled her eyes.

"Yeah, and I don't need another unsolved one."

"If we keep tiptoeing around, that's exactly what's going to happen," Kimberley challenged.

"People out there are scared, but they're still talking because they have faith in us. If we start pulling in anyone and everyone for questioning, townsfolk will see us as the enemy. They'll quit talking. We won't be able to shake anyone loose," he explained.

To Kimberley, it made zero sense. She didn't need people to talk in order to catch the person responsible. She needed evidence, facts, not town gossip. She wondered if Sam had ulterior motives for not wanting to bring Henry in. She knew he had had the public information session yesterday. What happened there? What about the press? He was an elected official. Was reelection coming up? Was he putting politics before police work?

"Henry has a history with her, and he doesn't have an alibi for the night of her murder, and he lied about how close they were," Kimberley pressed.

"So, should we pull every guy she dated in for questioning? One-night stands? Prom dates?" Sam crumpled the brown bag into a ball and tossed it in the garbage.

"Maybe. All we know is Isobel might be the link between Hannah and her murderer."

"We don't even know that yet. Until the paternity test results are in, it's just a hunch, and even then, we can't be certain."

Kimberley stood from her chair. "Alright then, I'll be in my office twiddling my thumbs."

"Just please be patient, Detective. We'll get this guy. Trust me."

Kimberley restrained herself from letting out a huff. Instead, she picked up her coffee and nodded. She left Sam's office, looking out into the main area. Deputy Hill was at his desk mulling over paperwork. All the other desks were empty.

"Hill, whatcha working on?" she asked.

He turned back to look at her. "Traffic violations." He held up a stack of paperwork.

She gave him a slight nod. With an open murder investigation, traffic violations should be the last thing anyone should be working on, but she understood the work had to be done.

"Carry on," she said, turning to face her office. She opened the door and twisted open the blinds that looked out into the main office area. She wanted the first glimpse, just in case Sam had a change of heart and decided to haul Henry Colton in early. They were wasting time with this "let's shake him loose" approach.

Kimberley walked around her desk and took a seat, looking up at the ceiling, swiveling her chair back and forth. There wasn't much else she could do other than wait. She had talked to everyone that knew Hannah, which wasn't many. She didn't really have any friends. Her only family was her mother and her daughter. Her relationship was private, and regardless of what Sam thought, Kimberley knew whoever killed Hannah Brown knew her intimately. This wasn't random. This was planned. Methodical. She closed her eyes for a moment, mulling over all the facts of the case. Where and when she was murdered—Deer Creek in the wee hours of the morning—indicated their meeting was a secret between them. The murder was quick. A gunshot to the head. So quick Hannah hadn't seen it coming. Evident by the frozen look on her face, her features in a neutral position, lips slightly parted, eyes open, not too wide, not narrowed, just like she was looking at somebody, somebody she knew, somebody she trusted, somebody she loved. But why the decapitation? Why leave Isobel there? Was it all a ploy to throw police off the scent of the real killer? Them thinking it was a copycat killer led them astray. Kimberley's eyes snapped open. That's all it was. It had to be. Sam and Kimberley had spent nearly two days tracking down a potential true-crime obsessive.

Kimberley let out a laugh for being a fool. During the time they wasted, the murderer had been mostly likely covering his tracks, staying one step ahead of the police. How could she have had such tunnel vision? She quickly wiped that thought away. It wasn't her that had laser focus on the true-crime obsessive, it was Sam. To him, that had been the only explanation. She shook her head and tilted it toward each shoulder, one at a time, to crack her neck. But really, she still didn't know anything. It was just a hunch.

Kimberley looked down at her desk. A piece of white paper poked out from her keyboard. She slid it out from under. A folded piece of computer paper with "Kimberley" written in the middle in cursive. She didn't recognize the handwriting. She carefully opened it, revealing a typed note. Her eyes scanned it.

The big city detective might not want to keep poking around something that should be left alone. A single whore, who is no more, is no great loss to anyone... Remember that.

Just like every time I close my eyes, I remember Jessica's adorable face.

The coffee Kimberley thought she had successfully swallowed pushed its way up from her stomach, burning her throat as it reentered her mouth. She wretched into the garbage can beside her desk a greenish, brown liquid. Sweat beads formed at her hairline. She stood up straight, wiping her mouth with the back of her hand. Grabbing her keys from the top of her desk, she bolted out of her office.

"Where's the fire?" Deputy Hill said lightheartedly. When he saw the horror on Kimberley's face, he stood at attention and swallowed hard.

"What's going on?" he asked.

Sam emerged from his office. "Detective?"

"It's Jessica!" she yelled over her shoulder as she pushed through the first set of doors.

Sam chased after her, but Kimberley was too fast. By the time he made it out of the police station, she was speeding off, lights on, sirens blaring. A cloud of dust behind her vehicle.

Kimberley drove too fast for the speed limit signs, but it wasn't fast enough for her. She needed to get to Happy Trails to make sure Jessica was okay. She had dropped her off an hour ago. Could something have happened? Did that fucking sicko do something to her? Did he take her? Surely, the daycare would have called. But maybe they hadn't noticed.

Kimberley's phone rang over and over. After the third call, she finally answered. "What?"

"Jesus Christ, Detective. What's going on?" Sam asked. There was concern and frustration in his voice.

"On my desk is a note. I need it analyzed and brushed for fingerprints." Her breathing was heavy. She wouldn't be able to breathe normally or think clearly until she saw Jessica.

"A note?"

"They threatened my fucking daughter!" Kimberley yelled, slamming her hands against the steering wheel.

She could hear Sam running, his footsteps were loud. They stopped and she assumed he was standing in front of her desk. He was quiet. She assumed he was reading the note.

"Jesus Christ," he said.

In the background, she could hear Sam instructing Deputy Hill to bag it up as evidence. "Careful not to touch it," he said. It sounded muffled, as if he was covering the mouthpiece.

"What the fuck," Deputy Hill said, almost inaudibly. He had read the note too.

"Where are you?" Sam said into the phone.

Kimberley swerved her car around a pickup truck that hadn't moved over and took a sharp right down the road that led to Happy Trails. Just five miles and she'd be there.

"On my way to Jessica's daycare."

"Okay, good. Where was the note?"

"On my desk, just the corner of it sticking out from under the keyboard."

"Shit. I'll talk to Barb. See if she saw anyone come in after she opened."

"What about security cameras?"

Kimberley pressed down harder on the gas. But the vehicle was already at its top speed. The wheat fields on either side of the road were a golden blur. She focused intently on the road, although there was no one else on it, nothing to watch out for. Her hands gripped the wheel at ten and two. Her fingers were turning white from lack of blood supply, but she kept clenching them as hard as she could, picturing the same hands around the neck of the person that penned that note, squeezing the life out of them.

"I'll pull Burns off the road and then have him review them. But we're not as set up as you'd think we'd be for a sheriff's station."

"What the fuck does that mean?"

"We're a small town with a small budget…" He paused. "Just don't worry about anything here. Get to your daughter. Make sure she's safe and call me."

Kimberley tried to push back tears. What if she was gone? What if she'd never see that smiley face again? Those rosy cheeks. Her little hands and feet. What if she never got to tell her how smart or strong or beautiful she was again?

"Okay," was all she managed to say before ending the call.

One more mile. One more mile. She conjured up the image of Jessica right in front of her eyes. Willing it to be real. Willing it to be the face she saw when she entered Happy Trails. She needed her to be there. Her body started to ache like it did back when she was still nursing. Her breasts throbbed like her milk ducts were full, but she hadn't nursed in over a year. She could feel her skin warm almost to a burn. Her stomach flipped and turned. It was like she was going through physical withdrawals at the very thought of losing her daughter. She wasn't sure if this was her motherly instinct that something was wrong, that something had happened to Jessica or if she was working herself up. She tried to take deep breaths, but each one came out like a howl of a cry.

She slammed on her brakes in front of Happy Trails, throwing her door open and running toward the daycare center. Kimberley hadn't bothered to even turn the engine off. Her mind was on one thing and one thing only: her daughter. She threw open the front door, running down the hall toward the toddler room, calling out for her daughter. She pushed her way through the closed door. "Jessica," she panted, out of breath.

Margaret whipped her head in the direction of Kimberley. "Kimberley, are you okay?"

"Jessica."

Kimberley scanned the room. It was full of kids running about. Some at tables coloring. Some playing with toys. Some playing kitchen. Each one she looked at wasn't Jessica.

Relief flooded her when she spotted her beautiful little girl, sitting in a corner with her legs crossed. She appeared to be pouting. Her head down, staring at her lap.

A hand touched Kimberley's shoulder. "Are you okay?" Margaret asked again.

Kimberley's eyes were glued to Jessica, who hadn't even noticed that she was in the room yet.

"Yeah. I'm fine, now. I'm okay." All the breaths she couldn't get out were escaping. She breathed heavily, trying to catch them.

"Good. What's wrong, Kimberley?" Margaret forced a smile, but she was still very concerned.

"Why is she in the corner?" Kimberley asked.

"She's been very upset today. I was going to ring you after play-time was over as it's a bit chaotic during free play. She really wants her elephant. Usually I wouldn't encourage this type of attachment behavior, but I know she's still getting used to everything and it comforts her. Would you be able to bring it here? I'd like to get her to participate in some of the activities this afternoon, and I don't think she will without it."

Kimberley nodded. "Oh yes. Of course. I can swing by the house and bring it right back. Can I talk to her for a moment?"

"Perfect, and yes, of course. She's your daughter."

Kimberley took the steps toward Jessica slowly, her eyes taking in every part of her. From her pouty lips to her messy brown hair, to even the small scar on her chin that happened on a walk in Bryant Park when she fell down trying to chase the pigeons. Jessica looked as though she had just lost a friend, and she had: her stuffed Ellie. How could she have forgotten her stuffy? Jessica loved that thing. Carried it everywhere and somehow, Kimberley had forgotten it. She had been solely focused on the case. Her daughter taking a backseat to her work, and now some asshole had involved her sweet, beautiful girl. This had never happened in New York City. So much for small-town USA being wholesome and welcoming. To her, this place had been as much a cesspool as New York City so far. How could she have let this happen? There'd be no more soft stepping or taking it slow. Now that her daughter had been threatened, she was taking this case into her own hands, regardless of Sam's thoughts on the matter. At the very least, she'd arrest the person that wrote the note. At the most, Kimberley would kill them.

She wiped her face, pushing her hair back, and forced the corners of her mouth to turn upward. She didn't want Jessica to see her upset. Children could sense when things were wrong, as much as adults liked to believe they couldn't. Kimberley remembered her own childhood. She always knew when things weren't right, which was nearly all the time. She could see the bruises on her mother's arms. And as much as her mother told her she was clumsy, she knew it was her dad that had left those marks. She had seen her mom's face, blotchy, wet, and red. Her mother would tell her she had just watched a sad movie, but the movie was her own life.

She didn't want any of that for Jessica. Kimberley wanted to protect her from the ugliness of the world around her for as long as she possibly could. Two-year-olds should believe in things like Santa Claus and fairies and unicorns, not in the boogeyman, not in evil, and not that their life is in danger.

"Jessica, baby," Kimberley said, kneeling down in front of her daughter.

Jessica looked up, a smile spreading across her face. "Mommy," she said, leaping into her mother's arms.

Kimberley hugged her tight, rubbing her back and running her hands through her soft hair. While she held her, she held back tears. She realized that home wasn't New York City or Dead Woman Crossing. Home was wherever her daughter was. She released Jessica, staring into her big blue eyes. "Margaret said you've been having a rough morning."

"Ellie's gone." Jessica pouted.

"I know. Would you like it if I went and got her and brought her back to you?"

Jessica nodded several times. Her face lit up and she giggled.

"Okay, sweetie. I'm going to be right back." Kimberley rubbed her daughter's shoulders and pulled her in for a kiss on both cheeks, her forehead, and the tip of her nose, making Jessica giggle even more.

"Be right back, my smart girl," she said, standing up and waving.

"Bye, Mommy," Jessica said, waving back.

Kimberley stopped over by Margaret, who was trying to diffuse an argument between two children over a red ball. "Hey, Margaret. I'm going to be right back with Jessica's elephant."

Margaret nodded.

"Would you mind keeping an extra close eye on her today?" Kimberley asked. Her eyes said more than her words did.

Margaret looked at her, spotting the concern on Kimberley's face. She could tell there was more to her worry than just worry. "Of course. I keep an extra close eye on all my kids," she reassured.

"Good. I mean, thanks," Kimberley said.

Once outside, she dialed Sam. He answered on the first ring.

"Everything okay?"

"Yes, Jessica's fine. I'm going to stop at my house to get her stuffed elephant and drop it off. She carries that thing everywhere."

She turned her vehicle in the direction of the farm and drove off. It wasn't far from the daycare center, just a couple of miles.

"Good. Glad to hear she's okay. Barb said the letter was in the sheriff's mailbox. She thought it was odd, but she didn't look at it. Thought it was a love note or something like that," Sam explained.

"Since you didn't mention security cameras, I'm going to assume there's none covering our mailbox."

"You would be assuming right. I sent it over to the lab to be analyzed. So, maybe we'll get something there."

Kimberley tapped her fingers against the steering wheel. She knew all that would be on that note would be hers and Barb's fingerprints. There was no way this guy would be as careless as to leave his fingerprints behind, especially after the crime scene and the body had been so clean.

"Is it possible to get a deputy to watch the daycare center for the next couple of days?"

"I've got Deputy Hill on his way right now. He'll finish his shift out there, which should be just around the time Jessica gets picked up. We'll make sure she stays safe," Sam assured.

"Thanks, Sam."

"If you've got to take the day off, feel free to."

"No way. I know I'm close. This guy's nervous. Why else would he threaten my family? Isobel is the key," Kimberley said, pulling into the driveway of the farmhouse.

She parked her vehicle and got out, walking along the stone path toward the cottage.

"I think you're right about that. I've still got Bearfield tailing Henry. I'm inclined to bring him in," Sam said.

"I thought you wanted to wait and see if something rattled loose." Kimberley couldn't help herself.

"Things are different now. When you go after one of mine, you go after all of us, and I won't have that in my community."

She imagined Sam puffing his chest out and raising his chin.

"I'm just getting to the house now. So, if you wait about a half hour, I can be there to question him." Kimberley pulled open the front door, walking into the living room.

The house was still and quiet.

"Alright. I'll let you have the honors of interrogating him. Thirty minutes," he said, ending the call.

Kimberley slid the phone into her utility belt. "Mom," she called out. "Have you seen Jessica's stuffed elephant?"

She walked down the hallway to her bedroom. Pulling the blankets and pillows, she searched the crib. Nothing. She bent down, looking underneath, pushing around some miscellaneous baby stuff. It wasn't there either. She searched her own bed. Sometimes Jessica would lay with her for an hour or so before bedtime. It wasn't there either, or underneath her bed. Where was the last place she'd seen it? The kitchen? Kimberley left the bedroom and walked down the hall, entering the kitchen, which was spotless. Her mother was such a tidy person. Everything had a place, she'd always say.

"Mom," she called out again.

It wasn't in the kitchen, so she walked back down the hallway. Maybe Nicole was taking a nap. She tapped on the bedroom door.

When no one answered, she pushed it open. The king-size bed was made. She must be running errands. Kimberly closed the door, trekking back down the hall.

Have you seen Jessica's elephant? she texted her mom.

Standing in the living room, she waited for Nicole to text back, tapping her shoe on the wooden floor. Where could it be? She never left the house without it. A repulsive thought entered her mind. What if that man took it? What if he had already been close enough to Jessica to snatch it away? Maybe she'd get it in the mail tomorrow or in three days with another sick, threatening note. What would Kimberley do then? Would she drop the case? Leave Dead Woman Crossing? Quit her job? She tried to calm herself down before her mind took her to dark places, places that were always hard for her to climb back out of. She looked back at her phone, willing her mom to text back. Maybe it was in her mom's vehicle. She had dropped off and picked up Jessica countless times. That made the most sense. Yeah, that's got to be it, Kimberley told herself.

Her phone vibrated. *Hi, honey. We watched* Frozen *in our bedroom last night. It might have fallen behind the bed or something. Are you at the house?*

Oh, duh. Kimberley had completely forgotten that David took over the living room with some western show, so Nicole took Jessica into their room to watch the movie. Of course, Kimberley hadn't remembered. She was too busy thinking about Hannah Brown, lying on her own bed going over the intel she had collected and the crime scene photos for the twentieth time. No matter how many times she looked at them, they never told her a different story.

Kimberley quickly texted back. *Yeah. Just picking it up to bring to daycare.*

She stopped herself from texting any more. She wanted to tell her mom what had happened, about the note, but she knew it would freak her out. She'd insist that Jessica come home immediately and then Jessica would be on lockdown for the foreseeable future. And Kimberley didn't want Jessica to know that anything was wrong. She wanted her to feel safe. She wanted things to appear normal, even though they weren't. Just before she put her phone away, Nicole texted again. *Okay, I'll be home in a few minutes to help you look. Had to grab groceries.*

Kimberley stowed her phone in her pocket and walked back toward David and Nicole's bedroom. She pushed open the door and flicked on the light. She hated to pull apart the bed, because it would mean her mother would have to remake it for a second time, but she needed the elephant. She pulled up the blankets, sheets, and pillows. Nothing. She checked beside both bed tables, but nothing there either. She attempted to pull the bed away from the wall, but it wouldn't budge. "Ugh," she groaned. Kimberley kneeled down to look under the bed, lifting up the frilly bed skirt. It was dark underneath, so she pulled her flashlight from her utility belt, shining a light on the dust bunnies and rolled-up socks, but no elephant.

Ugh. She should have put a tracker on that damn thing, she thought to herself. Kimberley went to push herself back up, planting her hand on the wooden floor, but she paused, when she realized the plank of wood was unstable. She pushed the palm of her hand down harder, the wood rose again, wiggling in its place. That's weird.

Kimberley stood all the way up and pulled out her phone, bringing up her mom's number. *There's a piece of wood by your bed that's loose. Might want to tell David to fix it.*

Her finger hovered over the send button, but something stopped her. Instinct.

She erased the message, putting her phone away. Kimberley kneeled down on the floor again, pressing on several pieces of wood until the unstable one popped up. The whole thing came loose, and she removed it. A hole sat under the floor.

Hesitating for only a moment, she reached her hand into the dark abyss, feeling around. A tickle on her finger. Cotton that stuck to her. Definitely a spider and its web. She had faced worst things in her life than a spider, so it didn't faze her. Then her hand touched something other than wood and insects. It rocked back and forth. She gripped her hand around it and pulled it out. A shoebox. Kimberley set the box down. Items inside clamored around. The noise didn't give any indication as to what it was. She slowly opened the box. Inside lay two items wrapped in white rags, almost as if they had been mummified. Kimberley cocked her head. She pulled at one white rag, unwrapping what was inside; a flip phone fell out into the box. She pulled at the other white rag, unwrapping it from its mummification, a 38-caliber pistol landed beside the phone. Kimberley looked down at the phone and the gun. Two pieces of a puzzle.

She reached for her own cell phone and pulled up her photo album. The image she was looking for was right at the front. She went to her keypad and typed in ten digits. Kimberley hit dial. The phone in the box immediately began to vibrate.

CHAPTER THIRTY-THREE

"Kimberley, Ellie was in my car," Nicole said, standing in the doorway of the bedroom.

Kimberley was sitting on the floor, knees pulled in. In front of her were her new discoveries, the missing puzzle pieces. Her mouth and eyes were wide as she was working through everything in her head, a hundred different possibilities for why the same type of gun that was used to kill Hannah and the phone that had called her on the night of her murder were in this house. The same phone that had been in contact with her over the years that wasn't even saved under a name. The same number Hannah had as a contact on her emergency form at the daycare. Why was it here? In this house?

Nicole looked at Kimberley and then at the wooden floor where the board had been pulled up.

"What did you do to the—" She stopped herself as her eyes scanned the box and the contents of it.

"Why are these in your house?" Kimberley narrowed her eyes, meeting her mom's.

Her mom was a possibility in all of this, as much as she hated to think that. But they were in her house, the house she took care of, the house she lived in, in the bedroom she slept in, just beneath the floor she walked on.

"I… I… I've never seen any of that." Nicole shook her head.

"What about this?" Kimberley pointed to the hole that doubled as a place to stash murder weapons. "Did you know about this?"

"You need to put those things back before David gets here. He wouldn't want you snooping around his stuff," Nicole warned.

"Mom! You're not getting it. This gun, this 38-caliber, is the same type of gun that was used to kill Hannah Brown. And this phone"—Kimberley pointed at it, careful not to touch anything as it was evidence—"I dialed a number that was in Hannah's call log. The same number that was listed on the emergency contact form at the daycare. This phone rang. Do you understand what I'm saying?" Kimberley closed the box and stood up.

Nicole shook her head. Her eyes swam with tears. "No... no."

Kimberley knew she understood what she was saying, she just didn't believe it nor wanted to believe it. She stood up, picking up the box. Her mom kept shaking her head.

"Did you know about any of this?"

"Any of what?" Nicole tried to stand up straight, still in denial, trying to put on a show that none of this could possibly be true.

Kimberley stared into her eyes. She knew her mother knew something. Instinct. It would explain why she didn't eat. Why she had gotten so thin. Why she had aged ten years in two. Why she wasn't sleeping well. Why she fawned all over David, vying for his love and attention. She couldn't believe she hadn't seen it. All the signs were there. She had been acting like a woman who knew her husband was having an affair. Who had accepted it, even though it was eating away at her, destroying her, she stayed and let it continue, for what, a house to live in, a stable life? But the question was... how much did she know? Did she know he was sleeping with Hannah? Kimberley didn't think she'd ever forgive her mom if that were the case. She hoped it wasn't.

She continued to stare her mother in the eyes, waiting for her to break. She knew she could outlast her. Nicole began to crack. Her lip trembled. She looked away first, her bloodshot, sunken eyes bouncing around the room.

"I knew something was going on. He became distant and unaffectionate, leaving in the middle of the night. He used to deny everything. Then he stopped denying it, just shrugging his goddamn shoulders, like it didn't matter, like *I* didn't matter. When the whole moonshine thing with Wyatt came out, I felt the biggest relief. Like that was what he was up to. But now... now. I don't know." Tears streamed down her face as she tried to work it out.

"What about the night Hannah Brown was murdered? Was that another night he snuck off?" Kimberley shifted her bodyweight, widening her stance; full-on interrogation mode. She needed the facts. She needed the truth. This man lived in the same house as her and her daughter. This man threatened to hurt her child while he slept one room away from her. This fucking man had played with Jessica, held her... Kimberley shook her head in disgust. How could she not have known? A killer in the same house. Hosting her. Sitting at the same dinner table. Praying to his God as if his God wouldn't be sickened by him.

Nicole deflated in front of her, dropping her shoulders and hanging her head. "I don't know. I've been taking sleeping pills on and off to help me sleep. I took one that night. I assume he was with me all night."

"You can't assume that. If you were passed out, you have no idea what he did or where he went."

"He wouldn't..." Nicole shook her head, crying.

"I can't do this right now." Kimberley pushed past her mom, carrying the box with the gun and phone.

"Kimberley, wait. Can we talk about this?" Nicole pleaded as Kimberley walked down the hall.

She turned back for a moment. "No. He threatened my daughter, Mom, your granddaughter. He left a note for me at work threatening to hurt Jessica. He's a monster."

Nicole cried harder, dropping her face into her hands. "He wouldn't do that," she blubbered.

Kimberley's eyes lingered on her mom. She felt sorry for her. All of her childhood, she had watched her mom stand by her deadbeat dad, and she would have continued to do so, if his liver had held up after the decades of alcohol abuse. She thought when her father died, it was a blessing, that her mother would finally be free, that she'd become whole again. Rebuild and reinvent herself. But all she had done was find another deadbeat man to standby, one worse than her dad. She didn't think it was possible, but David took the cake. Why was she so weak? Why didn't she value herself? She was like a pistachio with the nut removed, just a useless shell. She wanted so badly for her mom to be strong and independent, but she was witnessing her childhood all over again.

Kimberley turned back around, startled to see a large shadow cast down in front of her. She followed the blackness with her eyes to a pair of work boots, dirty overalls, the red curtain being raised again up his wide neck, David's face, and the vein, pulsating in his forehead. She took note of his clenched fists and his feet, shoulder width apart, pressure on the toes, heels slightly lifted as if he were getting ready to charge at her. David's eyes went from the box Kimberley was holding to Nicole at the end of the hallway, back to Kimberley's face.

"Mom, lock yourself in the bedroom," Kimberley said while keeping her eyes on David. She shifted the box ever so slowly to one hand, while her other went to her side, right near her trusty Glock. Three locking points stood between her and her gun. Her NYPD snap holster had two locking mechanisms, thumb snap and rock it forward, to remove the weapon. She had only been in possession of the level-three retention holster for a week and hadn't had a reason to pull her gun out quickly or at all. She hadn't even practiced speed of release with it yet, assuming she'd only have to use it to put some wild animal out of its misery after a car hit it. She never imagined she'd be in this scenario in Dead Woman Crossing of all places.

"No. This isn't what it looks like. He's a good man. He would never…"

"Shut up, Nicole," David yelled.

"David, tell her you wouldn't do this. Tell her. It's all just a misunderstanding, right?" Nicole pleaded.

"I said shut the fuck up!"

The level-three retention holster had the same first two releases as a level two—those she could get through quickly. The third was a pivot guard.

Kimberley heard footsteps behind her, forcing her to look as she wasn't sure if there were one or two threats in the hallway. Nicole wasn't thinking clearly. Her mom walked toward her or through her to David, she wasn't sure. She was still holding Jessica's stuffed elephant.

Thumb snap. Rock forward. Pull. Muscle memory had served her wrong this time. The gun stayed in its holster.

The box was knocked to the ground, the .38 caliber and cellphone spilling out. A hand was on her shoulders, throwing her backward into Nicole. She landed on top of her. Nicole cried out. Kimberley scrambled to her feet as David reached down for the gun. She leaped at him, tackling him to the ground, the gun slipping out of his hands. She straddled his chest, trying to hold him down, but he had over a hundred pounds on her, real strength that came from farming. He lifted her up cleanly, tossing her forward onto the floor, the .38 caliber just a foot in front of her. She hadn't checked to see if it was loaded. She reached for it; she was just short of it. She felt big hands wrap entirely around one of her ankles. Kimberley turned her head, flipping on her back instinctively. It was better to be on your back than on your stomach. She kicked as hard and as wild as she could. David yanked her toward him. She slid across the floor, her utility belt scraping the wood. He stepped over her, his focus lasered on the gun. Nicole huddled in the corner of the hall, crying, telling them to stop. Kimberley stood once again. She went after him as she went for her Glock. Thumb snap. Rock. Fuck.

Two large steps put her right behind him. She yanked on his overalls, pulling him back again. She reeled back her fist, sending it forward into the side of his head. He groaned, but it did nothing to stop him. David wrapped his hand in her hair, twisting it, and whipped her body into the wall, the drywall immediately giving out, crumbling and splitting in several areas.: an imprint of her left behind. Kimberley fell to the ground just as David bent down to pick up the gun.

She reached down for her trusty Glock again. Thumb snap. Rock. Pivot guard. It was free from its holster. David turned with the 38-caliber in hand. Kimberley quickly unclicked the safety and raised the gun.

Two gunshots rang out.

Nicole screamed in horror.

CHAPTER THIRTY-FOUR

Nicole crawled down the hallway with the elephant in hand toward David, who was lying on the ground, writhing in pain. A pool of blood around his head and arm. She screamed and cried, trying to comfort him.

Kimberley stood up quickly, her Glock still aimed at David. She walked to him, kicking the .38 caliber further away from where it lay just a foot above his head. The first gunshot had come from Kimberley's gun, hitting David in the arm, knocking the hand that was holding the .38 caliber to his head a few inches away. When the second shot fired, it nicked the top corner of his head. Turning a fatal shot into a flesh wound. David had turned the gun on himself, trying to take the easy way out of this. Shame and guilt had caught up with him.

"You're okay. You're okay," Nicole said, pressing down on the bullet wound on his arm and running her hand over his forehead.

David stayed as still as possible, his eyes staring up at the ceiling as if he had come face to face with his own God. His body twitched even though every muscle in his body was clenching. Kimberley holstered her gun and pulled out her cell phone, dialing Sam.

He answered on the first ring.

"Where are you? I've got Henry Colton here."

"Let him go."

"What?"

"We've got a GSW. I need an ambulance at my house right now," Kimberley said, ending the call.

She placed the phone in her utility belt, turning back to look at her mother and David. Nicole was still trying to comfort him as if he had been in a car accident and not in a scuffle with her daughter over a gun that he used to murder the woman he was cheating on her with.

"Get some towels," Nicole cried, looking up at Kimberley.

"The paramedics will take care of him. They're on their way." Kimberley's voice was cold.

"You can't just let him die." Nicole used the stuffed elephant to put pressure on the gunshot wound, soaking up the blood.

"He's not going to die." Kimberley shook her head.

"He's bleeding out."

"He's got a flesh wound and a gunshot to the arm nowhere near the brachial artery. He's fine. Just in pain. I actually hope those paramedics take their time getting here," she said, pacing back and forth.

"How can you say something like that?" Nicole seethed, leaning over David as if she were protecting him.

"Easily. He killed a woman in cold blood and chopped her head off. He deserves to suffer."

Kimberley opened the front door and walked outside, needing the fresh air and needing to get away from her mother, who was clearly in shock. She hoped she'd come to her senses when her brain started thinking straight again. Sam's police truck, an ambulance and three Custer County SUV's sped down the driveway around the farmhouse and onto the grass in front of the cottage. Sam leaped out of his vehicle, running toward Kimberley.

"Are you okay?" he asked, putting a hand on her shoulder and lifting her chin with the other, checking her over for bumps, cuts, bruises, blood. Her hair was a disheveled mess. She felt a searing pain across her face, where it had smashed into the wall. She was sure it was red if not bruised already. Her knuckles were torn open thanks to two punches thrown in the last twenty-four hours. Her body ached from being thrown around like a rag doll. Her heart broke for her weak mother. But other than that… she was fine.

"I'm fine."

Two paramedics with a stretcher and medic bag approached quickly.

Before they could ask, Kimberley said, "Inside."

They nodded and ran past. When the door opened to the house, she could once again hear her mother screaming and crying.

"Are you sure you're okay?" Sam asked, holding her face in the palms of his hands, looking into her eyes, searching them.

Kimberley nodded.

He pushed some of her hair back so he could see her better. "You've got a bruise coming on right here." He gently touched the side of her temple, running his fingers down her cheek, tracing the discolored skin. She winced slightly.

"You should see the other guy," Kimberley teased.

"Burns, grab me an ice pack from the ambulance," Sam instructed.

Deputy Burns nodded. Moments later, he handed over the ice pack.

"Go on and help them inside," Sam said.

"There's two pieces of evidence that need to be bagged and tagged. A .38 caliber and a flip phone. One's in the living room, the other in the hallway," Kimberley said.

Hill and Burns nodded and hurried inside the cottage. Sam held the ice pack against the side of Kimberley's face. "Hold it right there."

She didn't argue with him this time.

"I'm going to have one of the paramedics check you out. You might have a concussion."

"I'm fine."

"I don't need you to play tough detective right now. I need you to listen." He tilted his head.

The door to the cottage swung open. A paramedic walked backward, pulling the stretcher through, while the other pushed on the end. Bearfield and Sam immediately went to help as they were struggling with the rock-lined path and the fact that David was a massive lump of uncooperative dead weight. Nicole walked beside him, holding his hand, crying. Just as they started loading him into the ambulance, a voice screamed from the main house.

"Dad, oh my God, what happened?" Emily cried out, running toward her father.

She tried to get close to him, but the paramedics told her to back away.

"Dad!" she yelled.

His mouth and nose were covered with an oxygen mask, so he didn't speak. He wasn't even attempting to say anything as his daughter and his wife wept over him.

"Tell me what happened!" she yelled, this time directing her attention at Sam. "Tell me!" She threw her hands up.

David pulled his oxygen mask off. "Emily…" He tried to lift his head to look at her.

Emily turned back toward David. "Dad." Her eyes widened.

"I'm sorry," he said, letting his head drop back on the stretcher. He didn't have the strength to hold his head up high, nor the dignity to.

Emily took a small step back, crying into her hands.

A paramedic slid the mask back on him, and they lifted him into the ambulance, wheeling the stretcher in.

"Can one of you check on my detective?" Sam asked.

"We've got to get him to the hospital," the paramedic said.

"It's fine. We'll follow behind," Kimberley cut in.

Sam pulled out his handcuffs and cuffed David's wrist to the stretcher.

"Is that really necessary?" Emily cried.

"It is," Sam said. "We'll be right behind you."

Emily turned to Kimberley. "You've destroyed my family. First Wyatt, now my dad."

One paramedic hopped into the back of the ambulance. "Immediate family only."

Emily turned and climbed in without saying another word to Kimberley.

Nicole hesitated, looking at David and then back at Kimberley. Her face crumpled. More tears spilled out. "I'm sorry. I have to make sure he's okay." She turned her back on her daughter, stepping up into the ambulance. The other paramedic shut the doors and ran around to the front, hopping into the driver's seat.

The sirens blared and the lights flashed as they sped off.

"Hill, you got the evidence bagged and tagged?" Sam asked.

"Yeah."

"Good. Leave them with Burns and follow them to the hospital. He might be injured, but he is a tough bastard and very large, so don't let David out of your sight. We'll be there in a bit."

"Yes, sir," he said, running to his vehicle.

Sam let out a deep breath. He pulled his radio from his holster. "All available units to the Turner Farm. All available units to the Turner Farm off of N2440 road."

He put the radio back in his utility belt and walked back to Kimberley.

"I'm going to have the team do a clean sweep of the farm."

Kimberley nodded.

"Bearfield, I want you to take the lead on searching this place. Start with the outbuildings. Bag up anything that could have been used to decapitate Hannah Brown."

"You got it," Bearfield said, beckoning Burns with his hand. The two started off toward the back of the cottage.

"You did good today," Sam said to Kimberley.

"No, I didn't." She shook her head.

Sam tried to look her in the eye, but Kimberley wouldn't meet his gaze. She was ashamed that she hadn't seen the signs, that she discovered who David really was over the dumb luck of looking for her daughter's stuffed animal. Her instinct should have told her as soon as she stepped foot in the house that David wasn't a good man. She should have seen it in her mother's weakened and sad appearance. She should have known with how David acted around her. It was all right under her nose, right in front of her face. But she didn't see any of it.

"It's hard to see trees when you're standing in the forest, right? Didn't you tell me that?" he said, raising an eyebrow.

"Something like that…" Kimberley sighed, opting not to correct the saying. It made more sense to her that way.

"I kind of got a sense of what happened here, but ya mind sharing it with me on the ride to the hospital where you will be looked over by a doctor, and no, that is not a request. If it's too much, you can give your statement tomorrow, but I will not budge on the wellness check."

"Yeah, that's fine… hold on," she said, handing him the ice pack. She walked toward the cottage. The door closed behind her with a thud. Inside, it was still, the only evidence as to what had just transpired being the pools of blood on the floor. She wiped her feet on the rug, force of habit, and walked further into the house, turning toward the long hallway. The stuffed elephant lay covered in blood on the floor.

The door opened with a squeak and closed with a thud again.

Sam stood there with the ice pack in his hand. "Everything good?" he asked, taking a couple more steps into the house.

Kimberley bent down, picking up the stuffed toy. She tried to wipe the blood off, but it just smeared it more.

Sam peered down the hallway where the fight had happened, noticing the broken drywall. "Was that you?" he asked.

"It was my body, if that's what you're asking." The soreness in her back had returned, or perhaps it had been there the whole time, but she was blocking out the pain.

"Let's get you to the hospital."

Kimberley opened her hand, dropping the blood-soaked stuffed animal back on the floor.

CHAPTER THIRTY-FIVE

Kimberley sat on the edge of an exam table in a small doctor's office. She'd been fully examined and was just waiting on a prescription for pain meds from the doctor. There was a knock on the door.

"Come in."

Sam poked his head in first. She had refused to get into the hospital gown but did remove her shirt so the doctor could have a look at her back. She was dressed back in her uniform.

"How ya doing?"

"Concussion and a couple of bruised ribs." Kimberley shrugged her shoulders. "How'd it go?"

She wasn't concerned about her own injuries. She wanted to know about David. Would he fess up? Confess to it all? Make this an open-and-shut case so it'd be easier on his family and Hannah's family? Or would he deny everything? Demand a lawyer? Refuse to talk? She could see it going either way. He was a proud man, and proud men don't admit their wrongdoings.

"He confessed to all of it." Sam shifted his stance.

"Really?"

He nodded. "He said they'd been having an affair for over two years on and off. Hannah got pregnant shortly after they started seeing each other. Isobel is his daughter. But recently Hannah wanted more. She wanted to leave Dead Woman Crossing, take her daughter and find a better life. She blackmailed him, saying she'd go public with their affair and his fatherhood if he didn't pay her to keep quiet. She wanted fifty large, but obviously David doesn't have that type of money, and she didn't know that. Apparently, they met down at Deer Creek, and she flew into a rage when she realized he didn't have the money, tried calling Wyatt to expose David. And he shot her." Sam shook his head. "It's a damn shame."

"And let me guess, he staged it to look like Katie DeWitt James's murder to throw us off?"

"That's right."

"I mean, he got us to bite on that for a while but... what a fucking idiot."

"That's right too." Sam rocked back on his heels.

"Now, what?" Kimberley asked.

"I'll wrap this case up. You take it easy, spend some time with your daughter, and come back when you're feeling better. And I mean it. Take some time off." He cocked his head and turned on his foot toward the door.

Before he left the room, Kimberley said, "You know I'll be back in the office on Monday."

"I know." Sam smiled.

CHAPTER THIRTY-SIX

Kimberley lifted Jessica into her high chair, wincing from the pain she felt throbbing in her back. She locked the tray in and set down a bowl of Cheerios and a sippy cup of apple juice mixed with water. Kimberley was dressed in her uniform. It was perfectly pressed and creased in all the right areas. She had attempted to cover the bruise on the side of her face with some concealer, but it still showed through. It was Monday morning and she hadn't seen or heard from her mom since Friday when she hopped into the ambulance with David. She didn't know where she was staying, as Kimberley was still residing in the cottage. She figured she'd need to find a new place to live soon. Sam had the place swept and a forensic cleanup crew in and out by the time she brought Jessica home on Friday night.

Even after she had run the elephant through the wash cycle three times, she still couldn't bring herself to give it back to her daughter. It was tainted. Jessica had cried for an hour when Kimberley told her it had left and joined the circus. She spent hours searching for the same elephant online, but with no luck. She had decided that after work, and before she picked up Jessica, she'd drive over to Weatherford to look for a new stuffed elephant.

"Are those yummy?" Kimberley smiled at Jessica.

"Yeah," she said, pushing several into her mouth.

"Take a drink."

Jessica lifted the cup, taking a big gulp.

"Nana?" Jessica said, setting the cup back down on the tray. "Nana."

Kimberley's face crumpled for a moment. She quickly smoothed it out, not wanting to break down in front of her daughter.

"I'm right here, sweetie," Nicole said.

Kimberley turned around, finding her mother dressed in a long cotton dress standing in the doorframe. There was a cracked smile on her face, like she was both happy and sad, proud and ashamed. What was she doing here? Where had she been? Why had she chosen David over her own flesh and blood?

Instinctively, Kimberley stepped in front of her daughter like a lioness protecting its cub. Nicole's face crumpled. Tears streamed down her face.

"I'm so sorry, Kimberley."

"Sorry for picking a murderer over your own daughter and granddaughter?"

"No. It wasn't like that. I'm sorry… for believing him. I just… had to make sure he was okay."

Kimberley narrowed her eyes. "Were you with him the whole weekend?"

Nicole shook her head. "I stayed in a motel to give you space and to clear my head. He confessed everything to me, but I know deep down I didn't even need his confession. I knew he did it as soon as I saw the phone and the gun. I just didn't want to believe it."

Kimberley's lip trembled. She wanted her mother in her life, but how could she trust her around Jessica? Would she do the same thing again? Stand by a man that broke her. She had before.

"I know I screwed up. I can't explain why I did what I did. But I'll be better. I'm getting help. I'm getting out of this cycle I've been in my whole life."

Kimberley stared at her mother carefully. She looked different than she did a few days ago. Her face was a little fuller and brighter. The dark circles under her eyes had faded slightly. Her hair was combed. She had even applied makeup, which was now tear streaked with black mascara running down her cheeks. She looked as though she had eaten, she had slept, she had changed. Like she was clean from her addiction, David, and before him, Kimberley's father. Nicole had an affinity to damaged men.

"I love you so much, and I never want to lose you or Jessica. You two are my whole life."

Tears streaked Kimberley's cheeks too. For over thirty years, this was all she had ever wanted out of her mom: strength.

"I love you too, Mom," Kimberley said, walking toward her with open arms. They cried into each other's shoulders, holding one another tight. The embrace lasted longer than all of their hugs over their lifetime combined. Kimberley knew there was now a fracture in their relationship, and she hoped over time it would mend. But deep down, Kimberley knew it was only a matter of time before Nicole would need her fix again.

"Wuv you," Jessica said, giggling in her chair.

Kimberley and Nicole turned back to Jessica and laughed, wiping the tears from their eyes.

"Such a smart girl," they said at the same time. They smiled at Jessica and then at one another.

Kimberley glanced at her watch. "Oh, I'm going to be late."

"You're going to work?" Nicole immediately started tidying the kitchen up.

"Yeah, of course."

"Oh… I can take Jessica to daycare if you'd like." There was a plea in her mother's eyes.

Kimberley grabbed her messenger bag from beside the counter. "Why don't you keep her home and spend the day together?"

Nicole's eyes lit up and a smile spread across her face. "I would love that."

Kimberley nodded, saying goodbye to Nicole and Jessica. She closed the door to the cottage and walked up the rock-lined path to where her Ford Explorer was parked. She opened the car door and tossed her messenger bag across the driver's seat into the passenger's seat.

"Hey," Emily called out. She was standing on the large white wraparound porch, wearing blue jeans and a T-shirt.

Kimberley stepped out from behind her car door and took a couple of steps toward the house. "Hey."

Emily put her hands on her hip and glanced off into the wheat fields for a moment. She looked back at Kimberley. They hadn't spoken at all since the day David was wheeled away in a stretcher. She was fully anticipating that Emily would yell at her, tell her she needed to move off their property, that she wasn't welcome there. She thought she'd call Kimberley every name in the book, blame her for what happened to her family not once, but now twice.

"Do you wanna come over for drinks tonight?" Emily asked.

An olive branch had been extended.

"Yeah, I'd like that," Kimberley said with a nod.

Emily gave a small smile and disappeared back into the house.

"I'm so happy to see you," Barb said, standing up from her desk. She walked around it, carrying a pink gift bag.

"Hey, Barb."

"Some of the guys had bets on when you'd be back in the office."

"Oh yeah?" Kimberley cocked her head.

"Yeah, they clearly don't know you that well. Sam and I said you'd be back today. The rest of them bums said you'd take a week off."

"Glad I could be here to prove them wrong." Kimberley smiled.

"I got your daughter something," Barb said, holding out the bag. "Look inside." She grinned.

Kimberley reached her hand in and pulled out a gray crocheted stuffed elephant, with tan yarn to accent the ears and feet, pink yarn for rosy cheeks and white yarn for tusks and toenails.

"I heard what happened to her other stuffy, so I spent the weekend making this one for her."

Kimberley's eyes moistened. It was the nicest thing anyone had ever done for her or her daughter. Without saying a word, she wrapped her arms around Barbara.

"You're welcome," Barb said. "Now get to work." She was smiling as she walked back to her desk. "By the way, there's coffee and fresh-baked cookies on your desk."

Kimberley smiled and thanked her.

As soon as she entered the main office area, clapping ensued. The deputies rose from their desks, breaking out into applause. Kimberley nodded and flicked her wrist, her way of saying it wasn't a big deal. They whistled and hollered. Sam emerged from his office, joining in. His hands thundering together.

"Alright. Back to work, everyone. Hill, go ahead and give Barb my winnings too."

Deputy Hill nodded.

"Yeah, yeah, yeah, I heard you all bet against me." Kimberley shook her head.

"Burns said you got thrown through a wall. Shit, I would have taken two weeks off," Deputy Bearfield said.

"I didn't say 'through,' I said 'at.'"

"Did her body break part of the wall?" Bear asked.

"Yeah."

"Then you got thrown through a fuckin' wall. Anyway, you're tough for—"

"What? A girl," Kimberley cut him off, cocking her head.

"No, I was going to say, you're tough for coming back so quick. We're all real proud of you." Bearfield smiled.

Kimberley nodded her approval. "Thank you."

"Come on, Detective." Sam beckoned her into his office.

She quickly went into her office, dropping off her gift bag and messenger bag. Kimberley picked up the coffee and the plate that contained two large chocolate chip cookies.

Sam was seated at his desk when Kimberley entered. She sat down and extended the plate of cookies.

"Want one?" she asked.

"You know I do." He snatched one up. "Ya know, before you came along, I got way more baked goods."

"Well then, you're lucky I share," she said, setting the plate down and taking a sip of her coffee.

Sam broke a chunk off his cookie and tossed it in his mouth, smiling happily. "How ya feeling?"

"Good."

"False. You had a concussion, several bruised ribs, a back injury, and several contusions in the face just three days ago. So, you literally can't be 'good,' but I suppose that's your way of saying you're fine to return to work so quickly. But are you good, I mean, really? You don't have to play tough with me." He raised an eyebrow.

Kimberley nodded. "I'm fine."

"You know what it's going to be like now?" He tilted his head.

Kimberley raised an eyebrow, half mocking his previous expression.

"Well, now that the case is closed and most all of your newfound Oklahoma family members have been charged with crimes, it's back to traffic violations and breaking up brawls at The Trophy Room." Sam cracked a smile. "How does that sound?"

"Right now," Kimberley took a bite of her cookie, chewing and swallowing it, "that sounds fucking perfect." She smiled wide.

A LETTER FROM JENEVA ROSE

Dear reader,

I want to say a huge thank you for choosing to read *Dead Woman Crossing*. If you enjoyed it and want to keep up to date with all my latest releases, just sign up at the following link. Your email address will never be shared and you can unsubscribe at any time.

www.bookouture.com/jeneva-rose

I hope you loved *Dead Woman Crossing* and, if you did, I would be very grateful if you could write a review. I'd love to hear what you think, and it makes such a difference helping new readers to discover one of my books for the first time. If you loved what you read, feel free to get in touch with me on my Facebook page, through Twitter, Goodreads, or my website as I love hearing from and connecting with readers. Once again, thank you so much!

Thanks,
Jeneva Rose

 jenevaroseauthor

 @jenevarosebooks

 jenevaroseauthor

 www.jenevarose.com

ACKNOWLEDGMENTS

First and foremost, I want to thank the entire Bookouture team for believing in my writing and bringing me on for this incredible journey. To my fellow Bookouture authors, thank you for giving me the warmest of welcomes. To my editor, Lydia, thank you for being an absolute pleasure to work with. You've pushed me to make *Dead Woman Crossing* the best book it could possibly be, and I can't thank you enough for being so wonderful throughout this experience.

Thank you to my friends and family for supporting me throughout this crazy author journey, through all the highs and lows, from rejections to book deals. A special shoutout to Marissa Mielke. You're the best cheerleader, the kindest person, and I'm so proud to call you my friend.

Thank you to Rachel Salamon, Christina Behlke, Christi Mathew, Becca Merklein, Ashley Carlson, Kristine Johnson, Dan Salamone, AJ Paulus, Brian Kruise, Ashley Kruise, Meghann Roberts, Jazzee Behn, Himmy Mac, Mallorie Lehman, Hollie White, Shelby Esther, Katie Kocan, Aubree Lynn, Ryan Scanlan, and Kim Kauth O'Hara. Without your insight, the character of Jessica King would have been more like my English bulldog than a sixteen-month-old human. So, thank you very much for sharing your own personal experiences as parents of toddlers.

I also like to thank the people in my life that have supported me with little nods throughout my books. So, thank you to my father-in-law Kent Willetts who I transformed into Kent Wills, the nutjob of a ghost tour operator. To my mother-in-law, Andrea Willetts, who became Andrea's Café. Additionally, her personality mixed with my own mother's personality inspired the wonderful character of Barb. To the Cariello Family for their support, and a special thank you to Dominic Cariello for providing me with the expertise needed to give the character of David an accurate military background. My nod to you is Officer Cariello.

Thank you to my husband, Andrew, who has read every word I have ever written, the good, the bad and the ugly, and despite all of it encouraged me to keep going. I wouldn't be where I am without you.

Finally, I want to thank my readers. Thank you for taking a chance with a new author and a new story. I hope you enjoyed *Dead Woman Crossing*, and I hope you'll continue on this journey with me and Detective Kimberley King. I get to live my dream because of you, and I am forever thankful.

Jeneva Rose